THE PHOENIX FEATHER II:
REDBARK

ALSO BY SHERWOOD SMITH

The Phoenix Feather I: Fledglings

THE PHOENIX FEATHER

2

REDBARK

SHERWOOD SMITH

BOOK VIEW CAFE

Published by Book View Café Publishing Cooperative
304 S. Jones Blvd., Suite 2906
Las Vegas, NV 89107
www.bookviewcafe.org

ISBN: 978-1-61138-989-0

Cover Design by Augusta Scarlett
Interior Design by Marissa Doyle

ONE

OUR STORY CONTINUES, BEGINNING with Mouse, who stood on the deck of the supply ship, wondering why Commander Weken had sent Orderly Yaso along. Perhaps he could not conceive of a life without an orderly, even for a lowly second year cadet.

Anyway, the sailors were pulling up the ramp, and nobody seemed to be unduly worried about *two* orderlies coming aboard, for there was Shigan lounging up to stand next to Yaso.

Mouse retreated to the far end of the deck as the sailors began doing things to ropes and sails, putting the ship underway.

Mouse sat tucked up between a barrel and the hull, out of the chill wind. The sun warmed the top of her head, and the rocking of the ship made her drowsy. She was beginning to drift into dreams when a rough hand shook her. "Wind's shifted," someone said cheerily, as thunder rumbled in the distance. "Rain on the way. Best get below."

She dragged herself to her feet, wondering why she was still so very weary, after two days of doing nothing but walking and sitting on a rock staring at the sea. Icy splats of rain struck her cheek, rousing her. She got to her feet and went below.

This ship was not nearly as large as the one that had brought her to the training island, but it was also not as crowded. She saw shelves built along the compartment she was pointed to. Blankets rolled neatly at the ends indicated one could lie on them. But were they reserved for sailors?

She hovered uncertainly as conversation went on around her.

". . . Turtleback told me the moment the dock hands saw those longboats running in with no lanterns, they woke everyone and climbed to the roof with fish spears to hand. But the pirates ran straight up to the fortress, as if they weren't even there."

"Pirates," a big, broad sailor repeated scornfully. "I've seen pirates. I've fought 'em. Everything they say, those were hired swords. Mercenaries."

A tall woman whistled. "Mighty expensive expedition, that. For what? Everything they have there they grow, or *we* bring it."

Mouse spotted Shigan sitting against the hull, knees up, his long eyes open, reflecting the light in the lantern swinging overhead. Yaso bent over a basket of something. Mouse went that way, and sank down against the hull between the two, as the big sailor said, "They wanted into that fortress. My guess is they were after someone, or someones."

"But they raided the village," someone else said.

The woman nodded. "So Turtleback told us. They were chased out of the village, but not before they grabbed villagers. Maybe it was a slave expedition, sell them to the Western Islanders—"

The big man, who had sailed between the docks at the fortress and Te Gar, said, "I was *there*. Those were hostages. To force the fortress doors open. I've been fighting pirates off and on for twenty-five years, and let me tell you, those weren't pirates, or slavers. Not from what we heard. They wanted in, and since there isn't anything inside that fortress but a lot of boys eager for the kill, they were desperate to get at someone."

"Who would they want?" asked a sailor, with extreme skepticism. "I'm told it's all second sons and the like there. They also take anyone—carter's boys, sweepers, doesn't matter as long as he can hold a sword."

"Someone rich sent those hirelings," the big man said stolidly. "Why do rich people do anything? Maybe one of those second sons got himself kicked out and wanted revenge against the masters. Or there's a clan feud going."

"Clan feud," someone else repeated. "*That* sounds more

like it. The rich do love their clan feuds, though it's always the likes of us doing the dying."

"That's right. Unless someone even more powerful goes after them, then it's every head that bounces, from the clan chief's granddam to the newborns," another remarked sourly. "I've heard about those clan feuds. Ayah, the main garrison will be sending the inquisitors, and *they'll* find 'em out, ha ha."

"Food's ready," an older woman interrupted them, pointing to the galley. She turned toward the three passengers. "Crew gets served first."

The storm broke overhead in a roar of thunder as people moved to get their meal. When the rumble rolled away to the west, Shigan turned to Mouse. "Teach me your style of defense," he said in an undervoice.

From habit Mouse was about to refuse, for Heaven and Earth, and the martial arts style based on it, had always seemed to be part of The Story. She and Muin had kept it secret in case it somehow led back to Father — for the tassels knew their island of origin.

But now she was free, and if she told no one where she came from, then no one could trace her, or Heaven and Earth, back to Sweetwater. And Father had only made her promise not to reveal it to anyone in the village. "If you tell me what you know about joining the gallant wanderers," she said, "I'll show you what I can until we go our separate ways."

Shigan sat back, tension leaving his shoulders, his hands, his forehead. He didn't say anything more, but shut his eyes. A very short time later, when one of the sailors came around with grilled fish and sticky rice balls, he didn't react. Then they saw that he was sound asleep.

Over the next few days, Shigan mostly slept. Mouse found herself less listless each day, especially after Yaso brought her more of that medicine to drink. Its pungency was distinctive. Not bad, not good. More . . . odd. It tasted much as the ground smells after the first thaw of spring.

When Mouse asked what it was, Yaso said, "I had to use most of the precious herb on the wounded, but I did save a bit. I've brewed slivers for your tea."

Four mornings later, they sailed into the harbor at Te Gar Island.

Mouse had thought the harbor at her home island large, but it was not half the size of the one they sailed into.

The sailors expected them to help bring to the deck all the empty baskets and receptacles that would be filled again next month. Mouse was relieved to feel closer to her old self again. But too many days had passed since she had done Heaven and Earth, and she felt stuffy and crowded inside her own skin.

At last they dropped into the back of one of the longboats to be rowed ashore.

The ship captain said, "If you're going up to the garrison, I can show you the way."

Mouse took out the letters. Her heart drummed as she held them out. "Will you take these? I want to get in a day of liberty before I go."

The captain laughed, taking the letters and the tally. "I usually do, and it means a free meal for me. Oh, to be young again!"

Soon the longboat bumped up against a piling. They climbed up a barnacle-covered stone stair to the upper part of the dock, where boats tied on when the tide was high.

The sailors wished them a good journey, then headed off toward the warehouses as Mouse, Shigan, and Yaso started up the quay toward the main street.

As soon as they were alone, Mouse turned to Shigan. "Should we seek the Hall of Justice? There should be a wall with notices."

Shigan's brows slanted at a steep angle. "Why would you want that? All you'll see are warnings and capital lists — and there's sure to be someone watching to see who is interested in them. Which the gallant wanderers aren't. They have their own ways of communicating. We just have to find one who will talk to us."

"Oh." Mouse shivered at the idea of unseen eyes watching to see who read the notice boards. She was now glad that she was with Shigan, annoying as he could be.

They followed a stream of people up onto the quay, and then to a street that led into the city. Everything was new and interesting, from the ornamental trees to the accent the vendors called out in. But familiar smells drifted on the cold air, waking her appetite.

Mouse stared in a swooping combination of amazement and consternation. The street was fascinating, but had one common factor: everyone seemed to have a hand out for money. Her stomach reminded her that she hadn't eaten for what now felt like an age, and she was aware of a pulse of regret about the garrison. At least it would be familiar, unlike this world in which money was charged for lychee nuts, and melons. At home, when you wanted a snack, you picked and peeled the nuts yourself, and same with fetching a melon off its vine.

Familiar—and back to the old questions, she reminded herself as Shigan lounged along with scarcely hidden boredom. And Yaso . . . was just Yaso.

Under Commander Weken's orders.

Mouse stopped suddenly, and when the other two stopped, she turned to Yaso. "You've been really good to me. I don't want to lie to you. But I've decided to leave army training."

"All right," Yaso said amicably.

Mouse frowned, unsure whether Yaso was hiding something, or didn't understand.

"Ayah," she sighed. "I overheard some fourth and fifth years once saying something about deserters. I think they only behead you if you run from battle, but still, if you feel you have to report on me to Commander Weken, I'd rather we part now."

Yaso said, "I want to follow you." It was simply said, with sincerity Mouse could feel.

"Let's go, before those sailors finish up their other cargo, and see us standing around," Shigan suggested.

The three followed the crowd up toward a vast intersection with what appeared to be a main road, running parallel to the coast. Mouse stared avidly at the shrines, the performers hoping for coins, and the shops, the embodiment of the country bumpkin. The three of them caught the eye, Shigan for his striking good looks and sauntering indolence, wearing his plain dun robe as if it were five layers of silk. He ignored everyone and everything except for scraps of music, grimacing as if offended when he heard false notes, or fumbled rhythm. Otherwise he looked bored.

One of those whose eye followed them was a sharp-faced woman with long reddish hair worn high on her head and streaming down her back. Her robes swished beguilingly about her legs above her scuffed boots as she loitered outside the most popular inn for travelers.

She watched Shigan for half the length of the street before shifting her gaze to Mouse, the perfect clueless outsider. She matched their pace, drifting nearer, and finally, when the three turned a corner, she bumped up against Shigan, raised a hand around which she wore a bracelet of tiny bells, and as she shook these, and her targets' eyes went to it, with the other hand she reached for Mouse's sash pouch.

Which was completely empty, but five hard years had bred in Mouse a dislike of being touched. In a move faster than the eye, the woman found her hand knocked away.

She smiled beguilingly at Mouse, displaying sharp little white teeth as she said, "Looking for fun, sweet boy?"

"Only if it's free," Mouse said, wondering what this odd person's idea of fun might be.

"Free for you and fun for me," she replied, still smiling. "Come with me. Meet some friends? They'll treat you real well—" She stopped abruptly as her wide-set eyes encountered Yaso's limpid gaze.

The woman backed up a step, turned, and with a flick of her fluttering skirts that somehow resembled the flick and flutter of nine tails, she vanished into a crowd—from which a roar reverberated. Mouse gave a puzzled glance at Yaso, who hadn't said or done anything that she'd heard, but then she was distracted by the sounds of shouting and laughter.

There was a raised fighting ring off to the right, built between two buildings, boards hammered and poised on a multitude of barrels, and railed by wedding-red bunting. A burly man stood in the center of a ring, arms upraised as the crowd roared around him. Another man limped to the rail, climbed painfully over, and vanished into the crowd.

"I'll fight anyone here, any weapon!" the burly man roared in vernacular. "An imperial boater if you beat me!" He held up a silver, boat-shaped tael, which was astounding wealth to Mouse.

Shigan grinned, his eyes wide. "If we won that, we could get a room at an inn. Baths. Clothes. Maybe even a weapon."

Mouse frowned. "Neither of us could grapple that man. Look at the muscles on his neck. He's got muscle on top of muscle."

"He said any weapon. See the rack of swords and spears on the back wall of the ring? After two years I ought to have learned *something*." Shigan raised his voice, his vernacular Imperial-accented. "I'll try!"

Before Mouse could utter a protest, he pushed his way into the crowd. She followed after, Yaso behind.

Those nearest the ring howled, laughed, and shouted

mocking encouragement. Clearly they were there to be entertained—and to lay bets on the contestants, Mouse saw when she glimpsed the side table where a woman was taking money and handing out carved markers.

Another roar as Shigan climbed into the ring, and surveyed the weapons rack: a throwing spear, a halberd, a steel sword, a wooden sword. His hand reached for the steel sword, and the spectators uttered a low, "Oooooo!"

But before he could touch it, he snatched his hand away and picked up the wooden sword, which was very much like the ones they had used for scrapping for two years. He whirled it to warm up his wrist, but the spectators took it as posturing, and some *Ooooo*ed again, while others called mocking encouragement, or comments.

"He's rabbiting."

"Afraid of steel, eh?"

"Come on, pretty boy, let's see your sword swing!"

Shigan flushed, which puzzled Mouse until the innuendo caught up with her. She was so used to boys bragging and comparing and otherwise making remarks about parts that she didn't have, and didn't want to have—she thought her own arrangement, with everything nicely tucked inside where no one could kick or punch you, so much better—that she'd gotten adept at ignoring such blather. But Shigan was a boy, and it clearly irked him.

He snapped the sword up to the ready. It whooshed nicely, and this time the spectators *Ooooo*ed appreciatively again, though there were some more catcalls, too.

For the space of about ten heartbeats, Shigan whacked away fearlessly, his form so much better than it had been. But he fought in that stamp-and-jerk method that Mouse now suspected would be most effective in a line. Alone, and against a huge veteran fighter, he was a gnat attacking a tiger.

The burly man let Shigan get in enough blows to test him, and then he took the offensive. Mouse winced as she watched it happen. She saw the moment of decision, the smirk and shift of balance and tightening of the right shoulder as the man came on the attack. First he feinted, then slapped aside Shigan's thrust. The sword whipped around, then smacked Shigan on the arm hard enough to make him drop his weapon.

He could have backed up, but no. He whirled the blade around and smacked him across the face with the flat of the blade, not hard enough to wound. It was meant to entertain the watchers, but at the cost of humiliating Shigan, whose face now sported a telltale red mark. Then the sword arced a third time and whacked Shigan on the butt, knocking him into the rail hard enough to almost send him flying over.

The crowd roared with laughter as Shigan clutched desperately at the bunting strewn along the rail.

Mouse burned with indignation. Shigan could be irritating, but not right now. He'd volunteered to earn something for them all, and even if he had been his usual annoying self, knocking the weapon away was fair. But slapping his face with a wooden sword . . .

No.

Mouse pushed her way through the crowd until she reached the rail. She hopped up, and vaulted over.

As soon as her foot hit the ring, the laughter redoubled, some with tears on their faces as they pointed at her. She shut all that out as she picked up the wooden sword Shigan had used. It was damp with sweat. She used the end of her robe to wipe the handle so that it would not slip in her hand, and faced the man.

He stood with his head to one side. "What are you doing here, urchin?"

"Fight," Mouse said. She heard her own high voice, and flushed. But she held her ground.

"Fight," the man mimicked in a squeal. Then he tipped his head the other way. "I'd lose face to even consider it."

Mouse didn't answer. She waited where she was, her body humming with Essence. She hadn't entirely lost it!

The man sighed. "Will someone remove this puling infant for me?"

Two men clambered over and separated, each reaching for one of her arms. Mouse whirled the sword in an arc too fast to see, striking the first on the point of his elbow, and the second on the knee. Both stumbled, one falling, the other clasping his arm and dancing in a circle, cursing.

The big man's smirk thinned. "Interesting. Ayah, if that is the only trick you know, little worm, here's a lesson —"

And he struck.

Or, he meant to strike.

But Mouse had heard the intake of breath, saw muscle-tightening of intent, and neatly sidestepped so that the sword slapped the air. She brought hers around and smacked the man, hard, on the shoulder, same place he'd hit Shigan.

The crowd's noise shifted in tone, most staying with scorn, some surprised, and not a few laughing. Mouse shut it all out. Her unwinking gaze stayed on the huge man before her, as she breathed in Essence.

The man came at her again, this time testing, still fast, still hard, but watchful. But his breathing, his muscles, signaled every blow, every block, and she evaded him, often by a hair's breadth, and when she next struck, it was at his face.

His head twisted at the last instant—and the blow mostly struck his nose. She had pulled the blow the way he had, to slap and not to wound, but on a nose, any blow is painful. Worse was the unspoken lesson here: he had badly underestimated this runt.

He attacked once again, this time with full force and fury—to discover only air. Then pain blossomed too quickly to see: shoulder, opposite knee, and then a very hard poke in the ass.

The man dropped his sword, clapped a hand to his knee, and let out an unwilling laugh. "You win this bout, young master. We don't usually get gallant wanderers. What sect are you?"

The noisy crowd quieted, most of those in front wanting to hear the answer. Mouse took her time laying the sword in the rack, thinking fast. She ought to have considered that type of question! She could not mention Heaven and Earth, which was a style, not a sect. In fact, it wasn't even a style, but the names for two drills, in typical guard humor, Father had said: fighting upward against mounted warriors being Heaven, whereas Earth was fighting straight ahead and downward against foot warriors.

In any case, Mouse would never say those words around anyone but family, lest it somehow reach the evil emperor. Her mind cast about rapidly, then lit on a cherished memory, the Essence-drenched sacred space under the redbark trees . . .

"The Redbark Sect," she said.

"Why is your senior so bad?" The man pointed at Shigan, who stood beside Yaso, one cheekbone swollen slightly.

"He just joined us," Mouse said.

The man's voice quickened. "Where? Who is your master? Where can I find him?"

"We wander," Mouse said—and, remembering her hero tales, "If you are fated to find out more, you will."

To her relief, the crowd actually accepted that. But for how long? She knew she couldn't deal with any more questions.

She stuck out her hand. "I'll take that silver now."

The woman dealing with the betting stood up, holding out the silver tael. Mouse took it. The woman said something, but Mouse didn't hear it. The noise of the crowd was too loud, and Mouse didn't care. She didn't owe them anything. She readied herself, leaped to the top of the rail and then somersaulted over the heads of the crowd.

A roar went up, this time of approval.

As they turned, some shoving to follow, she said in Imperial, "Let's go."

They ran, Mouse heading straight uphill.

Two

SOME FOLLOWED, OF COURSE, but Shigan and Mouse had been training hard, and they soon outstripped the followers, who fell away one by one. Mouse and Shigan fell into the training rhythm and paced side by side until Shigan stopped so abruptly he swayed.

Mouse was about to ask why when she noticed a carriage some twenty paces ahead of them being pulled to the side, and all the foot traffic went to the side as well, as from above the thump of a drum and the thin, reedy sounds of music drifted on the cold wind. Shigan bent, leaning his hands on his knees as Mouse glanced back, relieved to see Yaso a little ways behind, crimson in the face.

Guilt struck her. "I'll carry my things. You don't have to be a grunt anymore."

Yaso hitched the tied bundle higher over a shoulder and said, "I don't mind."

Unsure what to say to that, Mouse surveyed the cavalcade coming from above that had forced everyone else to the side. First came two rows of guards in clattering armor with markings of green, blue, and peach worked into their breastplates, matching the intertwined salamanders on the banners borne by the next pair. After that, the musicians, followed by a horse-drawn cart, whose liveried driver applied some sort of stick that braced the wheels, sending up the sharp scent of hot wood.

The carriage itself was the typical box on wheels, gilded to the upswept roof corners, painted with salamanders and osmanthus. The silken curtains hid the passengers from view, though Mouse got the feeling that the passengers could see through the silk.

The foot traffic above all bowed, so Mouse did, too. Shigan remained where he was, stooped over as he breathed deeply. Yaso bowed and the carriage passed, with two rows of maids, five each, following. These maids didn't look a lot older than Mouse, their hair twisted up tightly in fox ears on either side of their heads, their modest robes green and gray with a thin edging of peach on their sashes.

Mouse wondered what their lives were like as they passed without glancing to either side, and then turned to survey the rest of this street. The buildings looked much finer here than that main street paralleling the quay. Here were discreet shops, lots of plants, and along the north side of the curving street, fine manors whose decorated doors had charmed guardian flying lion statues at each side, one to eat any bad luck approaching the door, and the other to draw wealth and health. Only the nobles and powerful clans were permitted to display these outside their doors.

The road curved upward, toward the private mansion of the governor, of which only two layers of swept roof were visible. On the upward points, no fewer than five statues, which meant someone connected to the imperial family at four degrees.

Shigan straightened up, looking around. "Let's find an inn. I really want a bath." He jerked his thumb backward. "But we won't find anything up there that would let us in for just that boater. If it even is one."

"Boater?" Mouse repeated.

"Slang for silver taels," Shigan said with a shrug. "The court tosses them to the crowd on festival days. Inns up that way probably demand to see gold before you stick your nose in."

Mouse accepted that, but said, "Shouldn't we look for gallant wanderers first?"

Shigan said, "They aren't easy to find, especially in cities. They are actually living outside the law, remember. Some governors will clap them up for forced labor, I found out that spring. What we need to do is go wandering ourselves and hope we see them, or walk the streets every day until we meet one who will talk to us."

"Oh."

They started back down again. No one was following them, or paying them the least attention, Mouse was glad to see. "Shouldn't we trade this silver for coins somewhere?"

"Inns can change them." Shigan held out his hand. Mouse gave the tael to him and he inspected it, then grinned as he handed it back. "It's truly a dragon boater."

"Is there a difference?" Mouse asked. She had only seen a silver tael once, when walking around the harbor that day so very, very long ago, with First and Second Brothers. A pulse of hurt wrung through her, regret and longing: she missed them both. She knew Muin was fine, but for the first time she spared a thought for Yskanda. Of course he'd be happy. He was finally getting his chance to draw to his heart's content.

Shigan said, "Any silver or goldsmith can make boaters, but they make them different sizes, and some even mix other metals in them, making them worth less, though when they get caught at adding impurities, it's a capital offense. But the *dragon* boaters — imperial taels — have to be a certain purity and weight or they don't get the dragon claw and tiger-eye stamp here at the bottom. There's a charm worked in that no one is able to duplicate."

They had been walking back downhill as he spoke. Mouse discovered she was glad Shigan was leading. She hadn't even thought about such difficulties as money, or inns. But she had to begin. After all, the heroes in the tales dealt with both all the time.

They reached a cross-street that ran parallel to the wide curve of the quay, which opened into the one on which they'd gained their boater. The hanging signs of jugs inside a square, the sign for travelers, had been worked into wood, with sun-faded banners and standing pillars all up and down the street.

Which one to pick? Mouse had never set foot in an inn in her life. A glance at Shigan disclosed uncertainty in his face as well. Then a scuffle behind them, a soft sound, caused them to turn. Yaso had dropped the bundle, and stooped to pick it up again.

"I'm going to carry my own things from now on," Mouse said, springing forward to help. To emphasize her point, she spoke in the vernacular. "Yaso, you don't have to carry my share. We're not cadets and orderlies anymore. Here's an inn," she added, pointing to a sign right overhead depicting a

beautifully rendered blue hibiscus. "Why don't we stay here?"
She peered at the door through a stream of people going in and
out.

Shigan headed for the door in his usual impetuous
manner. A big man with long sleeves, a brocade over-robe, and
a huge belt worked with gems scowled at him from the
doorway, clearly ready to knock him out of his path.

Mouse grabbed Shigan by the sleeve and yanked him back.
"Do you want to get beaten? Don't get in their way," she said
in an undervoice. "I saw that at home. These nobles will have
their bodyguard hit anyone in their path." She pointed to the
husky man following the swaggerer in brocade. He swung a
cudgel by his side. Behind both followed a pair of servants
who walked meekly, hands folded right over left.

Shigan glared after the brocade man, but said nothing as
Mouse led the way inside. Here, an innkeeper with gray at her
temples stood. She had been bowing and smiling widely, but
at the sight of Mouse, Shigan, and Yaso, her smile faded to
barely polite. "Yes?"

"A room," Mouse said.

The innkeeper's brows lifted. "Do you have money?"

Mouse held out the boater on her palm.

The innkeeper's tight mouth relaxed, though her smile
wasn't as wide as the one she'd given the back of the man in
brocade. "We have a room. Two beds will fit on the kang, and
your servant there can have a pallet by the door."

That sounded reasonable. "Can you change money?"
Mouse asked.

The smile widened to a smirk. Mouse caught side of a
movement beyond the innkeeper, where a teenage girl stood,
meek as one of the servants following the brocade man, only
not dressed as well. Mouse couldn't tell if this girl was looking
at her or not—she was squinting so hard that no pupil could
be seen—but then the girl gave her head a slight shake.

Mouse's gaze flicked back to the innkeeper's smirk as the
woman said, "Of course we can—we are happy to change
money, or perform any other service our guests desire."

Mouse took a chance. Stumbling a little over her words,
she said, "Thank you, that is very good to know. Ah, where is
the room?"

Evidently that was a reasonable question, as the innkeeper
didn't blink. She snapped her fingers, and without looking
round, said, "Petal, show the customers to Seahorse."

Petal bowed to the innkeeper's back, and led Mouse and Shigan upstairs and down a long hall past widely spaced double doors that had to have sumptuous rooms behind them. Mouse was distracted partly by the way the girl walked, sort of a stiff list, the way her peers often had after taking an especially hard fall or blow, for a few days. Mouse was also distracted by this first look into an inn. Each of those widely spaced double doors bore a plaque with a name on it—Kraken, Leviathan, Dolphin.

The inn girl Petal led them all the way to the end and then turned left, along an adjacent hall. The doors here were narrower, and closer together. The names were painted on the wall next to the doors, smaller sea creatures this time. Each name was framed in decoration.

All the way to the end, a little past the turn that would run parallel to the front—no doubt looking into a courtyard. The last door (with Seahorse written very plainly, no decoration at all) opened into a small room taken up mostly by a barren kang, with bedrolls stacked at one side, and a low table with flat mats around it. The window looked outward, over an alley that seemed to lead to privies, judging by a faint whiff wafting in.

Petal said, "I'll put heating stones under the kang. It'll be warm by nightfall."

As Mouse peered into the room doubtfully, Petal said in a low voice, "It's small—the smallest we have—but it's clean. I tidy it myself. Just keep the window shut if the wind dies. And like all the other rooms, put your shoes outside before you enter. The bond-servant comes around once an hour to collect them, so they'll be clean when you want them again. If you don't want them cleaned by us—some have very fine shoes, with gems sewn on and the like—use the shoe rack inside the door."

"The room is fine," Mouse said quickly. "I just... ah, if we want a bath. There isn't a separate room, or a screen?"

"There is a bath house at the end of the alley," Petal said slowly, peering at them as if to bring them into better focus.

Then she waved them over the threshold and into the room, where she said in an urgent undervoice, "You don't seem to have a lot of extra money, if you don't mind my saying."

Mouse held out the silver tael. "This is all we have."

Petal breathed out, then said, frank for frank, "First Mother will kill me if she hears, but she'll cheat you if you change it with her."

"Thank you," Mouse said. "I thought that's why you . . ."

Petal raised a hand, glancing nervously to the side, as if someone hovered there, a stick to hand to beat her with if Mouse said the words out loud. "The room costs are reasonable, to get people in. Where she gets you are the extra charges. If you eat here. Bathe here. Ask for laundry service or mending."

"Who does the mending?" Mouse asked.

"I do," Petal said. "At night, after the kitchen is readied for morning. For bathing, if you don't want us bringing the tub and water to your room, which is three hands" — she flashed five fingers, meaning five brass coins — "go down this alley to Silk Row and turn toward the sea. You can almost see it from here. There are bath houses the sailors use. They're nice, and a third of the cost we'd ask. And you can eat anywhere along the street. It will be good. No one lasts if it isn't good."

"Thank you," Mouse said. "Petal?"

The girl bowed.

"One last question. Where can we change this boater honestly?"

"Take it to the Haipen Silversmith up back where you came, fifth on the right, next to Rani the Fortuneteller. Haipen will be reasonable, only charges five tin."

The girl performed a stiff bow, one side of her face twisting in a wince, then she stepped back over the threshold and pulled the door shut behind her.

"Bath first," Shigan declared. He was speaking in vernacular now, slowly — as if thinking out his words first.

"I need to practice," Mouse stated in the common tongue they'd used in the military. She enjoyed being able to say it — though it came out sounding defiant. "I haven't moved for days. I'm doing that first."

Shigan's lips parted. "The bath can wait. You did promise to teach me."

"I can change the money," Yaso offered. "If you want to practice now."

Mouse held out the boater. She still had no idea why Yaso had decided to come with them. Maybe the orderly would decide that freedom was better than hauling someone else's stuff, and take off. With the boater.

But Yaso had always been honest with her, especially

about Essence. It felt right to trust Yaso. If it turned out to be wrong, she would find a way to earn money

Yaso left noiselessly. Mouse turned away from Shigan, her thoughts scattered around the vague sense that the room was too small. She moved to the window, pushed it open, and peered down. "It doesn't stink too bad," she said. "Best, there's a lot of grass between two fences and the backs of shops. No one will bother us."

"Lead on."

They found a back stair, Mouse not wanting to pass by the smirking innkeeper. There was no proof of anything Petal had said, except the fact that Mouse didn't like that smirk. Though maybe it was perfectly reasonable for a person running a business to look for rich custom. But being so obvious about it was scarcely polite.

She shook off thoughts about the innkeeper when they reached the grass. Shigan coughed, wrinkling his nose, but said nothing as Mouse walked in a small circle, stamping down the crackling grasses, and watching her breath cloud. She was trying to remember how Father had first taught her Heaven and Earth, then remembered Father saying that the real lessons had begun when she was small. But she didn't want to stand there talking all day.

She said, "Watch me once. It's warmups first, then moves against mounted, and after that moves against foot soldiers, all four sides."

Prickles ran over the backs of her arms and across her stomach at the idea of doing Heaven and Earth before a witness. She shivered involuntarily, reminded herself that she had promised, and anyway, they were far, far from Father and the island and anyone finding out and telling the evil emperor.

She swung into the first movement, and as habit took over, sheer joy put snap into her movements. She didn't look at Shigan. Couldn't look at him—she didn't want a distraction, so she did not see the wide, unblinking gaze of one who has at last witnessed the sunbeam finding the waterfall.

To Shigan, there was nothing in his life's experience to match the sight of Ryu Mouse's short, scrawny figure whirling through a complication of defenses and attacks, equal parts grace and strength and lethality. Distractions such as the grease stain on the butt of Ryu's robe, and the scuffed boots, the tangled, greasy topknot, and even the whiff of privy on the briny wind coming off the sea became irrelevant, outshone by the brilliance of that sword form.

Ryu had been exasperating and cagey by turns ever since their first meeting, but now all that was left was . . . intent.

Mouse came to the end, and the words wrung out of Shigan, "Teach me that."

She heard his tone as a demand, and scowled his way. "I *said* I would. But you have to do it in pieces. There's a lot that we learned as cadets that you will have to unlearn."

She picked up a twig, then bent to dig in the soft ground. She made Father's circle with the S dividing it, and around it, the small circles where the foot would land as one transitioned from one move to the next. "Equal balance, sun and moons."

"First, stance and breathing," she said. She'd switched back to the common tongue used in the military.

Shigan let out one short sigh of impatience, then composed himself, and silently followed instructions, eyes closing as he concentrated.

He had been taught breathing, so he caught on fast. She moved to the footwork, a concept he also knew from learning to dance. After two times through, she said, "You're getting it much faster than I did. You have to be able to land on each circle without looking, without thinking about it."

Precision footwork was nothing new to him. They kept at it until the sun gradually sank, and the deepening shadows blurred detail. He began to loathe the words, "No, again." But he kept a rein on his temper—and she saw the struggle, relenting at last. He really did seem to understand it, and much faster than she had, but he was also older, and had been trained to move by someone, though not in martial arts.

When they could barely see one another, Mouse glanced up toward their window, surprised to see the paper between the lattices glowing golden.

"We can start with the sword in the morning," Mouse said. Her body felt good again, strong, her muscles warmed and singing with natural Essence. It would be good to get back to practice every day.

"I'll be ready," Shigan stated.

Upstairs, they discovered Yaso in their shared room, the bedding laid out military-style on the kang (heads to the wall, feet pointed inward) and, in the tiny space left, the small, plain table had been set with dishes, a pair of eating sticks at each plate.

"There are only two," Mouse objected. "But we can split it

into three portions."

"I've already eaten," Yaso said. "Go ahead. I have to take the dishes back. They kept the rest of our money in case."

"This is wonderful, Yaso," Mouse said, ravenous. "But . . . money. How many brass did you get? We don't know how long they'll last." As she heaped her dish with rice, sweet potato, and grilled fish, she added, "I want to join the gallant wanderers, but there's no telling when I'll find one to point the way. So I guess I'll have to find a way to earn money first." And to Yaso, "Where did you find this food? It's so *good.*"

"It's better than what we've been eating," Shigan observed. "But then pretty much anything would be."

Mouse ignored that, and turned to Yaso. "Did you go exploring? Did you see a bath house? If we take the dishes back together, I can get some money and go bathe."

Yaso spent the rest of the meal describing the various shops along the street as Mouse and Shigan inhaled the food, right down to chasing stray grains of rice around the plates. They piled the dishes, grabbed their second set of clothes, and all three went out to carry the dishes back to the eatery Yaso had found, where they ransomed their coinage.

The bath house Petal had suggested was scarcely fifty paces away, a place with a modest front, but warm and smelling of herbs. Orchids grew in pots around it, carefully tended. "I didn't think Morningstar Robe grew wild this far north," Shigan said.

Mouse scarcely glanced at the orchids, a modest white — having lived all her life in an environment where orchids of every hue grew wild. But . . . "Morningstar Robe? I never heard that name."

Shigan swung around to regard her. "I thought you were so well read. It's a tale told to children, how the Morningstar Goddess as a girl was treated ill by her cruel older sisters, and when an important suitor came to look them all over, between them they used all the jewels in the house, so the Morningstar Goddess went out to the garden and decorated her robe and hair with orchids, and the suitor chose her." He laughed. "I suppose you wouldn't hear it, as it's usually a tale for girls." He was remembering how his youngest sister had loved it.

Mouse said, "Yes — " then stopped, remembering that she was a girl. But she still hadn't heard it or even read it. Maybe because it was a tale about how important it was for a girl to be beautiful, Mouse thought as she followed Shigan to the men's side of the bathhouse. Mother had scorned all such tales!

She firmly opted for a bath in a little alcove all to herself, to Shigan's surprise. "It costs more," he said. "Why? We were all together at Loyalty Fortress."

"I grew up this way," Mouse stated. "Modesty is one of Kanda's first virtues."

Shigan's unhidden surprise made her think that for all his affect of superiority, he must have grown up in a home even smaller than hers, with everyone on top of one another. Ayah, that was *his* life.

The important thing was, she decided as she sank gratefully into the steaming water and sniffed in the fragrance of clean-smelling herbs, she had two decisions to make. The most immediate was how to make more money, especially if she wanted to have baths all by herself. The second was, when to strike out on her own.

She leaned her head against the rim of the tub and shut her eyes as she moved her knees around, making the water swirl about her skin. At least she didn't have to decide right then what to do about the last part. And what if they discovered she was a girl? Did it matter?

She sat upright, calculating quickly. No, she still had time before she ought to expect another moon time. Until then, she just . . . didn't want anything to change.

Her reverie broke when a man came along the corridor outside the hanging panels yelling for any who wanted more hot water — three tinnies. The thought of someone coming in shook off the creeping lassitude, and she hastened out of the bath, toweled hurriedly, and was just pulling on her stockings when the hanging batted unceremoniously and here was Shigan, dressed except for his long fall of blue-black hair, which he was twisting up into his warrior's knot.

"There you are," he said. "I thought you'd fallen asleep."

Alarm had burned through Mouse. "I didn't invite you in," she snapped.

He blinked in bewilderment. "So?" Then his expression changed. "Were you born in one of those ascetic sects? How did you survive training, with us all in one hut?"

As he spoke, he tried to remember Ryu Mouse in the baths — or the privies — but then no one would have scoffed at Ryu. Their hut mates had respected fighting skills beyond their own. In any case, he didn't recollect seeing Ryu in the baths or the privies, but then he didn't remember ever looking, either, his own intent invariably to get in and out as fast as possible — especially the privies.

"Yes," Mouse snapped, slamming her booted foot to the floor, and continued unfairly, "As I said before, I was raised on the Twenty-Five Virtues, modesty being one of the very first." She shoved past him and out into the frigid air, and away from the entire subject, Yaso trailing behind.

They hurried back to the inn before the air could chill their freshly washed skin, and up to their room, where Yaso had left their single lantern burning.

True to her word, Petal had put heating stones beneath the kang. Mouse curled like a puppy into warm bedding.

Shigan lay awake, staring at the ceiling.

Memory arrowed him back to the sight of Ryu Mouse tossing aside bow and shield, then taking just a wooden practice sword, leaping from those stone walls like some kind of warrior prince from the *Tales of the Gallant Wanderer*. But . . . smaller.

Then came that amazing fighting, and the single blow that knocked the assassins tumbling . . .

He had to learn that. If a scrawny runt like Ryu could master it, he could, too.

He slept.

THREE

MOUSE WOKE FROM DISTURBING dreams involving trying to count tinnies that kept dropping and spilling, but it was desperately important to know exactly how many she had. When she opened her eyes, she knew she had to set about earning something. But where? How?

She turned her head to where Yaso sat in the center of a faint but distinct, lucent glow, hands on knees, legs crossed at the ankle. Mouse blinked and sat up. No, she was not imagining that glow. It was the distinctive glow of beeswax candlelight. But no candle burned – and the window was pale blue with impending dawn.

Mouse cast a glance at the quilt-covered hump that was Shigan, then scrambled over, close enough that she could smell that faint scent that always came off Yaso, like honey-comb. "Teach me?" She mouthed the words.

Yaso smiled, and mimed what to do: hands together, breathing slowly.

Mouse knew that Essence breathing. She sat across from Yaso, legs crossed, hands on knees.

Yaso's whisper was so soft Mouse barely heard it. "How did you learn? Through the five essences, or the four elements? There are many roads."

Mouse shut her eyes. "Four elements," she whispered back, remembering being small. Lying on her bedding, every fold of which hurt her feverish skin. Her head pounding. Even her eyeballs hurt. Her stomach roiled, and water tasted like marsh weed with blood in it.

The only thing she could bear was Ul Keg's hand gently holding hers as he kept saying, *Breathe with me, breathe with me.*

She remembered struggling and panting and whimpering and fretting as his slow breathing drew her like an invisible embrace, until she sank into the rhythm, and then, oh, and then, the pain didn't hurt so much. It was still there, like a vast fire, but she floated above the ground and the fire, in the third element, air.

Then he'd said, *Remember, you are made up of four elements. Fire is one. Fever is your fire, trying to burn the poisonous things that make you sick. Do you see them?*

No, she had whispered, but as she said it, she held onto the image of floating above the fire, keeping herself from falling into it again, where it hurt so much. And then she saw the wiggling, spiky blobs of a sickly blue-white hue falling toward the earth and trying to crawl into it to spread and branch. But the flames burned them to ash.

I see, she'd said. *I see.*

Then breathe with me, and watch the flames scour the ground clean. Breathe, and see your fire scour your vital waters clean. Breathe, and see the fires burn the things out of the air, until the air is clean. Then you will drink as much pure water as you can to wash the ashes away.

She watched and breathed, breathed and watched, and the things came slower and slower, then stopped altogether. *They are gone,* she'd said. *I'm still so thirsty.*

That's because your vital waters dried to help the fires burn. But now you can let the fires go, and drink this medicine, and let all your vital elements come into harmony . . .

Mouse opened her eyes, about to explain, when Yaso began to speak, even more softly.

"All thoughts are one, and one is the universe.

Let the Essence breathe through you, unifying the ground that is you with the air you breathe.

Let the Essence unify the fire in your veins with the waters of your body.

And when all is in harmony, bring forth the light."

Mouse didn't know if she were glowing or not, but she gained that detached sense of floating between earth and sky, all in harmony. Including Essence, which breathed in and out of her like a tide washing up and receding. It was there, and powerful—but as soon as she squinted over at Yaso to compare their glows, that sense was gone. Inside her mind, she thumped to earth.

She tried to compose herself, struggling against impatience. Then Yaso said, "That is a good beginning."

Mouse opened her eyes, astonished to discover the window was full of light. She jumped up. "I'm going to do warmups," she said loudly, in direction of the mound of quilt that was Shigan. If he woke, fine. If he didn't, ayah! At least it wasn't like Loyalty Fortress, where cadets got up for training or got in trouble.

This *is* training, she said to herself as she got into stockings and boots. That was an odd thing, too. Now she was used to boots; the last time she'd been able to work in bare feet had been in her secret garden behind the apple trees. It seemed so long ago!

But she did not like the idea of walking barefoot through those filthy gutters.

She stepped to the middle of the well-trampled circle and began swinging her arms as she engaged her Essence breathing once more.

Shigan arrived at a run. She obligingly left the middle of the circle to him, but otherwise didn't speak as she began the warmup, Shigan mimicking her. The small circles by now had been thoroughly trampled along with the stubby grass, but Mouse knew where they were, and had to admit that he hit the small circles perfectly with each step and turn.

It was time to keep her promise. It felt strange to be a teacher, and stranger yet that the student was Shigan Fin, but he had done all she asked—and there was the memory of that intensity as they sat in the hold of the ship, the way he breathed, the huge pupils of his eyes. She still did not understand what had gripped him, only that it was important to him, a person she'd assumed didn't take anything seriously.

"Now for the Redbark sword form," she said, having thought it all out. It felt a little like stealing, but she could not actually name its true name, lest that somehow lead back to Father.

First she put Shigan through the warmup one more time. Mouse watched narrowly, ready to pounce on the slightest error, but she had to admit that he learned fast. He moved so well, so *strong*. She recognized some of her reluctance for the poison of jealousy. Tchah! She breathed out hard to extirpate it, as if breathing out a ripe stench.

That enabled her to begin. She walked him through one side of Heaven, leaving the other three for later. They sped up slowly, repeating the form until a man ambled up, carrying two slop buckets to empty into the privy, and then from another direction, a dog raced along, tail waving, followed by a couple of children. When they'd halted for the fourth time, Mouse saw that the morning was already well advanced.

"Let's get something to eat," she said.

Shigan suppressed the desire to insist they stay and keep working. When they got inside, the innkeeper looked up from watering the flowering hibiscus in pots along the back window. "Good morning, customers," she said with a bow, and a very false smile. "Is everything to your satisfaction?"

"Yes," Shigan said. He spoke vernacular but he'd unconsciously straightened up, erect with his old hauteur.

The innkeeper's eyes narrowed as she examined him and his dun robe, her brows twitching slightly as she considered the anomaly of a boy who carried himself like a young lord dressed worse than her own servants. She cooed, "You have not availed yourself of our excellent dining area. Very private and quiet, but the best food on the street. Or maybe Petal was remiss in explaining?"

As she spoke, she shot a look at Petal, there in the background, that caused the maid's expression to pale to a sickly hue.

By now Mouse had identified what she did not like about this innkeeper. It was not just the falsity between smile and eyes, but the cruel note in her voice that reminded Mouse of Yulin, cruel as in cold anger, a relish for seeing others in pain.

Mouse stepped forward before Shigan could speak. "Oh, she did," Mouse stated. "She did her very best to get us to stay, so tempting she made everything sound. But we had already made promises."

"Of course you must keep those," the innkeeper said, bowing again and moving aside to address a group coming down the stairs.

"Why did you lie?" Shigan asked when they got to the top of the stairs. "I can see hiding that Petal told us about the cheating, but all that about promises?"

"Because Petal moves like someone who just took ten with a stick," Mouse said bluntly.

"I didn't see—"

A cough behind them caused Shigan to halt and they both looked back, to find Petal right behind them. "A message," Petal said, only her cheeks betraying that she'd heard herself talked about. "He paid me to put it in your hand."

Petal's fingers trembled as she held out a scrolled paper to Mouse. As soon as Mouse took it, Petal turned and fled.

Mouse didn't open it until they reached their room. Yaso wasn't there.

Mouse opened the note. Scrawled in vernacular:

To the Redbark Warrior: I spent all afternoon and evening watches seeking you. Three that match your description are said to be at this inn. If you want to earn some good money, come back to my ring. Old Rock.

"What's it say?" Shigan asked. "Or is it secret?"

She handed him the paper. He glanced at it, then at her, giving a low whistle. "I don't know about you, but I've been wondering if we're going to have to sign up to haul night soil."

She grimaced. "Why would we do that?"

"We don't know how long it'll be before we can find our way to the gallant wanderers, and unless you've got a few dozen boaters hidden about you, we'll need to eat. I found out that hauling night soil is the only job in most cities that always wants more drivers. You get to keep more of the earnings if you have your own cart," he added.

"You must have been a really rotten apprentice if hauling night soil was a better job than going home again," she commented. "Couldn't you at least try dancing with some other house or company?"

He gave her an incredulous stare, for he'd never actually *said* he was a dancer. But he hadn't denied it when the Mo cousins and the rest speculated about him being a thief, a criminal, and the rest, and remembering this made him laugh. "Their musicians stank worse than the night soil carts." He laughed again. "In any case, army training seemed better than both. Look, at least go listen to him. If you don't like his suggestion, ayah! I can find out where the carters go to get hired. It's usually where the barges are, where the river meets the sea."

The door opened then. Both looked up as Yaso walked in, this time with a wooden food carrier from which fragrances wafted. "Congee?"

Mouse rubbed her hands, hunger yawning cavernously inside her.

Old Rock was easy to find, near the great intersection be-tween the main street and the road from the docks, which they had traveled up the previous day after leaving the trade ship.

He was fighting staff to staff with a man even bigger than he was. The crowd was huge, almost all men, Mouse noticed. A great many of them carried belongings, as if they'd just come off a ship.

She turned her attention back to the fight, which lasted long enough for her to notice that the bigger man favored aggressive swinging over any training he might have had. Old Rock exchanged some testing blows — Mouse saw each coming — then got him off balance. Wham!

The crowd roared.

Old Rock leaped down at one side, and then two men climbed in. As they went to choose their weapons, the crowd roiled. Old Rock pushed through, and grinned at Mouse and Shigan.

"Want to make some money?" he asked. "When Lotus Pod" — he waved a huge, horny hand toward the woman at the betting table — "told me how much we lost yesterday, we thought, if we could find you and work up a scheme together, we could make it all back, and then some."

"By fighting?" Mouse asked skeptically, poised to run.

"I'll do it," Shigan spoke up. He breathed, "Better than shit-carts."

But Old Rock gave him a scornful glance. "I suppose a few might pay to see a pretty-boy knocked on his butt. Especially if he dressed fancy."

Shigan flushed, mouth twisting.

"But the real money would be in seeing the runt, here, come up into the ring. Look like a victim. We bet on you, the rest bet against, we clean up."

Mouse frowned, perplexed. "But surely it would only work once."

"We wait till the crowd changes," Old Rock said. "That's why I front up the high bribes to the patrollers for this spot. All the sailors coming off the ships with pay in their pockets, tired of being cooped up for days or even weeks, they can't resist my ring. Either to fight me, or each other, or to watch and bet. They watch for a while, then go on looking for food, drink, and so on. Lotus Pod always knows when it's a fresh crowd. She has an eye for faces. Or are you Redbarks too superior for the game? I've never heard of the sect — and no one I asked last night had either. All said it has to be some southern thing. Which matches your accent, I'm thinking."

"Southern it is," Mouse said, waving a hand southeast, rather than southwest, where she was sure Imai truly lay. "I won't kill anyone—"

"Never," Old Rock stated. "The Blues would be on us faster than flies on a turd. Everyone walks away. Maybe with a limp or a black eye at most, so that we don't look like mice pretending to be lions. The sailors all like a good fight, and bet high when there's action. In a few days it'll be Sky Lantern Day, and everyone far away from families will be wandering the streets if the weather lets 'em, looking for ways to spend money."

Mouse glanced Shigan's way, to see him making urging motions with his chin. She could almost hear him saying that it was better than hauling night soil, which seemed to be the only other easy hire.

Ayah, she could find out if that was true. Meanwhile . . . "I'll try it," she said. "For a few days, anyway."

"Great!" Old Rock grinned. "You just saved me arguing all day—I can be generous. A hundred tinnies a day—"

"Half the take," Shigan cut in, his vernacular sounding much more like the accent of the locals.

Old Rock shot a glance his way.

"Half," Shigan said again, rocking back on his heels. "Redbarks work hard, fight hard, and like comfort when it's over. Part of our oath."

Mouse shot him a startled look. "Our" oath?

"Three fives to us," Old Rock countered. "I've got the bribes, and the equipment to think of. No lower than that."

"Done," Shigan said, as Mouse caught up with the fact that they had been bargaining—and she'd nearly agreed to a terrible rate.

"Let's get started, before the storm comes in," Old Rock said, waving a hand skyward. "No one stays around in bad weather. Here's how it goes. The betting goes higher if you get them on your side, or against someone . . ."

He talked rapidly, so that Mouse began to get the idea of small stories in each battle. They almost matched up with the types of stories found in the hero tales—the Smallest Dog Wins, the Obnoxious Noble Loses being the most popular ones.

It sounded easy, but she discovered the moment she

climbed up into the ring that she became intensely self-conscious, and she was distracted by the crowd. *Don't make it look too easy,* Old Rock had warned. *The more of a fight, the better.*

Her attention splintered as she considered the watchers — and Old Rock's sword whooshed down. She barely evaded a direct hit, but the glancing blow was hard enough to knock her staggering.

That snapped her focus. The watchers shouted, but she no longer heard them. She let Old Rock come at her as she gauged his moments, and then she picked her moment to topple the tree, as she thought of it. Every opponent she had ever faced was bigger, and stronger. She had to rely on speed, and balance — keeping hers, and weakening theirs.

Four fast strikes and down he went, to cheers and jeers.

"Who else?" she yelled.

Two men climbed in, both smelling of brine. Sailors.

They began to argue about who was to go first until she said, "I'll take you both."

It was no more than she'd done sparring in training, but the spectators seemed to think it amazing. She settled into her stance, and let them come at her. Since they hadn't trained together except in hauling ropes, all she had to do was get them in each other's way, gauge their favorite strikes and retreats, and then come in fast, spinning between them then dancing backward as both fell hard.

The spectators hooted and roared.

She glanced toward Old Rock, who gave the prearranged sign for retiring. Though she'd recently spent days sparring, she dropped her sword and wrung her hand, which was Old Rock's cue to come forward, limping, and work the crowd again.

Mouse hopped out of the ring, and went over to where Shigan stood behind Lotus Pod, arms crossed as he watched her deal with the betting.

His grin was pure avarice. Mouse sighed, not believing it was so easy to make money.

The rain hit soon after, fast turning to sleet with the force of arrows. The ring hastily broke up, and that was it for the day — but they walked away with the equivalent of two dragon boaters, all in tinnies.

When they returned to the inn, they discovered wet clothing hanging everywhere. Yaso had laundered their things, but had pulled it all down from the courtyard line when the rain started.

The sleet hissed, no signs of abating. The two of them ordered a sumptuous dinner at the inn and ate there (Yaso having already eaten, as usual), and when Mouse later crawled into her bedding, it was with awareness of the loosening of that knot of apprehension. *I can do this.*

   . . . But not forever.

FOUR

YSKANDA EXPERIENCED THE DAYS following his entry into the imperial palace as a period of relative grace. *Experienced* and not *enjoyed* — there was no sense of ease, in spite of the plentiful food, the soft clothing, and the exquisite surroundings kept in pristine condition by an army of servants. Every melodic gong or bell-ring that marked an hour or a watch in which he was not summoned before the emperor was a relief . . . but sometimes, in the distance, he could hear the watch changes signaled by the imperial guards' drum tower, a reminder that his respite would not last. With proper food and rest had come awareness, his first realization being that, in spite of the harmonious setting, he was a creature imprisoned in a pretty cage for the emperor to toy with.

The second realization was that his family must have escaped capture, or surely he would have seen them, or been told. He no longer believed his kidnapping was random. Sweetwater was so isolated, with no roads, only paths known to the inhabitants. There was not so much as a signpost anywhere about — not in a place where most did not know how to read. So, he had to assume that he alone had fallen into some kind of trap, that early autumnal day in Imai Harbor. The first of the family to do so.

Therefore, he had two goals: to survive, and to protect his family as best he could.

To survive meant mastering the complexities of the huge

palace grounds, and the intricacies of the servant hierarchy within it. He also had to master the mysteries of palace protocol.

First in importance in that servant hierarchy, he learned the evening of his arrival from the chatty maid who sized his new gray-blue apprentice robes on him, were the denatured men in the gray robes and the tall hats with stiffened extensions to either side. These extensions did not exceed the length of the wearer's shoulders, but they seemed to Yskanda's frightened eyes to throw out an invisible wall that caused everyone in the servant category to make way. (As yet he had not seen any nobles, much less any of the imperial family. He was grateful for the reprieve.) These denatured men in the hats were elites with their own rank hierarchy, discernible in the shades of gray in their robes' sleeves and trim. They wore tallies carved of fine jade, though with no tassels appended. Chief Bitternail was very high up, having no fewer than five shades of gray in his robes, which meant he was one of the very small number permitted within arm's length of the emperor's person—and he could deliver edicts in the emperor's name.

The denatured—not eunuchs, an opprobrious term from less civilized days—were referred to among the servants as *graywings*, which had to do with the gray robes and those winged hats.

"You apprentices, of course, don't get hats," the chatty maid explained. "Your waist tallies are plain wood. Don't ever be caught anywhere without it. Especially now!"

"Why especially now, if I may ask?"

She liked this pretty, polite boy who had been so mysteriously boosted over a good part of the fierce competetion. "It's a new rule. Just happened. Get caught without it, and suffer a flogging. Or worse." She handed him a rectangle of wood about the length of his palm, with his name painted one side and a simple tiger-eye burned into the other. "That will get you around our parts of the inner palace. Don't go anywhere else without being summoned. If they want you in the inner palace, they will come for you, or more rarely, give you a tally to hold then surrender. Understand?"

He barely had time to mutter a *yes* before she was off again. "Hats. Everyone at the very bottom goes bare-headed. Apprentices who pass the Imperial Examination and thus become scholars, or are appointed through other special considerations . . ." (He heard in the word "special" that same tone people reserved for the wealthy and powerful.) ". . . get what they call *loaves*, because they're plain. No wings. Fit over your topknot, and look kind of like a steamed bread-loaf. A tassel comes with the next rank up. All right, you're done. Come back after the Tiger Watch three gong."

"Every generation of graywings," the shoemaker's apprentice said later as he measured Yskanda's feet for two pairs of the square-toed cotton-topped, hemp-soled shoes worn by servants in the palace, "gets a different category of names, once they give up their own family and submit to the denaturing ritual. Chief Bitternail's generation—Chief Bitternail is the one who carries the flywhisk, which marks him as the graywing chief, closest to the emperor—his generation, as you might guess, are named for teas. The old ones, most of them retired, or seeing to the dowager empress's pavilion, are all named for precious stones, and the graywing boys in training are all herbs. In my grandmother's day they were animals. Did you get your tally? Good. Don't ever go out of your dorm without it, unless you like beatings." He patted his own waist tally, which had a slightly better carving of a tiger-eye, though it was still wood. "Especially now—they've tightened security again, we've been hearing."

Yskanda had to learn protocols, which not only meant which bows for whom, but how these might change on ritual days. Or even different hours.

"But one rule supersedes," he was told by the earnest apprentice to the Department of Rites and Auguries to whom he was sent last. "If the emperor is walking, you go face to the ground, whatever you are carrying beside you. If he wants to sit watching the moon, you wait until he's out of sight before moving, unless specifically ordered. Even if you're crouched on ice. And if you meet any of the other imperials, especially if they are disturbed, go to the ground."

The first night, he slept in a tiny room no bigger than a closet. The second night Yskanda spent in a ten-bed dormitory with other male scribe apprentices. There was a kang all down the window side, with cubbies opposite. Their bedding lay side by side almost within arm's reach of one another.

Of course, his new dormitory mates peppered him with questions that next morning, but he'd had a day and a night of wakefulness in which to think. His mind kept coming back to Bitternail's grave face, and the utter detachment with which he had said, *It was so ordered.* If someone as important as this Chief Graywing Bitternail returned that as an answer, perhaps he ought to as well. Any other answer might lead to questions about his family, and he would not risk that if he could avoid it.

So, to *Why are you here?* and *What examination did you pass?* and *Where are you from?* as well as less neutral questions, beginning with, *How much did your clan pay to jump you over the primary level?* He replied — once they quieted enough for him to speak — "It was so ordered."

And it worked. No one dared go beyond that invisible, but mutable, boundary, which was reassuring in the immediate sense, but alarming, because it underscored the sense that anything bad could happen in the blink of an eye.

Like being grabbed off a street and flung onto a ship.

What he could not know was that Bitternail, without peer in understanding the complex tides of talk in the palace, had in the most delicate way let it be known that the ferrets had brought Apprentice Afan. That meant whatever reason he was here had something to do with the emperor, however tangentially.

That was daunting enough that nobody dared to haze him, or lie to him — which could easily be checked — but they registered their distrust of someone boosted over the heads of boys who had been there since they were ten, chosen after ferocious competition and testing, by leaving out a few of the rules they had grown up with. Such as the fact that certain routes were not open to someone of his status. An error he learned painfully the first morning he was to present himself to the scribes, wearing his new robes, his head stuffed with details of protocol he was still repeating to himself.

A pair of graywings going to court saw the lowly, bare-headed apprentice wandering along a corridor reserved exclusively to them (and their superiors), which caused such an affront they stopped what they were doing to administer a lesson.

The graywings, he discovered that morning, were experts at pain: their beating left no bruises that could mar the visible skin and so offend the eyes of any passing imperials, but they hurt terribly just the same.

Also, the time it took for the beating and accompanying lecture made him late. He entered the building he'd been directed to, into a long chamber with the lighting slanting down from high windows on both sides, opened their widest. Braziers burned on both sides of the room to counter the cold from those windows; along the walls, polished surfaces mirrored the light.

Everyone was already there, at work.

The chief scribe didn't even glance his way. A roving scribe scowled at him and stated in an icy tone, "You are unpunctual."

She had not posed her statement as a question. He had been told repeatedly that to speak out of turn would result in a beating. He could only drop down, face to the ground, and wait in sickened apprehension for another beating.

With his forehead pressed to the floor, he remained unaware of the glance exchanged between the roving scribe and the chief scribe. Both could see from the way Yskanda winced as he knelt that he'd already been beaten. They had a fairly good idea what had happened. And why.

The presiding scribe sternly lectured the shivering Yskanda about the importance of being on time when summoned, a lesson that totally bypassed him but did not escape the more alert among the listening apprentices: the Scribe Instructor, as the saying went, was scolding the prostrate dog in order to warn the hiding fox. They all were obliged to remember that when something did disrupt the smooth flow of palace life, questioning was invariably relentless. And painful.

Also, this lecture underscored the fact that this boy had been placed under the court artist by the emperor himself. No one knew why. One could not ask. To the apprentices, the reminder sufficed as a warning.

To the masters, it was a signal to discover what, if anything, made this boy stand out. That much was absolutely within their rights.

Yskanda was bidden take a seat, after which the scribe mentally rearranged her lesson. Thus the apprentices not in the ten-bed dormitory that Yskanda now shared at last got a look at the boy about whom rumor had been flying. Yskanda was utterly unaware of the effect of his ethereal profile, after so many days of scant meals.

Gazes watched him as he settled down at the empty desk. His shuttered expression eased a fraction when he recognized all the tools awaiting him as the very best.

That was a superficial relief. He was still sick with pain and shock; though Father had occasionally swatted him, First

Brother, and Mouse, when they had broken rules, it had stung but never bruised or raised welts. The only other time he'd been beaten was when the Sweetwater twins had lain in wait and pounced on him, and First Brother had dashed to the rescue before they could do much damage. His body throbbed with his heartbeat as he tried to concentrate, his first thought snagging on the observation that the court scribe, under whom he was supposed to be placed, was not even there.

"Ready your ink," came a familiar command.

With trembling fingers, Yskanda dribbled water onto the waiting ink stone, then ground a fresh ink stick as the scribe in charge ran them through a series of basic questions, then came the order to pick up brushes. They began with various scripts. These familiar tasks did more to steady Yskanda than any words could have. The familiar smells of ink and paper, the feel of a very fine brush in his hand, all enabled him to settle his mind, so that when the scribe began the test in how color is laid down, line and shade, composition and form, he had mostly shut out his surroundings, and the throbbing pain.

The last exercise was to pair off and sketch one's partner, each posing and sketching by turns, indicated by a sand measure. Yskanda stared into the girl he was paired with; his dreamy gaze narrowed to acute observation in such a way that it, in so beautiful a face, rendered her self-conscious enough to look away. Every time she glanced back she could not prevent a blush.

And so, what he captured was the tight line of her shoulder, her averted gaze, and the shading indicative of color in her cheeks.

The roving scribe, glancing down at the emerging drawing, had time to draw a slow breath when a very rarely heard gong rang brassily nine times from without: the emperor was coming!

Here? Looks semaphored between apprentices as they hastily set their brushes down, twitched robes straight, and then prepared to bow to the floor.

A hard elbow jabbed into Yskanda's side, recalling him from that place his mind retreated when he drew in freeform. He jumped, flinched from the pain of that jab on his bruised rib, and flung his brush down so fast that ink splattered across his drawing as he dropped to his knees beside his mat the way his fellows did.

When roaming inside the palace, the emperor seldom

brought any entourage numbering more than one or two graywings and a pair of imperial guards, unless he wanted to send a silent message to some courtier or other functionary, in which case he came with a long tail of armed guards and two rows of graywings.

Bitternail was one of the pair accompanying him now, opening the door into the scribes' training hall, where everyone waited in silence, foreheads to the floor. The emperor moved along the rows, glancing down at the apprentices' labors. He paused when he spotted Yskanda.

He glanced at the drawing depicting the self-conscious averted gaze of an otherwise thoughtful young girl — that much was revealed in the briefly sketched high forehead and tight shoulders. The drawing was ruined by a spray of ink, as from a brush jolted in the artist's hand.

"Afan Yskanda," the emperor said. "Have you met the court artist yet?"

That was definitely a question. "This unworthy apprentice of no talent has not, your imperial majesty," Yskanda said to the floor, consciously using the language he had been coached in.

"Not yet?" the emperor addressed the room, his smile of amusement causing every adult's jaw to lock. "Ayah, the scribes have their own way of doing things, it seems. Yskanda," he said. "Raise your head."

Yskanda did, and everyone there who dared a sideways peek at a boy whose actual personal name was used by the emperor — whereas they all had been there years, and were quite certain the emperor had no idea who they were — saw no smirk of superiority, but the blanched face of terror.

"Your imperial majesty," Yskanda whispered, the welts on his back and ribs throbbing as he tried to keep his head up while maintaining his crouched posture.

"In a few days we'll be celebrating Sky Lantern Day. I want you to join those chosen to sketch my family. It will amuse me to see them through your eyes."

"Yes, your imperial majesty."

The emperor walked on, pausing once or twice more to glance at a drawing here, and one there, before passing out of the room through the far door.

No one spoke as the lesson resumed, but wonder, question, and resentment flashed from eyes to eyes: there would be no trusting this newcomer until they knew more about him, but neither would there be any of the petty cruelties that were a part of the silent, ever-vigilant competition for promotion. The emperor's presence, his use of a personal name, had armored Yskanda as effectively as imperial guard war gear.

As the lesson ended, a little page arrived, summoning Yskanda to meet Court Artist Yoli. Yskanda followed the page, leaving behind him whispers of speculation. Those who had seen that look of terror assured each other that the rumor about the ferrets having brought him had to be true, which pretty much killed speculation, at least publicly. It was *never* a good idea to discuss anything having to do with the ferrets.

Yskanda's emotions had been swooping and diving like a wind-mad kite, leaving him feeling as if he existed in a dream. At least the court artist's studio was not far as distances went in the vast imperial palace, although it seemed farther because of all the twists and turns along narrow corridors and around tiny courtyards, and the pain that made walking agonizing.

The court artist's rank granted him an enviable place at the northwest corner of the complexity of buildings to which the artists belonged, a sizable space with a bank of west windows and two south windows, overlooking the rock garden called Serene Contemplation. As soon as Yskanda stepped over the threshold, there were the familiar smells of paint and ink, in a room crammed with the paraphernalia of painting and art, with hangings suspended from the vaulted ceiling as well as shelves and trunks and tables, all overflowing.

Court Artist Yoli Jiwa, an old man, tangled white eyebrows curling crazily above deep-set, pouchy eyes, said irascibly, "Ayah, come in, come in. I told the Household I was too old for any more apprentices, but . . . we do what we must," he finished in a grumble. "Why are you here?"

Yskanda bowed and said so faintly he was almost inaudible, "It was so ordered."

"It was so ordered. It was so ordered," the old man grumbled. "Ah-yah, then there's nothing to be done, is there? Let's see what you are capable of."

He then began a series of questions. At first Yskanda carefully framed his answers in what he hoped was the palace style, until Court Artist Yoli interrupted impatiently, "Never mind mumbling the humble-humble. You and I are here alone, so there is no need to refer to yourself as unworthy and all the rest of it. If you were truly unworthy you would not be here demanding yet more of my time."

Yskanda resumed using the pronoun *I* instead of the formal third person in his answers. Even so, the court artist barely listened to the answers before throwing another at Yskanda, as he shuffled through a table laden with scrolls, papers, books, and other items pertaining to the artist's craft.

He grilled Yskanda about the Six Principles of Painting, then flitted between subjects—brushes and technique, light and shade, complementary and contrasting colors, their meanings, ritual and symbols, and so on— until he gave a grunt, and emerged from the mess with Yskanda's old sketchbook. "*Here* it is. Now, let's take a look."

He began to page through it as Yskanda stood before him. The eyebrows bristled as the artist hummed and hemmed. He had a very wispy beard, which he stroked with one finger as the other leafed through the sketchbook.

At last he looked up. "I've certainly seen better, but also worse. At least you were given the proper fundamentals in brush handling, or I would send you back to the primary classes even if they beheaded me for it—it would be either me or you, and I'm older." He studied Yskanda's pale, anxious face, harrumphed, then in a somewhat easier voice, said, "I'm told you'll be sketching Them in a few days. This should not have happened for . . ." A shake of the head. "Ayah, no matter what this old sinner thinks. As you say, it was so ordered. There were enough witnesses."

He leaned forward, eyeing this boy who sat so stiffly. He suspected what had happened, but only tapped the sketchbook. "I will do my best to get ten years of study stuffed into you in two days. But the first and most important lesson is, whatever is said about a true sketch—what the eye sees—draw no flattery—you grant Them as much face as you can. More. There won't be a second chance."

He began to talk rapidly, sketching, and requiring Yskanda to sketch, all the while. The court artist did not say, but he was slightly heartened by what he saw: the first few pages of the sketchbook had conveyed an impression of good skills taught the basics, in rather outmoded forms, as one would expect from a far-off island that no one but its residents had ever heard of. But here and there among the later sketches in particular gleamed what the poets sometimes referred to as a captured bit of soul. The artists dismissed such whimsy as highly inexact (as well as inappropriate), for if one captured a piece of a subject's soul, would that not diminish the subject?

Artists called this rare gift the spangle of sunlight on water, for though one can be dazzled by the effulgence of what appears to be liquid sun on the water, there is no diminishment of the actual sun.

So it was with this talent. This boy captured in a line here, a shading there, the telling detail amid a morass of conventional decorative elements, that reflected, even revealed, the subject's inner being at that moment. Not just people, but blossoms, trees: he gazed down at a brief sketch of a pepper tree, knowing that were he to travel south to find it, he would know this tree in all its vigor. And there was a toucan, head cocked; the court artist fancied that if he were to travel to that flyspeck island, he would recognize that very bird among the thousands there.

Unfortunately, there were also the outmoded forms in composition and placement. This apprentice was not trained nearly as well as someone thrust into this position ought to be. One step into the perfumed air of court and he'd be climbing a mountain of swords and swimming in boiling poison.

The court artist glanced up consideringly. It was very clear this boy was all nerves, apparently living on air and fear, yet he made no complaint or accusation. Court Artist Yoli Jiwa found himself interested in spite of his long-inured skepticism, but there was simply no time for a carefully planned instructional strategy.

The boy had two days. Without any idea what lay behind this sudden whim of the emperor's, the court artist could only plan the surest, safest path up that mountain of swords.

Dark had fallen when he finally said, "I know the gong rang for your meal. Page!"

Another child appeared at the side door.

Court Artist Yoli waved his brush. "Run ahead to the scribes' dining area. Carry my orders. They are to set out hot food and medicinal tea for this apprentice. Run!"

The page bowed and pattered off.

"Now, you go eat. Then sleep. And be back here by the first morning gong."

"I'm not to go to class, then, sir?"

"With only two days to prepare, you must come directly to me."

Yskanda bowed, exited, then did as told, going to his dormitory after a meal that left him feeling somewhat better.

There he found a fresh outfit waiting, and someone

pointed to where the baths were. The entire palace was served by a mighty hot spring from deep below Mt. Lir, mixed with fresh water. Even the least of the servants could get plenty of water.

He was stared at overtly as well as covertly. There was no hiding the spectacular bruising down his thin frame; many winced and turned away, especially those who knew they ought to have warned him about the hallways, and hadn't.

They felt it especially at his politeness. There was no question from him, no accusation or heated glower, no sniveling or pouting. He just sounded tired.

Once he was dried and dressed, he made his way back to his dormitory, where he found his new mates lying in wait.

To the storm of questions he said in his mild voice, "You all heard: it's orders. I know nothing more." Then he bowed low to his peers, and spoke even more formally. "This wretchedly ignorant apprentice is in your hands; would you deign to enlighten this fool about the imperial family a little?"

Everyone looked at one another. Then lively Senye Tan, who Yskanda had already discovered loved the sound of his own voice, said, "You will be the envy of all, having an excuse to stare at First Imperial Princess Manon." Senye Tan was a tall, rangy young man just sprouting a wisp of beard and mustache, and a mobile face with which he made a lot of wry grimaces.

To this everyone agreed, and another added with his eyes half-closed, "Serene as the sky, cold as first snow, that is the first imperial princess. She's not just beautiful, she's perfect."

"So perfect," another agreed, "she's the only one permitted outside the palace, but of course she goes veiled, surrounded by an army of imperial guards, and she only visits the booksellers."

"Everyone tries to guess when she'll go," Senye Tan said. "In case a wind comes along to lift her veil and they can get a glimpse of her." He leaned forward, eyes wide as he whispered, "She went into the city yesterday, and the books must all have been bad ones as she was back quick as that." He snapped his fingers. "And Snowdrop, who does the linens in her pavilion, swears she was colder than ice, everyone tiptoeing. Scarcely breathing."

"Over books?" Yskanda asked.

The oldest boys exchanged glances nicely mixed with scorn and pity for such naiveté. "She's got a secret flirt, of course," one said. "Why else would she want to leave the palace?"

"And they quarreled," Senye Tan said.

"Who would quarrel with beauty?"

"Who would dare?" another murmured softly.

"The imperial children are *all* beautiful," a third spoke up. "I say nothing about Imperial Sister, for whom I have the greatest respect. But I wish you luck in getting any of them to sit still for you."

Yskanda had learned from the graywing who taught him protocol that the First Imperial Consort had had a Spring Festival child before she entered the palace. The emperor had bestowed the title "Imperial Sister" on this girl when he adopted her.

"If First Imperial Prince Jion were here, he'd be still. Because he'd be asleep," Senye Tan cracked. "You'd have to pretend not to see the drool as he snores."

Some muffled laughter at this, then the serious one said, "But you won't find Prince Jion there. Or Second Imperial Consort Su."

The levity vanished at the mention of the second imperial consort.

"Is their absence something I should know about?" Yskanda asked.

"The first imperial prince is on a tour to the silk islands," the same boy said. "Wait. By now the tour would be over, and he's established as a governor."

"A governor who won't actually do any governing," Senye Tan put in sarcastically. "He'll be too busy in the hunting field, or eating and drinking. Or asleep!"

"Hush, Tan-Tan," someone said, and the others made warding signs, or looked away.

"What's wrong with that?" Senye Tan asked, widening his eyes in a fake-innocent look. "Personally, I'd *love* to be a nongovernor. All the fun, no work!"

As others shot insults at him, claiming he didn't work anyway, a boy leaned toward Yskanda to murmur, "We don't know what happened with Second Imperial Consort Su."

Everyone sobered, and another whispered, "She had her favorite maid carried out feet first."

"And the emperor confined her to her pavilion to reflect."

"Her first maid carried out feet first," Yskanda repeated — then realized it meant *put to death.*

"It happens," Senye Tan said, lifting a shoulder. "It can happen to anyone. And there's always ten waiting to jump into their place."

"So shut your mouth," another muttered, elbowing Senye Tan.

Who sighed, turning his gaze heavenward. "If you were going to rat on me, you would have by now, wouldn't you?"

The conversation staggered on from there, with much side-commentary, from which Yskanda gained the impression of covert competition between the imperial consorts on behalf of their children, though everyone seemed to believe that First Imperial Prince Jion and First Imperial Princess Manon were favored for the heirship. Second Imperial Prince Vaion thought himself funny in a way that sounded to Yskanda the way raucous village boys in Sweetwater thought themselves funny. Second Imperial Princess Gaunon, everyone seemed to agree, was as harmless as a bunny, and about as smart, her head empty of everything but dancing.

No one—not even Senye Tan—dared to whisper a word about the emperor.

But one thing Yskanda could ask about was the letters home. "Am I correct that everyone is to write to their families?"

"Haven't you seen us all writing, late at night?"

"I thought it was only for those who had been here for at least a year," Yskanda said. "Forgive my ignorance."

Senye Tan waved a careless hand. "Writing home each year is one of the privileges of our being in the palace," he assured Yskanda. "But the farther away you live, the sooner your letter has to be done, in order to get it there by New Year's. You'll find the sailing schedule at Bright." *Bright* being what the students called Azaleas Brighten the Summer, the annex where their masters worked when not teaching, and where schedules for everything could be found.

They went to sleep after that, Yskanda thoughtful. So the letters were universal, and not merely a pretense at discovering where his family was. The emperor could send an army to Imai to tear up the island if he wanted, and no one could do a thing. He might already have done so, which was how Yskanda was discovered—he simply didn't know. And he dared not ask, lest he say the wrong thing and somehow condemn his family, assuming they hadn't been caught. That was the worst thing, not *knowing*.

After much worrying he came to the conclusion that—at present—his position was very much like one of those history-ies Ul Keg gave Yskanda and Mouse to read, in which the eldest child of royal and noble figures was often taken to the house of an enemy to be raised. Usually as the result of a treaty.

He decided he must live as a hostage, though his family had no political importance whatsoever. His being here surely had to do with the emperor wanting revenge against his parents. Nothing else made sense.

So, as a hostage, ought he to write a letter or not? He was certainly not exempt from retribution—that had been made abundantly clear when the graywings beat him so badly—along with the ever-present reminder that his life was at the disposal of the emperor's whim. He must walk softly. Cautiously.

Over the following two days, he agonized over this letter. During daylight he thought he ought to write—he even went so far as to find the date and the ship headed for the islands nearest Imai, which was very soon—but at night he could not shake himself from the conviction that one of those ferrets would be delivering his letter. His one comfort was the conviction that if Mother somehow knew the imperials were coming, she would use some of her hoarded Essence papers and put together charms to help the family escape to the temple at Burning Rock Island. But nothing would help if they were taken by surprise.

The fine paper the students had access to sat among Yskanda's scant belongings, the inkstone ready, the brush dry.

FIVE

ON SKY WISHES DAY, when Ghost Moon hung low and round on the horizon, Yskanda rose early, in spite of considerable pain from his bruises, to go to the temple. He had followed the Snow Crane god along with his family and the village, and he had listened to Ul Keg's stories of the Phoenix Moon god, but his own inclination had been toward the Ghost Moon god, bridge for souls to the world unseen.

He had been shown the temple that the servants went to. He went to light incense and pray for his family as well as for his own survival, and made it back in time for a hasty breakfast, unaware of the silent graywings and guards who had observed his movement away from his dormitory. But he had only entered a temple then returned, and so he remained oblivious to how closely he was watched.

On Imai, Sky Wishes Day had been celebrated during the afternoon, kites with wishes written on them sent high to chase the sun to Heaven, and carry their cargo of wishes to the gods. The entire village had their wishes inscribed on one kite by the shaman, as paper was a rare commodity — made by Mother and Yskanda.

As he had ever since his apprenticeship with Master Bankan, Yskanda hoped that Mouse was helping Mother with the paper, and he mentally sent his wishes skyward.

He reported to the court artist for a day of hasty training; the rest of the apprentices were dismissed in the afternoon, but to his surprise, he wasn't. "The imperial family follows court custom," the court artist told him. "Celebrate at night. They put lanterns in the kites."

An expensive custom! It surely would be beautiful to see, but Yskanda would rather have missed it, if it meant being in proximity to the imperial family. To the emperor, with his sardonic eye.

A graywing called Melonseed came to fetch him after the evening meal. Once again everyone watched, speculating in whispers as Yskanda picked up the shoulder bag that Court Artist Yoli had given him.

Melonseed took Yskanda to the emperor's own pavilion, where he soon found around twenty richly dressed people gathered in the imperial garden, around a picturesque lake.

This was his first glimpse of the imperial family. A quick, searching gaze: the emperor was not among them.

There must have been close to a hundred servants there, beginning with six carefully chosen apprentices from Yskanda's wing, all at least three years older than he, most older. An army of maids attended on the imperial consorts and other relations, graywings gliding here and there overseeing more menial servants with braziers, food, and other supplies, as the young imperial relations decorated lantern-kites.

Bitternail was in command; when Yskanda reached him and bowed, Melonseed murmured so that only Yskanda could hear, "There is a table set aside for you." At least the low table looked like the other six scattered about the garden, so that the drawings would cover every angle.

Yskanda went to his table and knelt very carefully in his new court robe, which was the same subdued color as his apprentice robe, but made of much finer fabric. He made certain that none of the folds extended beyond his mat, as the ground looked damp.

Then he brought out the fine papers that Court Artist Yoli had recommended, and laid out his tools. He quickly began grinding ink as he looked around at the people in their beautiful silks, which the flickering candlelight loved.

Two lamps had been set on either end of his table, so that none would make a shadow. As he smoothed the paper, preparing to sketch, several youths near his age, but slightly younger, scampered up, long sleeves fluttering, the silver and pearl ornaments binding their many braids winking and in the torchlight. None of these wore gold — that was reserved for the emperor's own family.

The most elaborate, fantastical kite-lanterns Yskanda had ever seen lay waiting for the imperial family's pleasure in inscribing their wishes and sending them heavenward. His heart squeezed when he saw impatient young fingers grabbing the fragile constructions, and sometimes poking holes in the exquisitely colored and fitted paper. More than one lantern was then smashed by careless hands, which made him sorrowful.

But eventually the young ones seized what they wanted, and then most of them began to prowl around. A couple came his way.

"Who are you?"

"What are you doing?"

He had no idea how to address them, as he did not know their various identities, so he made a general low bow, and addressed the ground. "This humble apprentice has been honored with the task of sketching the imperial family."

"We've never seen you before," the older one pointed stated, pointing at his bare head and his robe. "You have to be *new*." The word "new" was a disparagement, akin to "beginner."

"It was so ordered," Yskanda said — and even the exalted imperial relatives accepted that.

"Draw me first," declared the youngest, a solid child in shades of rose and green. He struck a pose.

"No, draw something on my lantern," another demanded shrilly, stamping her foot. Then she darted away, as Yskanda cast a frightened glance up at Melonseed. He was supposed to be sketching the imperial family! Weren't these others there to decorate the lanterns?

But he received an infinitesimal nod, so when the girl returned and thrust a lantern peremptorily at Yskanda, he bowed, took the fragile construct carefully, then bowed again as he said in the mode he had been coached in, "Is this humble apprentice to inscribe a wish, or to make something else?"

"Wishes are stupid," declared a very spoilt imperial cousin, who even at a young age knew that to write her true wish (to be adopted by the emperor, instead of being a mere cousin) would be considered treason. "Draw me a phoenix! No! I want the Vermilion Bird."

Yskanda was going to point out that he only had black ink, but Melonseed's head moved minutely, the extensions on his hat shifting as he shook his head once. Apparently one did not say no to imperial relatives.

Yskanda picked up a brush. Just wetting the tips of the hairs in the ink, he sketched an upward flying bird shape with a long, curling tail. The girl—one of the royal cousins?—clapped her hands, snatched the lantern, and pattered away, shrilling, "Cousin Gau-Gau, look, look! Where's my candle?"

Yskanda saw the other apprentices surrounded by silk-clad imperial children. The older imperial children were in fact snatching up the lanterns made by servants and demanding a drawing from each apprentice, then flinging them skyward without a second glance as they went for yet a new lantern.

Yskanda turned out two tigers, a phoenix, and a dragon. Not once was he asked to inscribe a wish. Did they have so much that there was nothing more to wish for?

Servants set tiny candles into the lanterns so the smaller children could have the pleasure of letting them rise from their fingers. They children chattered happily with upturned faces as they watched their offerings rise slowly into the sky, blending in golden points among the distant stars.

Then a voice called out, "The emperor approaches!"

All the servants went to the ground, Yskanda and the apprentices included; the imperial family performed deep bows.

The emperor entered, impressive in the golden robes that only he could wear. His magnificent outer robe was embroidered with white cranes, their eyes jeweled. His hair was bound up high in a complication of braids and secured with a jewel-topped hair clasp. From it long braided tails with golden ornaments swung behind his straight back. Behind the train of his robe walked his entourage. Yskanda, watching out of the corner of his eye, did not see him speak, but a signal was made for them to rise.

At once everyone was in motion, the imperial relations surrounding the emperor like a flock of gaudy birds, reminding Yskanda of Ul Keg surrounded by hundreds of birds of all kinds when he tossed seeds to them. The emperor said something, lifted a hand, and the elders among the emperor's family settled down at tables to eat and drink, as the younger relations returned to gather more kite-lanterns. Soon the air was filled with them, a soft glow scintillating in the air.

Yskanda was enthralled by the profligate beauty of the scene. But a tiny cough from Melonseed jolted him back to the present—and his orders!

He dropped to his mat, and began sketching, brush moving swiftly as he captured the outline of the scene. Then he began filling in details, remembering the court artist's lecture on placement: emperor at the center, of course, and all other figures four-fifths of his size, except for the dowager empress at his right hand. She was rendered a size midway between that of the consorts at his left, and the emperor.

When it came time to concentrate on the finer details, such as features and clothing, the task became exponentially more difficult, though on the surface, making such a handsome family look good should have been easy.

But Second Imperial Princess Gaunon could not stop playing with her silken tassels as she marveled at the sky filled with lanterns glowing in jewel colors, and as for Second Imperial Prince Vaion, every time Yskanda looked his way in order to try to get characteristic features down, the prince made horrible faces at him.

The Imperial Sister was very still, but her long, angular face above a strong jaw with a cleft chin was not flattered by her open-mouthed expression as she watched the floating offerings, so Yskanda turned to First Imperial Princess Manon, who sat demure and so still that even the golden ornaments hanging from tiny chains in her hair pins did not so much as sway.

The boys had not exaggerated her beauty. Yskanda concentrated on her. As he worked, he remembered comments from the boys in his dormitory, how everyone in the palace had only to see her to fall in love with her, how every scribbler in the place could not resist drawing her, though it was strictly forbidden. Pictures of her sold very well in the streets.

She had perfect features, yet she sat there so composed she looked no more lifelike than a carving. There was no hint of character in those smooth cheeks, the lowered eyes, the tranquil mouth.

Yskanda glanced at the second imperial prince when he turned to laugh at something one of the other boys was saying. He sketched quickly.

There was little Yskanda could do to make them look like themselves, without sacrificing all the other requirements: the importance of painting grace into their poses, and the details of headdress and clothing. But he thought he got a little of the second imperial prince's grin when he laughed with those other boys. The rest of his picture was safely generic in its flattery, which the court artist had assured him would be expected.

Generic and flattering. Yskanda did not even try to capture whatever fleeting signs of real personality lay behind the composed smiles of the two present consorts and the emperor's mother, much less the emperor. Each feature was meticulously rendered according to traditional styles signifying imperial dignity and grace.

Yskanda was working on the details of the headdresses when the emperor abruptly rose to walk about, waving off the entourage.

He had covered half the circuit before he stopped beside Bitternail, a flick of one hand making the entourage drop back.

The emperor glanced across the decorated garden, illuminated by the fairy lamps, at Yskanda's bowed head as he painstakingly employed a tiny detail brush. "What has he said?"

"Nothing, your imperial majesty," Bitternail replied, firm in his conviction that his carefully selected spy in the dormitory would be truthful and accurate. His life depended on that.

"And to the court artist?" the emperor asked, brows slanting.

"Nothing but questions pertaining to instruction," Bitternail said, having assigned two pages to trade off listening at the court artist's door.

The emperor lifted his head, contemplating Yskanda, who—aware subliminally of that scrutiny—did his best to hide the shaking of his hand.

"The letters are shortly to go out," the emperor commented. "See to it he has time to write one." And he moved on, eventually coming to a stop behind Yskanda—who bowed to the ground as the emperor stood, silently gazing down at that gorgeously sketched, absolutely correct, and utterly lifeless scene.

Almost lifeless.

The emperor gazed down at that bent head, wondering what thoughts lay hidden there.

"You caught my younger son's smile," he finally said, and moved on.

Yskanda and the apprentices were dismissed shortly thereafter.

Sky Wishes Day came and went in Te Gar Harbor.

Mouse used her day's earnings to buy a kite, and write on it her wishes for the new year coming up—and as she set it free, and watched it rise with all the others, she thought about the days when she and her brothers would discuss endlessly what they might wish for. Her wish was for her family to be safe and well. She hoped it would reach Heaven by the New Year.

The following day, she went back to looking for gallant wanderers among those who disembarked from ships down at the wharf, as she worked at Old Rock's ring. The earnings were irregular. That first day was a good day. The following day it rained so hard, there was no ring at all. The third day, the weather was fine, the crowds were large, but they weren't betting.

The day after that, a huge, drunken sailor got all his crowd betting, and when they did, others followed. It was a good earnings day—which was lucky, as they had to pay for their room.

She had no idea what to do with money after basic needs were met, as she was far too frugal to want to spend it if she didn't have to. She left the coins on their shared table, and Yaso took what was needed for their meals, leaving the rest there. Shigan helped himself to it, buying what he considered necessities for the room—a rug so that he wouldn't have to sit on the cold floor, a better pillow.

And finally, a new (to him) robe of blue silk and a crimson sash, bought from one of the stall vendors who sold worn clothing, and a silken headband of a darker shade of blue.

He was packing up his fortress clothes to try to sell to a vendor when Mouse noticed. "If you're not wearing that anymore, can I have it?"

"Of course," Shigan said, surprised. "But why? Though I would not call anything along our street fashionable or stylish, you can find something better than those abominable rags."

"I'm used to them," Mouse said. "And I don't want to waste money. We don't know how long Old Rock will let me fight in his ring."

She said nothing more, but it unsettled Shigan. Perhaps he ought to strike out on his own . . . no. He looked down at Second Ryu's untidy head, rejecting that idea. He was finally learning that sword form. And Second Ryu was not just a good teacher; he was becoming a kind of little brother. Oh, not at all a replacement for the little brother Shigan secretly missed, but good enough to want to stay. Except he felt guilty for touching that communal coinage, meager as it was. Especially as Second Ryu spent nothing in spite of being the wage earner.

The following day, instead of watching at the ring, Shigan went strolling with an eye to possible ways to earn money that were not night soil hauling.

But what? As he walked down the busy main road, his feet kept pace with a crowd of newly arrived gawkers—he had always found safety in numbers. There were far too many scholars sitting out in the cold weather with their little tables, inks, and brushes, to write letters for those who could not read. They always seemed to be waiting for someone to come up to them, and of course only the poor would need their services, which meant they earned a pittance for their toil.

Then there were the augurs, but though Shigan knew the rudiments, he had no talent at augury. Of course the world was full of fake augurs, but he hated the idea of doing that outside of a game. There were those who insisted that the unseen world eventually caught up with the fakes, the truth of which Shigan had no interest in testing.

The gawkers lurched to a stop where the street ended, and he jolted to awareness of his surroundings, exactly where he least wished to be: the double-roofed government buildings looming over him in a horseshoe, built against the jutting rock that formed a natural barrier (and defense) of the east end of the harbor. The garrison lay directly above.

The crowd shuffled sideways to goggle at the notice board on the other side of the great drum outside the Justice Building. He stayed with them, his attention divided between the notices and those who read them. Also, those in the background. But there was nothing of particular interest in the notices, which were the usual mix of criminals at large (his name not among them, at least there was that), edicts, and whatever news the governor thought fit to impart. When the gawkers turned about and started down the street again, he moved with them.

Back to the problem of what he could do. As always, he was distracted by music. Most of it dreadful, some even painful to the ear. But then there were rewards—here, a vendor with a beautiful voice, singing the poems of Ar Laq set to eastern melodies. There a trio of people his age with woodwinds, probably apprentices trying to make some pocket money, as any earnings they made would go to their master.

And then he passed by a pleasure house through whose open doors excellent music drifted out to entice passersby.

Ayah, why not?

He walked up, past the greeters who took one look at his clothes and dismissed him. He made it as far as the door, when a huge man put out an arm like a tree branch. "Let's see your coin, boy."

"I'm actually here to see if you need musicians. I can play three instruments—"

"We train our own." The arm did not move.

Shigan turned away. All right, try again.

The second place, an artfully decorated restaurant, did not let him get past the word "three" in "three instruments" before saying, "Go back to your master, boy."

By the time he'd been rejected the sixth time, he was getting very tired of the word *boy*. No one would let him even try: for some it was his obviously worn, cheap clothing, for one it was his lack of a local master, but for all it seemed to be his age. Even using Imperial did not work—if anything, it got him rejected more firmly, with a growled, "We hire no guild runaways here."

He sped away fast, deciding never again to use Imperial.

The shadows were stretching out longer than his length when he gave up for the day. The air was turning bitter and his stomach gnawed itself with hunger, a familiar sensation from the fortress—but there had always been a plentiful meal waiting.

He made his way back to the inn, where he discovered Yaso unpacking a food basket from which the smell of onions, herbs, and braised fish rose. Mouse sat cross-legged at the little table.

She looked up at his entry, noticed the tight face, and said, "What happened?"

Annoyance flashed through Shigan at letting his defeat show. He shrugged it off. "I tried to find work. Even the shabby teahouses wouldn't let me in the door. Too young."

"You play instruments?" Mouse asked, surprised.

"Three," he replied shortly.

He was a runaway apprentice *musician?* Mouse caught herself before she blurted the question. It was pretty obvious that had to be the truth, and it was also obvious why he hadn't said anything, being a runaway. And since she hated personal questions, it was not fair to ask why a musician would want to run away.

He sank down on the other side of the table, still graceful even in a slump, muttering, "If I had a jar of acacia gum I'd glue some hairs to my lip for a mustache and go back."

Mouse grinned at the idea of Shigan with a false mustache, and said as she accepted a dish of still-steaming dumplings, "Then you'd have to cut your hair every day."

"Not if I could make a mustache," Shigan said as he picked up his sticks. "We used to do plays for . . . I wish I had that room full of costumes and character accessories now."

"I can make you a mustache," Yaso said.

"You can?" Shigan asked.

Mouse was half a heartbeat behind. "You can?"

"It's simple enough, using a piece of silk and some hairs," Yaso said.

"The herbalist probably has acacia gum," Mouse pointed out, grinning at the idea of Shigan wearing a disguise. Then she studied his face. "If it was a thick one, you'd look funny. Because your eyebrows are so thin. And . . ." She traced an extravagant slant over her own straight brows. "They already stand out."

"I wore white ones once, curled all the way to my ears," Shigan said with a reminiscent grin, thinking of a certain irascible figure he was gleefully mocking under the guise of a mythic role. "I was dressed as the Snow God in *The Fox and the Turtle*."

Mouse had read the play, as it was common for beginning scholars. She couldn't imagine what it would be like to see a play acted, even one that was a long lesson in proper virtues, disguised as a play.

"I can make eyebrows, too," Yaso said. "It's little different from making a mustache."

"If you do that, I might have a chance." Shigan sat back, mentally assembling a role. He wanted to earn money of his own, but his motivation right now was to get past those sneering door guards.

Mouse said, "You ought to stuff your clothes, too." She flapped her hands at her body. "You're tall enough. You just need to be . . ." She eyed his body, trying to find the words for his lean form, muscled like a cat. "Not so skinny."

Shigan wasn't going to argue about the fact that the world contained plenty of very skinny men. Adding bulk to his body would definitely change his presence, which might even be fun. And certainly warmer, with winter coming on in earnest.

They finished their meal, and went off as usual to the bath house. On their return, they found the dishes gone, and Yaso sat sewing.

Mouse bent to look at the tiny, delicate strips of fabric. "Are those going to be the eyebrows?"

"Yes. I need the hair, then I can sew it to the silk," Yaso said.

Shigan pulled his hair clasp out, and held out a hank of his hair. Yaso used a sewing scissor to clip a finger's width of hair, and sat down again to sew. Mouse realized that Yaso was going to stitch it hair by hair. "That's a lot of work," she observed.

Yaso smiled. "I like to sew. I like to mend things. It's another way to cultivate Essence."

Shigan rolled his eyes at the word *cultivate* but said only, "I'm very glad you like it, because I sure wouldn't." Then wrapped up in his bedding.

Mouse, feeling something more was needed, said, "Thank you, Yaso. You are turning out to be the most useful of us all."

Yaso said mildly, "I am here to help."

Shigan turned over, one eye narrowly observing Mouse. "He's a servant, so he serves."

"He is not a servant," Mouse stated, then amended, "At least, I don't think of you that way," turning to Yaso. "I think of us all as . . . as brothers, the way they are among the gallant wanderers."

Shigan sat up on his elbows. "So you're saying that I'm saying being a servant is a bad thing, when I'm saying it's a thing, part of the order of things?"

Mouse scowled, trying to pick her way among what she now recognized as shoals. "I never had servants," she said finally. "Everyone divided the work, according to what you can do. And according to tradition. Like the men going out in the boats spear-fishing. Though girls could learn it." She felt herself straying into dangerous territory, and paused, wondering if it was time to confess that she was one of those girls.

She glanced at Shigan as another rush of inchoate feelings rolled over her, a tidal wash that left her feeling awkward. No. There was no reason to confess and make things uncomfortable, because the rules of virtue were firm about females and males living separately until married. Not even touching. But she and Shigan hit each other all the time in sparring, and nothing evil happened—because Shigan thought she was a boy? As long as she kept on living as one, then she wasn't really being unvirtuous, was she?

Shigan's thoughts had gone in a completely different direction. Was he perceived as arrogant? He'd already made that mistake, a very hard lesson. Order—that is hierarchy, he had decided, was not innate, but all in the head. Everyone's head. So . . . when was it unquestioned, and when not?

One thing he could do now. He looked across at Yaso, to whom he had never spoken except to give an order, because that was the order of things *he* had grown up with. He said, "Thank you for making the mustache and eyebrows."

Yaso's head bowed in acknowledgment.

Silence fell as Shigan turned over again and dropped into sleep.

Mouse lay awake. She was used to them all going to sleep at the same time, but here was Yaso with a light burning. Mouse had kept her bows to her parents secret for so long that she hesitated, watching Yaso's bent head. The orderly had never said a sarcastic word, ever. Barely spoke, even.

She glanced Shigan's way, on her right side. He was wrapped up in his bedding facing away from the light, the only thing visible the end of his loose sleeping braid. She turned to her left, where Yaso sewed peacefully, shadow outlined against the wall.

She composed herself as best she could—still feeling exposed—and performed her bows to the southwest. In her mind, she spoke her nightly prayer to the Crane God on behalf of Mother, Father, and Ul Keg.

Yaso never moved.

Relieved, Mouse settled down to sleep.

SIX

NEXT MORNING, WHILE SHIGAN and Mouse worked through the Redbark Sword Form three times, she asked if he was going to go buy acacia gum, and really try to find a job. "Won't they expect you to have an instrument?"

"Maybe. Some places will have a guqin, or a guzheng. Even more instruments, except for flutes. Those are usually personal."

Mouse accepted that, and with an eye cocked skyward: "Let's spar now. I don't know how long the weather will hold." Bad weather meant scant food, and worry about paying for their room—or even going back to Seahorse, which probably wouldn't smell as bad in winter, but who wanted to try?

But when they got back upstairs again, and changed out of their practice clothes (now that they had enough clothing for that), they found congee waiting, along with a small jar of acacia gum, and what appeared to be three hairy caterpillars laid out on a square of silk. Yaso was not there.

Shigan propped thumbs and forefingers on his skinny hips as he looked down at the items. "I don't know why Yaso is still with us, but he sure is useful." He shook his head, then looked around. "I wish we had a mirror. I don't want to put these on crooked."

"I'll do it," Mouse offered.

Mouse knee-walked up beside him. Shigan sat down cross-legged, and tipped his head back. His face was smooth, except for a very few tiny dark hairs sprouting on his chin. His eyelashes were so long! Weren't boys supposed to have short ones? She stared, aware of an odd, prickly sensation, being so close, though she'd just been sparring, and thought nothing of physical contact then. She disliked the sensation, and twitched, trying to shake it away.

He sensed it and opened an eye. "What's the matter? Is there a giant pimple forming?" He scowled, fingering his face.

"No. Just the cold."

Shigan remembered that Second Ryu came from some southern island where they had no real winter, and mentally shrugged, as Mouse carefully spread acacia gum on the back of the mustache silk. He tipped his head back once more and sat still as light fingers delicately applied it to his upper lip.

"No. Too high," she muttered after scooting back. She peeled it off, then reset it. "There."

Shigan fingered it carefully. "Do I look old?"

"You look like you with a fake mustache. Sit still, let me put these on."

Keeping her sticky forefinger in the air, she held one eyebrow up to his face, first aligning with the extravagant slant of his natural brows. No, that just brought attention to them. Then she turned the silk, and held the false brow straight over his eye, obscuring that slant.

"Oh, that's it! And Yaso made them a little longer, so I can put them closer in over your nose . . ."

She moved back. The effect was startling in the way it changed his face, making it look bonier, his eyes set deeply below those bristling brows. Even adding a lot of fake warts was not going to make him less handsome, but the idea of pointing it out led to that vague sense of discomfort. So instead she said, "You look like the drawing of Pirate Bain in *Tales of the Wanderers*."

What boy wouldn't love to hear that? He flushed and grinned — looking very much younger.

"Don't do that," she exclaimed. "You look like you again, and the mustache bunched up."

Shigan pressed his lips into a line and narrowed his eyes.

"That's perfect," she exclaimed. "Now you look old."

The temple gong sounded in the distance. Mouse jumped up. "I must run!"

Shigan took off his winter robe and added more layers

underneath, then replaced it. That added some bulk to his body. Satisfied, he went out, head down past the innkeeper tending her indoor garden, until he reached the street, and bent into a nasty wind.

He'd forgotten the weather, which was going to get a lot worse before it got better. He revised his plans to begin at the other end of the street. He did not want to spend the winter slogging a long distance through this weather if he didn't have to.

He hadn't walked far when he came abreast of a low, rambling corner teahouse he'd passed the day before as being too shabby, the music coming forth painful to the ear.

Today, he heard the sound of a flute larking up and down the scales. It was good! Maybe he'd been too impatient the day previous, or maybe it was merely the clouds overhead threatening sleet, but he turned in.

"A table, sir?" A young woman appeared, wiping her hands on her apron.

Shigan exulted at that "sir." Consciously lowering his voice, he began, "I'm a traveling musician looking for —"

She cut in, saying, "Over there, sir." She vanished through a darkened doorway.

The place smelled of tea, with a faint trace of heated wine. The room had low, plain tables. The support beams were bare, planed wood, decorated with strips of paper with what looked to Shigan like student calligraphy in one or another of the scholarly languages. More decorated the walls, the poetry either famous ones from the ancients, or what had to be student poems, employing much-used expressions. The whole was lit by four lanterns in the corners.

Shigan made out a raised platform at one end, on which three musicians sat, one old and two teen-aged. The tables were mostly empty except for three, two of them with a single man sitting, and one with a pair talking quietly as they ate.

The two young musicians, one on the pipa and one the guqin, accompanied the older man who played the bamboo flute. He was quite good. One of the two girls on the stringed instruments sounded to his ears much like he'd sounded when he was still growing in adult teeth.

Heartened, Shigan suppressed the impulse to touch his mustache as he headed for the tea master, a small man with the largest yam of a nose Shigan had ever seen. The tea master's wispy graying hair began at the back of his head, as though in full retreat from that mighty proboscis.

"Salt!" The tea master squeaked as he ran about, apparently seeing to several tasks at once. Or trying to. "Spoon!" And after a couple of clanks and the rattle of a bowl dropping and spinning on the floor, "Onion!"

Shigan began backing away, but then the nose turned his way. "Custom?"

"Musician," Shigan said, trying to keep his voice low, though the tea master's was almost as high as Second Ryu's. "Looking for work."

"Baste!" The tea master threw something into a sizzling pan, and through the steam piped, "Instruments?"

"Guqin, guzheng, pipa. I can play the dizi, but not as well as he does." A tip of the head toward the old man.

"Hah!" The tea master snorted, a much deeper sound than his voice. "Not two in this city can play as well as he. I can try you." He waved his hand toward the stage.

The girl playing the guqin got up silently and went to a table to collect dirty dishes left by the pair of men—clearly the tea master's daughter.

Shigan went to the guqin, and gave the strings an experimental pluck to check the sound. This one had silken strings instead of brass. A quick turn to two pegs, and he was ready. What to play? Something traditional, a song a grown man might play.

He plucked a string, listening; the instrument's body was tired, but sound enough. It was an elder among instruments, the dragon's gums worn, even notched. He changed his mind about the song, choosing "Waterfall above Peony Peak," a contemplative melody that would not strain a venerable old instrument.

He could hear his own errors, but they were small, mostly due to lack of practice for nearly two years. At the end he looked up.

The tea master had not stopped bustling about his labors, but he had been listening. "My custom is mostly apprentices and students from up the hill. They swarm in at midday, and again at the end of the day. They all think they're great talents, and we don't say anything because they pay to play. What I need is someone who will accompany them. Sometimes this, sometimes that instrument. Hold your temper. You get a third of the take, and of course you can keep anything they throw to you. It won't be much," he warned. "They being apprentices.

The scholars are mostly wealthy, but they spend on themselves. Rice wine," he finished succinctly.

Elated, Shigan said, "Start?"

"Today. I need my girls for the tables."

The other girl laid down her instrument, tied on a waiting apron, and began setting out lanterns on all the tables, but the old man with the flute sat where he was, eyes closed. It had to be nearing noon, so Shigan decided to warm up his hands properly, reflecting that warming up was a very different matter from warming up for Redbark Sword.

He looked down at his hands for the first time since the previous spring. They had changed. That first month had been torture, both the making of the blisters that broke and bled, and the hiding of them. He had calluses across his palms now. Like military men.

A huge, unseen brass gong reverberated from somewhere on the hill, louder here than at the inn; shortly thereafter a rush of footsteps heralded a swarm of dull blue apprentice robes, and the slightly finer robes of a few young scholars who had not yet found a position. All the tables filled in what seemed the blink of an eye. The two girls whirled out the tea trays, never spilling a drop, as the air filled with the fresh scent of tea. The man brought out plates of food for those who could pay for it.

The old flute player vanished without a word. The silent girl came back once the tables had filled, and picked up the pipa, an easy instrument to play. For a short time there was a low hum under the clack of sticks in bowls, and then the first to finish their meal set up a Circle board, as a crowd gathered around to watch. The next two came toward the stage, first throwing a moon, or brass coin, into the bowl—a string of which coins would make up one dragon boat.

Those who played wind instruments brought their own, and invariably barked the name of a song in Shigan and his partner's direction. The very first song, Shigan did not recognize the name. He was trying to figure out how to say so in the fewest possible words, but the boy had already launched into playing, the girl began accompaniment, and Shigan recognized he was there merely to provide background music. Improvisation was easy enough—he had done a great deal of that—and so the midday hour went.

Once two boys came up, and the girl laid down her pipa. The two boys each threw a coin into the bowl. Later, toward the end, Shigan found himself waved off imperiously, as three coins landed in the bowl: three girls, almost the only girls among the sea of boys, clearly liked playing together.

They were the best of the volunteer players, none of which were prodigies. Now he understood the provenance of the lackluster music he'd heard the previous day when he'd passed by.

The swarm left as suddenly as it had come, and then Shigan was told he was free until the afternoon watch. The evening went much like the midday; at the end of it, the tea master handed Shigan his share of coins, saying, "My name is Mu. Be prepared to stay late on festival days when music is permitted. Otherwise, nights will be like this until summer, when the sun goes down later."

Shigan bowed, thinking that he and Second Ryu surely would find gallant wanderers before summer. He exulted — right now he had a job that was bearable, and he'd earned money.

In triumph Shigan made his way back to the inn, where he found Second Ryu and Yaso sitting in that stupid Essence-meditation, a form of which Shigan had endured far too much of as punishment ever since his earliest days. "I got a job," he said loudly, and dropped his coins on the table to join the others — almost half a string.

Mouse gloated over the coins as if they were diamonds and rubies. "Now I won't worry too much about winter coming, and the ring being closed." She rubbed her hands. "I'm hungry. Let's find dinner."

Mouse was surprised and pleased that Shigan had found a way to earn money, which pulled some of the burden off her shoulders. Yaso didn't bring in money, but took responsibility for their laundry, and for finding food, and mending. And of course there was the Essence breathing. Mouse wasn't learning anything during those morning sessions so much as practicing drawing Essence into herself and breathing it out.

When Shigan woke early, he invariably went down to their habitual drill spot to stretch the way he'd been taught as a child, and then to work on Redbark Sword form. As soon as it was light, Mouse joined him. He'd mastered the form much faster than she'd thought he would. They ran through it without weapons, and then with weapons they borrowed from Old Rock. Then they sparred, Shigan rejoicing in the rhythms, the gains in strength and precision. The first time he landed a touch on Second Ryu filled him with wild triumph.

Mouse grinned proudly and exclaimed, "Good one!"

But there was never enough time, for when the temple gongs rang, it meant they had to head for work, he to Mu's Teahouse and she to Old Rock's ring. On laundry days, they got their own congee, since Yaso headed out as soon as the Essence-breathing finished.

Mouse bought from vendors as she jogged to the ring. She was getting used to city life. The chaos of her arrival had sorted into three types of life. Actually four, but she mentally erased the governor and the nobles who lived behind those fine carved gates up on the hills.

There were the street vendors, who walked all day, in all weathers, selling their wares. Then there were the stall owners, who had at least a place to sit, though they, too, were out in all weathers, and had to dismantle their stalls each evening then set up again come morning. Finally, there were the store owners. Mouse always tried to buy from the vendors first.

She finished her pancake before it could get cold, and jogged the rest of the way to the ring. Lotus Pod finished setting up her table and Old Rock put out the weapons, swinging his favorite sword and stamping as he warmed up his muscles, breath clouding.

As soon as a few spectators gathered, they started.

Mouse had become famous along the street—those who relished such bouts admired what they called "the mouse who bites the tiger." In this case, there was added mirth in the fact that their favorite really was named Mouse. Many locals enjoyed sitting at the tables in front of the local teahouse to watch The Mouse flatten some obnoxious brawler. The Mouse was so quiet, so modest, it was a pleasure to watch those bouts, no one revealing even by a hint what was to come. The locals just never bet against The Mouse.

The only problem for Mouse in an otherwise satisfactory life was the lack of gallant wanderers. She finally put a question to Old Rock one day. "Don't gallant wanderers come to this island?"

Old Rock laughed. "They pass us by all the time! Ayah, now and then," he amended at her round-eyed surprise. "I guess you don't notice them. Most of them dress for the road, not in silk or colors. You can recognize them by their walk. By the way they carry themselves. But you have to be watching as they never come to my ring."

Mouse was ready to ask why not, but he turned away, roaring a challenge to a group of noisy newcomers, and the day passed without a chance to ask.

She decided to watch for herself.

One cold day, when Old Rock's nose was suspiciously redder than the weather warranted, she caught a whiff of hot wine about him. His fighting ability wasn't any less; he was just more talkative, especially after four people all wearing brown and green robes, sashes, and headbands sauntered by. Their packs were suspiciously bulky, their weapons clearly wrapped up, as this was an Imperial harbor. Though it was well known that the local garrison didn't bother anyone who didn't brandish bare steel, or cause trouble. The local merchants had that strong of a presence: they didn't care who their custom was, as long as they paid.

As for these four, only one of them giving the ring a single glance of such obvious contempt that Mouse — ready to leap over the heads of the crowd to pester them with questions — faltered to a stop.

Old Rock watched them go. "Snobs, every one of those damn gallant wanderers. They don't come near *us*," he said, his back turned toward Lotus Pod as he swigged from a flask. He let out a satisfied sigh, then clapped her hard on the shoulder. "The ones to watch out for are the half-trained ones tossed out of their sects for bloodlust and thievery. But I know how to spot 'em. Don't you worry. I have some vicious tricks I save just for them. You keep doing what you do and we'll make out fine."

Mouse reported that the next morning, while she and Shigan began sparring. He had improved enough for them to exchange occasional talk while moving through attack, feint, defend.

"He's good," Shigan said. "But I think the fifth years back at Loyalty Fortress would all be better."

"True." Mouse's blade whirled around to tap Shigan — who wasn't there. He sidestepped, and came in low, third combination in the Earth portion of Heaven and Earth. Or rather, Redbark Sword. "I know there are better warriors out there. Better than me, certainly. Better than Old Rock. He's got size and strength, but it seems . . . I think he's what they called in my village a two-day fisher."

Shigan flashed a grin as he sidestepped another attack.

"Which means . . .?"

"Fishes two days, dries his nets for three. It's not to say he's a bad person," Mouse added hastily, as her words felt disloyal somehow. "He's kind in his own way. He and Lotus Pod seem to be pretty honest, as far as I can tell. And he does a thing he likes doing. But I don't want to do that forever. I don't even want to do it a year."

"Nor I. So we both have to be on the watch," Shigan said.

SEVEN

WHEN THE WEATHER TURNED foul, happening more often as the sun's arc dropped farther each day, the ring had to close early. They began to depend on Shigan's earnings, which went up enough for them to move to a better room on the next corridor, labeled Haddock. This room was larger, the table bigger, with good cushions around it. Best of all was a brazier, which Petal lit every morning well before dawn, so that they did not have to climb out of their warm bedding into a room so cold the water in the pitcher would have a thick coating of ice.

Shigan had settled in. He had begun his life as a musician talking as little as possible to hide his own voice. As a result few took any interest in him. The Mu family was polite; he called the daughters Tea Master Nieces One and Two, and they called him Uncle. Tea Master Niece Two was actually a fine musician, but the students were more interested in themselves. The only times they paid attention to her was invariably after drunken poetry contests, when she would create a melody to the winning poem on the spot. Shigan figured out how to provide an accompaniment, which sometimes netted them an actual silver boater now and then from the richest scholars.

Otherwise, he was lucky to make half a string of cash a day. Between that and Mouse's earnings, they were able to buy better winter robes, though used, to layer over their other clothes, and bed shoes as well as slippers to wear inside the room.

Shigan also bought some fabric, with which he stuffed his

clothes, changing the shape of his torso into what he thought might be more manly instead of like a boy. Mouse had noticed, and decided not to observe out loud, that he looked like someone who ate far too many mooncakes and egg pastries.

With time on her hands, and no one to spar with when Shigan was at the teahouse, Mouse gravitated to the booksellers. She did not spend any of their precious earnings on books, which would have to be carried, but she read voraciously, looking for anything related to heroes using Essence. She also consulted the Herbal of childhood, which she comprehended much better now. Mindful of the movement of the two moons, she visited an herbalist, and secured the necessary ingredients for the Cramp, though she regretted the necessity to pay for herbs she once could pick in the wild.

Her first cramp came the week after Sky Wishes Day. The remedy was as painful as she'd remembered. She took to her bed, claiming she'd eaten something bad from a street vendor.

The next day she insisted she was fine, though she looked a little wan, and even Old Rock could see Mouse's gritted jaw. Just as well the weather turned foul early that day. She retired gratefully to the inn to drink hot medicinal tea and then nap.

The same happened the following month; she made herself rise the second day, though her innards were tender from the force of that herb wringing her out. At least she knew what to expect. Which was as well; as winter set in for the duration, though there were as many ships coming and going in the harbor, passengers were fewer, and the sailors who had liberty showed a tendency to turtle their heads into jackets and cloaks and head for the nearest inn that catered to their kind. The streets were not a place to linger.

Nevertheless, the harbor city began setting up for New Year's Two Moons, banners and posters with fat, smiling, dancing pigs everywhere, the symbol of contentment and plenty. As Mouse jogged toward the ring one morning, she thought back, recollecting the last Year of the Pig mainly by all the cakes and good things they'd had to eat.

Sometimes Shigan came to watch her spar, and they walked back together at sundown, he going back to Mu's Teahouse, and Mouse to the inn — or she occasionally joined him at the teahouse to drink hot tea and warm up.

Shigan had just joined them one day when he stared at someone in a way that caused Mouse to look more closely at the spectators. Her gaze caught on a short, solid young woman who stood like a trained warrior. She had a frizzy nest of brown hair that reminded Mouse of her own squirrel-tail hank of hair, but the young woman's was worn in a long braid. She seemed a couple years older than Muin (which looked old to thirteen) and wore a plain traveler's winter robe over loose trousers and high boots, with a warrior's headband. Her stance was tranquil readiness. Her pack had the wrapped tube-shape that indicated a sword.

Next to her a tall boy of about Shigan's age stood. He resembled the woman through the eyes and the shape of their ears, though his hair was darker and a lot smoother, though not nearly the silken ribbon of true black like Shigan's.

A group of sailors, already well lubricated against the chill, judging by the dull red of cheeks and noses, were nudging and guffawing as they tried to jolly each other into volunteering. Finally one climbed up, to a roar from the rest.

Old Rock indicated himself and Mouse. "Who'll you fight? I should warn you, this boy here trounces me regular."

The usual scorn howled and roared, a booming voice proclaiming, "You just say that to get the betting higher. We're not stupid!"

Not stupid maybe, but definitely predictable. The man picked Mouse, of course, spat on his hands, chose the biggest of the wooden swords, and swung it around, posturing for his friends. There was no style in those swings, and nothing but heaviness in his stance.

Mouse settled into readiness, but as she did, she sensed assessing gazes. A quick look, and there were the two travelers' unwinking stares.

The fight went as those fights usually did, but she was distracted by those two watchers. Trained, she thought.

Mouse won, of course, the spectators shouted and laughed and roared, and then the two pushed forward.

Mouse turned to Old Rock for clues.

His big, rough hand scrubbed at his jaw as he stared, bemused.

Mouse watched as the boy and the woman conferred, then she gave him a nod, and he vaulted so lightly over the rail that Mouse's nerves chilled: this one had training. "Challenge," he said clearly, gaze on Mouse.

Another glance at Old Rock, who came up beside Mouse to face the new challenger. Old Rock spoke, his voice rumbling too low for the spectators to hear. "Why don't you fight me, instead? My boy here just finished a bout."

The challenger said, equally low-voiced, "He didn't even break a sweat in dumping that drunk on his ass." And to Mouse, "I can see the evidence of drink in your partner's face, which might explain his being here, but you should know better than to sell your skills like this." A contemptuous gesture toward the ring.

Mouse's temper kindled. "Not your business what I do or don't do to earn a living. Nobody gets hurt here."

"That's something," the boy replied seriously, still with that steady stare of judgment, which irritated Mouse. She breathed in, pulling Essence into a ball within her as they squared off.

Most of the spectators did not know what to make of the beginning of their bout. Instead of the wild swinging, roaring, stamping flail of the previous fight, these two stepped softly, cautiously, each watching the other for tiny signs. When at last they moved, it was lightning-fast, testing and questing, then back.

A couple of spectators groaned. "What are you afraid of!"

"This is more boring than watching ice melt!"

"Shut up," Old Rock boomed. "Just you wait."

And indeed, when the challenger finally decided it was time to teach Mouse a lesson, he came on fast.

By now Mouse was used to facing brawn, but she had not faced an opponent who could give her a challenge of skill since her last bout with Muin. It took all her concentration, and strength, to hold her own; she could not predict this boy's moves, and she'd faced this kind of speed so seldom that she sensed herself lagging, out of rhythm.

He pressed his attack. Infuriated, she brought up a hot gout of Essence, throwing it into her strike at his blade. Wooden sword met wooden sword —

CR-A-ACK!

The boy flew backward, fell, then rolled to his feet and shook out his hand, where a spray of splinters had scored the flesh.

Mouse flinched away half a heartbeat before a wooden splinter as long as her palm could strike her right eye. It slashed her hairline.

Mouse froze, unaware of blood dripping down her face as she stared at her challenger, who stared back in equal dismay, his bleeding hand gripping only a handle. "That was . . ." he began, at the same moment she quavered, "I didn't mean to . . ."

Old Rock came forward quickly, always with an ear cocked for the local authorities. "No harm done, no harm done," he said loudly. "We'll call that a draw—bad drill sword—it can happen to anyone. Everyone gets their coin back, fair and square."

Robbed of the sight of more blood, the spectators turned to the next most immediate need: reclaiming their money. As they crowded up to Lotus Pod's table, Old Rock began sweeping up the splinters.

Mouse got herself out of the ring, fighting the light-headedness that came after a hard thrust of Essence.

"Are you all right?"

She blinked again, aware that the boy was peering down into her face, having repeated his question a few times.

Lotus Bud stepped up, silently offering the boy one of the bandages they kept for accidents. Then she turned to Mouse. "Ryu. Let's wrap your head."

Mouse twitched away without thinking. "I'll do it." She tied the proffered cloth over the stinging cut as she turned her attention to the ring, where one of the drunk's friends was challenging Old Rock.

The boy joined her on the outskirts of the spectators. Mouse heard him say in northern-accented vernacular, "Good enough, Cousin, good enough. It's all superficial cuts," and then, "What sect are you?"

Mouse drew in a startled breath. Could it be *at last* they'd found their gallant wanderers?

Shigan had come up to stand next to Mouse. "Redbark."

The young woman murmured, "I've never heard of the Redbark . . . style? You cannot be a true cultivation sect."

Mouse scowled. "Why not?"

The young woman replied in an even tone and the steady gaze of conviction, "I do not want to believe you belong to a sect dedicated to evil."

"Evil!" Mouse repeated at the same time as Shigan's incredulous, "Evil?"

The young woman flushed slightly, shifted her stance, then changed her tone, "Is this why you worked to attain your skills, so that you can perform for gawkers and drunken wagerers? Have you no sense of honor, of justice?"

Mouse grimaced, hot to the ears. When she first started to

read gallant wanderer tales, the stories were full of honor and justice and loyalty, and one old one even referred to a code.

Ul Keg had said, "The so-called code of honor is old, very old."

Mother had said, "The Sage empress spoke against it, for in ancient times it was understood between men, and she said anything that concerned half the population was useless to the whole."

Father had said, "Be careful of words like honor, and even justice. What one means isn't necessarily what you mean."

To which Ul Keg had finished, "Quite right. Even now, too often what nobles define as honor involves face, and rank, and who shall prevail over whom. Whereas the commoners usually define it another way, closer to trust between clan, neighbors, community, so that all can live together in peace."

Mouse longed to join the gallant wanderers, but still she pointed at the wrapped sword on the woman's back as she said, "Selling your sword on the wander is so much better?"

"Our Eagle Island Sect does not *sell* our skills," the young woman said, still in that even tone. She was speaking to Shigan — she took him for an adult, Mouse realized. "Our oath is . . ." She stopped, looking away. "That can come. I am aware that the wandering world is full of snakes and rats as well as the tigers and dragons everyone wants to hear about. We strive to better our skills, and the lives of those around us. That is what cultivation truly means."

"I'm here to earn money so we can eat," Mouse said trenchantly. *While looking for you.* But she did not trust them enough to actually say it. "And nobody gets hurt," she added in an undervoice.

The boy spoke up. "Are you going to try for the Sky Alliance Prize?"

"Prize?" Shigan and Mouse asked at the same time.

"Never heard of it," Mouse stated, as Shigan shut his mouth — his voice had sounded to his ears far too young.

The boy began with enthusiasm, "It's only the best competition in all the northern islands — "

"Peace, Cousin Matu," the young woman said, and then folded right hand over left fist, forearms horizontal in the gallant warriors' bow as she inclined her head, bowing first to Shigan as the elder, and then to Mouse. "Ki Tenar, of the Eagle Island Sect. And this is Cousin Ki Matu." She indicated the smiling boy, using the term for father-cousin of a younger age.

Mouse was thrilled to learn the gallant wanderer bow at last. She'd seen it referred to many times in the hero tales, but never described. Everyone bowed the same. No hierarchy, unless it was earned by merit within a sect. And then it was merely a deeper bow. One only bowed forehead to the floor when taking a master.

"Ryu . . ." She halted there, aware that she had ceased thinking of herself as Mouse for quite a while now. It no longer fit, like shoes grown too small. But she wasn't Second Ryu either, not with Muin gone. However, she could be Ryu — and keep that connection to him.

She repeated firmly, "Ryu. Redbark Sect."

"Shigan Fin, Redbark Sect," Shigan said, when Ki Tenar glanced his way.

The clouds that had quietly gathered while all this was going on chose that moment to send a flurry of snow, harbinger of much to come.

Cries of disappointment rose from the spectators as Old Rock declared the day's competition at an end.

"Redbark Brother Ryu," Ki Matu repeated, wondering if Ryu of the Redbark Sect was even younger than he'd guessed — which was no older than twelve or thirteen. And far too young to be on the wander without a guide. At least so it was with responsible clans and sects. He knew that little boys could be very sensitive about size, so he shrugged awkwardly, his smile crooked, as he said, "I just wondered how old you are . . . but likely any day you'll start shooting up tall as a pine."

He meant well. Most boys preened at predictions of prodigious height.

"Oh," Mouse said absently. She gave a little nod. Ryu. Shigan never called her anything but that. Yes, that definitely ought to be her gallant wanderer name.

Which means it is time for me to begin referring to her as Ryu for this part of her tale.

A strong buffet of wind, bringing huge, messy clumps of snow, caused her to bend into the wind and start toward the inn. She said nothing more to Ki Tenar or Ki Matu. She wasn't certain if she wanted them to follow or not, so she left the question to them and began walking as fast as she could.

They followed, Ki Matu saying eagerly, "The Sky Alliance Prize competition draws competitors from all over the wandering world. It's not just sword. You have to be good at riding, and other martial arts. The winners get offers from the

Alliance sects to fill any blank seats from the year before. The top five get to choose because everyone with an extra seat wants them."

Ki Tenar paced on Ryu's other side. She glanced skyward at the gray clouds moving lower as she said, "We just arrived in the harbor to look for a ship going north, but the weather is getting so bad that we decided to find a place to winter, and work on our skills. We'll recommence our journey north as soon as the spring thaw comes."

"Are there masters among the competitors?" Ryu asked.

"Yes. And it's masters who do the judging," Ki Matu said. "Are you interested?"

"Yes!"

Matu then asked, "Where do you come from?"

Ryu had prepared for this question a long time ago, as a last resort. It seemed time to use it. "An island far from here, so small that you wouldn't know the name even if I told you. And we never say it. I'll just add that to leave, we first must go in sampans over treacherous waters filled with rocks, called Dragon Teeth Pass, between two islands so close no ship can sail between them. Then overland through dangerous forest to a harbor, to wait for a trade ship that might take a season to reach us—"

She had plenty more, but at that moment the sky began unloosing its burden.

The wind worsened at every step, and by the time they reached the inn, snow swirled around them. Petal was there at once, sweeping the snow out the door, her red-rimmed eyes lowered. Ryu noticed a smudge on her cheek, but on second glance, her stomach curdled when she recognized a bruise.

Shigan and Ryu stamped their way inside, not seeing the innkeeper bar the way for the Ki gallants. "We are full up," she said with her poisonous smile.

It wasn't true, but she was an expert at evaluating potential worth, and young gallant wanderers with worn clothing were never in possession of much. She had five rooms left, for which she fully intended to charge a swingeing price for desperate travelers caught stranded.

The two pushed back out into the snow, bending into the wind as they sought for another inn.

"I don't know which of us would have won if that sword hadn't shattered," Matu shouted to his elder cousin.

"Was it that close?"

"Close, yes! I think Redbark Brother Ryu would have taken me in a real fight. Though I pressed him hard. He's not as strong as I am until he uses Essence, and then he's far past me. But he can't be older than twelve!"

"I saw," she replied, cupping a hand around her mouth. "We didn't see Redbark Brother Shigan fight. We don't know how much better he is. Or what he is, master or apprentice."

"I'd like to find out more about their sword form."

"All right. But now, shelter."

EIGHT

YSKANDA HAD LEARNED THE layout of the palace, in particular where it was safe to walk and when. His tutoring with Court Artist Yoli Jiwa now took place during afternoons, except when Yoli was summoned to court; then Yskanda had assignments, sometimes sketching rock gardens, trees, and the complicated decorations of various buildings in this or that light, despite very cold fingers. When the weather was bad, he was copying fragile, faded masterworks as Yoli focused on refining his line and precision.

Morning classes he spent in the general academy, which was taught by a mix of scholars and graywings. Yskanda sat with his peers among the scribe apprentices, trading off studying ancient texts for next spring's Imperial Examination, and preparing and making books and scrolls. He found he was not behind: Ul Keg had taught Yskanda and Mouse the traditional five-point essays that students for generations had called the five-talon. The length could be as short as a page or as long as a thick scroll, but all followed the same structure: introduction, presentation of idea, traditional references, argument, conclusion.

Yskanda had loathed this form almost as much as Mouse had — and he discovered soon that his feelings were generally shared, especially by the scribes.

At least he was included among those partial to the decorative arts, rather than the scholarly side of being a scribe.

Instead of writing piles of five-talon essays on paper he had made himself, his studies of the classics incorporated lessons in calligraphy as well as embellishment. Since Yskanda had memorized most of those classics under Ul Keg, his instructors encouraged him to concentrate on perfecting his strokes, and the execution of decorative symbols.

The day before the imperial ship going to the islands near Imai was to leave, he was assigned to paint the rock garden outside the enormous warren of buildings making up the Library of Splendid Literature, which included the archive.

The library was open to all who had access to the imperial palace. The archive, which occupied the southwest end, was only open to scholars, students, and ministers. The "students" designation included those studying at the general academy, Yskanda was told. He had yet to explore it, and as he walked out to find a likely spot from which to paint, he glanced at that building promising himself a visit when he had time. Alone.

Solid, square Yut Hak, one of the quieter boys in Yskanda's dorm, joined him.

That didn't surprise Yskanda. They were usually put in pairs, sometimes more, after which they would compare works and critique each other.

Yut Hak had only painted for a brief time before he put his brush down. "I've been asked to collect the letters home," he said. "Have you finished yours?"

Yskanda's hand jerked, causing his brush to splatter. He covered the splatter by stippling shadows on the rough stone he had been drawing as he said, "I haven't written one. I only just entered the palace. Everything is too new."

That much he had planned in imaginary conversations.

The boy looked up at the gray sky, then down at the gray rocks in the raked gravel, before saying, "Writing home is a privilege. It's never a good idea to refuse a privilege. Can be taken as a slight."

Yskanda set his brush down. "I am not . . ." He stopped there, his thoughts winging ahead: they were alone, a rarity. Making him suspect that Yut Hak's primary purpose right now was the letter, and not the painting lesson.

Once again, Yskanda sensed the invisible bars of his cage. He clasped his hands and bowed his head. "Thank you for the reminder," he said. "I will get it done."

Yut Hak's expression eased. He stayed for the remainder of the period, also painting, but that one unhidden reaction had told Yskanda what he needed to know: Yut Hak had been told to corner Yskanda about his letter, and perhaps not to accept a negative answer.

He no longer wavered over whether or not he had to write. It was clear he had to; perhaps the next reminder would be more forceful. This existence as a kind of hostage was like playing an invisible game, with rules he had to puzzle out. Including what would happen if he guessed wrong.

He had learned about invisible games, as he'd told Ul Keg the last time they saw one another. One of the unspoken rules he'd managed to figure out during the first year at Master Bankan Evnet's house was not to ignore questions that were actually interrogations. That only caused the interrogator to fill the silence with increasing pressure, even threat. Instead, he had learned to fill the silence with words, which allowed him some control of the content.

That night he sat writing at his desk in the dorm, aware of Yut Hak coming by once or twice. It occurred to Yskanda that Yut Hak might be the graywings' ear among the apprentices. Surely they had one. Maybe more than one.

And so, next morning, his letter lay in the pile, addressed to Master Bankan Evnet, and inside, the text apologized for his abrupt disappearance, and went on to describe, in detail, what he was learning. He did not describe how he'd left Imai. He did not say where he was. It was a letter filled with chatter about scrolls, scenery, inks, lessons in line, and so forth—a written version of the prattle that he knew quite well had led to his fellow apprentices at Bankan's thinking him odd but harmless as a rabbit.

He guessed that it would be ferrets delivering his letter. He could not prevent the ferrets from searching for his family, but he was not going to help them; his hope was that that if Mistress Anise stopped at the master scholar's house on her twice-yearly tax delivery, it would be long after the ferrets had given up and left. Meanwhile, surely the master scholar would give her the letter to carry to his parents. If they were still there in Sweetwater.

Yskanda's second fear, beyond their being captured (but *surely* Mother would not be caught unawares?), was that if Father knew Yskanda was a prisoner, he would risk his life to come and rescue him. The long descriptions of what he was learning were meant to convey that he was not in prison; he was doing what he loved. And again, surely, if he could reflect that Father coming to the rescue would be exactly what the emperor wanted, Mother and Father could see that, too.

His letter vanished with the others, and he waited tensely for repercussions. There were none. Life went on, full of art — which began to change as armies of bond-servants, under the direction of the Household graywings, began putting up fresh calligraphy around doors, furbishing up the door gods, and hanging banners for New Year's Two Moons.

These banners with their golden tiger-eyes surrounded by exquisite embroidery were so magnificent that it hurt Yskanda's heart to see them, but the reminder every day, almost every breath, that he was living in a cage tempered the exhilaration and awe. He hoped that the emperor would be far too busy with the elaborate New Year's rituals, and with his family, to bother with Yskanda. But he couldn't count on it.

He remained vigilant to any mention of the emperor, and learned that those closest to the imperial presence recognized every shadow in his expression and shade in his voice. Every sighting of the emperor, no matter how brief, was discussed endlessly, the better to determine what those expressions might mean, and at least in public discussions, how best to please him. It was generally agreed that his most dangerous expression was a certain smile that might or might not have anything to do with laughter. It, unlike anger, was never predictable.

Yskanda had seen that smile the day he was brought.

He moved through his days, alive when he had a brush in his hand. The only time he ventured out alone was to Ghost Moon temple when the moon was full.

Spies and peers alike gave him cautious approval. He was invariably thoughtful, kind, discreet, exceedingly talented with that brush of his, and appeared to be singularly free of ambition, though he worked very hard — when Court Artist Yoli summoned him, the two of them might be at their inks and papers for several watches, but when the young apprentice finally emerged, no complaint was ever heard, even if he had missed meals. Nor did he ever make special demands.

The palace ferrets and the inner circle graywings separately agreed that even though they knew absolutely nothing more about the boy than they had the first day he arrived, it would be terrible indeed if the order came to end his life; at least they could make it painless. Unless, of course, there was an order about that, as well.

The end of the year for many of the common folk was celebrated with a ritual acknowledging the Kitchen Fire God, but in the capital city, New Year's Two Moons was nigh when they woke to the Day of Sealing Up of the Seals, wherein the courtiers, in their formal court wear, paraded not only with their jade batons of office, but their seals, to be safely locked up while their offices were closed.

In the city, businesses closed for a formal reckoning of accounts, paying of debts, and then commencing a frenzy of cleaning and preparation for the new year, from stripping old sayings from outside doors to sweeping detritus from the back entrance. No one wanted any residual dirt, mixing with bad luck, to linger into the new year.

Two days before the festival, as servants outside the palace and within it labored to shroud all the decorations in mourning-white cloths, Yskanda's dormitory mates began happily discussing what they would do with their liberty. Yskanda was not left to wonder long if he would have liberty; it was Bitternail who caught him leaving the morning session, on his way to the midday meal, to say, "You have been selected to paint the imperial family during the New Year's Two Moons ritual and celebration."

Yskanda bowed, his mind bumping once again against the bars of his gilt cage. The emperor was toying with the hostage again.

That afternoon, Yskanda was to meet with Court Artist Yoli. As soon as he got there, Yoli eyed him from beneath those curling snow-colored brows, moved to the door to tap certain talismans engraved within some carving around the door frame, and then said, "What's wrong?"

"All is well insofar as this ignorant and unworthy person is aware, Court Artist Yoli," Yskanda replied promptly. And then he repeated his orders.

Yoli had been informed earlier. Once could be considered whim. Twice pulling a half-trained boy, however talented, into the exalted realms to paint before the masters declared him ready indicated something else. Add that to the mysterious way the boy had appeared, and it caused the court artist to set aside his own work to think.

He knew the identity of every important individual in the

palace and in the court, and Afan Yskanda was no connection to any of them. The only time in the emperor's highly ritualized, circumscribed life Yoli did not know much about was the brief period more than twenty-five years ago, when the then Second Prince Enjai had lived outside the palace, at the end of which the Empress yanked him back inside, as wild rumors circulated about a heels-up chase clear to the river. Wasn't that when he was first supposed to be married?

Yoli had access to all the archives; given that it was midday, and most were at their meals, he slipped out of his wing and traveled back routes to the archive. The old graywing in charge glanced up, and, seeing Yoli's long-familiar face, returned to his reading.

Yoli prowled along seldom-visited stacks and racks, until he came across the drawings made at that time . . . court events . . . ritual parades . . . oh yes! There it was, the official selection for a bride. The last such, as it happened, though until then it had been a centuries-old tradition.

Now intensely curious, Yoli took out the entire stack related to that search, including the ones he'd contributed himself when the five young women had been chosen for the Second Prince's future wife.

He unrolled the papers with one hand. There were the five final choices, so very young. One, two . . . and Yoli whistled under his breath as he stared down at a female version of Yskanda's features, sketched by his own hand.

The bride who'd disappeared.

Gossip flooded back to his mind, all speculation. No one knew what had happened. Only one thing was clear: the emperor himself had not forgotten — if Yskanda's resemblance to this Alk Hanu wasn't coincidence. In which case, was young Yskanda here as a privilege or as a hostage?

The court artist rolled the drawings back up, replaced everything exactly as it had been, and withdrew thoughtfully to his chamber to figure out a strategy.

When Yskanda turned up for his lesson, Yoli abandoned the exercises in brush discipline that he had planned. "It is time to begin learning the fundamentals of court painting," he said.

Yskanda's eyes widened. "I thought I was."

"You were. And are. In the general sense. Those lessons I will be leaving to your morning classes. I'm going to begin with lessons for dealing with the imperial presence. You're ready enough — don't waste breath denying humbly. Save that for outside this room."

The court artist uttered a short cackle as he moved about the room, touching every one of the talismans he had bought at great expense and placed to suppress sound going beyond the confines of the room.

He patted one, a plain inkstone — one of the many in the room. "Don't ever speak your mind until I have a chance to employ my talismans. I am reasonably certain that half the pages, and all the graywings, keep their ears to the door when they pass by. Not that I have ever talked treason, but I do speak bluntly, a privilege I feel I am owed within my own four walls."

Yskanda had no objection to that. He wished he could do the same.

"Now. You need to learn what I do. And why. It has little to do with technique, which you are adequate enough with. Time will refine that skill. We are going to embark on illustrations of historic moments. Without looking at the records first. Then we will compare, and discuss yours and the former court artists' choices. In here we have the luxury of speaking plainly, without the flattery and self-deprecation that is part of courtly etiquette. Out there, if you ever do anything well, it is due entirely to the emperor's merit, understand?"

Yskanda said, "I understand."

"If the emperor orders you to drop the formal court manner, and he does sometimes, what you do is shorten the flowery language, cutting short the expressions of gratitude for whatever is under discussion. You might even venture into a personal pronoun, if he is insistent. But in no other respect do you set aside formality. That," he stated, "should keep you alive."

Yskanda noted that he had not said *would*. Was that a general observation or was that directed specifically at him?

Yoli smoothed a sheet of paper as he said, "To all eyes, it seems my life has been one of ease and plenty, pageantry and renown. It is true."

"But?" Yskanda asked, testing the limits of this room's freedom, without venturing to his own situation. "This unworthy student ventures to observe that there might be a but."

Yoli flashed a sardonic grin his way. "But. It's true that I have never faced dangerous attacks. My moments of danger all occurred in court. For the purposes of our discussion now, these have included times when I was required to record an important event."

Yskanda said, "But you told me that artists have to be objective."

"Who is ever truly objective? Is it even possible? We might debate, had we the leisure, the ancients' writings on that. We could also debate the idea of objectivity, which is as important, at least to me. But we don't have the time. You ought to have begun these lessons when you were small, so we must do what we can."

Yskanda bowed, as always taking the words as a remonstrance — which suppressed questions Yoli did not yet want to answer. "Every choice you make says something that transcends words. The way you place the figures, the colors you use, the symbols you choose — and even if you claim to be neutral, much will be read into what you draw. But there is only one opinion that truly matters."

"The emperor's?"

"Why do you make it a question?" Court Artist Yoli smiled thinly. "What you, or I, might consider objective won't matter. His opinion does. So we will learn to find a way between what we find objective and what has been accepted into the archive. We will begin with the obvious historic moments, such as the Peace at the Bridge of Autumnal Sighs, during the Mei Dynasty. Now, listen as I read two eyewitness accounts, and then what the court historian wrote . . ."

The day before New Year's dawned with a silent procession from the inner palace toward the Shrine of the Emperors, winding its way up the long street of steles put up by previous emperors to their forebears. The emperor would pray alone for peace and plenty on behalf of the Thousand Islands.

Those permitted outside the city lined the streets to watch the regiment of imperial guards, all with white mourning headbands tied over their helms, and white sashes at their waists; the courtiers in rank order, also in white; the graywings again in white, bearing the banners, the great fans, and the imperial canopy, then the palanquin carrying the emperor. After that, rows of handmaids in white.

They walked past storefronts and booths and houses, all with white draped around doors and windows.

This was the one day a year that the crowd did not shout in unison, wishing the emperor ten thousand years: they bowed down in silence, knowing that the following day they would make up for it when he made his triumphant return on the first day of the new year, and at his appearance all the white shrouding would be whipped away, revealing the glorious decorations in all their color.

For those who had to remain inside the palace, they could only hear the muffled drums and the periodic bawls of the great horns, until those died away. It was a day of cold food and quiet everywhere, as the emperor disembarked from the palanquin at the great Gates of Memory, and proceeded alone, on foot, up the road past tombs of former dynasties, and even past the Jehan Dynasty's tomb, to the Shrine.

The tombs were grand enough, visible from the entire city below on very clear days; these were decorated by various emperors to their own and their family's glory, but the steles along the Memorial Path could only be put up by one's progeny: Which posthumous name would they give you?

Each of the years he had made this journey, his eyes had caught on the grimly plain stele of Emperor Milo Giha — whose posthumous name, Milo, could be roughly translated as "He who was lost"; and Giha, though superficially bland, was a single stroke away from "Demon spawn."

But our tale does not concern the emperor's subsequent thoughts that day, on this trip he had been making since his coronation, in good weather and bad.

Instead, we return to Court Artist Yoli, who had begun thinking of Yskanda as his parasol tree (symbol of integrity and innocence, excellent attributes in the world, but impossibly dangerous in the rarified atmosphere of imperial court), and we return to Yskanda himself.

Yskanda's mind plunged into a newly assigned set of challenges, scarcely aware of the world around him, outside of the smoke from braziers and stoves and incense burners that seemed to hang motionless in the air.

It was a relief to have work to focus on, enabling him to shut out the world around him, as he strove to get his mind around what Yoli was trying to teach him.

At the end of a very long day, Yoli sighed and sat back. "I wish I had a year, even a month. But we have what we have. At least I will be there to help you, but you must remember not to let your mind go wherever it is when you draw like this."

Yoli held up one of Yskanda's most skillful drawings, of a small page looking open-mouthed at an aerial tangle of nightingales against the bare, ghostly branches of a tree. The drawing was superlative in the way it caught the child's expression — which would get that child beaten for wasting time, if it fell into the wrong hands.

That same ability to reach deep into the soul could equally get Yskanda killed . . . privilege or hostage? So far, neither emperor nor boy had broken the silence.

"Whatever happens tomorrow, you *must* remember the compositions we talked about," Yoli went on. "Including elements you must not add that might be perceived to detract from the imperial subject's face. Even if you find those elements inspiring. They remain in the background, their proper place, and they cannot attract the eye."

They had constructed three separate possible arrangements, right down to the size and placement of each figure. All Yskanda would have to do is get the general features indicated, and work on the details of dress and hair ornaments.

NINE

THE GENERAL ROUTINE WAS to bathe before bed, and wash up in the morning.

As the emperor's grand procession wound down from the tombs at dawn, Yskanda went to the bath he shared with the apprentices, and asked for a concoction of carrot seed, cedarwood, chamomile, clary sage, cypress, and lavender to ward the throbbing in his temples. It was not quite a headache, though his skin hurt a little. He paid scarce heed, troubled by a sense that the thoughts and images crowding into his head made his skull seem too small to contain them.

At one time he had welcomed that sense, because when he had it, he always found it easier for his mind to slip away from his surroundings to *there*, that peaceful place from which he could draw what he saw inwardly as well as outwardly.

But he could not indulge that sense, not now! He stayed in the bath as long as he dared, breathing with relief as the throb eased. Then he scrambled out and shivered into his best robe, which was stored in a cedar chest. After he dressed, he stood with his arms out as the servant all the boys shared aired the robe with aromatic smoke from incense. He held his breath; for some reason his lungs ached when he breathed, which usually did not happen.

Yskanda met Court Artist Yoli Jiwa at the latter's wing. The court artist was almost unrecognizable, with his wild hair neatly brushed up and skewered with a fine hair clasp. Even his wild eyebrows were brushed. He cast a frowning glance at Yskanda, and gave a short nod and a grunt of approval, giving no hint at how startled he was by Yskanda's unconscious beauty, enhanced by his thoughtful brow and modest dove gray clothing. There they waited until a page arrived, saying, "The imperial procession is nearly at the imperial garden."

"Let us go," Yoli said, leading the way.

Yskanda carried his brushes in the shoulder bag that all apprentices used, and a roll of the finest paper.

The two paced in silence toward the imperial residence end of the palace, where more imperial guards were to be seen, and quietly gliding graywings appearing and disappearing through discreet doors obscured by budding plum trees and various evergreen shrubs.

Typically, there was no sign of anyone watching the two, but when they approached the modest east door, it opened, and a graywing whom Yoli addressed as Smokeleaf bowed in greeting. Yoli sent one last scowling look toward the bank of clouds gathering on the horizon, then led the way inside, Yskanda at his heels.

The hum of voices met them before they saw the royal family in the emperor's residence, which Yskanda had heard everyone refer to as the Golden Dragon Pavilion. Here was the secondary, less formal throne room, outside of which were heard higher children's voices threaded with women's voices, and the deep tones of the male singers. It all blended into the soft, complicated music played by musicians along the side of a chamber decorated with green, gold, and crimson, with blue highlights. Vivid colors for a gray season, though this weather, Yskanda had been surprised to hear, was considered warm by the northerners.

The voices quieted when the horns and drums signaled the approach of the emperor. The imperial family gathered in rank order.

The emperor entered, and the family bowed, while the waiting servitors went to the ground, Yoli grunting with effort as he did so.

"Rise," the emperor said.

From a distance he looked tired, as well he might, if he really did spend the night praying up at the temple at the tombs. But of course he wasn't the only one. His entourage had had to stand through the night outside the Gates of Memory — Yskanda had learned that only the hardiest were picked for this duty, but their reward was to keep whatever was left of the gold that they tossed to the crowd on the way back to the palace that morning.

The imperial family crossed the private court that opened into the ancestral shrine. Yskanda and Court Artist Yoli were permitted to kneel under the lower eaves of the triple-roofed Golden Dragon Pavilion, the servants behind them.

Yskanda looked into the courtyard. His gaze strayed to the arched, beneficent branches of a redbark tree, which Ul Keg had taught him was sacred. Two trees grew at either side of the shrine, sheltering chrysanthemums and gardenias. Even in the cold, Yskanda could almost smell the bark. The air fingering through those branches seemed somehow purer, the light on the bark clear, almost luminescent.

A rustle recalled his attention as the sacrificial dishes were borne to the door and then handed to the youngest princess, who passed each to her brother, and so on through the consorts, and finally to the dowager empress, from whom the emperor accepted each dish to be placed on the altar table. The emperor lit the incense sticks, set them up, then led the family in bows and one last prayer for a year of peace and plenty.

And then it was done. The emperor and family left the shrine, returned to Golden Dragon, and trod up the stairs to the formal dining room.

"Come," Yoli whispered to Yskanda. "We have to get up to the balcony, and secure a spot at the side where we can see everything, since the weather has held off so far. Remember, even if the emperor speaks to you, never face south. Always eastward. You can look about you, but your body must remain in one position — at least if the weather turns bad we'll have wind at our backs."

Yskanda peered up at the hazy sunlight. "You think a storm is coming?"

"I feel it in my bones." The court artist rubbed his elbow discreetly. "There will be a play. Usually is."

They exited through one of the discreet side doors, and climbed steep stairs to the upper floor, above the high ceiling of the inner throne room. This building with its three stacked roofs, each corner guarded by the twelve animals of the stars plus three mythic guardians, crowned the hill at the north end of the palace grounds. It was the highest point in the entire palace, excepting only the watchtowers at the corners of the outer walls.

Court Artist Yoli motioned Yskanda to a balcony overlooking the Imperial Garden, which was the largest of the
many gardens in the imperial palace. It was centered around a
stream-fed lake, with covered zig-zag walkways leading to
pretty arched bridges built over the winding canal. On the
island in the midst of the lake a terrace had been built, with a
fine three-tiered pagoda at one end, roofed in what looked like
pure gold. Walls winding here and there created secluded
areas, each connected by a round moon door, and opening to
scenery beautiful from every vantage, through every season.

Overlooking this fabulous garden was a long balcony.
Drawing tables had been placed at either end. The court artist
waved Yskanda to one, and took the other, both low tables
facing east.

Yskanda set out his paper, brushes, and ink, then swept his
gaze over the magnificent view. He lifted his eyes, taking in
the structure of the inner palace: the consorts' and princesses'
pavilions to the east—visible only as high walls and rooftops—
and the princes, young and old, housed to the west, within a
maze of courtyards and small gardens.

Beyond the high wall to the south, the Hall of Glorious
Harmony, the grand governmental building, with two of the
three lesser governmental roofs partly visible at right and left.
And far to the east, the northmost side of the buildings
Yskanda lived and worked in. He turned his head toward the
west, which he had never seen. He couldn't see much now but
rooftops over the high walls, but he'd learned that south of the
princes' pavilions lay the garrison of the imperial guards, and
the sinister prison called the House of Eternal Peace. Between
it and the garrison lay the infamous Lotus Blossom Square, the
execution ground.

Quickly he glanced southward again, and realized that the
palace was not built on flat ground, but lay on a gentle slope
above the lake. Far to the south he made out the towers over
the main gate that opened into the city, barely visible in a
glinting haze, its winding streets marking by steep, swept
roofs. And beyond them, the bay, now the color of brushed
steel as clouds advanced in a line.

Bitternail and Melonseed emerged through the main
doors, holding them open, and the imperial family filled the
balcony in a ripple of silks and dancing tassels.

Court Artist Yoli caught Yskanda's eye and nodded
meaningfully: it was time to make ready for whichever

command came.

The emperor raised his hand, and a line of colorfully dressed and masked players pranced out to the terrace, surrounding a dancing figure in a roly-poly costume, wearing a pig mask.

Yskanda painted quickly, memorizing detail for adding later. When he'd captured the outline of the imperial family, he showed his sketch to Court Artist Yoli, who nodded.

Yskanda smiled to himself. He was about to rise and take his things down to the garden, where a table had been set behind a pear tree so that his unsightly presence would be slightly obscured, but he would still be able to see the balcony. He could then add in the imperial family observing the play, for most of his paper was empty awaiting the addition of the august play-watchers.

He glanced down at the players for one last check, but his eye was drawn by movement to the side. He turned his head. Alarm flashed painfully through all his nerves when he saw a mass of imperial guards streaming toward the prison. They surrounded wretches stumbling along, their heads and hands imprisoned by big, heavy-looking, cruel racks.

His family? The thought was instinctive, but though the figures were far away, none had any familiar lineament: he would have recognized his father's tall form, and mother's short, slight one. First Brother's and Mouse's as well, though they had probably grown in the time he hadn't seen them. But he'd know them, he was sure.

These were all male, two very husky; in the few heartbeats he had been staring, the others also saw them.

Court Artist Yoli caught his eye and flicked a meaningful glance toward the stairs. Yskanda swept up his materials and moved to the servants' stairs. The door exited into the garden. As he traversed it, a cold sting on his cheek caused him to glance up. The light was fading before the tumble of clouds overhead.

But no orders had been given for withdrawal. The players still cavorted, the musicians still played, sound oddly muting as the light dimmed.

"News!" The single syllable rose above the music, a distant bawl, then closer, "News!" And an imperial guard bolted into the garden and flung himself flat below the emperor's balcony.

Yskanda flung open his paper and began sketching in the imperial family as they stilled, looking down curiously. One of the graywings emerged through the garden door to fetch from the guard his written report.

By the time he reached the emperor to hand off the report, a couple more stings of tiny hail struck Yskanda, and tapped his paper. He shook them away as he glanced up to his left — and saw the emperor's face harden to marble.

The entire world stilled, or so it seemed. Yskanda's heart raced. The back of his neck gripped. The throb in his head increased. He knew his painting was all wrong, as wrong as porcelain shattered to meaningless shards.

He rolled up that paper, and smoothed a new one, anchoring down the edges with his ink as a breeze began to fret them. Overhead lightning leaped from cloud to tumbling cloud. The charged air, the emperor's cold fury — felt, rather than seen — the building storm coalesced into impressions that his hands raced to capture. Splat! Pok! Tap! More hail. Larger hail. He flicked the ice crystals away, then worked the blotches they left into the wet ink as his mind slipped into that other place, and his hands labored to capture what he saw.

He lost track of time, starting when a gnarled hand reached down to yank the paper away. His brush left a long streak across the painting as more hail dropped. Yoli thrust the paper into his robe, smearing it and crumpling it badly. Then he flicked a half-finished drawing down in front of Yskanda.

"Paint—" he began. And stopped.

Both looked up.

First Imperial Princess Manon stood on the other side of the pear tree, the rising wind rippling through her long, glossy knee-length hair. She wore layers of silk in white and peach and ice blue, her outer robe with its long sleeves embroidered with hummingbirds and begonias. She didn't move, or even blink despite the smack of hailstones.

For her, this first close view of the astonishing young god in gray, fine wisps of hair blowing about his face, caught at her breath.

She had never seen anyone so beautiful.

She fought for clarity, and won. He wore the gray of a servant, and were those *dragons* on that painting? The scorch of anger at his temerity burned away the effect of that first glimpse of his face, and her eyes lifted from the paper to his bewildered expression, as if he knew not what he did, or even where he was.

Court Artist Yoli bowed to her, then turned to Yskanda,

pointing silently but insistently at the paper. Yskanda looked down at the carefully posed drawing in traditional poses, groping to make sense of it.

Lightning flared, this time with a crack of thunder. The hail intensified, then abruptly turned to snow. Yskanda shivered, realizing for the first time that his hands and feet were fast turning numb. "I don't think I can paint," he said apologetically.

"Let's try from somewhere more sheltered," Court Artist Yoli said, and shoved the folded paper firmly under one arm, and pressed it to his side.

The servants' stair required extra steps, of course. When they reached the top, before they could look for a spot, Bitternail approached. "His imperial majesty summons Court Artist Yoli and Apprentice Afan."

As they turned the corner on the steep stair, Yoli grunted with effort, hissing under his breath in the ancient tongue, "I'm too old for this, too old."

Too old for . . .? Yskanda wanted to ask, but thought it better to keep silent.

They were led to one of the back chambers, where not only Bitternail and Melonseed stood attentively at either side of the emperor's chair, but a row of imperial guards waited impassively at the back. The rest of the imperial family was gone, excepting only First Imperial Princess Manon, from whose appearance the damp and dishevelment of that brief hail storm had vanished save for a telltale blotch of wet here and there on her flowing silks. Her maids waited against the adjacent wall, as still and silent as statues.

Yskanda remained behind the court artist, and when the latter dropped to his knees and pressed his forehead to the floor, Yskanda did likewise. The emperor said, "I am told Afan Yskanda was in the middle of painting an augury, and you attempted to hide it, Court Artist Yoli?" His voice was the soft one everyone dreaded hearing.

The court artist spoke from the floor. "Hide? No. This incompetent old fool intended to destroy such a scribble not worth polluting the eyes of Heaven's chosen. Apprentices are all too fond of the worn styles of ancient days, in their ignorance thinking them impressive."

"First Imperial Princess said it was a picture of dragons fighting among clouds?"

"One water dragon," Yoli stated. "Of three claws only.

This old scribbler will display the offending paper if your imperial majesty wishes, but his fumbling intent was merely to avoid offending the purity of your imperial majesty's eye."

"Never mind the flattery," the emperor said, but his voice was a shade less furious. "Explain."

Yoli spoke rapidly to the floor. "The apprentices are traditionally set to copying ancient scrolls. This is how they learn the enlightened traditions of the empire which has been blessed by heaven with your imperial majesty's presence. This incompetent court artist makes no claims whatsoever as to whether the world in the days of our ancestors was filled with dragons, or if they were imagined. What can be attested is that apprentices tend to choose the most fanciful images, in their efforts to awe and to please, though the modern style is to appreciate what is actually before our eyes. Since the heavens sent a storm today, this ignorant apprentice chose the most traditional form to sketch it. Please punish me for not teaching him well."

The emperor glanced to the side. He waved a hand toward his daughter. "Is that satisfactory, Imperial Daughter?"

The first imperial princess cast one last glance Yskanda's way, for already she had ceased to believe that first glance. But his rain-washed face if anything was more luminous, color bright in his cheeks, his long-lashed eyes wide.

She wrenched her gaze away and bowed. "Yes, Father Emperor. Forgive this stupid daughter for adding to your burden—"

"Yes, yes, never mind that. Go along. Inform your mother and the other consorts that I will join them presently."

The princess bowed again in a rustle of silks, and exited noiselessly, her maids closing the door softly behind her.

"Rise. The both of you," the emperor said.

Yskanda and Court Artist Yoli got to their feet, Yskanda's heart still racing as the emperor turned his way. They stood close enough to see the color of the emperor's eyes, so dark they looked like two chips of obsidian. Yskanda dropped his gaze quickly.

The emperor said, "I trust you'll know better another time, Apprentice Afan?"

"Yes, your imperial majesty," Yskanda said.

"He's got years before he'll produce anything worth saving," Court Artist Yoli commented, with the freedom of decades of service.

"Perhaps," was all the emperor would allow him, and then, in the same tone, "Yskanda, what can you tell me about Prince Jion's disappearance?"

Yskanda's head came up, his bewilderment plain—for a moment he couldn't even recollect who Prince Jion was. Then he remembered the prince who was a governor in name at some distant island. "Your imperial majesty?" he managed.

The emperor saw that confusion, and sat back. Conspiracy definitely existed—and he meant to delve to the root of it, for imperial princes did not simply vanish without help—but it was equally plain that Afan Yskanda knew utterly nothing about it. The timing truly was coincidental.

He waved a hand in dismissal. Yskanda and Court Artist Yoli bowed themselves out.

As they descended the servants' stairs, the wily old court artist caught the look of question in Yskanda's face. When they reached the exit, he mouthed the word, "Wait."

They scurried around the perimeter of the court, slipped past the fantastic spirit screen, a single block of exquisite moon-hued jade, and then hurried through the snow back to relative safety. When they reached Yoli's own suite, he shut the door, then touched the Silence charms one by one, reflecting as he did so that he still had no proof charms like these actually worked, except that he was still alive—and that might be due to a number of reasons.

Nevertheless. "What possessed you to draw this?" Court Artist Yoli asked, taking the wet paper out. Wet, but not sodden. The paper quality was too good for that.

He unfolded the mess, and laid it out on his table. As he'd intended, most of the ink had smeared into a morass, except for one strikingly vivid image of a dragon's face against a cloud, whiskers waving. A sinuous curve of neck, the rest vanished into the vaporous cloud, which in turn became a vast smear. But Yoli remembered the whole vividly: no fewer than three dragons tangled in battle, amid lightning branches, against the backdrop of a mighty storm: not water dragons at all, but one of fire, one of gold, and one of shadow. "I will probably have to light incense and eat vegetables for half a year for lying to the emperor, but *is* it an augury?"

Yskanda shook his throbbing head. "I don't know. I truly don't. I just draw . . . what I see."

"What you see," Yoli repeated, and uttered a hissing sigh. "Unfortunately, the princess saw it, too. And went straight to her father."

"Why? Did I anger her?"

"Drawing dragons right under the imperial family's noses might indeed have angered her, so presumptuous at the very least, and dangerous if she saw it as an attempt at inauspicious prediction. Who knows? I cannot tell you. I have never exchanged a word with First Imperial Princess Manon, though once in a while she comes by to examine what I might be painting."

"Is it forbidden for them to speak to you?"

"If it were, then First Imperial Prince Jion would have been in permanent confinement for reflection, as he was always chattering in my ear. Until they sent him off to the Silk Islands. It might be misplaced anger," the court artist mused as he hunted over a shelf, then selected a bottle with a red cloth stopper. "It is said that of all the imperial children, First Imperial Princess Manon and First Imperial Prince Jion are the closest to one another. She has to be almost as upset and angry as the emperor at this news of the prince's disappearance."

Privilege or hostage? Yoli was fairly certain by now that Yskanda was in a precarious position indeed, balanced on a knife edge between the two. He unstoppered his wine and took a drink before sinking onto his cushion, and rubbing his watery eyes. "Too old, too old . . ." he muttered.

Yskanda debated inwardly, then said, "It seemed as if the emperor was ready to blame me for that missing prince."

Yoli saw the stress in Yskanda's face, and waved the bottle, which sloshed. "I will say this very seldom when it comes to our emperor, but in this particular case, worry not. What you heard was a father desperate for a reason for what otherwise would seem impossible. Prince Jion left here with a veritable army of guardians the emperor picked himself, but still the prince vanished? Vanished — no one know if he lives or died. At least there has been no body, or the process would have been very different." His tone was severe.

Court Artist Yoli swigged from the wine again, then sat back. "You saw how fast the emperor dropped that line of inquiry. He knows very well you had nothing whatsoever to do with it. Perhaps for a moment he hoped, for then there would be a reason conveniently to hand." Or he thought immediately of a father who might have done to him what he had done to this other father, but that thought he would not speak at all, and looked away. "Though I will say, if those wretches we saw being herded toward the prison are innocent, Heaven help them. No one else will."

He grunted, looking up fiercely under his wild brows, which had lost their groomed look in the storm. "That would be another reason for the princess to be angry. There will be no trips outside the palace now. The rules tightened around the time you came, but those days will seem lax compared to what is to come, I suspect . . . it was an open secret she likes visiting the bookstores herself. Ayah! That is now a thing of the past, you can be sure. And meanwhile the army will be scouring every island Prince Jion visited on his tour."

He shook his head and helped himself to a third swig. "What we need to do is keep our heads down, and our eyes on our work. And *you*." Another slosh of the bottle. "We were two ants on the same burning rope. Did you realize?"

Yskanda paled. "I endangered you?" He dropped to his knees, head bowed. "I am so very sorry."

"Get up, boy, get up. You simply have to learn to keep your mind away from wherever it goes that makes you want to start drawing five-clawed golden dragons right there under the emperor's very eye. Believe me when I say you really don't want to commence foretelling disasters. It never ends well for anyone, especially the augur."

"What do I do?" Yskanda asked.

"We will address that." Yoli took a fourth swig, thinking petulantly, why couldn't this boy be plagued with pimples, or a nasal whine, or some such? I, thought the court artist grimly, must have been the worst sulfurous sack of sin in a previous life, to get burdened so late in this one.

He scrabbled through the tiny drawers of a chest carved all over with albatrosses in flight. "Ah. Here. I knew this would be useful one day."

Yoli pulled out a smooth stone of dull gray flecked with brown, an ordinary-enough stone. The engraving on it was so worn it was almost indecipherable. He handed it to Yskanda, saying, "It was a gift from the last empress. Put this in your sleeve every day. When you think you are going to find yourself in that sort of trouble—" Here he waved his bottle at Yskanda's ruined drawing. "—you take out the stone and hold it tight. Or at least get it as close to your skin as you can. The charms on it should keep you firmly . . ." He had been about to say rooted, then recollected the way Yskanda had stared at the holy Redbark trees at the imperial shrine, and said instead,

"It should keep you *here*."

"Thank you, Court Artist Yoli." Yskanda bowed, sorry that he had clearly upset his master.

"Fine, fine. Go change out of your court robe, my hapless young parasol sprig. Take time to burn some incense at one of the temples — the gods know you will need as much protection as you can get — or whatever you wish to do this day. Then I suggest you come back, and we will initiate the new year quietly with some work."

Yskanda wanted nothing more than quiet. He bowed and withdrew, leaving the court artist alone. Yoli set aside the wine and pulled fresh paper to him. Swiftly, surely, he drew everything he remembered of that remarkable picture, which in his mind already had a name: Three Dragons Duel. He tried to hint at the detail Yskanda had only begun to work in, such as the greater dragon on the right, having features that called the emperor to mind. At least that part had been well obliterated, the single dragon still visible being anonymous. This dragon had muted golden highlights, a relatively benign figure, as dragons go. But who was the shadow-dark dragon in the middle?

He expected Yskanda would make his way back as soon as he'd burned an incense stick in New Year's Two Moons prayers at one of the temples. He rose, shook out the paper to dry it, then rolled it and Yskanda's ruined one together. He stored them in an old casket, put the casket at the back of his clothing trunk, and returned to set up for what he hoped would be an otherwise normal day.

TEN

THE YEAR OF THE Pig meant sharing, as the pig stands for generosity, wealth, and happiness. Before the sun came up, Ryu went to the temple of the Snow Crane, carrying food she'd bought from a vendor, and a cup of wine. After adding the spirit food to the loaded table before the altar, and pouring out her libation, she lit incense and prayed for her family's well-being.

Her heart was buoyant when she emerged. This was the year she would join the gallant wanderers! That brought a pang of regret for Mother, but as Ryu made her way back to the inn, she reflected that Mother had known she was unlikely to make a good scholar. Whereas if she became a wandering hero, dispensing justice, Father would be very proud, and Mother would come to see that this was as good a life as struggling with ancient lists of affinities.

When she got back to the inn, she found Shigan alone, rubbing Yaso's salve into his upper lip. Yaso was gone – to another temple, Ryu assumed. "You don't want to light incense for your family?" she asked Shigan.

He made a curious grimace. "I believe my family will go on as always without my adding to the general smoke." He waved upwards. "Let's spar."

A last daub of salve to his lip, which had become irritated from the acacia gum until Yaso found this solution. They went down to their usual spot, which Eagle Island Brother Matu had cleared of snow while he was waiting.

The cousins were waiting outside Ryu and Shigan's inn when the two came out, Ryu to go to the ring and Shigan to the teahouse. As they exchanged greetings, both cousins eyed Shigan uncertainly in the clear light of day, Ki Tenar suspiciously.

Ki Matu smiled. He gave his cousin a glance and rubbed his upper lip significantly.

Ryu said abruptly, "Shigan, can you pull off the mustache? I think they think we're a couple of bandits."

"No, we would never be so rude," Ki Tenar protested, bowing.

Ki Matu grinned. "We had a wager. Over your age, Brother Shigan."

Shigan reddened to the ears, but when Ryu said, "He needs the disguise to get work as a musician," the elder Ki cousin's expression cleared, and Matu leaned toward Shigan, muttering, "I wish I'd thought of that. They won't let me wander alone until I *turn eighteen*." He said it as if eighteen was at least a century away instead of a year.

"It's your voice," Ki Tenar said earnestly. "Yesterday when it was cloudy and dark, I didn't notice, but in this sunlight, your young voice and . . . the rest of you . . . it looks . . . odd. I take it you're not the Redbark master?"

"No," Shigan said, reddening.

"Told you," Matu said under his breath, looking up at the sky. "Anyway," he said to Ryu and Shigan. "We came to talk about training together. If you will honor us by demonstrating your sword form, we'd be glad to show you the Eagle Island Sect's knife form." He spoke in a tone that made it clear he expected them to recognize this name — and respect it.

"Yes," Ryu exclaimed, delighted at this chance to get to know genuine gallant wanderers.

The four made plans to meet at dawn the next day.

Ki Tenar watched that next morning, and liked what she saw enough to agree to her younger cousin continuing on. She explained that she'd have to spend her mornings making and baking desserts at a place known to gallants of their sect, in order to earn the cousins' keep.

As winter settled in, the three — sometimes four — met in all but the worst weather, which Ryu and Shigan had gotten used to during their training. "War," they were told often enough, "doesn't wait for a nice spring day."

Their practices extended well into the morning, and occasionally beyond, when — as happened more frequently — Old Rock's ring was closed for days due to intermittent snow. Ryu would run down to check, then run back while Shigan and Matu practiced grappling.

Ki Matu freely agreed that Redbark Sect's sword form was superlative. What he brought to their sessions — besides a formidable challenge, as he was strong and reasonably quick — was a much better style of knife fighting than had been taught at Loyalty Fortress. There, knives were for finishing off enemies — the difference yet again between attacking in a mass, and defending yourself when you are alone.

The other skill was grappling, which they began if the ground had dried a little, between Shigan's midday and evening shifts at the teahouse.

At first, Matu reserved his true strength for wrestling with Shigan, who was larger, so he assumed that he'd be a far better match. With Ryu, he concentrated on showing her methods of breaking holds and getting bigger adversaries off balance, which she found very useful. "You won't get any size for years, and even then, you might end up one of those wiry men," he explained earnestly, glancing doubtfully at Ryu's small, square hands and equally small feet in their boots. "So your strategy is to be slippery."

That worked until he discovered that Ryu, when using Essence, turned into a ball of whipcord and steel. He had no idea that these moments happened when Ryu feared that Matu was about to discover through feel what she wanted to keep hidden.

At least they wrestled with clothes on. For one thing, their ground was scarcely ideal in the first place. Anyone could come by, situated as it was in the open, between buildings, and near the privies for the warehouse on the other side of the alley. But people so seldom came around that they'd gotten careless in checking.

One day early in the grappling lessons, when they had ended up covered in mud, the two older boys insisted they go to the baths right away. Ryu tried to say she'd wait, but sensed that a protest would raise curiosity — who would want to stay covered with icy, slimy mud? When they reached their favorite bathhouse, and she paid for her usual tiny, private alcove, Shigan swept Matu along to the next one down, his speech rising clearly over the screen between the alcoves. "Let Ryu be. Redbark seems to be a modest, monkish sect. He likes to bathe alone."

"Oh," Matu said.

Ryu spent the rest of her bath listening to their two voices as they talked about boyish things. She liked their voices. Both still sometimes squeaked the way Muin had when he was a third-year, but otherwise they were different, Shigan sounding more like . . . more like a singer, in a way. There was a ring in his voice that made Ryu think he could sing, and well, if he had a mind to.

Matu's was flatter, slightly husky, but it was pleasant to listen to, too. She grimaced, wondering if she sounded like a pig squealing to them. Ayah! If she did, it couldn't be helped.

Over the next stretch of days, as Phoenix Moon waned then waxed again, chasing Ghost Moon across the sky, Ryu, Shigan, and Matu fell into a routine, which was occasionally broken by Ki Tenar, when she did not have a banquet of some sort to prepare for.

Her sword skills were well-trained enough to put all three on their mettle when they sparred, and her critiques were excellent afterward, but where she truly excelled was in knife skills. She fought with two knives by preference. She had a flickering, wicked style that depended entirely on fast reflexes and precision of eye.

Ryu invariably tried to wheedle extra sparring time from her, leaving the boys to grapple together. "I'm too scrawny," she pointed out several times. "They just have to hold back with me. Whereas if I get better with knives, then no one will get close enough to grab me, yes? And you're so *good*."

Ki Tenar was a serious, dedicated sort of a person, always striving to cultivate herself to a higher level, and she was not proof against such earnestness.

And so the days turned into weeks, the three younger ones — as will often happen with young people — so busy they were never aware, until much later in their lives, how very happy and carefree they were during those wintry days.

But time brings change, and so it happened as winter began to wane over Te Gar Island.

The streets had been largely empty during a last, nasty storm that kept switching between sleet, hail, and soggy snow for four long days and nights.

But then one morning the inhabitants woke to clear sky, the air dry and chill in a world of drips and tinkles as overflowing gutters drained and icicles slowly began to melt in the rising sun. As usual by now, Ryu and Shigan slipped out after watching warily for the innkeeper. Luckily she seldom rose at this hour, as during winter potential customers never arrived before midday at the earliest.

Matu was there, waiting. "Our training ground is an ice pond," he said, then squinted skyward. "At least it ought to melt off today. Maybe by afternoon. My cousin is at the baker's already. I'm coming with you to the ring. Maybe Old Rock will let me have a go."

"I always run," Ryu said.

"I'll meet you there," Shigan said. "I don't want to shake all my stuffing loose." He ran his hand over his torso, stuffed with extra cloth. "I doubt Old Rock will even be there yet. Nobody has been able to come into the harbor for weeks."

"I think he will," Ryu said. "May the Goddess of Plenty grant he does, or we're going to starve."

They all knew that a lot of the Young Masters from the hill who brought the most coin to the teahouse had been confined at home to study. The teahouse had been mostly filled with the poorer scholars huddling over tea, in preference to their unwarmed rooms, which meant no extra money for the musicians. But a handful of tinnies was better than nothing at all, for that innkeeper made it very clear she would toss them out even when rooms lay empty if they didn't pay promptly. Shigan had even suggested they move, but Ryu had refused, her gaze sometimes lingering on Petal with a furrowed brow.

Ryu and Matu bolted down the street, Ryu glad to stretch her legs. She'd been running rather than jogging lately, as practice had been so intermittent.

When they neared the ring, she let out a triumphant "Hah!" There was Old Rock, scowling.

When they slowed, the big man turned their way. "Look." He pointed at the boards—where ice had warped and even split the wood. "I've got to replace these. Help me pry up the bad ones?"

Old Rock was in a sense a senior, though not really a boss. Ryu got to work, and Matu offered to help, as he had nothing else to do. Shigan caught up with them, surreptitiously straightened his padding, then began to help them carry the last planks to the wheelbarrow Old Rock had brought.

When they finished, the tide had turned out in the bay. The big gong on the promontory below the government buildings reverberated on the cold air, and the three turned to glance idly out to sea.

Then Shigan stilled.

Ryu blinked. "Aren't those navy ships? A lot of them," she added, thrilled at the grand sight of ships slanting into the bay of gray-green, choppy waves, the slatted sails full.

A passer-by, waiting for the wrestling ring to be set up, whistled, saying with an admiring look, "Those have to be the imperial navy. Look at those tiger-eye banners! There must be ten war ships out there. How do they sail so close to each other without bumping together?"

Shigan's head turned jerkily, and he said with an odd smile, "I think it's time to go to the teahouse."

Ryu glanced at the sun. Seemed a little early for the teahouse, but the wind had come up, blowing coldly about her ears. He would not want to risk getting his mustache and brow glue wetted for nothing. "Some tea sounds like a good idea."

Matu agreed, and the three started away as Old Rock looked morosely at his ruined ring, mentally calculating which would be more costly, paying someone to replace the flooring or taking the time to do it himself. And here were boats full of imperials, probably loaded with silver.

"Let's run," Shigan said.

Ryu gave him a surprise glance. "What about your stuffing?"

"I'll try this," Shigan said, folding his arms across his chest and stomach. "I haven't had a good run in weeks."

Ryu accepted that. Running had been a habit all her life. Matu accepted it, too, always ready for training in any form.

The three of them pounded up the street, slowing when they neared the teahouse. Shigan touched his mustache and eyebrows. "Looks good," Ryu said. "Especially when you puff out your cheeks and do that frown thing."

Matu nodded, about to add, "It's your voice that gives you away," but decided against it. While Shigan took criticism without a squawk in practice, at other times his moods made it seem like touching a boiling kettle.

The three entered the teahouse, Matu marveling that the Mu family so valued Shigan that they permitted him to come in and out the main door like a customer, instead of going round to the back.

Only a few poor students were there, warming themselves. The instruments sat in their shadowy alcove — Tea Master Mu not having put the candles out yet. Ryu and Matu sat well away from the door and its cold rushes of air, near tables of patch-robed scholars hunched over their tea. Two had brought out the Circle board, and judging by the number of black and white stones jostling around dragon forms, were nearing the end of their game.

"White . . ." Ryu whispered, after a glance, and made a surreptitious motion meaning *is getting slaughtered.*

Matu looked down, puzzled, then whistled softly under his breath at how fast Ryu had assessed that board. Then one of the daughters was there with the teapot, having recognized Ryu, who invariably had only tea, nursing it for hours through stormy days.

She gratefully wrapped her fingers around the cup, casting a glance at Shigan, who sat hunched over his guzheng, his fingers warming up. He had to be even colder than she was, judging by how his fingers trembled.

"He looks like an old man when he slumps like that," Matu said under his breath.

Ryu scowled, and Matu flushed, though no one was paying them the least attention.

Slowly scholars began to trickle in, then, quite abruptly, a flood of them, talking in excited knots while glancing back at the door. The Mu daughters began putting lamps in the center of the room, where the wealthier scholars inevitably sat — and then froze in place when the door slammed open.

In clattered armed warriors, weapons at the ready. At least they were not in helms and battle armor. The leader wore the feathered hat and silver panther chest embroidery of a seventh level captain — two up from the bottom, where Muin would be next year. He shouted, "No one move."

Ryu and Matu exchanged startled looks. The captain strode into the room, cloak swinging as he glanced around. "You." He pointed at Tea Master Mu. "You. You . . . you." The mailed glove pointed at the daughters, and then at Shigan in his shadowy corner. "Out."

The captain pointed toward the kitchen.

"The rest of you line up against that wall."

One of the wealthy students straightened to an offended height, his long silken sleeves rippling as he began in a high voice, "My uncle is the First Magistrate —"

The captain held up a tally, and turned slowly, so that all could make out the tiger-eye carving. "Imperial orders," he snapped. "Move."

In silence, Ryu and Matu joined the others, until they were wedged between the boy in the silk robes, which smelled of costly incense with a hint of anise, and an aproned roofer's boy, who obviously had no work while everything was icy. Ryu trembled — was her disguise about to be revealed?

One by one the boys were motioned to the middle table, where the captain stood, arms folded, next to an aide. This aide held up a scroll.

The lamplight shone through the paper a little, enough to reveal not words, but some sort of drawing. From the way the guards began scrutinizing every face and form, it seemed that it was indeed a drawing. This was a search for someone specific.

It couldn't be for me, Ryu was thinking miserably. Could it? Commander Weken had given her that tally, but she had believed they weren't serious about deserters unless it was in the middle of a battle . . .

One by one the boys shuffled left, and then it was her turn. She held her breath. The captain barely glanced at her and jerked his chin toward the rest of the rejects. She moved away, relief washing through her in waves.

Matu followed a moment later.

They stood with the rejects as the captain went through the rest. One after another got the silent chin-jerk of rejection, until suddenly, "You. Over there."

Everyone stared at the black-haired boy in the pumpkin-colored robe over dark green and light green. He appeared to Ryu to be about her own age, a boy with sharp cheekbones and chin and extravagantly arched brows. His pouty mouth pouted even more as he exclaimed indignantly, "My father is the quartermaster in the garrison. I study at the Academy of Sublime —"

The target was clearly a rich boy.

"Shut up," was the curt reply.

Silence fell as the captain worked through the remaining half dozen — and once again, second to the last, pulled another boy out. This one was not rich. He wore an apron splashed with paint. The only features he shared with the rich boy were black hair and a sharp chin. He spoke more humbly, beginning with, "You can ask my master, who sells porcelain on Prince Ratha's Miracle Victory Way—"

"We will," stated the captain. He pointed out pairs of burly guards to escort the two boys out, and then said to the rest, "All of you. Return home, or to your school or master. Stay there until you hear the garrison watch gong release you."

The army warriors clattered out, leaving everyone shaken as they whispered, as if imperial ears still listened.

Ryu moved toward Shigan out of habit. She was within a few paces when Tea Master Niece One cut in front of her, to confront Shigan. Ryu heard the teahouse daughter's low voice—barely—as she said, "This daughter dares to suggest you go."

Owner Mu was now darting hither and yon to little purpose, and Tea Master Niece Two had gone to make sure her beloved instruments had not been damaged by tramping boots.

Shigan turned a questioning gaze to Tea Master Niece One, as Ryu stopped where she stood, uncertain whether to join Shigan or to retreat.

Tea Master Niece One murmured, "My uncle is too short-sighted to see that your mustache is false. I don't know why you do that. I don't care. You play well and the customers like you. But he's going to be frightened, and ask questions, and whether or not you have *anything* to do with whatever's going on, from here on every day you're here will feel like crossing a mountain of swords and swimming across a lake of boiling poison. You'd better go." Her voice trembled on the last words as she lifted her hand not toward the front door, which he had always unconsciously used, but toward the kitchen door into the back court.

Shigan shot a strained glance at Ryu as Tea Master Niece One turned away and pushed past Ryu without seeing her.

Shigan retreated through the kitchen, Ryu following, and Matu on her heels, muttering, "What was that? Was she accusing Shigan of something?"

Ryu made a violent motion to shut up. She didn't understand anything. She plunged through the kitchen door into a narrow alley, and glanced toward the gate to the main street. Shigan stood there, leaning against that gate, one hand resting against it and his forehead on his hand.

ELEVEN

WHEN RYU CAUGHT UP, Shigan straightened with an effort she could feel, and gave her and Matu a sickly semblance of a smile. "Ayah! That was humiliating," he said. "But an old player did tell me once that there's a difference between playing a character and becoming the character. He said, 'However cleverly you dodder about, you will always be yourself playing an old man, until you understand what it is to be old.' Funny thing, I feel . . . old. Right now."

Matu had been frowning, but his expression cleared. "The army captain thought you really *were* old, or you would have had to go through that line with us."

It was meant to be reassuring, but Ryu could see that his words barely registered as, with trembling fingers, Shigan yanked off the mustache and eyebrows. "I've lost my job, that much I know," he admitted. He bunched up the silk, about to toss it down, then changed his mind and put it in his pocket.

"Let's go," he said, unlatching the gate.

"I wonder how long their search will take," Matu said at Ryu's shoulder. "Usually this is a cage situation."

"Cage?" Ryu repeated.

"I keep forgetting, you don't know the—" Matu stuttered to a stop when they stepped into the street, to find—

"Petal?" Ryu exclaimed, as all three stopped.

"There you are," Petal exclaimed, squinting up into Shigan's face. In the sunlight, Ryu noticed for the first time that one of Petal's eyes focused, while the other stared somewhere in the distance. "Listen. I came as soon as I saw First Mother run off." And to three expressions of incomprehension, she said quickly, "There were imperials searching through the inn. For a boy, who looks your age, and even a little like you. Enough that First Mother ran off to find the commander in charge."

"What?" Shigan whispered.

"Because she said, if there's a reward, an underling will try to cheat her out of it. But a commander surely wouldn't dare. Even if it's not really you, she thinks there might be a partial reward for trying, and gold is gold."

Ryu opened her mouth, but no words came out. Unbidden, Inspector Shaz's dry voice spoke in memory, outlining the different types of search. She peered upward at rooftops to see if crossbowmen lurked there. The situation had suddenly become so unreal.

Petal went on, "Ki Tenar is waiting at your practice place, she said only for the time of a finger of an incense stick. Yaso went to find you." Petal pointed at Matu. She squared her shoulders. "I came because I — "

But Shigan and Matu both started running, Ryu at their heels. Petal followed, stumping grimly behind.

The inn wasn't far. Shigan did not go to the door, but ducked around the side of the building to where they saw Ki Tenar pacing back and forth over the mushy ground on which they had been drilling all winter. At the sound of their footsteps, she whirled. "Matu! There you are. The cage is going up."

"Cage," Shigan repeated.

"When the imperials cage a city, that's when gallant wanderers leave," Ki Tenar said.

"I was about to explain," Matu put in. "Can we take them with us?"

"If Uncle has space," Ki Tenar said — using the polite form for "uncle" meaning an elder whose authority one acknowledged. "There are some other gallants from three different sects who will also be going. But we can try."

That was when Petal grabbed Ryu's arm with both hands. "Take me with you."

Ryu stared, startled — she had been about to ask Petal if she wanted to join them.

But Petal could not read minds. "Take me. I'll follow

anyway," Petal said through gritted teeth. "Or else I'll run my
head into a post and kill myself." Her fingers dug into Ryu's
arm painfully. When Ryu pressed on her wrist to loosen her
grip, Petal dropped her hands and jumped back, reddening. "I
know I should not touch a boy without leave, but I have to go.
I have to."

Ki Tenar put out a hand. "We can't take underage people
on the Wander without permission. That would end up being
a kidnapping offense."

"I can cook, I can clean, I can sew. I've even been learning
your fighting things, whenever I can," Petal said in a quick,
breathless voice. "Watch!" And there, before their astonished
gazes, she thrashed her way through the warmup for Redbark
Sword.

She was awkward, her movements jerky and completely
lacking foundation, but it was all there. "I watched you
whenever I could, through the window up there. And I
practiced in the cold room. When I could."

Ki Tenar said in a kindly voice, "If you get permission from
your parents, or your master — "

"*My* parents are *dead*," Petal said fiercely, tears gleaming
along her eyelids. "My mother must be crying in the
underworld at the way First Mother broke all her promises
and made me her slave. She'll kill me before she would let me
go. She will kill me anyway — it was she who did *this*." She
widened her eyes, so that the listeners were forced to look at
the blind one. "To her I'll always be a slave — all that matters is
gold. She even sold her own daughter in marriage to that
terrible old man for gold, she said you can't spend love, but
gold is always gold — "

The stream of words ended abruptly at the sound of more
footsteps. Yaso appeared.

"The cage is closing," Tenar said.

Shigan said, "We need to get our belongings — "

"Uncle won't wait for us past one incense stick," Tenar
said. "Maybe not even that."

"I'll get them," Yaso said. "Where to meet you?"

"At my bakery. You know where it is," Tenar said to Yaso,
who nodded; the bakery was adjacent to the herbalist for
whom Yaso had been volunteering.

Ki Tenar said, "We'll go the back way." She pointed past
the privies, and started off.

Petal started after her, face mutinous in spite of the tears running down her face. The two Ki cousins looked her way, but then Ryu said, "Come with us, Petal."

"But she's underage," Tenar protested, without slowing.

"No I'm not," Petal declared. "I'm near eighteen."

They all looked dubiously at Petal, who was bony and gaunt, no taller than Ryu. "When you go hungry all the time, you don't grow. Look into the bond-pen someday, you'll see," Petal stated flatly.

"I feel like at least I ought to talk to the innkeeper," Tenar said, not quite wanting to call Petal a liar.

Shigan shook his head. "A nightingale's song will never come out of a rat's mouth."

Tenar gave him a puzzled glance, and Ryu said flatly, "Did you see all her bruises?"

Tenar shook her head, now looking unsettled. "I'll let Uncle decide."

No one spoke as they all began to run, but Petal sent Ryu a glance of desperate gratitude that Shigan and Matu did not miss.

They fetched up at the bakery's outbuilding, where Tenar — scrupulous as always — explained to a wiry older man about Petal, who stuck to Ryu's side.

The man turned to Petal. "You are a runaway apprentice?"

"No," Petal stated, her voice high and thick with unshed tears. "I'm *not*. My father was the owner and I the daughter of his first wife. Then he married that woman, who makes me call her First Mother. She treats me as a bond servant, but I wasn't born one. It was she who put the bond yoke on me whenever she sent me on errands, just so I could never dare to run away. But today she was in such a hurry to chase the imperials in hopes of getting gold that she forgot the bond-collar." And she pointed at Shigan. "To report him."

All eyes turned to Shigan, and Tenar said slowly, "Are they searching for *you*? What did you do?"

"Nothing," Shigan stated.

Impatiently, Ryu said, "Nothing," and added, "I know you might think I'm lying, but it's true. In fact, I never told you, but we both were in army training for two years, but we left, for me to seek an Essence master. Which they don't have there. The commander even gave me a tally for Te Gar Garrison, but, ah, we think the wander is better. If Shigan were a wanted criminal, Commander Weken would have been the first to turn him in. Anyway I saw the drawing. It was a foxy face on a boy maybe twelve or so. Shigan looks a *little* like it. But the rest of the drawing was of a very rich boy, with a fine headdress and the like. At the teahouse, we saw two boys taken away. Both had foxy chins."

Faces began to relax at the complete conviction in Ryu's voice.

Ki Tenar said to Shigan, "Ah. I thought I saw signs of military training."

The older man added, "You were right to leave. Our sect styles and army styles are difficult to reconcile."

Ryu sighed. "Ayah, we learned that. Anyway," to Petal, "I've been worrying about you. But I wasn't sure what to say. Or how to say it. I would be glad to take you with us."

Yaso appeared, burdened by three bundles. "I left coins to pay for our room the last three nights."

Yaso had bundled up their clothing into their cloaks, tying the corners in knots that they could slip over one shoulder.

Shigan took his, saying with a rueful glance back, "I sure hate leaving that fine rug to that terrible innkeeper."

Petal said with bitter satisfaction, "She'll have to hire four bond-servants to do the work I did. At least think of that. She'd rather have teeth pulled out than pay out a tinnie."

The man said, "Let's go. We have a long run ahead of us."

And they ran.

As Shigan's feet pounded the ground, his toes pushing painfully against the inside of his boots — seemed his feet had grown again without his noticing it — he tried to wrest his tumbling emotions under control. Instructor Shaz's dry voice spoke into his inner ear: *The basics of a search are similar, but no actual search is like another. Let's examine the essentials . . .*

"Terrain," Shigan muttered, his breath puffing. "Number of searchers, number of targets. Stationary or moving target. Orders. Time."

A splash, and Ryu bumped up against his arm. "What?"

"Nothing."

"You're talking."

"I'm trying to remember what Shaz said about searches . . . to distract myself from . . . the fact that my boots are too tight. . . My toes are killing me."

Ryu noticed he was puffing hard, the padding in his tunics slumping ridiculously around his middle.

Finally they fetched up against an ancient, crumbled wall. Stones all over the place, many of them grave markers of

ancient soldiers—the mounds long ago blown by the wind—
had kept anyone from building in the area. They were well
outside the harbor city now.

The others were also breathing hard. They clearly hadn't
grown up running, or learned to trickle Essence while pacing
themselves. Beside Ryu, Shigan pulled out all his padding and
stuffed it into his makeshift carryall.

A short time later the uncle said finally, "We're nearly
there. Right now they will be going through the manors on the
hill, but then they'll spread out. We need to get to the cove
before the search shifts to the shoreline."

They picked their way among the old stones, which had
gaps here and there where people had fetched rock to carry
away for building. In single file they squeezed through one of
these gaps, and down a winding path carved by a trickle of
water that soon would become a stream as the snow began to
melt in earnest.

Over a hill behind a small fishing village, and then down a
treacherous, slippery path full of dark, liquid mud, to a rocky
beach where wavelets washed up in a narrow lagoon. As soon
as they appeared on the path above, a longboat put off. It met
them at the shore, and carried them to the ship; Petal stayed
near Ryu, her face pale, her gaze darting everywhere as they
clambered aboard.

"Go below, go below," a white-haired granny rasped. "On
the tide turning, we will sail."

As soon as he got into the boat, Ryu saw Shigan slip the
crumpled wad of false mustache and eyebrows over the
gunwale and watch them sink away.

A short time later they bumped up against a worn deep-
sea fishing junk, from which someone threw a hempen ladder.
They clambered up one by one.

Once again Ryu found herself in the bowels of a ship. She
squatted on the dank wood that smelled strongly of fish, as
others tried to find somewhere to sit amid the jumble of nets
and baskets and barrels everywhere. Shigan sank down next
to her, drew his knees up, crossed his arms, and put his
forehead down on them.

Ryu wondered if he were really upset that the Mu teahouse
daughters had seen past his cherished disguise. Ayah! She was
used to his sudden moods by now, without understanding
them in the least. Why shouldn't he be as delighted as she was
that at last they were on their way to a gathering of gallant

wanders!

Hot, strong, smoky tea of an unfamiliar flavor was passed around. It warmed Ryu wonderfully. After that, the familiar sticky-rice balls with grilled fish, cabbage, and peppers.

She had finished when someone came below to announce, "We've sunk Te Gar."

That meant no one could see their ship from the island, so those who wanted to could go on deck. Shigan was the first up the hatch, Ryu on his heels.

In the west, the sun was already sliding toward the sea. She turned her right shoulder to it, making her mental bow to her parents and Ul Keg, and sending a joyful thought that her new life was about to begin.

Shigan shut his eyes and smiled.

TWELVE

YSKANDA DECIDED AFTER A restless night, during which he kept sliding the ward stone from under his pillow and turning it over in his hand, that he had to learn something about imperial hostages.

There was one auspicious element to an otherwise inauspicious situation: he was not only close to what had to be the best collection of records written by, and about, past hostages; he was even permitted to use the library. All the apprentices in his level were expected to, as traditional symbols and styles lay at the heart of their study.

Following the relatively subdued New Year's festivities, they were told to resume their regular schedule. Yskanda decided to go while most of his peers lingered over the evening meal.

The archive was huge, but neat labels for subject, dynasty, and era marked each standing set of shelves.

Yskanda had just found the one for treaties—which he figured had to turn up something about treaty hostages—when a whisper of sound warned him of someone coming, and there was a graywing he didn't know. "May this individual help the student find something?" he said. "I am an archival assistant."

"This grateful student believes he has found what he needs, thank you," Yskanda said, bowing.

The graywing did not go away, but instead took the scroll

out of Yskanda's hands. "Treaties?" he asked, his tone mild.

"It's for an assignment," Yskanda said.

"What kind of assignment? I ask because perhaps I might better direct you."

"We are learning historical symbols and elements," Yskanda said, his face burning. "It seemed to this incompetent student that, surely, such historic occasions as treaties would be accompanied by drawings of those making the treaties. Which I can copy."

"Ah," the graywing said. "A very clever notion, that. Alas, that particular scroll contains no drawings. It's all details of diplomatic missions." He gently replaced the scroll on its shelf. "Come over to this side – this area is off limits except to certain ranks and above, and must be cleared with the Grand Historian. Over here are the general records. The few sketches are not worthy; the only students who find these useful are the scribes when they study old scripts. You'll find better examples in the archive used by the artists and illustrators." There was a question in his voice, still mild.

"They have been pawed over by many hands," Yskanda said.

"That is inevitable," the graywing commented, and glided to another alcove altogether, where he helpfully pointed out this and that scroll. Yskanda chose one at random, and had to sit down and begin sketching before the graywing went away. Yskanda made himself stay in place until he finished the outlines of a sketch, as that sense of being watched never lightened its grip on the back of his neck.

He left, and had not gone a hundred paces when Yut Hak rounded a corner, then stopped his eyes widening with relief as he exclaimed, "There you are. I was looking for you. You haven't eaten."

Not *Have you eaten?*

Avoiding the question entirely, Yskanda proffered his rolled drawing, glad he'd stayed. "I was not hungry." Which was true. His throat was scratchy, and the headache that wouldn't go away kept him from feeling hunger. "I was working on the elements assignment. I chose an old treaty to use as my model." And he talked about that picture all the way back to their dormitory, where their mates were preparing to go to the baths.

The next morning, Yut Hak emerged out of the swarm heading to eat breakfast. He walked next to Yskanda and talked about their prospective assignments. Occasionally he turned to Yskanda, asking what he thought; as they walked, Yskanda found himself wishing that Yut Hak would say straight out that he was there to monitor him. The pretense at friendship rang as false as a cracked bell.

But Yskanda would never deny anyone face. He submitted to the questions, and to Yut Hak sitting next to him while he forced down an unwanted bowl of congee. By the time the meal ended, he resolved to skip as many meals as possible. Just as well he was used to eating twice a day from childhood, and not even that during the humid heat of summers on Imai. The children had gone all day eating little but fruit they snatched from laden trees and shrubs, with the occasional dried fish, and then nuts when those began to ripen and fall.

On the way out, he walked slowly, and when Yut Hak turned his head in response to a comment by another peer, Yskanda veered near the basket of bean-paste buns and snatched two, one for each pocket, then scurried out to follow the others to class.

There was always a soft buzz of gossip before the instructors walked in, but ever since New Year's the ambient tension raised the note of the voices, and flattened them to a susurrus of whispers as people stood in knots. Then, at the sound of instructors' footsteps approaching all scurried to stand behind their seats.

Yskanda, who loathed bloodthirsty gossip, tried to shut his ears, but especially in the dormitory it was difficult not to catch words and phrases. So far the talk seemed to be less about the missing prince (most of that was speculation about whether or not he was dead) and more about the prisoners brought in on New Year's Day. Yskanda did not want to speculate on what the prisoners had done any more than he wanted to know what the inquisitors were doing to them.

It was a relief when the chief scribe entered, scowling around the room as they bowed. The lesson commenced, for a time returning life to a semblance of normality. Yskanda gratefully let his mind sink into his work, reluctantly returning to the world around him when the deep, melodious temple gong shivered its brassy note through the wintry air at midday.

Yskanda had hoped to slip away, but as soon as he got out the door, there was Yut Hak waiting for him, amid a cluster of others from his dorm. Snow was falling fast as they headed for the dining hall. When Yskanda slowed, so did Yut Hak—and Senye Tan looked back, laughing, expecting to see others laughing with him. He slowed, too.

Senye Tan always needed an audience. "Dead, I tell you. Dead as a squashed roach."

"No," someone exclaimed on an outgoing breath.

Someone else said, "You saw the corpse, of course?"

Senye Tan retorted, "Oh, sure, with my imperial prison tally. Cricket—you know, page to the Household—said the guards were full of it. The pretender was found dead."

"Surprised he lasted this long," someone commented.

Another said with careless relish, "Those inquisitors are too good to let someone die before they're given the command. They can make tortures last months."

Senye Tan was walking backward, sleeves flapping, eyes bright with glee. "Dead—of poison!"

"I don't believe it."

"No chance, Tan. Nobody would dare poison a common prisoner much less someone in the clutches of the ferrets, and how else could they do it?"

"Right, no one could get past the army of guards to strangle or stab him!"

"Cricket swears it's true."

"It's true," said a new voice, low and urgent. "And if you want to be carried out in a shroud, keep talking. They just beheaded a row of servants and guards, *and* two graywings, for letting it happen."

Silence fell with the shocked suddenness of a slap.

Even Senye Tan looked uneasy, and then, with a forced laugh with no humor in it, "So who has extra green ink for the commentary on Dan Bi's *Poetry from the Royal Island Progress*?"

The conversation turned to those who took scribe classes in the afternoons, while Yskanda was with the court artist.

"What do you think?" Yut Hak asked Yskanda.

Yskanda said in his blandest voice, "I don't have the class doing Dan Bi," and dashed through the door to the dining hall, making a noise of brushing snow off his clothes. "I need the privy," he added, and plunged in that direction.

At least Yut Hak didn't follow him there. Yskanda headed that way—then when he should have turned right, he turned left, and he was free.

He pulled the bean-paste bun from his pocket. It had gone cold. He gnawed at it as he made his way along a circuitous route to Bright, where he drifted along the board depicting various departments' schedules.

One of these was the library. He noted a different graywing named for the midday shift today, and so once again he headed there. This time he walked as soundlessly as he could, drifting along the various shelves until he reached that secluded alcove. He was not supposed to be there, but he comforted himself with the reflection that he would do no damage. No one would know he was even there. But a hostage had to protect himself . . . somehow.

Why was this area secluded? Instinct insisted this was where he ought to look.

The records were, as usual, divided by dynasty.

This time no one interrupted him. He chose three scrolls marked by the word "treaty" and took them out of the alcove to one of the little desks in corners around the warren of shelves. He opened two of them, one being the one he'd wanted, and the other waiting to be looked at. But before he began reading, he helped himself to paper, ink, and brush waiting at the little table by the door, and set up the outlines of a sketch.

The first scroll—the one he'd been caught trying to read the previous day—turned out to be exactly what the graywing had said. It described the rituals of the treaties, down to the speeches. There were two hostage situations, both princes sent to former enemy courts, and one princess sent to grow up in the allied court, to marry a prince. Nothing was said further about any of them beyond their names.

The second scroll was even more useless, being entirely composed of the formal language of treaties following a war, but written and ritual, with a lot of notations about augury. This might be important to someone, but he understood little.

The third, which had been isolated in its dynastic location, concerned a treaty between two northern islands, back when the capital had moved away from its present location for the duration of the Tan dynasty. Yskanda almost didn't read through it. The paper was brittle, smelled odd, and had turned a dark yellow, which made the faded ink difficult to read. But the sight of a slashing scribble in the same ancient script, though dark black in color, meaning it had been added far more recently, caught his eyes.

Yskanda scanned past the long description of the treaty ritual, followed by the treaty itself, down to the emperor's instructions. Included were the words, *You shall tender unto me a report each day detailing everything he sayeth, and everything he doeth, right unto what he weareth and eateth.*

Next to that, the scrawl, *And some things never change!*

Judging by the color, that ink could not be any more than two or three decades old, if that.

Intrigued — and confused — Yskanda unrolled the remainder of the scroll, but that was the only comment. The rest concerned the conduct of the treaty party.

But at least Yskanda had a name: a Prince Noh, during the Tan dynasty.

A bell rang. The midday break was already ended.

Yskanda hastily replaced all the scrolls and made his way to Court Artist Yoli's, noticing furtive knots of conversation here and there. Quick glances to see who might be listening, or walking by, then breaking up. Tension made the frigid air seem even colder. Yskanda was shivering when he walked into the court artist's workroom, where heat-stones glowed in all four corners.

Yskanda set about readying his materials as his mind caromed between the things he had heard and read. As he did, the court artist rose with a grunt, and touched his Essence charms for silence beyond the doors. "What's troubling you? I want your mind clear."

Yskanda considered what to say. Court Artist Yoli had already stated that he hated politics, and refused to get involved, and Yskanda suspected that being a hostage would be political. He'd found the warning comforting, because it meant the court artist would not ask questions Yskanda was not ready to answer.

Yskanda frowned at his row of brushes, then said, "I don't rightly know if this is political or theory, but what exactly is a pretender? Everyone is talking about a pretender being poisoned. The only time I saw the word used was in histories, when someone started a war and called themselves the new emperor but was defeated."

Court Artist Yoli grunted. "Ah yes, flapping lips. In this case — and I know nothing beyond this single fact, and don't want to know — it appears that someone or other in the prison, now dead, apparently masqueraded as Prince Jion."

Yskanda looked up, startled. That was *far* more political than being made a hostage on a whim. He suppressed the thousand questions sprouting in his mind and said, "I'm ready."

The lesson was entirely on color, specifically what could be said with contrasting colors, and what must not be said. They talked well past the dinner hour about the difficulties of finding materials with which to create the subtler shades — and keep them from fading, or turning.

When Court Artist Yoli got to his feet, stretching so that his old bones cracked, he said, "So I'm going to keep you on decorative elements until you master the gradations, before we even think of beginning on the human figures."

Yskanda stood, bowed, then sat down again as the door shut behind the court artist. He smiled at his desk, happy with the assignment, as it gave him an excuse to work with the superlative hues only afforded by a generous imperial budget. As he carefully painted wisteria blossoms down the left edge of his paper, he gnawed at the second bean-paste bun, which was quite stale and hard by now. Better that than being forced into pretense of amity with a spy.

He forgot all about Yut Hak and pretenders, his mind filling with attempts to capture the exact hue of blossoms just as the sun was coming up, until he was startled by the gong signaling the night watch.

He hastily put away his materials, and since the court artist had already left, conscientiously touched the Essence Silence stones to end the charm, then headed back toward the dorm, arms held close against his body and shoulders bowed against the frigid, snow-filled air.

Halfway there Yut Hak shot around the corner and nearly ran him down, a lantern stick in his hands. The lantern's swinging light revealed then concealed the tight stress in Yut Hak's face; when it swung back again, Yut Hak flushed as he exclaimed, "*There* you are. I thought . . ." He looked away, his lips compressed so tightly they were bloodless.

Yskanda clamped down on a sarcastic rejoinder as he remembered that single line from the long-ago emperor about the hostage Prince Noh. *Everything he says. Everything he does. Everything he eats.*

Yut Hak was clearly afraid, and Yskanda wondered for the first time not what his orders were — he had a pretty good guess about that — but the penalty for not carrying them out.

"I had to work late," he said. "But I finished."

"You can't skip meals," Yut Hak replied tersely as he turned about and fell in step beside Yskanda. "I mean, it's no way to treat the body your parents gave you, especially in the cold."

Yskanda wondered if Yut Hak had spent the midday and evening meals looking for him. "Yes, I agree," he said pacifically. "Thank you for your concern."

As they joined the others going to the baths, he reflected on what he'd seen in the old treaty. Perhaps he did not need to read everything about hostages and how they survived, at least right away: that single line made it clear what he needed to keep in mind.

But who had scribbled that comment?

There was no chance to find out as the days marched on. Yskanda had begun winter determined to endure a season that others considered a regular part of life, but he never seemed able to get warm, shivering in his layers and layers. Some of his dormitory mates made fun of him for being a weakling, which he accepted with a tranquil, "I never saw snow before. I didn't know it would be so cold."

The ever-present headache pounded, and the scratchy throat turned into raw soreness. He said nothing to anyone, but within a day the low fever that he'd begun to regard as a part of winter life mounted dramatically, flushing his cheeks and making his eyes look, the court artist said, like those of a dead fish.

Yoli sent him straight to bed, and then admonished the duty pages to see that the graywings in charge of the dormitory got food and medicine to Yskanda — a piece of well-meant interference that affronted the graywings and so might have had the opposite effect had not a report reached the emperor that Afan Yskanda was quite ill.

He summoned the Imperial Physicians, and said, "See to it that boy recovers."

Six words, but the physicians heard the tone that meant if he dies, you die, and they considerably startled, then frightened, the graywings in the lowly apprentice dormitory by arriving in a group, looking like rusty crows in their sober garb.

By then Yskanda was delirious with high fever, muttering in his home dialect, which none of his dormitory mates understood. He dreamed of immersing himself into the cold, clean sea, a desire that he had been trained out of in his waking life.

The physicians in turn checked his pulse, stuck needles into his nerve-conduits to strengthen his flickering life force, then ordered him to drink vile-tasting medicines, which were so hot both in temperature and taste that his eyes watered, but the internal heat burning him up began to bank, and he once more recognized his surroundings.

He was ordered to stay in bed, where he lay insensible while the fever burned; he was too sick to eat, but the frightened graywings brought him food and tea. His dormitory mates, who had come to like him, sneaked in delicacies in hopes of tempting his diminished appetite.

They felt sorry for his missing Fire Festival. And once his fever abated, leaving him weak and hoarse, they brought him not only medicinal teas that their various families swore by, but delicacies from the city vendors. Senye Tan smuggled a Circle board into their dormitory, where they took turns playing against Yskanda even when they discovered that he invariably won.

"I've never seen a strategy quite like yours," the oldest said one day as the icy wind rattled their windows.

Yskanda could not tell them that he liked the game because it brought memories of those warm days when it would rain and rain, keeping him and his brother and sister indoors. First Brother had found playing Circle infinitely preferable to reading, so the three had played endless games. Initially First Brother won, which was the way things ought to be, as he was best in everything. But then Mouse, around the age of eight, began beating them both—if she could be got to sit still and finish the game. At the time, how she had maddened First Brother and Yskanda, stopping halfway, or even sooner, and declaring that she knew how it was going to go, and that was boring!

Oh, how innocent they were, how happily *ignorant!*

A cough shook his frame. He blinked, finding everyone looking expectantly at him. "I'm nothing, compared to . . ." he began to say—then caught sight of Yut Hak there, and wondered if this kindly act of bringing in the game was yet another interrogation attempt. Weary and sick at heart, he coughed again to cover the pause, then said, ". . . my tutor, who always won."

No one exhibited surprise at this—that was the nature of tutors the world over.

"What else did you expect?" Senye Tan cracked, and the

moment passed.

By Earth Festival the next month, he was on his feet again, but had a lingering cough. For all that time, Yskanda had been too sick to visit the temple, though that had become the single haven of solace. As soon as he was able, he went back to the Ghost Moon temple—alone. This temple, too, had a young redbark tree. He paused to breathe beneath its sheltering branches, reveling in the heady sense of limitless sky above him, and below, the graceful dance of all living things, very much like fireflies moving with purpose through soft summer nights.

Otherwise Yut Hak remained at his side at every meal, and at liberty times, but Yskanda resorted to his old tactic of filling silences with what he wanted to talk about, which was color, line, composition, style.

He avoided group whispers, his internal name for gatherings to gossip, but he couldn't help but overhear the occasional bit of rumor, especially at night while the dormitory was preparing for bed, or in the baths.

Prince Jion, it seemed, was far more interesting while missing than he'd ever been while doing what he was supposed to be doing. The air was constantly filled with speculation about where he was, how long he'd been gone, and whether or not he'd been abducted.

"All my best ears say the pretender never talked," Senye Tan said one day in the baths, after his friends made sure no one was outside the door. It was only their dormitory inside the huge chamber full of hot water and steam. "So no one actually knows if he was there the entire two years—which I for one do not believe—or for a week, which is more likely."

"I hope he was the entire time," someone commented. "If you're going to end up poisoned to death before you get your first chin hair, it's better if at least you got to live like a prince for two years."

"Would you do it if you knew you were going to end up dead at the end?"

"Who said he knew he was going to end up dead?"

"I'm just saying, if. Two years of no work, whatever you want to eat, drink, do."

"No."

"Yes!"

"I'd take it, and then I'd have two years to figure out how

to get around the poison," Senye Tan said.

"The pretender didn't."

"But who says he had two years? It's said he had a week at most, and got caught. Maybe it was less than a week. That makes the most sense. How else would all his servants and guards not notice a new face? Unless the pretender looked just like him?"

Yskanda left the bath as the others kept debating what the pretender had looked like, and how he'd managed to swap places with the prince.

As he settled into bed, he added the day to his mental tally: any day on which he did not catch a glimpse of the emperor, much less hear his voice, was an excellent day. Each tally that added up to a Phoenix-moon month was a cause for quiet gloating: he had survived so far. Enough months, and perhaps the emperor would forget him . . .

THIRTEEN

OUT IN THE HARBOR, no one noticed a small trader slipping in among the bigger craft.

Fai Anbai and his carefully chosen team of four were tired and worn from their long journey during which they dared not stay longer than to get new supplies in any harbor.

The wharfs had ships along them being loaded and unloaded. By the time the ferrets' courier ship, which looked like a trader, anchored, boatmen were already rowing out to meet them—a result of sending a pigeon at dawn.

As always, Fai Anbai waved his team to one boat, saying, "Liberty until morning. By then gods grant I have good news for that long-overdue liberty."

The team laughed and cracked jokes back and forth as Fai Anbai dropped alone into the second boat, which would take him directly to the secluded wharf reserved to the palace guards and the ferrets when under orders.

The boatman leaned into his oars, head bent so that all Fai Anbai could see was the top of his conical straw hat, worn by all the boatmen along the quay. His hands gripped the oars—familiar hands. He was not wearing gloves, though the air was bitter.

A jolt to the core, then he said, "Still testing me, Father?"

A quick glance from under the shade of the hat caused another pang. His father's expression was too grim—answering another question Fai Anbai had wondered at previously. His father had maintained that he meant to spend his life in his garden, tending his miniature trees. And so he could usually be found. But apparently he was still very much aware of inner palace life, and of course kept all his old skills. All anyone outside that boat saw was yet another boatman, indistinguishable from the others.

"You were sent to identify that boy you took during the fall season?"

"Correct."

"Is he the son of Danno and Alk Hanu?"

"Who?" Fai Anbai asked. "Wait. Those names . . . why are they familiar? Were they on the Capital List?"

"They once were." Old Fai's breath steamed briefly as he sighed. "One of my friends among the graywings thought he recognized that boy's features. I went over to take a look — and he's Alk Hanu to the life. I had to supervise the making of the target drawings after she and Danno vanished, and have never forgotten that face."

"I remember something about a runaway consort," Fai Anbai said. "This is related to that old story? The most I remember is that the reorganization of the imperial guard happened around then."

Old Fai gave a five-sentence summary, adding, "Of course you don't remember much. You were, what, nine? Ten. And no one dared talk after the empress yanked the imperial prince back behind the palace doors."

Fai Anbai whistled under his breath. A twenty-five year grudge? "Afan Yskanda's family isn't — "

"Tell me later. We have only until I reach the dock, and I don't know who's watching. Whatever the truth of the matter, you'll discover that security has been tightened ever since you left."

Fai Anbai puzzled at that for about a heartbeat. "Ayah. He's expecting Danno the former elite imperial guard to come for his son?" The last of the mystery seemed to be solved.

"The imperials went on high alert as soon as you left. Their commander will apprise you after your interview with the emperor. Is your tally ready? Good. This couldn't come at a worse time: the imperials failed to find Prince Jion. *And* word came of an attack on one of our training fortresses."

"What?"

They were within fifteen paces of the shoreline. Less, if anyone was in earshot.

"He will be in one of his moods," Fai Senior said — no need to say who "He" was. "You'll have the time it takes to walk to the interview chamber to decide what to say."

Rain began to fall.

Ordinarily the long walk would be another irritation in a long list of frustrations and irritations, but Fai Anbai welcomed this chance to think. All this time he had assumed that the emperor had caught wind of incipient treason, or rebellion, to be quietly and effectively rooted out while innocent subjects went about their lives.

But this was merely a personal matter, it seemed.

He was sworn to obey direct orders. But this realization did shape what he would say.

At the outer city gate, though Fai Anbai recognized both sentries, as well as the four auxiliaries, they demanded his tally. He held it out and the guard on the right inspected it closely, as another wrote down who he was and what he carried.

There was another check on his identity at the palace's west gate — used only by the military — where Fai Anbai discovered Bitternail waiting with a hot cloth and a fresh robe.

Fai Anbai washed up as best he could while walking, exchanging the fresh tunic for his grimy one lest he offend his emperor's eyes and nose, and when his hands were clean, handed off the tip he had prepared just in case, which Bitternail accepted with his customary dignity.

Outside the emperor's private interview room, Bitternail handed the towel and tunic off to one of his underlings, and entered with the chief ferret.

The emperor flicked a single glance at Bitternail, who, successfully interpreting it, closed the door, and waited outside as Fai Anbai crossed the floor swiftly and then began to prostrate himself.

"Rise, rise. Your report, Chief Fai?"

"Your imperial majesty's orders," Chief Fai Anbai reminded the emperor, "were to conduct the investigation discreetly. There were no traces of Afan Yskanda's family; we did go to the imperial tax records, to discover that the island is riddled with tiny villages of five to ten houses, some connected, others isolated. Nearly all the inhabitants illiterate. No post delivery whatsoever. With the agents I had I estimated it would take at least a year, probably longer, to go from village to village — no doubt with word running ahead. So I put my people in various positions, including at the scribe house where Afan Yskanda had apprenticed, while I continued to comb records. For a time all my plant at the scribe house gathered was gossip about Afan Yskanda — nothing about his background. There was absolutely nothing else to be found."

"Interesting," the emperor observed.

"Before I left, Graywing Scribe Melonseed had assured me that they would see to it Afan Yskanda would write a New Year's letter along with the apprentices. With this in mind I waited for the imperial ships and I was the first to inspect all post — and so I saw his letter. He wrote to Master Bankan, the chief scribe — "

"I saw it," the emperor interrupted mildly. "Which is why it went with the rest of the letters, instead of being carried straight to you."

His face and tone were even, but Fai Anbai sensed impatience, or perhaps import, and hastened his words. "Once he read it the chief scribe threw the letter away; my agent said the scribe was quite open about the fact that there was no one to hand it to, no one to report to that the boy was missing. But in the talk that stirred up, we discovered that once or twice, Afan Yskanda was visited by a Phoenix Moon monk on his Ul wander — whereas most of the island worships the Crane God — and afterward by an old woman. No letters exchanged hands, which caused no surprise as the villagers are known to be largely illiterate."

The emperor waved a hand, saying, "And yet Afan Yskanda isn't."

Fai Anbai, who had endured a frustrating search during the intense heat of a southern island summer, and quite humanly desired acknowledgment, wrenched himself from an itemized to a succinct summary.

"I checked the tax records, to discover that for years a monk of the Phoenix Moon had delivered the taxes for three connected villages before he left to wander again. He was replaced by this same old woman who had visited Afan Yskanda."

"Phoenix Moon monk. They're all teachers. That might explain Afan Yskanda's education." *Might*, not *would*; after all that labor, still nothing was concrete. Fai Anbai suppressed an impulse to speculate as the emperor went on, "You found his home?"

"Yes and no," Fai Anbai reported. "His village lay at the

very northern end of the island, in sight of an even smaller island. Using the guise of a trader, three of us traveled to Sweetwater, where we discovered that the Afan family had lived there, but they had recently been contacted by some relation from an island further south, from which they had originated. Something about the expected death of an elder, who summoned the descendants home."

The emperor leaned forward. "What did you discover about this family?"

"They were well regarded. The man is named Afan Olt, a wood-carver, and one of the leaders of the spear fishers."

"Nothing about weapons?" the emperor asked.

"No. The woman, the local herb-woman, is called Ugly Iley—"

"*Ugly* Iley?"

"Yes, your imperial majesty. All concurred that her face was corrugated worse than a turtle's back, though there were various claims as to the cause—the fire they escaped before they arrived—disease—punishment from the gods. All attested to her ugliness. Three children, the middle one being Yskanda, meant to study for the temple, but sent to the scribes."

"What of these other children?"

"Afan Muinkanda is the oldest, sent off to the army. We had no orders, so we did not follow up on him, but a cursory check furnished no Afans among the garrison guards at Imai."

The emperor said, "He can wait. He ought to be easy enough to find, if he is already in my army. And the third?"

"A daughter, Afan Arikanda, also trained by the monk, and intended for the temple."

The emperor waved a hand. "She, too, can wait."

The emperor was thinking. A search for the older boy in his army could be done by low-level scribes. Searches among monks and nuns could be more difficult, especially if they surrendered their names on joining, as some temples required—but it wasn't impossible. And monks' and nuns' acolytes stayed put until they took their vows.

He was certain he could lay his hand on these two any time he desired, but that would be a waste of time until he was absolutely certain of the parents, who still might or might not be Danno and Alk Hanu. His only evidence, if it could be called that, was Afan Yskanda's face.

The search had stalled. But he could wait. If Afan Yskanda

truly was Danno's son, even if there were two other children — ten — he expected that Danno would eventually turn up to find him. And the palace was ready. The night Fai Anbai left, the emperor had decreed that every man who entered or left the palace must be identified and his presence documented, and patrols had been increased to line-of-sight at all times.

Danno might at one time have been the best warrior on the imperial island, but he could not waft himself in and out of the most closely guarded palace in the empire.

The emperor smiled with anticipation, then leaned over and picked up the report he had been reading. "Before we go further, tell me what you make of this."

Fai Anbai stepped forward to take the report. He glanced at the neat lettering on the outside of the folded paper, opened it, then scanned a report twin to the one he had received at his last supply stop aboard the ship. "Pirates attacked Loyalty Fortress."

This report was far more detailed, written in a flat, detail-heavy style he immediately recognized. He read on rapidly, then looked up, frowning. "Tek Banu is always thorough, your imperial majesty. She ought to have sent someone on to Te Gar to collect the younger boy, the Essence talent—"

"She did. That report is also there, though there is nothing to be learned: the boy listed as Second Ryu never turned up at Te Gar. The ship captain carried Commander Weken's communications to the garrison, as usual, but declared—as did the sailors—that they lost sight of Second Ryu, and what they mistook as two orderlies, on the quay. One of those apparently proved to be another cadet, a deserter."

Fai Anbai glanced down. "Shigan Fin?"

"Another from one of the eastern islands between here and the Silks," the emperor said dismissively. "From what Commander Weken said, apparently could not deal with army discipline."

"Deserters." Fai Anbai frowned, knowing that cadets who ran off, especially at the lower levels of training, might be written down as deserters, but no one bothered pursuing them; they had rendered themselves worthless by running. However, if their names turned up on a crime list somewhere else, the desertion became a capital crime, carrying an automatic sentence of beheading.

He shrugged off Shigan Fin as someone else's problem, and turned his mind to this issue, which appeared to be a state one. He really did not want to expend his force, and his time, on the personal quarrel if he could avoid it — even an imperial one. "Two possibilities occur. One: the mercenary hirelings were lying in wait, and snatched them as soon as their feet reached ground. Or, second, this Second Ryu was trained by some renegade who might have found one of those mountain cultivators who insist on living outside the law, and seen his Essence talent. Taught him long enough to instill a few tricks before the Ryu boys took the test for entry."

"Ryu," the emperor commented. "A common name in both army and navy."

"Mostly in the north, but yes," Fai Anbai said. His fingers slapped the part of the report that detailed Commander Weken's testimony to the effect that Second Ryu had been ill for days after a demonstration that he would not have believed but for the number of eye-witnesses. ". . . so Second Ryu was taught a little about Essence, but likely ruined for army discipline. My guess is that if the mercenaries did not capture them, the three might very well have vanished among the criminals."

"Criminals" being one of the common army disparagements for the gallant wanderers.

"But all, from Weken — whose record is excellent — on down, claim that Second Ryu's discipline was as good as First Ryu's."

"I've found that people will put the best face on those they like, or to cover their own lack," Fai Anbai said with a slight shrug. "That's merely a guess, as I was not there myself to hear how the questions were asked, or to put my own. It's also possible the Essence harmed Second Ryu's mind in some way. Drove him mad, even — we know that can happen to Essence talents. We won't discover for certain unless he turns up again. I can add Second Ryu to the internal Watch list, rather than the public Watch list, since no crime was reported other than possible desertion. Essence talents rarely stay hidden forever. Once he turns up again, we'll nab him."

"Do that," the emperor said. "And so, to my final, and most pressing matter. I'm afraid," the emperor said — though both knew that was merely a rhetorical fear — "that I must reward your excellent work with more work. My son Jion is missing. I sent the army out. The search so far has turned up nothing. Until I see a body, I will not believe he is dead. Find Jion, Chief Fai. Track him down, and you shall have whatever promotion you desire — a manor of your own — a noble consort if you want a second one, some time to enjoy them. Find Jion and bring him home," he finished in that gentle voice that caused the entire palace, from the loftiest dukes to the smallest bond-servant, to walk softly.

Chief Fai bowed himself out, thinking: well, you wanted a state matter. You got one.

He returned to his own quarters in an otherwise undistinguished building on the west side, in hopes of having a little time with his wife. She welcomed him, but with a muted look — and he soon discovered why. Here, in his tiny outer room, spite of his earlier words about liberty, the team that had gone with him was waiting, and a little apart, Tek Banu.

She always sat apart. Her nature was solitary, her conversation abrupt and so flat in tone she looked and sounded surly. She was older than Fai Anbai, a legacy from his father's day as chief. After his father was wounded so badly that the Imperial Physicians did not think he would recover, he had used every argument he could to get his son to lead the ferrets, at first temporarily, then permanently.

Tek Banu is second in seniority and expects to replace me, but the ferrets under her would be worse than wolves in the city walls and rats in the temples, Fai Senior had said from his sickbed.

Fai Anbai had agreed with that. In the brief times he had worked with her, he had discovered that she disliked partnering with anyone as much as they disliked working with her.

She's more experienced but you have a far better record working with others, so I've convinced the emperor to assign you as my aide, and I will shift responsibility to you gradually . . .

Chief Fai said to his team, "We are not finished." To the quiet sighs and fallen faces, "We have new orders — and if we are successful, it will mean promotions for everyone. No, *when* we are successful. There is no *if* in this case." He turned to Tek Banu. "Your previous mission is superseded. We are tasked to find Imperial Prince Jion, or his body. However long it takes."

He knew, and she knew, it was nearly an impossible task. But that was the sort of mission she liked best. "We'll find him," she promised. "Or if not him, his bones and teeth. And then we'll hunt down those who dared to lay hands on an imperial son," she added with a rare display of emotion, a vicious anticipation that was far more disturbing than her customary flat tone.

FOURTEEN

KI MATU LOATHED TRAVEL by ship because he always got sick.

The cousins had spent a month with a relation who lived inland of Te Gar Harbor. Matu had been recovering after several short journeys between islands. They had been arguing about whether to risk the seas with winter storms coming on, or stay on that island, until the encounter with the Redbark Sect pair. Ki Tenar agreed to stay. She had learned that surviving in a prosperous city was easier than in an unknown countryside—she loved to bake, and everyone in a city needs to eat.

But now they were forced to sail, and within a day Ki Matu was violently ill.

Usually they headed for the nearest island. Granny Mang, the ship-owner and a connection to the Eagle Island sect, was concerned.

"I thought we ought to gain a good distance from Te Gar before we try another island," she said.

"If you can take us to the next island without imperial navy, we'll stay there," Ki Tenar replied, looking anxiously back at Matu, who couldn't even keep down boiled water. Petal sat beside him, ready with a rag in case he was seized with another bout of dry heaves; she had volunteered to help when everyone else fled. Even Ki Tenar, who could shovel out a barn, got queasy at the smell of human vomit.

"I've cleaned up everything," Petal said. "And I want to earn my way if I can."

Granny Mang gave her a terse smile. "Everyone is going to have to earn their way, with all these extra mouths," she said, and they sailed through a fiercely rocky night as the storm blew around them. The next day they came in sight of a harbor — then Granny Mang shouted, "Come about!"

Her sailors yanked the clattering sails around, worked the rudder, and they headed back into deep water. "Imperials. Ten in harbor," she reported.

Shigan turned to Ryu. "All I saw were bumps and blurs."

"Ayah, I as well."

To similar mutters from the other gallant wanderers aboard, Granny Mang said, "Seventy years walking a deck, and you learn the rigging of every type of vessel. Those were imperial warships, the fast ones, not the carriers bringing big weapons and horses and the like. But bad enough."

"Another search," one of the gallant wanderers commented. "Once might be happenstance, but twice in two islands is a very bad omen. Can you take us straight to Tortor Island, and give us one of your lifeboats? I have two golden dragons."

Granny Mang frowned, weighing danger against how long her supplies would last with this many extra people. She said, "You can have one boat, but we need the other."

"Not everyone will fit into one," someone observed.

Granny Mang turned to Ki Tenar, who had come up on deck, her face blotched with cold and worry. "If your cousin can make it to Tortor, it's only three days more to Ten Leopards."

Ki Tenar looked at the range of faces, and gave a short nod.

"What's Tortor Island?" Shigan asked a sailor.

"It's got no harbor, the beaches are all treacherous with rock and geysers, and the land is all forest. Bad stories about it, but the gallants will go there and vanish when there's trouble. The imperials don't touch it."

"Done," Granny Mang said promptly, accepting the two golden taels, but with a worried look toward the hatch, below which Ki Matu lay.

While everyone was on deck, Yaso emerged from the galley at the back end and crouched down beside Ki Matu. "Here, sip this."

Matu turned his head, but then the smell of whatever it

was wafted to him with the gentle steam. It cleared his head briefly, and better, numbed for a single breath the unremitting nausea. He sipped and slurped, then lay back, breathing fast. But the brew did not come back up.

Ki Tenar clambered down, and ran to them. "What did you give him?"

"It's ginger, with a bit of turmeric and some other herbs."

"Blrghle," Ki Matu moaned.

Yaso bent to help him sip the remainder of the little cup, aided by Petal.

Ki Matu fell asleep, his breathing slowly easing.

"We'll need to get water into him," Yaso said.

"I can do that," Petal offered. "Give me a spoon. I'll give him a tiny sip to begin with."

"At least there's plenty of fresh water," Ki Tenar said as the sound of sleet began hammering the deck above them: she'd seen the rain catchers set out.

Granny Mang took the ship into deep gray-green waters, past treacherous reefs and between rocky outcroppings that invariably were named some variation of Dragon's Teeth. When they were enveloped in blizzards, the ship slowed to a crawl, bucketing in excruciatingly wild waves—forcing Yaso to dispense more of the precious ginger root, turmeric, and a tiny pinch of precious ancient Longevity Root, which Petal patiently fed to Matu, drip by drip.

Everyone worked. Ryu, the smallest, was given the job of cleaning dishes once everyone ate. That left her with plenty of time. Some of that she used in a tiny, dank compartment meant for holding fish for trade. There was just enough space for her to work through Heaven and Earth in the dark, adding a balance challenge as the ship tossed about. Sometimes Shigan joined her, though they could only drill one at a time. More often they did handstands, competing with one another in who could keep their balance longest.

Ryu invariably won, a benefit of her years of learning to balance on bamboo poles, but she noticed that Shigan was now far stronger than she was, unless she burned Essence. He could do a handstand and lower the top of his head to the deck, then straighten his arms. She concentrated on her Essence breathing, trying to build up more Essence within her as she worked on head-to-deck handstands. It was torture. But if *he* could do it, she would do it, too.

When she was so sore she was trembling, Ryu stayed on

deck, hands wrapped around a small jar of boiled water, and watched the great leviathans disporting within coral reefs. Once they glimpsed a surging bridge that caused the sailors to freeze, then run about. Ryu and Shigan saw why when the bridge rose higher, became a loop, and then one end of a massive tentacle snapped up, tossing some object sky high — as it came down, one of the sailors wailed, "It's a shark! As long as a house!"

The shark and the tentacle splashed down again as the captain lit incense and everyone prayed to hide the ship from the great kraken. Either the gods listened, or the creature had no interest in them, as it sank below the waves and vanished.

The morning after that, Ryu woke with a familiar and unwelcome cramp low in her gut. She made it to the head before the first gush of the monthly. When the cramping eased, she slipped down into the hold and went to her bundle, though she was very afraid what she would find there. She had a distinct memory of keeping her Cramp herbs hidden in her bedding. Which now lay days and days of sailing behind them.

But she was desperate enough to search anyway, in case she had misremembered and rolled the little container in her socks, the way she'd first carried it when she left the army.

Sure enough, there was no sign of it.

She returned slowly to the deck as cold wind swept its length, wondering which of her few clothes she could sacrifice, and how could she rinse them out without everyone discovering what she was doing?

To her surprise, she found Yaso at the rail where Ryu usually stood, holding two cups of something steaming. The wind whipped the summery smell of ginger tea toward her, familiar now with poor Matu drinking it every day. Except that Yaso was clearly waiting for her.

She trod cautiously toward Yaso, glancing to either side to make sure no one was around. The sailors were all in the rigging, doing something to one of the clattering sails, or down below. No one else in sight, preferring to remain out of that bitterly scouring wind.

Yaso's face was noncommittal as always. "Those herbs are not good for young bodies, did you know that? Unless you have made the decision to never have a child. There are better ways to slough that blood."

Ryu stared, in a panic, and once more glanced around. But no one was in sight. And Yaso merely waited.

Ryu whispered, "You knew . . . I'm a girl?"

Yaso said, "I know you were born with a girl's body."

Isn't that the same thing? Ryu was going to ask, but she didn't care about the answer. "How long?" she asked cautiously.

"Since the beginning," Yaso replied, still calmly, as though they discussed the shape of the clouds overhead. "If you do not wish to be unfilial by harming your body, you ought to be using your Essence, and a talisman sign, to relax the muscles, which you will find far less injurious."

Ryu stared. "My mother made me read about the herbs," she began. A clatter and a shout overhead caused her to stop abruptly.

"Perhaps she did not have time to finish the lesson," Yaso suggested. "The herbs are one very old method, rarely used now."

"Old method?" Ryu repeated, and remembered her mother reminding her that she had to teach herself herb healing. And that she was dependent on whatever books Ul Keg could scour from booksellers, usually the old, picked-over ones.

"It was used by the very poor, and by women who for whatever reason did not wish a child to result from a mating. They would use it the following day. But you needn't use such force. Your Essence is sufficient." And then, in a low, easy voice that did not carry, Yaso told Ryu what she needed to know, and taught her the talisman sign to inscribe on the skin directly over her womb.

When Ryu said she understood, Yaso walked away, leaving the ginger tea. Ryu gulped it down, then retreated to the head, and put into practice what she had just learned. At first her limbs trembled in anticipation, and she braced, muscles tight—which set off another cramp. But then she did Essence breathing, and went through the steps again. This time her body did the needful, as easy as peeing.

She walked out to take the empty cup to the galley. As she did, she glanced half-fearfully for Yaso, wondering if the orderly was going to say something. *From the beginning.* For the first time, Ryu began to wonder about Yaso's own story, but as always, she shied away from even thinking questions. That path was dangerous. Far better to leave things as they were, especially if Yaso said nothing.

Over the next stretch of days Ryu did her job, avoiding the main hold where poor Matu lay in misery, where despite Petal's vigorous scrubbing the acid tang of puke still loured in the air. Gradually she relaxed, trusting that things had gone back to normal. "Normal" being Shigan, and others, unaware of her secret.

Ryu was too absorbed in her own problems to spare much attention to Matu, now that he seemed to be surviving.

But that was not true for Petal.

One of the earliest and harshest lessons of her life so far was that nobody else felt your pain. If you were lucky, someone might sympathize, but you could be in agony while others stood within arm's length, feeling absolutely nothing.

Ever since then, she'd looked for the signs of pain in others. It seemed to undo some of her old pain when she did something to ease theirs. She didn't know how that worked, just that it did. Taking care of Eagle Island Brother Matu was that way. Each little sigh of release, each grateful closing of his eyelids, and easing of his tight mouth that indicated the clawing nausea he suffered had loosened its grip just a bit evoked a small release within her.

They fell into the habit of conversation. Not much. It cost him too much effort. He was better off sleeping. But little exchanges—*Is the medicine too hot? No, it's perfect this way, I hardly taste it*—and so forth gradually made it easy for them to talk, though they had begun this journey as strangers.

Ryu, usually so aware, noticed none of this as she avoided the stinky hold after bringing food from the galley so that Petal would not have to leave Matu to fetch it. She also worried about what Yaso might say, and to whom—though she knew Yaso had never been a blabbermouth. It was the fact that Yaso *knew* that unsettled her so much.

And she watched Shigan, who was everywhere, constantly asking questions about sailing, and volunteering for every job. He practiced with her, but otherwise he worked willingly, more interested in the ship and sailing than in Ryu and whatever she might be hiding.

The biggest of the sailors, a hearty man nearing thirty, made it his business to answer all Shigan's questions, explaining how the battens controlled the sails, and promising that one day Shigan might be permitted to handle setting sail himself, and maybe even catch a glimpse of the precious charts.

"This is how pirates find their prey," this man said self-importantly. "They steal charts, which list common routes. Traders, for example, go along certain ways."

"I thought the imperial navy goes everywhere," Shigan said on a note of question.

"Oh, yes, they do, but they have favorite routes, centering around their naval yards. Then there's the nobles' routes, which we stay away from as much as we do the navy. Like what they call Journey to the Cloud Empire, mid-spring when the rest of the islands celebrate Kraken Boat Festival. Everyone stays well away from the belly of the dragon." The sailor sketched a vague outline in the air, suggesting the map of the Empire of a Thousand Islands, then poking his finger at the middle section.

The sailor gave Shigan a slightly condescending smile, saying comfortingly, "You might not have heard of it, but the nobles and imperials go on sampans all decked with gold and jewels along a narrow passage between islands with a lot of waterfalls and suchlike. Musicians play, and there are poets and singers."

"Oh," said Shigan.

"Anyway, we never let anyone see our chart, and our markings are in a code only we know. Maybe I'll let you see ours, once day." He grinned at Shigan.

All this was watched by the chief helmsman, a grizzled individual whose sparse hair had turned white. But there was nothing old or hoary in his acute, amused gaze.

Shigan noted that gaze once or twice. He mentally shrugged it away, but one rainy day when his sailor teacher was on deck for his duty, and Shigan found the only space to sit and eat was next to the old helmsman, he sat, then said, "You seem to be laughing at me. I'm trying to fix my ignorance."

The helmsman did not answer directly. "You can always tell a big islander from a small. Your little sect brother there is a small islander." He nodded at Ryu on the other side of the companionway, carrying two steaming bowls for Petal and Matu.

"Oh?" Shigan said.

"Knows boats," the helmsman said. "Got on board, knew where to go, where to stay out of the way. Knows sail in a general way."

Shigan gazed in surprise—the old geezer could tell all that

at a glance? "And me?"

"Big islander." It wasn't even a question. "Know nothing about boats—swallowing all Fin Noa's brag, when everyone knows sails are easy. Even a child can handle 'em. Helm, though? Now, that takes some work."

"I have actually been on boats. Twice," Shigan said, and at the pronounced amusement in the helmsman's face, he added, "but I wasn't allowed on deck. Is Fin Noa wrong?"

The helmsman chuckled. "Nothing he says is wrong, just . . . you seem to believe it as said, without seeing he's trying to impress you."

Shigan's brows slanted in surprise, and he looked warily at the helmsman. "Impress *me*?"

"Because he likes pretty boys, of course."

"Oh." Shigan blinked, his *Is that all* evident, if unspoken, making the old helmsman wonder what sort of life this boy was running from. "I guess I ought to have seen that." Shigan tried to sound indifferent, but succeeded in sounding exactly as inexperienced as he was.

The helmsman chuckled again. "Come on deck some night. If you can hold the helm, I'll tell Captain to explain the charts to you."

Shigan wanted nothing more than to get to con the helm himself; and Fin Noa was left to philosophical thoughts about the butterfly natures of youth.

Shigan was so diligent that the helmsman spoke up for him as promised, and Granny Mang permitted him to look at her precious chart, a wonderful complication of the Houses of Heaven—the constellations—and details of reefs and shoals and landmarks of islands, all carefully inscribed.

FIFTEEN

AT LAST THEY CAME to Tortor Island. All the gallants except their party crowded into a lifeboat and rowed toward the shore, where everyone could see waves splashing high against jagged rocks.

The ship put about with a great creaking of battens and the shuddering of the rudder. By now poor Matu had become dangerously thin, as all he could keep down was a rice ball or two a day. But true to her word, on the third morning out from Tortor Island Granny Mang came down into the hold where the travelers slept, and announced, "We'll reach Ten Leopards today. See that nick a little west of north? You're almost home."

"Ten Leopards? I thought you came from the Eagle Island Sect," Ryu asked.

"We do," Ki Matu said, rising up on his elbows at the prospect of land. "Ten Leopards is Ki clan. It's said the first gallants here were known as the Ten Leopards." He smiled weakly. "Island was probably called something else by the imperials. Back when the capital was up in the north. During the Tan Dynasty. Eagle Island isn't far. The clan descended from the eldest brother. Second brother came here. Now we have both islands."

With Yaso's and Ki Tenar's help he levered himself to his feet, and by the time they sailed into a narrow harbor with sheer cliffs on either side, he had managed to get onto the weather deck.

A single pier bisected that wedge-shaped harbor into two very narrow wedges. Matu was the first one off the ship, followed by everyone else. They walked up a curving path into a typical village built around a square, houses behind set at angles, so that there was no straight road along which demons could prowl.

Ki Tenar led them to a house with a large horse barn adjacent. Inside, they were offered tea and hot food. Matu was already looking better, now that he was on firm ground. A small meal helped further restore him. Then Petal, the cousins, and Shigan clambered into a cart that had been readied while they ate.

Ryu took one look at that closed-in, stuffy cart and said, "I'm going to run."

"Nobody runs up the hill," Matu said in a thready voice. "Unless they're being punished. And it takes all day to go up that hill."

"I'm used to running." Ryu shrugged.

For some reason even he couldn't quite parse, Shigan promptly jumped out and ran beside her.

For a time they enjoyed the run, until the road began to steepen, the path narrowing to switchbacks. The animals, used to it, slowed to a steady pace. Shigan slackened to a walk, putting on bursts to catch up. These bursts got farther and farther apart — by then Ryu had slowed to a jog as they wound up a twisting, narrow path past spires of striated rock and canyons that echoed the clopping of the horses' hooves. Far above, raptors drifted on the air currents.

Ryu did not need Essence until the steepest portion of the hill, and even then, she discovered that it took less effort than she had used those long-ago days when leaping to roofs and doing tricks on her bamboo poles.

Shigan forced himself to stay on the road until Ryu, concentrating on her Essence and completely unaware of his struggles, looked around with interest. The shadows had begun to slant dramatically when they rounded a curve to discover tall, crumbled statues so weather-worn it was difficult to recognize which gods the figures were to represent, other than that they had folded wings.

As they passed, Ryu looked across to Shigan, and said in a low voice, "Perhaps this was once a huge gate."

Shigan also kept his voice low in that oppressive

atmosphere, heavy with the weight of lost history. "It has to be . . . at least a thousand . . . years. More." And then, it was either fall down in a faint or catch the cart with one hand to help him along.

Nothing they saw subsequently corrected that impression as they came abreast of the ruins of a mighty fortress. Wild pear trees grew in the loam between fallen rocks, already beginning to bud. Gnarled apple trees also grew, the descendants of a long-ago orchard.

Shigan's legs had turned to water, and the horses were sweating in spite of the cold air when at last they reached what appeared to be a vast plateau. Ryu was whooping for breath, but looked happy and smiling and curious. Another short distance and the plateau proved to be the curving shore around a lake. On the far shore jagged mountains scraped the sky, white with snow.

A fair-sized village had been laid out along the lake shore, the buildings sturdy with freshly thatched roofs. The horses knew where to go; they pulled into a yard, where stable hands ran to see to them, as Ryu goggled, wiping her forehead on her sleeve, and Shigan tottered in a circle, breathing like a bellows. Matu clambered out with Yaso's and his cousin's aid to enter a low-ceilinged room with ancient carved ceiling beams. It smelled of savory spices and strong tea.

Ryu brimmed with delight and curiosity and a little bit of worry about being accepted among gallant wanderers at last. Shigan collapsed, his entire body aching as greetings and introductions sounded around him. He still wasn't quite certain what he'd proven, especially as Ryu seemed unaware that there had been a contest.

He was right. She looked at the Ki clan with avid curiosity. They all spoke in the northern-flavored vernacular that she was used to from Matu and Tenar, and they were a bewildering mix of Brothers, Sisters, and Cousins all designated by birth order—except for three or four elders before whom everyone bowed. But other than the birth order number, they seemed to move about with equality, and they were dressed alike.

Ryu wanted to believe that skill, and not birth or wealth, was what determined one's place below or above that invisible line; Petal, with years more experience observing people, spotted the more subtle signs of a complicated family hierarchy, as the teenager girls in particular began side-eyeing

Shigan with an intensity that meant he was shortly to become their target.

Though the Ki clan did not have bond-servants—part of cultivation in the world of the gallant wanderers was shared labor to keep the living environment orderly—here were distant relations who handled most of the kitchen work. Petal migrated toward these, who welcomed her with gratifying smiles when she bowed very properly to the nook containing the little shrine to the kitchen god, then said, "I come from inn work. What can I do to help?" And when they said the usual things about guests, she said, "I feel more comfortable working. I wouldn't know what to do with myself else."

Then the smiles were genuine, and she reveled in that simple welcome, a first in her life.

Ryu was too bewildered by the sheer number of new faces to notice where Petal went. As the entire clan gathered for a meal, she tried to catch the names thrown at her—Mountain Walking Ki also known as First Uncle Xiulu, Second Uncle Yslu, Flying Egret Ki also known as First Aunt Meilu—though no one was introduced as Matu's mother or father. Maybe they were wandering, or on a patrol.

Ryu's attention snagged on Second Uncle Yslu because of his name "Ys" before the generation name Lu, for the great poet-warrior who wandered about dispensing justice and posting poems exposing corrupt governors and others in powerful positions. Hearing "Ys" again made her think of Yskanda, knotting her heart. Of course he had to be happy, far, far to the south at Imai Harbor with his inks and brushes.

Some aunties fussed over Matu, to his embarrassment—his seasickness was well known—as the newcomers helped themselves from the bowls of plain food, mostly vegetables cooked in several ways, some fresh-water fish, and always rice. They didn't notice Ki Tenar withdrawing with Second Uncle Yslu to a quiet room, where the two sat on cushions at a low table carved with leaping dolphins, as a young cousin brought in a tray of hot dishes.

"So, Third Niece. You brought these newcomers into our home," he said, mildly enough. "Tell me about them."

"I had to," Ki Tenar said. She felt like a little girl again before her uncle's steady gaze. "There was a sudden cage, imperials searching Te Gar—"

He raised a hand. "Searching everywhere. We heard. But that does not concern us."

She had been about to ask what the search was for, then shrugged it off. "Three are the last of Redbark Sect. Petal was at their inn, ill-treated by an evil stepmother."

"I understand about Petal," said Second Uncle Yslu. "Your aunt interviewed her, and said she bears scars. She's already proved to be an excellent worker in the short time you've been home. I mainly speak of these others. I've never heard of Redbark Sect."

"Nor I," Tenar commented. "But from what I saw, their sword form is better than anything we have. Better than anyone's except Sky Island," she added. "Redbark Brother Shigan, the black-haired boy, is fast and strong but I think he lacks discipline. No," she corrected herself, her head tipped. "He is very disciplined, when he wants to be. He acts like he might have come to their sect from an entertainer band, or something similar, before he joined Redbark. They did say he was recently sworn in. But Redbark Brother Ryu, the smaller boy, he's been well-trained in sword. They both are at least adequate in spear and knives, and they say they know archery, though of course we could not lay hand to a bow in a city due to the laws. I think . . . I think he might have an Essence gift, but not trained."

"I'm told Redbark Brother Ryu ran all the way up the road," Second Uncle observed.

"They both did. Though I was afraid Redbark Brother Shigan might collapse along the way. He was struggling at Heartbreak Curve."

Second Uncle gave a grunt that meant, *Who doesn't?*

"And as for Brother Yaso, he doesn't seem to know any martial arts."

"If you vouch for them, you know you must take responsibility."

"I know," she said, serious and sober. "I guess I could have left them behind, but Matu likes them. He was learning from them. And he was teaching them our knife form. Ayah! And then on the ship he was so ill, and Brother Yaso, who acts as their orderly, was the only one with a remedy. He used all their precious digestive herbs, and I truly believe that he and Sister Petal saved Matu's life. I don't think Matu could have survived so long at sea else. There was certainly nothing I could do."

"This Yaso is their orderly?" Second Uncle asked, brows raised. Gallant wanderers did not have orderlies.

"They went into the army for a year or two after their sect

was wiped out, then left again. Brother Yaso was their orderly in army training, and came with them."

"Oh, is this Yaso a healer, then?"

"I think so, though he claims to be a mere learner. Anyway, that day in Te Gar, when the imperials came, we had to leave so fast I forgot all about stopping at the herbalist. We used up all their ginger root and precious herbs. I felt I owed it to them."

"Quite right," Second Uncle said reassuringly. "We pay our debts, and we will welcome them as guests. Anything else, of course, must wait on Grandfather. Eat up, niece!"

Another snowstorm closed in, a blessing for Shigan, who was in painful shape after that run. Well before dawn after their first night, he went to the outhouse, then limped to the barn, which he'd noted when Matu showed them around the day previous. It had plenty of clear space, and the hard-packed ground was kept swept clean between the stalls. He forced himself to stretch his knotted muscles, torture especially after all that time on the ship, when he couldn't find the space, or the privacy, to do his own warmups, the ones he'd as yet showed no one.

At least when he was done he could walk again, though it was going to be a couple of days before he could run.

Ryu, of course, was ready for another run by the next day, but she had terrible trouble telling all these bewildering people apart. Having grown up in a tiny village in a family of six, counting Ul Keg, she was completely unused to the way clans squabbled, made up, laughed, and cried, some of them all the course of a single day.

She completely missed how suddenly the teenage girls' braids were shiny from being freshly brushed and retied with a bit of silk, their sashes tighter around their slim waists as they circled around Shigan at the midday meal and again in the evening. The only behavior Ryu recognized was the way some of the teenage boys just getting hairs on their chins squared up to Shigan after Matu invited her and Shigan to the barn to play around. But there wasn't any playing. From the snide comments, Ryu understood that these big boys had taken that run up the mountain as a challenge.

But instead of bragging, Shigan spread his hands, saying, "Oh, I'm not the expert. Ryu over there is. I'm a mere beginner."

The boys laughed, and the biggest cousin made a crack about being overly humble as they all swung a stare Ryu's way.

Shigan seemed to be in one of his odd moods that she could never figure out. He added mockingly, "Now, if it's dancing you want, then I'm your expert. I like to dance. I can sing, too. Not well, but adequately."

"Anyone can dance," the biggest cousin scoffed. And, because he was bored, he eyed Ryu, who Matu and Tenar had both sworn ran all the way up the mountain. To him, Shigan might be a worthwhile rival or competitor, but Ryu was just a scrawny urchin. Sure that there was some sort of joke going on and he was the butt, he sneered, "You dance, too?"

Shigan answered before she could. "Not as well as I. He's still learning."

And then—before Ryu's astonished eyes—he lifted one leg. Everyone gaped when he kept raising it until it was straight up over his head, making one vertical line from toe to toe. Then he turned his shoulder and hip, reached up behind, and pulled his foot down toward the back of his head, his knee still pointed toward the ceiling.

Down came the leg and he said, "I'm stiff. Haven't really stretched in weeks. I'd rather just watch you and learn." He sauntered over to sit on a table next to horse gear.

The boys promptly showed off, doing the knife form warmups that Matu and Tenar had taught Ryu and Shigan. Then they challenged each other, doing various tricks like handstands and flips—none of them all that good, but they were clearly trying to impress the visitors. Ryu remained where she was, watching from a corner, until someone rang a bell in the distance.

The boys stampeded out. Ryu and Shigan followed more slowly, he trying to hide his limp. At least his muscles hurt a little less after that stretch, brief as it was.

Ryu said, "I never knew you could do that. With your leg. I sure can't."

"It's a dance warmup."

"You can really dance?"

Shigan shrugged. "Anyone can dance. Do I dance well? That would be up to those who see me, wouldn't it?"

"You never did any dancing," Ryu said, eyeing him—she sensed something missing. Why would he suddenly do it now?

He just shrugged. "There was no time for it at the fortress. Or at the teahouse," he added.

Ryu was going to point out that at Loyalty Fortress on the festival days, a lot of the boys had done sword dances and the ancient fan dance, but then she remembered how aloof Shigan had been in those days, keeping to himself as he read through all Instructor Shaz's books in the library or shot arrow after arrow at the targets. "I wish I could dance," she said wistfully. "I'm terrible at it."

"Your—*our*—Redbark Sword form is a dance," Shigan said. "And I've seen you do handsprings and the like. How can you say you don't dance?"

Ryu was going to deny that was dancing, but she couldn't find the words to explain the difference, so she sighed. "I wish you'd teach me anyway."

"All right," he said. "When there's the right music. But the barn is perfect for Redbark. Tomorrow morning, before they get up? Surely the cows won't smell any worse than that privy behind the inn did."

This far north the sun was rising perceptibly higher each day as winter began loosening its grip. All the talk was of the Sky Alliance Prize competition, which always ended with the Spring Festival celebration.

Those under a certain age slept, boys and girls together, in the attic loft of one wing in the rambling house. Ryu was given a pallet among them. Shigan was put with the teenage boys — but he always found at least one, usually several of the girl cousins lurking around when he came out of his shared room.

The teenage girls utterly ignored Ryu, to her relief, but still their quick, high voices intimidated her, especially when, a few days later, the third day of the third lunar month fell, which meant gathering in the ancestral hall to dust the tables, polish the memorial tablets, and scour the floor before the ritual, as the delicious smell of pancakes wafted through the air.

That evening everyone dressed in their best, which meant the girls braided ribbons through their hair, and wore embroidered robes. Ryu had never learned to braid her thick hank of hair, nor had she owned a nice robe. She had worn her brothers' outworn clothes since birth, and twisted her hair into a topknot. Thoroughly intimidated, she was glad she had been relegated to the attic with the young ones, even if they tended to stay awake far too long with tiresome games like farting contests, which they thought the pinnacle of humor.

The girls crowded around Shigan, wanting to kneel next to him for the ritual. Ryu was glad to stay at the rear with the children and the extended family, Petal among them.

After that, life settled into a new routine. Ryu rose early in the mornings from habit, bowed to the southwest as always, then rolled her bedding army-style, for she had learned that the youngsters cleaned the floor each morning after waking. But there was no Yaso for Essence breathing—Yaso was sleeping somewhere else. She found she missed that, though by now she knew the routine. She rose and dressed before the other children stirred, then ghosted through the house until she reached the barn, which had a large open space.

She and Shigan met at the barn before anyone else their age was awake, and Matu joined them when he didn't have family responsibilities such as feeding the horses and mucking out their stalls. The three of them moved through Heaven and Earth with no interruption, watched by sleepy cows on one side, and horses on the other, Matu still counting his move-ments under his breath. But he was getting noticeably sharper.

The rest of the day, under the rooftop drum of sleet, the clear space in the barn was used by the cousins, who were all chattering about the Sky Alliance competition. From age sixteen up, they rotated in pairs for three day shifts to watch the narrow harbor from huts on the mountain, as that was the only place a ship could reach.

The rest drilled in the barns while winter spent its last force in messy snow and sleet. Ryu sometimes watched the big cousins from the hayloft, miming the knife form where no one could see her; she was surprised that no one used Essence, though perhaps they saved that for sparring. They certainly knew what it was—or Matu had, she remembered, the first time they met. After drill and sparring, everyone helped with sweeping, scouring, and feeding the animals.

In the evenings, many of the young people made music and sometimes danced. Shigan was circled by teenage girls like raptors over a bunny. He listened to those who played, head cocked, then said, "If I play the guzheng, then you can dance."

Ryu, listening from outside as she contemplated going in, heard what the older girls did not hear—his distaste for what sounded to her like reasonable music (better than anything she'd heard in Sweetwater)—and, deciding that Shigan was in one of his moods, she withdrew to read now that the library was empty of any except a couple of the older aunts. She sensed undercurrents among the teens without understanding any of them. But it all felt a lot like the undertow off Hundred Rocks back at Sweetwater.

SIXTEEN

MIDWAY THROUGH THE MONTH they woke to a significant thaw at last. While the adults went elsewhere to drill after various household chores were done, Second Uncle Yslu, who was the clan's martial arts instructor, took all the young people out to the lake shore, where smooth rock, worn down over centuries, made an ideal training ground for weapons forms, while others set up targets for archery.

Shigan and Ryu joined at the back, which was proper and humble for guests, performing the warmups that the Ki cousins had taught them. They moved through the knife forms, and sparred with the cousins as Second Uncle paired them off, walked back and forth tapping limbs and bodies into alignment, and called directions.

Ryu was included among the teens, paired with those her age and a bit younger. She held her own well in the Ki knife fighting, which made her grin with glee.

Then it was time for sword work. Ryu and Shigan didn't know the Ki sword form, as both Matu and Tenar had agreed that Redbark Sword form was far superior. They followed along in the Ki drill, which was in some respects much like the Loyalty fortress drills. That caused them to occasionally make false moves, quickly corrected.

Second Uncle noticed, keeping a frown from his face. The guests were adequate with the knives, which was impressive if they had only recently been introduced to the form, but they wouldn't be placing any higher than the middle of the rankings for teens at the Sky Alliance competition. Their sword warmup, following the Ki pattern, was even less impressive — then he remembered that they had a different form altogether.

Time to see that after some sparring, he decided. It would only be humiliating to expose them to all eyes now if it turned out Tenar was mistaken, and denying guests face would shame them all.

He paired everyone up, putting Ryu with a fourteen-year-old, and Shigan with a sixteen-year-old with good if not spectacular skills. "Now," he ordered, and swept his eyes down the line.

Good form, good form, a startlingly fast move from Shigan which the cousin barely blocked. Second Uncle kept moving, coming last to Ryu and her partner, who stood there, the Ki youngster wringing his hand.

"What happened?" he said, striding over to them.

"Ryu here knocked my sword away in two strikes." The fourteen-year-old's voice squeaked in indignation.

"Sorry, sorry," Ryu said, blushing. She bowed, saying, "I didn't mean to . . ."

Second Uncle waved that off, saying sternly to the fourteen-year-old, "This is sparring, not a child's game." He turned his head. "Matu, you've sparred with Ryu. Come show us."

Matu took one glance at his uncle's skeptical face, and with an air of *You'll see*, squared up to Ryu, who was a full head shorter than Matu and much lighter.

With a new cousin, Ryu would have held herself back, but with Matu she didn't have to. Matu gave her a twisted grin and whispered, "Show them."

Ryu's eyes widened.

"Now," the uncle said.

Glorying in having a wooden sword in hand again, Ryu whirled into attack — five moves later, Matu's sword went flying.

The cousins stared, mouths open, eyes wide. Matu stood off to the side smiling as he enjoyed watching the reactions.

Second Uncle pointed with his own sword at his son, a big boy of nearly nineteen. The son walked up slowly, still trying to translate that blurring attack as a fluke, squared up, and when the signal came, he came in hard.

Ryu was driven back two steps as she blocked and deflected two cracking blows, then Essence surged up in her, and she followed with three rapid attacks impossible to see — and stopped with her blunt wooden blade at the son's throat.

The uncle cleared his throat. "Perhaps you would care to demonstrate your sword form for us?"

Ryu cast a glance at Shigan, who grinned as he jumped to his feet. The two of them snapped and flowed through Redbark, the cousins' eyes drawn to Shigan's handsome face, his perfectly proportioned body graceful and lethal. But the uncle, with vastly more experience, saw the latent power in Ryu's shorter, lighter body — sensing, though he didn't quite see it, the glow of Essence, far more powerful than anyone in the family had access to except for Grandfather.

After that Ryu went through all the cousins, winning against each of them. It wasn't until they began sparring two on one that she faltered, feeling that light-headed sense of having expended too much Essence. Her hand was slippery. Her wrist bent awkwardly on a hard block and she dropped her sword.

The two big cousins backed away instantly as Second Uncle came forward, saying, "I think that's enough."

"Good bout, Redbark Brother Ryu," the biggest cousin said with slow, still-bewildered respect, eyes wide.

The other bobbed his head in agreement, and in the background someone whispered the word *qilin*. And then, what sounded like ". . . fan form."

Fan form?

Ryu blushed, figuring she'd heard wrong, and regretting being out of practice. She worked her wrist, completely unaware of the speculative glances the older cousins were sending her way as she retreated to the back of the lines. She wondered why none of them had used Essence — was she not good enough? No, it wasn't that. If she hadn't, she still would have won most of those fights, except against the big cousin who seemed to be Second Uncle's son. Was it possible they didn't sense Essence? No, that wasn't it, either. The big cousin did, though not very much.

After that there was general sparring — and no one used Essence. Second Uncle said nothing about Essence, either. His only comment was that Matu had improved quite a bit. "There's a snap to your movements that echoes our guests' excellent Redbark Sword form. Keep learning it!" The uncle turned from Matu's red face and pleased grin to glance at the sky, and grunted at the massing clouds. "We should have just enough time to shoot five arrows apiece. Then, if it rains, we'll have grappling in the second barn. Run!"

Three targets had been set up against the back wall of the barn. Ryu no longer felt she had to pretend to be bad. She was out of practice, but came respectably close to the bull's eye. Shigan, she noted, had superb form—he hit the center five times, but frowned, not pleased with either his speed or precision.

Matu shot equally well, as did most of the cousins. Then, as predicted, the rain began. Second Uncle had them collect the arrows and run around to the front of the barn.

Ryu trailed behind. She'd been watching them from the hayloft for a couple weeks now. Was she going to be included or not?

She was. Second Uncle paired her with cousins her own size, against whom she held her own. She was too tired to pull Essence, so she shook her head when the bigger boys offered to spar with her, waving her right wrist.

They were dismissed for the midday meal, and Second Uncle went to report to the rest of the clan elders. They listened in growing surprise to the account of the sword sparring. He finished by saying, "I feel we ought to wait for Grandfather before we invite the Redbarks to join us, but if they do, our standing will rise in everyone's eyes."

"Let's see what Grandfather says," First Aunt Ki Meilu stated. "If he comes down."

Grandfather was their elder, who ever since his wife died spent all the winters—and occasionally the rest of the year— high in the mountains on the other side of the lake, cultivating in peace. Though two of the uncles were now grandfathers, and Grandfather Ki Lin was actually a great-grandfather many times over, everyone knew that "Grandfather" could only refer to one man.

Over the next few days, Ryu tried to adjust to the dramatic shift in the way the Ki family treated her. Not so much the ones under ten. But the adults now noticed her. Even more unsettling, she could sense them talking about her when she happened upon a group of them. Afraid of the questions they might ask, she avoided encounters, and when she could not, she was polite but monosyllabic, and the adults did not press her, having settled it among themselves that only a terrible tragedy could have set two young people loose in the world to fend for themselves.

She also learned why Matu's parents were not there: his father had been taken by the imperials and sentenced to work in a mine, and his mother had gone to seek him and rescue him if she could. Then Matu's paternal grandparents went. None had returned.

Much more difficult to avoid were the female cousins ranging from a year or so older than Ryu to twenty or so.

They began offering her snacks, and tea, and footbaths. Two of them even cornered her, giggling in high voices, one twitching her shoulders and the other toying with her long braids as they offered to tend her laundry — to mend anything she wanted mended — to listen to stories of her exploits.

She was already wary of them, after seeing how they flocked around Shigan. It wasn't that the boys she was used to living among had ignored looks. They hadn't. But the way girls either praised or dissected everyone's features was completely new to her, and when she heard the same girl flattered to her face and then disparaged behind her back in a lightning-swift shift in tone, it left her mentally reeling. This, she thought, related to Mother's lessons about beauty.

Four dawns after that day at the lakeside, she met with Shigan and Matu at the barn as usual. Matu joined them with renewed enthusiasm and the three sparred until they were dripping. The two boys took a water break as the rest of the younger generation began turning up.

But Ryu disappeared. Several girl cousins appointed themselves a search party — with no success. "Redbark Brother Ryu must have gone for another long run," one declared.

While finishing up buns to be steamed, Ki Tenar overheard that not ten breaths after she glimpsed Ryu slinking into the kitchen through the back door. Ordinarily she went dutifully to practice from early morning food preparation, for it was important to her mother that she keep up her knife skills. But when she heard her shriller cousins calling for Ryu amid gales of giggles, she retreated to the kitchen, and peered into the side-room off the well, where sure enough, she found Ryu drying dishes with Petal.

Tenar said, "My cousins are looking for you."

Ryu flushed to the ears. "I know. I, ah, thought I would help Petal."

"Shall I tell them that?" Tenar asked.

She—and Petal—didn't think a person could get any redder than Ryu already was without blood bursting out their ears, but it happened as Ryu said, "Yes. No! I don't want to be a bad guest, but . . ."

Tenar sighed. "They don't mean any harm. Truly they don't. If they have been teasing you, it's habit."

"I don't know what they want," Ryu mumbled, not quite daring to say, "They get too close."

Tenar gave a short laugh. "They want what most people want, to become . . ." She paused and eyed Ryu. ". . . friends with a future hero. It's a mark of great respect. Their way of trying to get your attention is by flirting."

Flirting! Ryu knew what it meant—vaguely. It was part of the mystery of what the poets called *matters of clouds and rains*, which to her suggested the tears and deaths of songs about love affairs (usually ending drearily), a subject she had no interest in whatsoever. Her nose wrinkled as if she'd just stepped into a privy where someone and their digestive organs had recently had a violent disagreement. "I wish they'd flirt with Shigan."

"Oh, they are." Tenar smothered a laugh. "It's just that you're now coming in for your share, a little. It's going to happen, Ryu," she added earnestly. "When you get older, and especially if you become a hero. You might as well learn how to deal with admiration before it's any more serious than a sly smile and a comment from others as young as yourself."

"I'd rather hide," Ryu mumbled.

"You are the guest," Tenar said, bowing with clasped hands, gallant wanderer-style. "Whatever you prefer."

She went out.

"She's right," Petal said.

"Right?" Ryu replied, as Petal handed off a bowl to be dried. "About what?"

"Getting used to being a Talent."

"I'm not a Talent," Ryu mumbled. She struggled too hard to be a talent. In the stories, talents did everything perfectly their first time. Effortless, easy.

Petal tipped her head. "According to the aunt who teaches the children, you are. All the elders agree. That much I overheard while waiting for the instruction for the children. They even wanted me to show them what I'd learned from you. Though I told them what you said on the ship. That I need to learn the foundations."

Ryu lightly slapped her own cheek. "I need to teach you that. I'm sorry I forgot."

Petal said, "It's all right. I want to learn their basics first. But Tenar is right about learning how to be around flirting."

"I don't want to flirt. And none of it is real anyway," Ryu burst out, disgusted at the very idea. "I hear what those girls say to each other, and then about each other. It's all . . . all fox and rat." She snarled her fingers together, then snapped them apart. "No, worse, because fox and rat honestly hate each other, but these are sweet one day, and nasty the next."

Petal lifted a shoulder. "You'll hear a lot of that sweet talk if you are around people. Especially when they want to attract someone of a higher rank."

"Rank? In?"

"Among each other. People do ranking. About everything, not just birth. Looks. Skill. It's human," Petal said. "Were you really raised in a temple?"

Ryu was going to say *small village*, but swallowed the words. "Something like," was all she said.

Petal gave a decisive nod. "I thought Redbark might be halfway to a temple sect. Following the Snow Crane, yes? I have heard they don't even eat chicken."

"Some will eat no bird, others will only eat birds that don't fly," Ryu said, as a troop of cousins brought in dishes from the adults' eating area. She fell into the shaman's cadences as she added, "The Snow Crane taught that migrating birds are the most worthy of creatures. They fly in orderly flocks, never abandoning one another. That is virtue. If one dies, they cry in mourning, which is righteous. They do not attack other creatures, but fly with reeds in their beaks, which is knowledge, and every year they go from north to south and then from south to north, which is faith. These are the five attributes that even humans cannot always display. . . ."

She noticed then the others' silence, and blushed. She finished drying her last bowl and set it down, saying, "Let me know when you're ready to learn Redbark Sword form."

Petal said, "I will."

Ryu made her way to the library, where she slid into a nook with an old scroll of gallant wanderer tales that she had never seen before.

When the cheery yellow jasmine bloomed and the great white swans that wintered at the north end of the lake near the hot springs took to the air with their young families to fly south, Grandfather Ki—once known throughout the gallant world as Sagacious Blade—came down from his isolation to rejoin the family.

Rowing his boat out into the deep waters got harder each year. He was aware of the weight of years in all his bones and joints, and as he rowed toward the opposite bank, the sky filled with low, wispy clouds that diffused the light to indistinct gray. He wondered if this visit might be his last.

He blinked, but it was not age making the world difficult to see. The edges of the lake, distinct when he set out, had been entirely obscured by mist drifting toward him. It was so very quiet, so peaceful, even still as the fog gently enclosed him. He wondered if, after all these years, he would lose his way and expire there on the lake, rowing in circles.

If so, there were worse deaths, caught between sky and water, he told himself, and yet his wrists trembled, and his lungs drew in more air to aid his laboring heart: his body was not at all ready for that.

Overhead he heard the cries of swans, then one long cry, both curiously evocative of command and of reassurance. He sat back, resting the oars, as he cocked his head and gazed up into the featureless white of fog.

Out of it materialized the graceful shape of a long-necked bird. A swan? No, a crane, the largest he had ever seen. It glided in and out of the wreathing drifts of vapor, circling around him in a manner no crane had ever yet done. He was not entirely surprised when the crane's shape dissolved, and then reformed into a long, slim personage dressed in undyed cotton robes, who settled into the opposite end of the boat.

Was this the dream before death? Shock seized his nerves, then pooled in his stomach. Belatedly he cast aside the oars and dropped to his knees in the dampness at the bottom of his boat, which was as old as he was, if not older. He tried to prostrate himself—only right when a heavenly being manifests to you—but the figure put out a hand, drawing him to his seat again.

"I am only a learner." The voice was not unlike the hoot of

a wind instrument, mellow and quite kindly. "I was sent."

Before the sun set, excited cries echoed through the house, "Grandfather is here!"

The family stampeded out, drawing the guests with them. They gathered in a half-circle, elders at the front, younger family behind, and all bowed as a lone white-haired figure rowed into shallow waters. Then the huskiest men dashed forward to pull the boat well up onto the pebbled shore so that their elder would not have to get his feet wet.

He stepped on shore, a short, neat man of venerable age, his thin hair worn in a topknot, his equally thin beard braided.

"Grandfather! Welcome back!"

"Grandfather, I'm sixteen now — they said I can go to Sky Alliance if I . . ."

"Grandfather, grandfather, see, see? I lost a tooth!"

"You look tired, Grandfather. Will you stay for good now?"

Aunt Meilu's voice rose above the others, scolding with heartfelt concern: "It is too cold up there, Grandfather. If you were ill, how would we know to come nurse you?"

"It's well, it's well, niece," Grandfather said, patting her hand with his gnarled fingers. "Up there, I am closer to your great-aunt, and if some summer one of you comes up to find my old bones on my pallet, bare to the sun and stars, why, that's as it should be."

He was as kind as ever, but his voice trembled a little, and a sheen of tears was seen in his eyes — but before anyone got up the courage to ask, it vanished, replaced by the crinkles of good humor as he greeted the elders, then their own offspring, and then the grandchildren and great-grandchildren, looking into each face with a searching gaze full of interest — seeing traces of departed loved ones as he listened to their tumble of words.

He came at last to Shigan and Ryu, who were brought forward proudly by Matu and Tenar. Grandfather looked at them with curiosity tinged with a certain pity, thinking that these two fresh young faces apparently had no idea what sort of watchers had taken an interest in them. No one ever had an easy life, nor necessarily a long one, when greater powers bestirred themselves to interfere.

Though the Ki clan's main ancestral shrine was on Eagle Island, they had a shrine on Ten Leopards as well, and Grandfather Ki conducted a ritual there, attended by the entire household.

The following day, he oversaw a practice on a foggy morning. Ryu and Shigan both thought everyone had always worked their hardest, but under Grandfather Ki's benevolent eye, there was a hum to their movements never before seen.

When Second Uncle dismissed the younger ones, they raced off toward the enticing smells of a meal like arrows from a bow. But the elders plus the one truly expert cousin remained behind in a deliberate way that caused Ryu to linger.

She didn't hide, nor did she presume to join them. She stayed where she was, at a distance, uncertain. She was about to turn away when a group of four broke apart. She saw that they had been distributing something between them.

Fans? Yes, it looked like fans in the uncertain light and drifting vapors. Then, as she watched, the four—including the cousin—lined up before Grandfather Ki, and performed a slow, deliberate martial arts form. But Ryu was skilled enough to recognize the difficulty of that drill in the slight sidesteps, the leans and twirls: they were getting inside the reach of an imagined opponent holding steel. Yes. They turned and performed the drill again, this time each at one of the stuffed targets. This time the fans tapped with smart force at various parts of the body.

This was a martial arts form that targeted acupoints. Though Ryu had learned plenty about nerve conduits, Mother had taught her very little about acupoints. She had figured some of them out through helping Muin who came back bruised so often from encounters with Yulin, especially those first couple of years, until he was adept enough to defend himself.

The Ki family had a secret form! Well, not really *secret*. But clearly not everyone was taught it.

She turned away thoughtfully.

SEVENTEEN

THAT NIGHT, SHIGAN DANCED for them at last.

He had deflected invitations with a joke, a yawn, or by moving to the guzheng and whirling out a storm of chords, encouraging others to dance.

All this changed when Grandfather Ki, who had been gazing out the window at the full Phoenix Moon glowing with silvery light, picked up his flute, shut his eyes, and began a simple melody. It was so pure, so exquisite that the entire clan quieted, and Shigan's head snapped around. He stilled, sensitive as a creature with antennae.

Grandfather played the same melody through, and the more thoughtful of the clan heard a gentle rebuke in the plaintive notes, a reminder that true cultivation was more than just martial arts expertise: music was one of the great arts.

To Shigan, music—good music—was far more than that.

The melody altered again, the mood shifting from yearning to playful. Grandfather Ki's white head wagged and bobbed as he added adding flourishes that begged the limbs to move.

Shigan rose, eye half-shut. He picked up a fan from one of the side tables, lifted his arms, spun on one foot, and with snap of the fan he leaped and twirled as easily as a leaf drifting on the wind, began to dance.

Anyone who responds to comeliness would have watched him at least a little, but within a few airy steps, in which he seemed to float in the air, he could have had a face like a fish for all the attention anyone paid to it. Except that his face was a part of the whole, a celebration of grace, beauty, and strength. The flute, the crack and rush of the fan in counterpoint, and the rustle of Shigan's clothing were the only sounds. The family sat motionless; they always respected skill, but here was skill plus the ineffable, often defined as art. Or as divine.

When Grandfather lowered the flute, three boys continued the rhythm with drums, Second Uncle Yslu had brought out a guzheng, and other instruments were fetched, one by one joining to the compelling rhythm of the drums that was both challenge and invitation.

Shigan set the fan aside and snatched up two knives from the rack on the wall. His dance became a whirl of glittering steel.

The Ki clan shouted their approval of what they took to be a compliment to their particular form. As it was. But Shigan's dance was more than mere flattery. Yes, it was a celebration of skill: it was also, though none of them could know this, a dance of defiance aimed at someone they had never met, and never would meet.

Ryu stared, unable to look away, her entire body afire with sensations she had no words for. Embarrassment first, at the sheer intensity. Soon gone, for these feelings were larger than that, as if the sun had sprung out of the sky and stood beside her.

At the end he leaped up into the air in a perfect split, toes pointed, the knives clashing overhead. The drummers pounded to an enthusiastic finish, the other instruments halted. He came down lightly, and grinned, breathing fast, his black eyes reflecting the golden lamplight. The family clapped; the older girls crowded around Shigan, shrill with praise and then whirled about—"Watch me!"—and they began to dance.

Ryu closed them all out, aware that she didn't have to define those feelings. Now the dance was a memory. She could compass memory. She could take it out and relive it, and maybe understand all the feelings, one by one, over time.

A month later they lined up and Second Uncle Yslu chose those who were to go to the Sky Alliance competition. Tenar had been edged out by a cousin a year older and more experienced with the fighting daggers, Ryu was sorry to see;

as yet she did not have enough experience to discern that Tenar was quite satisfied to remain at home.

The chosen ones, along with the guests, happily prepared to depart. Those not chosen turned back to the day's routine, their ears ringing with exhortations to work hard. There were far fewer complaints and wry looks than there might have been over winter, because Grandfather was there, speaking consoling words.

Under his benevolent eye all his progeny had worked hard and studied earnestly, trying to their various abilities to cultivate their better selves. Shigan had spent as much time at the archery targets as he could, no longer distracted by girls competing for his attention; Ryu, too, had found her days easier, spending her free time running along the lake shore as birds swooped and dived over the rippling water. There had been music at night, and sometimes dancing. Even Petal benefitted from everyone's determination to strive, as she was incorporated into the children's learning at last.

The only one who did not participate was Yaso, who used these weeks to roam the ripening meadows and mountain slopes to gather healing herbs, such as fresh ginger root, and high on a cliff under a redbark tree, a single precious Longevity Root, harvested from a group of three.

The scouts reported the Eagle Island ship's approach. It was time to depart.

The night before they left, Grandfather sent for Ryu.

"When you are ready," he said, "come to me in the mountain to study Essence."

Ryu made the gallant bow, sighing inwardly: when she was ready had to mean she wasn't yet. Then remembering what she'd seen on that foggy day, asked, "May I learn that fan form?"

He stroked his long white beard. "We will see what you have learned."

He glanced at Yaso. She missed that as she bowed again and spoke her thanks. Inwardly she sighed even harder.

Early on a sunny spring morning those chosen to go to the Sky Alliance competition dressed alike in green tunics, with green kerchiefs tied around their heads instead of headbands. One carried the Eagle Island Sect's banner, which was green with a brown eagle on it, brown streamers fluttering from the banner as they marched down the mountain singing, and made their way to the single pier, where the ship from Eagle Island lay waiting, sides lined with expectant faces.

Yaso's ginger had been dried and ground to make tea, and put into a flask. Before Matu approached the ramp, he drank the bitter brew down. Then, hiding his extreme dislike, he boarded with the others and followed them to the deck to greet distant cousins and old friends among the rest of the sect.

Petal followed behind Matu, quietly watchful. Yaso observed benignly from behind them. No one had ever thought of stuffing Matu with Longevity-Root-laced ginger before a ship journey before.

The ship put out to sea. Matu paled, but in spite of teasing from some of his Eagle Island cousins, he remained upright, though at the side. Following Yaso's advice, he kept his gaze on the horizon and managed to keep his stomach from revolt.

Second Uncle Yslu, in charge of Ten Leopards Island's competitors, sought out the Eagle Island chief, and introduced the guests.

Ryu was the youngest there, earning some skeptical glances from the Eagle Island gallants. She had expected that, and contrived to stay out of everyone's way as much as she could during the two days of the journey.

Matu did well until the last day, when they woke to a restless gray sea full of white waters, ominous clouds riding in on a rising wind. He was swallowing frequently as the ship rolled and bucked its way toward an island jutting on the horizon. It appeared to be roughly three times the size of Ten Leopards Island, which was basically a single forested mountain with its top blown off during the long-ago days when the world was filled with embattled dragons and demons.

Matu kept his gaze on the island, gulping now and then. A few of the bigger boys made puking noises and called "Watch out," and "Ware spew!" until chased off by the Eagle Island chief.

Yaso came up and gave Matu another cup of hot tea, then took one of his hands and pressed a thumb into the underside of his forearm above his wrist, staying there until the ship reached the calmer waters of the island's little bay.

"Is this Sky Mirror Island?" Ryu asked.

"No," one of the cousins said, in the tone of the seasoned traveler initiating the raw country visitor. "Oh, you'll hear some call it Sky Island, but this is where everyone meets, according to an old treaty – it's neutral ground. You can't see it, but there's a much bigger bay around that promontory and half a day's sailing north. That's a trade town, run by independent merchants. They guard it themselves. The imperials don't come around much, mostly watching for Westerners this far north. The real Sky Mirror Island is the sect's stronghold. They don't share it with anyone."

Matu was the first off the ship, Ryu squeezed in the jumble right behind. And so, at last, she arrived at her first actual gallant wanderer martial arts competition.

Everyone headed toward the open temple at the head of the trail, and one by one bowed to the image of the Fox God, champion of wanderers and freedom. Ryu stared up at the smiling fox-headed figure, liking his sly smile, and the way his pose expressed a sauntering liberty, three of his nine tails curling up around his sword arm. The other six curled up behind him in a way that suggested movement. In his left hand he carried a mask. A mask! The Fox God liked disguises. That heartened her!

Each newcomer lit one of the sticks of incense waiting in a fine vase, and then set the stick among all the others in a great sand vessel, bowed, and withdrew. Ryu followed Matu, mimicking his movements. Her eyes streamed from the thick swirls of incense as she rejoined the others.

Once they passed the temple, they headed up the trail toward a broad hollow between two low ridges, one of them heavily forested, the other, which stretched into the sea, mainly a tumble of rocks.

Some of the older teens began pointing out famous gallants, as the wind kicked up dust and fingered sleeves and tunic skirts.

"There's Mountain Tiger and his crescent spear!"

"I see Iron Tiger and Iron Ox . . ."

"There's Duck Bill Tang with his famous bow . . ."

"Is Lion's Mane here this year?"

Would that be Waoji Lion's Mane, the famous defender of justice? Ryu looked around quickly – until the answer came, "They say he's dead."

"Ayah! That's what they always say! If I had a boater for every time he's been reported dead, I could buy me a palace and a hundred song and dance boys. He's not dead – no one can beat him."

"You should ask the Sky Islanders."

"I did—but they just shrug."

"Oh, look, there's Chu . . . Hiya, Chu Gar! Back from the south? I was given a letter for you—given to me on Spring Peace Island . . ."

"Spear! Ayah, Righteous Spear! Did you see my brother?"

"Got a letter for you, right in my pack . . ."

Ryu tried to see everywhere at once, gaining an impression of mostly men, everyone speaking vernacular, their weapons not wrapped up or hidden, the way weapons were carried within the empire, but worn openly. Gradually she noticed other differences: most wore clothes of dull, undyed, or variations on blue, which she knew was the cheapest and easiest dye available as indigo grows everywhere. But here and there strutted wanderers in bright colors.

Some also wore their hair down, or half pulled up, braided and decorated with feathers or decorative clasps. Ryu gazed after them, wondering how they managed all that decoration without servants to do it for them. All her life the first thing she did on waking was wind up her thick hair into a topknot, before she even rinsed her mouth, a habit that had been universal at the training fortress.

Most were men around Father's age or younger. But not all. This one was graying, that one so young he barely had a wisp of beard. Teens there were a-plenty. Ryu saw three women chatting together, as one of them handed off something that looked like sealed letters. Of course gallant wanderers would send letters, too!

Ryu liked the sight of these three women, one wearing a sword, one long knives at her back, and one with a bow and arrows as well as a knife. But it seemed women were few among the total.

Then there were the ones wearing the black and silver panther masks. A few people stared after them, and Ryu noted people giving them wide berth, but everywhere else people clasped their fists in the gallant bow, and talked freely, without deferring the way ordinary people deferred to nobles and officials.

"The masked ones," Ryu said. "Are they . . ." She hesitated to say the name in case she was wrong.

Matu's usually pleasant face tightened as he looked away. "Shadow Panther sect," he said flatly. "Masked sects usually don't come. A lot of their competitions are fights to the death."

Ryu stared after three of the sauntering figures, amazed to

actually be in the presence of the infamous Shadow Panthers, who were in a lot of stories from recent years, more often villainous than not. One consistent element across all the stories: they did a *lot* of fighting.

Matu lowered his voice. "Everyone is welcome, as long as they bow to the god, which means they will respect the competition truce. And the first rule is, no duels to the death. Uncle told us when we first came that the competition is for improvement."

"Maybe they want to improve?" Shigan observed. "They certainly could improve what's said about them."

The cousins snickered.

Second Uncle Yslu cleared his throat for their attention. "Stay together until we get everyone entered into the list," he cautioned.

One of the older cousins pelted up.

"Chief says we ought to get the tent up now. We need more hands. The wind demons are awakening."

Ryu sighed inwardly. But she wanted to be a good guest. "I can help."

The cousin clasped his hands in a quick bow, and Ryu followed him. They darted between a lot of people running back and forth as competitors struggled to get their tents erected. Big splats of rain warned of a coming deluge.

The elders of the Eagle Clan had used one of the waiting carts to haul the big items up to a cleared area near the forested ridge. There was little there except for some small constructions, no more than a roof with four supports, to keep the rain off low brick stoves for wok and steaming over low fires. Tents in various states of readiness flapped and rippled in the rising wind, as people ran about with ropes and mallets and tent poles, shouting and swearing.

The Eagle Clan chief stood at the side, yelling directions at people who obviously only helped set up a tent once a year, if that. Ryu discovered Yaso at her shoulder. Together they began doing it the army way, working so quickly that the others took notice.

Ryu had never actually worked with Yaso before. She was surprised to discover that the long, lanky orderly was enormously strong; Yaso held the wooden support with seeming effortlessness as Ryu swiftly stretched the ropes to the pegs and then used the mallet to sink them. Everywhere else around the circle it took two of the bigger boys and even two men to hold the poles still against the wind.

As they moved to their second pole, Ryu looked up at Yaso. "Are you using Essence?" she asked quietly.

"Of course," Yaso said. "I told you, bring it with your breath."

Ryu banged away with the mallet, suppressing the impulse to say, *That's what I've been doing!*

As though she'd spoken, Yaso looked down at her with a kindly expression. "You will one day trust the Essence to flow through you. But you must learn how to do it and learn also its consequences —"

Second Uncle stepped up, nodding approvingly. "It looks to me like you were in the military?"

"Orderly," Ryu said, for that was the pertinent part right now. "Both of us."

The chief raised his voice. "Follow these two!"

More rain urged everyone to put in their best effort, and the subject of Essence dropped — Ryu letting it go with a sense of frustration. She hated being told she still had to learn something she thought she'd been learning. She avoided Yaso as everyone bustled around to get the tent erected, and when they came together again, the former orderly did not bring it up.

In spite of the wind, they got the tent set up, the ropes taut, the panels tight and flat. By then everyone had gathered, and formed a line to shift all their gear and supplies inside.

They were bringing in the last baskets when the rain let loose. Bad weather or good, the Sky Island contest always followed a certain schedule. Some unpacked and began food preparations while others leveled the ground within the tent, preparing sleeping places and stacking folding tables and mats. The young people all did what they were told, aware that there would be a big feast that evening, contributed to by all the clans.

It poured until the second half of Horse hour, after which everyone left their tents, slopping around in mud as they began bringing supplies to the huge open pavilion at the other end of the tent city. It had a roof with upswept corners, on each of which three carvings sat to ward bad luck, bad spirits, and demons: one figure with wings, one a land creature, and one aquatic.

Beneath the pavilion roof was a floor made of fine, fitted wood that Sky Island apprentices were busy cleaning and polishing.

As the sun began to dip below the western hills, from all the tents came lines of sect members, bearing mats and their contributions to the feast. This included the Shadow Panthers, carrying racks of delicious smelling yams that had clearly been cooking all day.

Upon the dais in back (which was also a kang) sat a half-circle of chairs. Ryu discovered that the gallant wanderers had a hierarchy, but it was predicated on martial merit rather than imperial merit or birth.

In the center of the half-circle, the place of highest honor, sat the chief of the Sky Island sect, and at his right last year's prize winner. Then all the chiefs of the sects in an order dictated by past wins of sect members. Every sect had at least a headband or a sash in a similar color, brought out for this feast. Most had robes that matched their banners. Only independents like Ryu and Shigan wore their everyday clothes.

Ryu and Shigan sat with Matu.

"Are there always this many gallants without a sect?" Ryu asked.

Shigan had been thinking the same.

Matu glanced around. "No—yes. It looks like there are a lot more than usual."

"Isn't the competition open to all?" Shigan asked. "I was expecting ten times the number I see."

"Yes, it's open, but the sects do the same as we did, hold their own competitions and only send their best. Also, this isn't the only competition, just one of the most famous. On account of Waoji Lion's Mane having been the winner for years, then a judge. Before he disappeared."

"Nobody told us we were being judged," Ryu said. "I guess if we were terrible, Second Uncle, or someone, would have told us to go away?"

"No, you could stay on Ten Leopards as a guest if Grandfather invited you. My sister spoke for you until he arrived. But Second Uncle would have told you if he thought you needed more training," Matu said. "Before you got on the ship."

Shigan put his fists on his knees. "I had no idea. We shall have to try not to embarrass you."

Ryu said, "What will we be seeing tomorrow?"

Matu used up the rest of the mealtime to explain how this

year's judges were no doubt busy making up the competition lists, initially by age group and weapon. The contests would go on until all in a given group but one were eliminated, then there would be a new list made up, and so on. At the end, anyone of any age and weapon could face anyone. "But we'll be watching by then."

After the dinner, each sect took away its dishes for cleaning and readying for morning. Some youngsters ran back and forth pushing polishing cloths over the floor, after which those inclined for entertainment gathered in a huge circle. Clapping and shouts propelled a popular storyteller to the middle of the circle.

"Would you like to hear the story of Bi the Whirlwind and Waoji Lion's Mane, when the two of them defeated the evil Yulin Enk?"

Ryu jerked upright at the name "Yulin," as the listeners howled their approbation, clapping and drumming their hands.

"I wasn't there, but my Third Brother was, and this is what he saw . . ."

Ryu listened enthralled as the storyteller recounted the tale of the famous pair of gallants who took on the private army of a corrupt tax commissioner. It was funny and exciting and sad and exhilarating—sad, Ryu reflected, at how many ordinary folk died in the fighting, yet it seemed that Tax Commissioner Yulin ("fourth generation cousin to the governor!") got away.

After the storyteller finished, a group came forward with musical instruments and offered to play for anyone wanting to dance. The lute player seemed to be the leader; when he began, the others joined, a little ragged at first, but they found their rhythm and plied away enthusiastically as people got up to whirl, stamp, and leap.

Matu leaned over to Shigan. "You're a far better dancer than any of these. Why don't you get up?"

Ryu could only see Shigan's profile as he said, "I need the right music."

His tone was even, his profile unrevealing. Ryu sensed his scorn rather than heard it for music that sounded wonderful to Ryu. Oh, maybe that boy on the pipa was a bit behind the others, and two of the flute players hit a few false notes, but the overall effect was stirring. But then, she knew she was ignorant about such things.

She stayed where she was, happy to listen, as her mind

began to wander back to that question of Essence. Letting it flow through her. She thought she was very good at that now, after all those mornings of sitting with Yaso and breathing Essence in and out. But that was because she was sitting and concentrating on breathing it in and out.

When she was fighting, she needed the burn of Essence in her core so she wouldn't have to concentrate on breathing it in and out, because she was concentrating on the bout. She'd need two brains, one to pay attention to Essence and the other to the fight, wouldn't she?

She sighed, feeling very much like a beginner: if cultivation was a climb toward a pinnacle of perfection, she'd just been booted back down the trail.

Her mood was somber when she followed the rest of the Eagle Island group back to their tent, and settled down to sleep.

EIGHTEEN

THE SKY WAS BLUE, the ground merely damp the next morning. She woke to others already stirring. She faced southwest, mentally petitioned the Crane God to protect Mother, Father, and Ul Keg, then joined the line for wash water.

At least Muin and Yskanda had to be doing well. This was Muin's fifth year at Loyalty Fortress. Yulin was supposed to be gone by now, which meant Muin and his friends would be the leaders of the fifth years — the leaders of all the cadets. One last year, and then on the path to greatness!

That was a cheering idea. She wondered where he would be next spring. If only she could find out, she might be able to find a way to him? Or even make her way back to Sweetwater . . .

No, that had to be after she had some merit to report, enough merit so that Mother would not be disappointed that Ryu wasn't going to be a scholar. The idea of memorizing lists and lists of affinities and conduits was unbearable, the more ever since she'd realized that some of the books Mother had acquired so slowly and painfully, and studied so hard, were considered old. Not old in the good way, but outdated.

"Ryu?"

She looked up, startled, at Shigan's face.

"They're calling us," Shigan said. "What's wrong?"

"Nothing," she said quickly, and picked up the wooden blade she'd borrowed from the Ten Leopards family.

His lips quirked as he twirled his own borrowed blade. "Of course you'd say that. Why did I even ask?" He laughed, and added, "We're over here with the apprentices. Matu says none of them have earned hero names yet." He pointed across the broad expanse, which now had targets set up at one end, divided off by rope-rails to keep people from wandering in front of arrows, and elsewhere, various groups milling around, weapons in hand.

Ryu was distracted as a pair of Shadow Panthers walked by, hands on the hilts of their swords. One wore only a fur vest with no shirt over voluminous striped riding trousers and boots, his hair pulled up in a high horsetail of braids, revealing a tattoo of an extended panther claw at the base of his neck, where it joined his shoulder.

Most of the Eagle Island sect had elected to fight with daggers, but there were two teens, both from Eagle Island, who preferred swords. Shigan and Ryu joined them, Ryu swinging her arms. She wished she could have warmed up, but of course if you're actually wandering around seeking injustice, and find it, you won't be able to ask a wicked villain to wait while you do your drills first. She would test herself by doing the competition without warming up.

She broke out of her reverie when the two Eagle Islanders gave Shigan a short nod, then looked her up and down with skepticism they did not bother to hide.

Ryu sighed inwardly, wishing she could put on a fake mustache to make her look older. Fifteen seemed centuries away, much less sixteen.

A horn blasted suddenly, followed by a gong so vigorously applied the sound bounced back from the hills behind the pavilion.

"Let us begin!" someone roared.

Close by, an older man with a paper stood by a little table at which a child of ten or eleven sat, brush poised, ink ready.

"Ver Goti of the Water Dragons facing Enau Fan, independent!"

Everyone in their group backed up, making a wide circle as Ver Goti and Enau Fan stepped into the ring. Both had real steel in hand.

The judge said, "Remember, drawing blood is grounds for instant rejection. If you compete with steel, you must demonstrate enough control not to break skin."

Both Ver and Enau clasped their hands in the gallant bow,

and began to fight.

Shigan and Ryu watched intently, as did everyone else. Enau came on fast and hard. Ver blocked, but Ryu sensed he was half a heartbeat behind, and as Enau's attack didn't let up, he retreated a few steps.

After a wild exchange, Enau made a plunging sweep, a dark bruise on the base of his neck revealed. No, that was not a bruise, it was a tattoo. Ryu focused on Enau's neck as the fight went on for another ten moves. There it was again—a panther's claw.

Then it was gone. Enau halted, the tip of his blade a finger's breadth from Ver's throat.

"Halt," the judge bellowed. "Enau wins!"

If Enau was part of the Shadow Panthers, why didn't he have a mask? Ryu didn't want to sound stupid by asking, and anyway everyone was watching the bouts. She shrugged away the question when she heard the judge bawl, "Shigan Fin of the Redbark Sect against Ban Tirig of the Old Marsh Sect!"

Shigan beat his opponent in fewer than ten moves, and retired to the winners' side, grinning over at Ryu.

Whether on purpose or not, she was second to last, put against a weedy boy of sixteen. He gripped a steel blade. She had her borrowed wooden blade.

The judge held up a hand. "Wood against steel—you can demand your partner match your weapon," he said to Ryu.

"It's all right," she mumbled.

And it was. By now she had a good sense of the others' skill, which was not much different from that of similarly aged cadets at Loyalty Fortress. She hadn't seen anyone use Essence, which surprised and dismayed her; maybe she ought to have expected that, after her experiences with the Ki family?

Her partner gave her a skeptical glance, but said nothing as they bowed to each other. He shook his blade, stamped his foot, and came on with an overhead strike. Ryu didn't need Essence. She moved from the hip, whirled her blade up, struck his blade at the precise angle at which his grip was weakest, and knocked the sword from his hand. The steel glinted in the air as it spun through the air.

People backed hastily away and it landed on the ground.

"Ryu wins!"

"I wasn't ready," the boy began, his voice cracking in disbelief.

"Ryu wins," the judge said again, louder. "Ze Nanyi of Sky

Island faces Shaoban Ys, independent."

That bout, the last of their group, lasted longer. Once Shaoban won, the judge began pairing the winners off, which was to go on until he had one name to turn in.

Ryu hoped that if she won her next bouts, she would be up against Shigan, so that they could get in some hard sparring, which would at least be fun, since it seemed she wasn't going to find an Essence warrior to watch and learn from. And it looked as if she would get her wish until the very end, when only four were left.

By then, Ryu's first partner had stopped glaring at her as if she'd cheated her way through that first win. She'd knocked two blades from hands in one or two blows, and the rest she fought longer, but no more than half a dozen moves. All these boys were stronger than she was; she knew she had to strike fast to win. She saw all their weaknesses in their first moves, and so she did not have to exert herself beyond her capacity, much less draw on Essence.

Then Shigan faced the biggest of their entire group, a boy named Sig Han Ar, whose age might be nineteen, but in all other respects he had a man's height and strength. Sig even had a small crop of black hairs on his chin, of which he was inordinately proud, the way he fingered it as he watched the bouts.

Sig and Shigan went at it with such vigor their wooden swords cracked on the air, causing people to wander over from other groups whose bouts were not as entertaining. Ryu was distracted by two of the black-and-silver masks showing up to watch. Sig was fast for such a big boy, and enormously strong, but Shigan was a little faster, his strikes cleaner after half a year of daily sweating through Heaven and Earth.

They fought for a while, until both were dripping, their faces crimson — though the spectators with inclinations toward beauty noted that Shigan was just as spectacularly handsome with the upper portion of his robe damp and clinging to his body, sweat flying off him.

They were both breathing like bellows when strength (and the advantage of three years of age and growth) edged out speed and Sig's blade slid up a magnificent block by Shigan but a heartbeat too slow, too unfocused, and stopped at Shigan's neck.

"Sig wins," the judge declared. And he added for the first time, "That was a very fine bout."

Everyone in the circle clapped. Ryu noted that a couple more young men had joined the two masks, all four whispering together.

Sig and Shigan bowed to each other, and as they moved to the bucket to get some water, Sig said, "How old are you?"

"Sixteen. No, eighteen," Shigan said. "I keep forgetting to count."

Sig laughed as he pulled off his headcloth to wipe his face, then tied it back on. "Get a couple more years on you, and I wouldn't bet on myself against you."

Shigan bowed again, then moved to the bucket, as Ryu looked at his back, wondering why she'd never heard a consistent age from him. Maybe he was like Muin and letters, only with numbers?

Ryu's name was called — and it was time to concentrate.

More people had come around to watch. She wondered if the pair without the masks, standing with a Shadow Panther, had that tattoo. She had to shut them out and focus.

Her partner was a head and a half taller, staring at her with unwinking assessment. She breathed in, pulling Essence from her core . . . and went on the attack. His feint hummed past her ear. She sidestepped and retaliated, fast as a hummingbird against a tiger. Tap to the knee, tap to the opposite elbow, distracting him — and there was the tip of her sword against his heart.

A shout rang against the far hills. She blinked, her attention widening to those around her. She caught the word "Redbark" here and there as she bowed to her opponent and then moved to the water bucket, desperately thirsty.

"I've never heard of Redbark." One of the two without masks who'd been with the Shadow Panther followed her to the water. "Where is your base?"

"We're the only ones left," she said, inwardly testing the idea that Shigan had joined First Brother Muin in that word "our."

"What happened? Who was your master? I ought to have heard of him."

Usually people stopped there, or she managed to get away, but she was hemmed in by others crowding around — including the two masks.

But she'd had time to prepare for this question. Mother had explained once that the name Danno was from the northernmost islands, which had a lot of words from when the

Western Empire had ruled those islands centuries ago. It meant "loyal." The closest name in the southern dialect was Duin, which is why her parents had picked the rhyming Muin for First Brother's name—there would be a connection between Father and First Brother, but only the family would know of it.

She said, "Master Duin."

The gong's brassy hum shivered the air. Ryu was surprised to see long shadows. She and Shigan headed for the Eagle tent, where the smells of simmering garlic, onion, and sesame oil woke their appetites. "Is Duin a clan name or a personal name?" Shigan asked.

"Just the one name," Ryu said flatly.

"Ah," Shigan said. "Of course. Typical for a gallant wanderer." He was intensely curious, but hesitant about being the first to break the wall of reticence that he and Ryu had tacitly maintained.

Matu joined them, and when Petal brought food to them, Ryu said, "Aren't you hungry, too? Sit down with us?"

Petal flushed, turning her head with quick, habitually defensive movements, her one eye scanning the boys' faces for disapproval. When she was satisfied, she sat slowly next to Ryu.

The boys went on talking about their bouts; then Ryu leaned forward. "Did you notice that there are some people with that same tattoo that the Shadow Panthers have? Well, one," she amended.

Shigan turned a narrow look her way. "No. I didn't. What I've noticed is how many Shadow Panthers are here. I overheard someone saying to our judge that it was the first time they'd ever seen so many of them here."

Ryu grimaced, hoping that the fun wasn't going to be ruined by trouble.

But nothing happened during the remainder of the meal, or afterward, when once again those who wanted entertainment gathered at the pavilion, where people brought out their musical instruments. This time, two storytellers offered tales.

NINETEEN

THE NEXT MORNING DAWNED cloudy. Ryu looked for Yaso, who brought over hot water. "No rain, but warm," the orderly murmured.

Ryu grinned as she splashed her face. When the brassy tones of the gong reverberated between the hills, she and Shigan trudged up the field to a huge fenced corral for the riding competition, with a row of targets at one end.

The contestants in their group had to catch one of the loose horses, then ride down a marked path and shoot at the targets. The judging was twofold: speed and accuracy.

Bows and arrows waited on a rack. Ryu had just noted these when she was startled by her name—"Ryu of Redbark Sect and Xiu Ren of Ski Island!"

Ryu had no idea what to expect. When Xiu Ren took off toward the clump of horses nosing the ground, she did the same. The horses promptly scattered.

Now what? This sort of thing was considered useless trickery in the army, where there were always orderlies to ready your mount. Ryu spotted Xiu Ren sprinting alongside a horse, red-faced from effort. He caught a handful of mane, then jumped up to scramble onto the horse's back, his bow and quiver banging on his back.

Ryu was too short to do that. She fixed her gaze on a slow horse moving at a steady pace, took a few running steps, and vaulted in a somersault to her horse's back before she remembered her quiver. A shout from the spectators rose, but she didn't hear it.

Three arrows had fallen out, the rest were halfway to escape. She shook them back in and clutched at the horse's mane, then wrenched herself around. Bareback riding was another thing the army scorned, though many had practiced that anyway. Shigan certainly had, and the Mo cousins had mocked him for it.

She'd tried it once, and remembered to grip with her thighs so that the animal's spine didn't gouge her in places she didn't want to be gouged. But how to guide the horse without a rein? Luckily it seemed to be willing to follow Xiu Ren and the rest of the herd, at least long enough for her to grip the bow, pull an arrow and —

She winced when she discovered she'd already passed one target. There, respectably within the second ring, Xiu Ren's arrow quivered.

She aimed at the next target, but felt herself slipping without stirrups. She clamped her legs hard to the horse, which launched from an easy canter into a gallop. She shot, but there was no time to see where the arrow landed. The next target was already coming up.

Three more times she pulled and shot; Xiu Ren had already finished the course, and every one of his arrows had landed, though only one in the bull's eye. Ryu glanced back. None of hers had hit the bull's eye, but at least they were all in either the second or third ring. Except for the target she'd missed.

Still, she was not surprised when the judge bawled, "Xiu Ren wins!"

Ryu slipped off the horse as a couple of young Sky Islanders ran out to retrieve the fallen arrows, and pull the ones from the targets.

Ryu joined Shigan, who said, "You hit the targets, at least. Except the first."

"It was dismal," Ryu said, shrugging as she forced down the unexpectedly sharp disappointment in her failure. "You do better for Redbark!" She tried to laugh it all off.

Shigan grinned. "I will."

Ryu felt even more dismal when the next pair, a girl and a boy, both did really well, the girl, who seemed to be Ryu's age, with only one arrow in the second ring, but all the rest within the bull's eye.

However, the pair following were even worse than Ryu.

The taller one managed to get himself on the horse, but his arrows — shot with obvious strength — hit the edge of the target except for the last two. By then he was slewed around nearly shooting backwards, and the arrows sailed over the targets altogether.

His competitor was right behind him on his horse, his arrows hitting the target, but none near the inner three rings.

"You can tell who's big island and who's small," Shigan commented.

"Big and small?" Ryu asked. "Big and small islands? How can you tell?"

"Most big islands have horses. Most small ones don't. I know there are exceptions, but . . ." He opened his hand toward the next pair coming out. "You can really tell who's been riding a long time."

Ryu could see it now. As the competition went on, there were more like her, obviously not horse-trained all their lives. Shigan was definitely horse trained. He'd never talked about his early life, but she hadn't either. She'd thought entertainers didn't ride, but maybe they did — after all, how would they get around on islands big enough for them to earn money going from town to town? Entertainers rarely came to small islands like Imai, where pay was mostly likely to be in a meal. Or maybe some extra sitting mats.

At any rate, Shigan heard his name next. He gave a grunt and jogged over to pick up bow and quiver. When the judge called "Go!" he bolted, running fast. His competitor did, too, but veered toward the nearest horses . . . just to see them disperse in what the horses clearly thought a fun game.

But Shigan had chosen a specific horse. He knew exactly how to catch the animal's attention, and then veer away — making the animal curious. People whooped with laughter when it looked like he was running from a horse, but then he turned, vaulted, and in a breathtaking movement caught the animal's mane and landed on its back.

This was the wildest of the horses, the one that so far had successfully evaded all the humans. It tried for a few steps to get rid of the rider, but Shigan leaned in, smacked the animal's flank — and it shot forward like lightning from a cloud.

A huge shout rose from the watchers as the horse galloped around to the lane marked off for the targets, guided entirely by Shigan's knees as he nocked and readied an arrow. One breathless moment while he sat there poised, his form perfect from arrow to the opposite elbow pulled back so far his fingers were by his ear, then *spang!*

The arrow slammed into the very center of the target. *Spang, spang, spang!* Perfectly timed, each succeeding arrow shot straight to the bull's eye.

His competitor followed several horse lengths after, his shooting good—against anyone else he probably would have won—but everyone cheered Shigan as the judge called his name.

He soon reached Ryu's side. "I take it," she said, "you're a big islander."

"I am," he said gravely, but she sensed a smile, though she couldn't see it.

"Taught early to ride."

"I was four when I sat my first horse."

"And to dance."

"That, too," he said, still gravely, though the smile had faded.

She paused, her hesitation stretching to a silence. They had in their months together gradually come to talk about most everything, except their lives before Loyalty Fortress. She couldn't tell him about her own. It was a sacred promise. And she knew that it all would have to come out, or nothing.

So she didn't ask.

He didn't ask.

She looked away—straight into the eyes of one of the masks. The face below the mask didn't appear to be much older than First Brother Muin. The masked wanderer smiled at her; she couldn't tell if the smile was friendly or not, because the expression of the eyes was hidden, so she turned away, uncomfortable.

From then on she was conscious of the Shadow Panthers everywhere. It felt as if they were watching her. She saw two of them talking to that big boy Sig Han Ar, who'd fought so well against Shigan. The big boy smiled—from his expression, he seemed to be flattered at being picked out by the masked ones.

She scolded herself, of course, for imagining dire consequences to being picked out like that. *I'm just another urchin,* she told herself. *Nobody important. No one has ever heard of Redbark, so they can't be assigning any importance to it, either.*

But that impression stubbornly persisted, especially when

she glimpsed another of the ones with a tattoo on his neck talking to one of the masks while she was at the standing archery competition. She made it halfway through that before being defeated. She stayed to watch the Eagle Island cousins until they were defeated one by one.

"We should have practiced over winter," Matu said. "But we'll do better with knives!"

"I'm looking forward to that," Ryu said as they walked back.

The sun had set when Ryu met Shigan coming back from the privies. He said, "There's more Shadow Panthers than any other sect. Twice that, if you count the ones with the tattoos. I've been watching."

"Twice?" Ryu repeated. "Is that normal?"

"I asked Matu. He hasn't come often enough to know, but he gave me that 'everyone is welcome' talk they all do." Shigan looked up at the stars, then at Ryu. "Maybe I'm just jumpy, but if we were still cadets on a game, and I were captain, I'd be planning for Tiger Crouched in the Grass."

Ryu considered that. "Wouldn't the chiefs be aware?"

"Would they?" Shigan asked. "Everything I've seen, they train for individual defense, not . . ." He waved a hand that took in the entire island.

"Army maneuvering," Ryu said, nodding. "I noticed that during Second Uncle's training, but didn't think much about it. I think we ought to tell him. He'll know what to say."

Catching Second Uncle Yslu when he wasn't surrounded by others was unexpectedly difficult, as there always seemed to be one or another cousin wanting to talk to him, then there were people from other sects coming over to share a drink and chat.

Second Uncle Yslu's cheeks glowed after all these congenial toasts when the two finally caught him alone between the pavilion and the Eagle Island tent. It was fairly dark by then, Ghost Moon dominating the sky, and Phoenix Moon still hiding behind the horizon.

They halted halfway to the tent, as Shigan outlined what they'd both seen, in the proper report format that Instructor Shaz had insisted on. Ryu noted once again how much better he was at it than she was—not the principles, which she understood, but he didn't hem and haw and backtrack the way she couldn't seem to cure herself of doing when giving a report. Which was one reason why she hated talking any more than she absolutely had to.

Second Uncle Yslu listened, then he laughed. "Of course the judges have seen them. Talk about nothing else. In the morning, you ought to take a little walk up the other ridge. You'll see Sky Islanders on the watch, just out of sight. I heard the same about the promontory."

Shigan shot a glance at Ryu, his mouth twisted with self-mockery, and she knew he was thinking that here the two of them had assumed they were the only ones aware of what was going on.

"I don't think anyone expects trouble of the sort you're thinking of," Second Uncle went on reassuringly. "What would they get out of it? There's nothing here that anyone would want. The Shadow Panthers are scouting recruits. I'm surprised they haven't already been at the pair of you. But that was observant of you. Tell me more about Tiger Crouched in the Grass. Part of your army training?"

Shigan fell in step beside him. "Have you ever read *The Way of the Blade*?" The title slipped out in Imperial.

But Second Uncle didn't react. "Yes — of course. That is, I glanced through it. But it's mostly about army maneuvers, which is useless for me. I was more interested in the writing on the cultivation of the warrior, but there was very little. We have better writings about cultivation, from more traditional sources . . ."

Recruiting?

Ryu slipped away without being noticed, leaving Shigan and Second Uncle to chat about writings for cultivation. She already knew that there was nothing in the Ki library about cultivating martial arts with Essence, which is what she badly needed training in.

She turned her mind to the problem at hand. Everything she had read about the Shadow Masks had presented them as villains. If so, why did the Sky Islanders let them come to the competition? She did have to admit that they hadn't done anything villainous. That she'd seen. Oh yes. The Sky Islanders had been watching.

Ayah! Not her affair.

The next day dawned to thin, glaring light under a mackerel sky. Ryu did not have to ask Yaso to know that rain was on the way. By the time they finished their morning congee and started for the next round of competitions, it was already getting sultry.

Spear was her worst category. She had no interest in using a spear, and, being one of the smallest, lightest of contestants, could not throw or fight with it without expending too much Essence. This she was unwilling to do, especially with the Shadow Masks watching, and she was eliminated in the second round. By now she was so conscious of them that she looked for tattoos on the necks of anyone watching her, if they didn't wear one of the black and silver masks.

Sig Han Ar won in this category, and sure enough, one of the masks was waiting when he came off the field.

As Ryu walked away, one of the maskless ones whose tattoo peeked above the neck of his clothes came up to her. "You show good form. You'll improve when you get some size and strength," he said.

She knew it was meant to be a compliment, but it still annoyed her. She suppressed her reaction. It was never a good idea to deny someone face, and snarling at a compliment was a sure method of doing that.

She said, "You're very generous but have overpraised. I know I'm weak."

She tried to walk away, but he fell in step beside her. "Have you pledged to a master in the Eagle Island sect?"

Again she bit back a retort. "I'm Redbark," she said. "I'm a guest of the Eagle Islanders."

"So you could be recruited by anyone," he said with a knowing grin. He looked about nineteen, with a hint of beard. He was tall, but still hadn't grown into his bony wrists and hands. "With your talent, that will happen. I've never heard of Redbark Sect." His tone made it clear that because he hadn't heard of Redbark, of course she'd want to leave it.

"There are only two of us now," Ryu said, then wished she hadn't said even that much.

Sure enough, he said, "What happened?"

How to get out of this conversation without rudeness? She looked up, then down, and mumbled, "I swore a vow of silence."

There, that should do it.

Two, three steps. He still hadn't gone away. He clapped her on the shoulder. "Time heals all. Especially when you find a new sect, a *better* one. A place where defeat won't happen. Where grief only happens to your enemies. That's for the *best* warriors."

"Hey, Water Cat!" someone called.

The gadfly—Water Cat—gave Ryu another clap, and he walked away, leaving her unsettled and irritated.

Her mood stayed sour despite the euphoria of the Eagle Islanders, who were really looking forward to the knife fighting that afternoon. She smiled and nodded to all Matu's encouraging remarks, but when she saw Water Cat, and two masks, watching from the spectators, she dropped her knife in her first round, and lost.

Then she rejoined the others, arms crossed, and pretended not to see Matu and Shigan both staring at her.

Shigan was called next, which kept him from saying anything.

As the afternoon went on, Shigan and Matu both did well, Matu lasting one round longer than Shigan. The first and second places were both taken by big Eagle Island cousins. They whooped and howled; to avoid questions that she could see in Shigan's face, she slipped way, and wandered until she came to the pavilion, where the competition between the top masters was taking place. A man with two steel swords faced another with a crescent spear. Within a few moves Ryu found herself focused intently, everything else fading away. Unconsciously she fell into her breathing, until time seemed to slow. The two before her sharpened into diamond clarity, even to the hiss of their breathing, and the snap-whish of the skirts of their robes.

For a brief, strange moment she was inside that fight, first facing the spear wielder . . . he was dangerous, as volatile as lightning and as hard to predict. Then she faced the sword master, and though he was fast, strong, and good, she saw the moves he would make in flick of eye, turn of shoulder, angle of hip then foot, before he made them, and she knew she would win . . .

One sword went spinning, watchers backing away, the other dropped as the sharp crescent blade came to rest against the swordsman's neck. Then both bowed to each other, as the watchers began to speak in praise of both.

Ryu was herself again, but had to blink before she regained her surroundings. And here was Shigan. But when he spoke, it wasn't about her dropped knife. "One of the masks was asking me all kinds of questions about Redbark."

Ryu stared. "Oh?"

"I told him I was the latest recruit, and when he asked

where our stronghold was, I repeated all that you told Matu and Tenar, the sampans and the Dragon Tooth rocks and so forth. I told him that since I'd never actually been there, I didn't know any of the other names of places."

Ryu nodded. "All right."

"All right?" he repeated, then gave her a narrow look. "You don't want to be recruited, is that it?"

"That's exactly it," she said, relieved the subject was over.

Though it wasn't over. Yet. His mouth twisted in a skeptical not-quite-smile. "Seems to me that saying 'no' is easier than dropping a fight." A memory flickered in his mind, too quick to catch. He reached for it, but then she spoke.

"I'm thinking of leaving."

"Leaving? Now?"

She hadn't meant to speak. But she'd sensed questions in him, ones she didn't want to answer. "Not right this moment. But after the Spring Festival. I want to start really being a gallant wanderer." And find an Essence master — though she didn't say it.

He whistled under his breath. "I wondered about that. I must say, I like the Ki clan, but a long winter shut up with them beside that lake is not what I thought of as wandering."

"Exactly." Relief washed over her, just as the first big splats of a rainstorm chuffed in the dirt, splatted on her cheek, and the top of her hand. "I was thinking I ought to tell Matu, Yaso, and Petal. They might want to come. Or not."

"Aren't they part of Redbark?" Shigan asked.

Ryu made a wry face — she kept forgetting that some might think Redbark Sect was real.

She'd find out if that was true.

That night, after a rain storm blew through, she went around to Matu, Yaso, and Petal. They went out into a cool spring night smelling of white peonies and sweetgrass. Ryu said, "As soon as the Spring Festival is over, I'm going on the wander. If anyone wants to come with me, you're welcome, but if you don't, ayah, that's fine, too." She grimaced down at her hands, hearing how awkward her own voice sounded.

Matu's intake of breath was the first sound. "Last year the elders made me go with my cousin, as you know. Tenar is an excellent senior," he said hastily. "But we ended up spending most of the summer and autumn resting after I was sick on the trip down, the second time being at my third cousin's on Te

Gar. I'd like to go with *you*. Learn Redbark. I'll talk to Second Uncle."

He worried about what the elder would say; it would be years before he understood that he ought not to have. The clan elders had talked before the young people even got on board the ship, expecting something of the sort, and Grandfather Ki said, "Remember what Kanda teaches: there are three ways to learn. By education, which is best. By mimicry, which is worst. And by experience, which is the hardest on body, soul, and mind. If Young Matu wishes to follow Ryu of the Redbark Sect for a year, and learn by experience, I believe that experience will benefit them all."

And so the following two days passed swiftly as the last bouts were held, with crowds of watchers at each event; Ryu kept away from the Shadow Panthers, and any stranger who showed a tendency to want to talk to her before and after she managed to lose her last two competitions.

She slipped into the growing crowd at the pavilion, where the final bouts of the sword competitions were held. Watching with close attention, she learned two things: though many were superlative, none were Essence masters. She overheard muttering that neither would have lasted three moves against Lion's Mane, and she turned away, convinced that she might very well have won against half of them, with the level of Essence she had now.

She was still determined to find an Essence master. Some-day Muin might need her to help him on the Phoenix Path.

Spring Festival! Everyone who brought musical instruments brought them out, along with cherished jugs of fine wines. A grand feast celebrated the winners, who proudly took their places on the dais. One of those was the oldest Eagle Island cousin, who won the double knife competition. He was toasted repeatedly by the clan.

Ryu got to taste her first wine as a gallant wanderer. A single cup went straight to her head, making her agreeably muzzy. She watched the dancers, enjoying the movement in the flickering light of many lanterns. She tried along with the younger cousins to get Shigan to dance, but he refused, and so finally Ryu fumbled her way back to the Eagle Island tent, oblivious to older couples slipping off into the soft air of the woods, where fireflies were just beginning to circle lazily in the scented air.

She woke with a dry mouth. Petal brought around hot tea, her face blotchy. Ryu squinted up at her, dry-mouthed after her first night drinking wine. Having never before encountered the results of someone crying all night, she said only, "I really need to stretch." Then, remembering her promise, "Do you want to come work on the Redbark Sword form before we depart?"

Petal's entire face brightened. "Yes." She breathed the word.

"I'm coming with you." That was Matu's voice, muffled by his bedroll.

Shigan said nothing, but joined them, as Yaso prepared their belongings for travel.

And so, amid the noise and chatter of the camp being broken, the five of them departed for the road. Ryu's spirits soared: at last she was truly "eating in the wind and sleeping in the dew," just like the heroes in the gallant wanderer tales.

TWENTY

ONCE YSKANDA RECOVERED FROM his illness, he was grateful for days in which he could immerse in the world of art and forget where he was, and why.

There weren't many. As the last days of winter blasted through, and the plum trees burst out in exquisite blossoms, the subject of the missing prince swiftly gave way to more immediate concerns, especially as there was nothing more to feed rumor. None of the mysterious prisoners were ever seen again, which happened most of the time anyone went into the imperial prison.

Much more vital to the interests of Yskanda's peers was the fact that the Ministry of Rites had chosen an auspicious day for the Imperial Examination. The trickle of thaw and the emergence of fuzzing green on the trees meant spring was coming — and with it, the examination. Apprentices spoke of little else.

Yskanda was considerably surprised when Court Artist Yoli said one morning, "The Imperial Examination is coming up. Your masters speak well of your knowledge of the classics."

"Is it not too early for me to test?"

The court artist shrugged. "Yes. No. Everything about your appearance is irregular, and I'm told you've memorized more than most of those snake-in-the-sun lazy seniors already sprouting beards. And there are those few who test far younger than you, though admittedly most of those have been

tutored since they could hold a brush. Why not try? Even if
you fail, you'll have learnt what to expect."

Yskanda wavered. He preferred to avoid anything that
might draw imperial notice, and at his age, not many were
invited by the masters to test. His best days were those rare
ones in which he was so absorbed in art he forgot himself and
his surroundings; his good days were ones in which he did not
see the emperor at all, for even when glimpsed across the
width of a formal courtyard, he could feel the imperial gaze. A
heartbeat's glance was all that was needed to remind him of
how tenuous was his position, his life entirely dependent on
the emperor's whim.

He never failed to lie sleepless and worried after those
distant encounters, the ward stone under his pillow, or even
clutched tightly in hand. Sometimes he railed against his own
worthlessness. If First Brother Muinkanda had been taken, he
would no doubt have found a way to escape by now. Even
little sister Mouse would have—she'd been so good at
winnowing in and out of trouble when they were all small.

But they weren't here, and it was disloyal, not to mention
unfilial, to even imagine them taken instead of him, so
Yskanda tried to keep himself so busy he didn't have time to
brood on these things. But there was no controlling dreams.

It didn't help that for once his peers failed to sidetrack him
away from gloomy thoughts. Even Yut Hak was entirely
absorbed in study—Yskanda still saw him numerous times a
day, but Yut Hak tended to look distracted, and the questions
like swarms of stinging insects had vanished.

For the first time, the dormitories and dining areas as well
as the libraries and archives were full of students bent over
books and texts, the only sound the rustle of paper, and the
soft whish of brushes on paper.

"At least," Senye Tan stated one day as he whirled in,
sleeves flapping, and slapped his books down on one end of
their shared table in the dormitory, "the examination will
happen right before the Spring Festival. Or we would have
had the most miserable festival in history."

"It's not the examination so much as the posting of the
results," tall, serious Xek Arkanda (known generally as
Gloom) murmured.

"What are you glooming about, Gloom?" Senye Tan
retorted.

Another spoke up. "Ah-ya! Green smoke rising from

Gloom's ancestors' graves as they go around the nether world bragging about his first-rank placement."

Gloom blushed and retreated to hide behind his pile of books, as the others went on to grouse about how boring it was to study madly, how many thousands of times they'd read the classics, yet in their dreams every night they sat down to a blank paper and could not remember a word. A few recited bits of poetry that made very oblique reference to family pressures. Especially the unfairness of those whose elder generations had swanned about enjoying the family wealth without attaining any merit on their own, resulting in parental pressure on the present speaker to bring glory to the family lest they lose rank.

This last complaint caused Yskanda to reflect on the irony of First Brother and the Phoenix Feather. Whatever merit he gained in the future would belong to the new name Afan, instead of bringing the Alk clan back to its old respectability. The gong rang in the distance, and Yskanda slipped out, wondering if Mother grieved over the disappearance of the Alks, the way she had grieved over the lack of proper ritual on holidays.

Over the weeks, especially during the unaccustomed cold of winter, Yskanda had formed the habit of cutting through the Garden of Serene Contemplation in order to reach Court Artist Yoli's chamber. He would never have dared to venture a step into the place had the imperial family ever used it, but he had learned that they had more private gardens at the north end of the palace. This particular rock garden lay at the southernmost reach of Imperial Garden — it had once, he was told, been the Concubines' Garden centuries ago, when the palace was first built. Because the imperial family was known to step into Serene Contemplation very rarely, the apprentices were often set to drawing tasks in it. In this way Yskanda got to know its paths, and the occasional venture into it when he might be late to the court artist had gradually become habit.

As always he looked around before venturing farther into the somewhat forbidden space, but without stopping. Once again he came up against a reminder that, however much he wanted to remain effectively invisible, he wasn't.

"There you are!"

The piping voice belonged to a young girl. Yskanda cast a quick glance aside, hoping that he was not the one addressed.

There stood Second Imperial Princess Gaunon, dressed in

layers of silk, the outermost a robe of the palest eggshell blue threaded with gold. It was woven in the difficult leaping dolphin pattern, so that it shimmered as she moved, calling attention to graceful embroidery of plum blossoms twined with little swallows in flight. She had chosen one of her very best robes in order to impress the beautiful apprentice, but all he saw was the expensive silk with that exquisite embroidery representing many hours of hard work being carelessly dragged over the raked gravel.

She had caused her maid to do up her glossy blue-black hair with gold hairpins decorated with jade to match the plum blossoms, with tiny chains dangling down beside her cheeks — hairpins ordinarily only granted to older girls. But this princess, spoilt by fond relatives, had collected such treasures and wore them whenever she could get away with it, steadfast in her belief that she walked through an enchanted life looking like a cloud princess, admired by all who saw her.

Secure in this belief, she had laid her plans, and — clever when it suited her — had executed the first part by using her maids to discover when, and where, the beautiful and mysterious new apprentice went about his daily tasks. And here he was at last.

Seeing her, he stilled, and then bent into a formal bow.

She came forward, hands outstretched. "Oh, none of that. You must help me," she said, having planned this much. "It's you who has to draw me dancing."

"This talentless apprentice does not dare, imperial highness," Yskanda said, backing up hastily.

"Oh, but you must! It's for a gift. For my father!"

He stilled, hiding his extreme dismay. What he was hearing was tantamount to an imperial command. "I have the musicians and everything," she said naively, for she was far too young to even think about the consequences of being alone with him.

"Your imperial highness," Yskanda said, desperate to get out of what he knew was going to be trouble. "This lowly apprentice is honored by your imperial highness's notice, but Court Artist Yoli must give his permission for this unworthy student to take time away from studies . . ."

"Of course," Imperial Princess Gaunon interrupted airily, certain of herself now. "But he will. Tell him it's to be a surprise, for Spring Festival. We all give each other gifts, you see. They have to be something *personal*."

"Forgive this stupid lout of an apprentice for his lack of understanding, but would not personal be . . . something her imperial highness made herself?" Yskanda asked, with faint hope he'd found a way clear.

Imperial Princess Gaunon smiled the smile that had got around her doting relatives all her life. "I know," she admitted forthrightly, abandoning her grand manner. "But the *only* thing I'm good at is dancing. So I thought a picture of me the next best thing. But it must be made by *you*. You're the best," she said, thinking this would please him.

A single gong struck.

Yskanda bowed as he explained that he must report to the court artist. The imperial princess, who now was late for lessons, said quickly, "I'll send my maid tomorrow, at this time, for your answer. Let her know when the court artist will release you." She said this last over her shoulder as she began to run, long silken sleeves fluttering like the tail feathers of her swallows, her long black hair rippling down her back.

Yskanda cursed himself for his inattention—he ought to have seen her and slipped away before being seen. He hurried to the court artist, and explained what had happened.

Court Artist Yoli grunted, scowling as he fingered his beard. "This is bad. She ought to have sent one of her servants to consult with me, as court artist. Or better, she ought to have gone to one of her cousins, who have all been trained to draw. There's one who inherited his father's talent, though he prefers the fleshpots of the city to ink and brush. But instead she went to an apprentice, a newcomer. When she's questioned, and she will be, she might say anything—and she'll be believed. You won't. There are those up there who, let us say, will insist on seeing this as an underhanded ploy on your part to gain advantage through the innocent child."

"With all my respect, I . . ." Yskanda began to protest, then sighed sharply.

"*I* know. *You* know. But *they'll* believe what they want to believe. However. There's no getting around an order, and at least you had the wit to come to me first. It seems I'm going to have to force it into my schedule . . ."

Yskanda was about to thank him when the court artist turned his gaze skyward and sighed sharply again, so hard that not only the mustache fluttered but his eyebrows as well. "No—I can't. I'm on call at court tomorrow, and I cannot predict how long it will last. . ." He shook his head, muttering

low, the only words discernable being "in the tiger's jaws." But
then he straightened up. "You're smart. And cautious. You'll
survive if you always make certain there is at least one woman
in the room with you, preferably more. Whatever that child
does in her dancing, the symbols you draw must be spring and
innocence, and only the most decorous of poses. The Swan is
the most trustworthy. Now, let's get to our lesson while you
still have a head to think with . . ."

At first Yskanda was going to avoid the imperial princess
and her maid, but he feared if he persisted she would send the
maid questing for him, drawing even more attention. The next
day, as soon as class ended, he went out into the garden of Serene Contemplation, where a sudden rain shower had begun.

He found the maid waiting, her clothes sodden, her body
shivering. "Third hour of Horse," the girl said, her purple lips
clearly numb, her teeth chattering. "Heavenly Harmony." She
turned and ran before he could ask her if she would be there
as well.

Heavenly Harmony . . . he ran over the names of the
various buildings, then had it: one of the two elaborate
pagodas in the Imperial Garden, where musicians often sat to
play. At least it was semi-public, which was both good and
bad, in that it was more likely to attract attention if anyone was
in that garden at that time of day, but so public a spot would
not look even remotely like some sort of assignation.

He ran to the court artist to report, and when the gong rang
the third hour of Horse, he made his way to the pagoda there
in the Imperial Garden, his arms laden with more drawing
material than he would possibly need. He'd already secretly
begun the work with an elaborate border filled with spring
flowers and butterflies.

The princess showed up with a bevy of maids holding a
rain canopy over her head to ward the world of drips. Yskanda
rose and bowed low. The musicians were already there,
instruments tuned, faces lowered.

Yskanda rejoiced to see all those maids, a buoyant feeling
that vanished when the imperial princess entered the pagoda
and then waved them off. They retreated — four sets of eyes
and talking mouths — and Yskanda suppressed a groan.

The imperial princess nodded regally to the musicians. She
had spent the last two hours warming up. In her mind, the
handsome, mysterious apprentice would be struck dumb by
her springing directly into dance like a fairy from a story. Not

only was she creating a dazzling picture for the ages, but surely he would fall into desperate love and write poetry to her
beauty as well as draw her — and *not* First Imperial Princess.

The musicians played.

The princess began to dance.

Yskanda watched only long enough until he saw
something resembling the pose he'd already chosen. Having
been granted his moment of verisimilitude, however brief, he
began concentrating on the gorgeous colors of her layers of
silk, and fell into the painting as his fingers reproduced the
tiny bunches of cherries, the iridescent hummingbirds, and the
twining golden vines on the outer robe. His focus filled with
the subtlety of color . . . so driven was he to finish quickly but
well that he, as well as the princess dancing out her dream,
both started violently when a cold, clear voice lanced across
the space: *"Second Imperial Sister."*

TWENTY-ONE

A DISCORDANT JANGLE AND the music stopped.

The princess tripped over her trailing hem and went down in a welter of silk and coltish limbs. Yskanda's brush jerked in his hand, smearing a blob of blue ink across the lower part of the drawing, spoiling it. He threw himself face down, along with the musicians, as First Imperial Princess Manon stalked into the pagoda, a vision in silver and ice blue with a hint of pale peach in the third layer at neck and sleeves and the long sweeping panels.

Her first thought: it was *him* again.

Anyone the imperial children came into contact with, her mother knew to ten generations who their forebears were. Her steward had reported that he was a commoner from some inkblot of an island down south.

The young princess scrambled to her feet, wailing, "Now you've spoiled everything!"

"Recollect yourself, Second Sister," was the cold response, and the musicians trembled.

"It's for Imperial Father," the younger princess whimpered. "Dancing is my best thing. Imperial Father even said so."

"*Not* before the eyes of the lowborn," First Imperial Princess Manon murmured, loud enough for the prostrate servants to hear.

For that encroaching *him* to hear.

Princess Gaunon shrilled, "The court artist himself sent the apprentice over, and Mama let me have the musicians." She gulped on a sob, and fled in disorder.

The first imperial princess started out, pausing at the door. "Do not move."

She swept out, leaving silence, and a mixture of tension and bewilderment on Yskanda's part. He rested his forehead against the cool floor, relieved that at least Imperial Princess Gaunon had said that about *the court artist himself*. He listened to birds trill in the distance, and the soft clatter of a windchime somewhere nearer, until he became aware of the hissing breaths of someone weeping.

He turned his head minutely, peering out of the corner of his eyes in the way he'd learned since his entry into the imperial palace. One of the musicians sobbed into her hands, the only sound her shuddering breathing. He turned his head the other way. No one in sight.

"What?" he whispered.

"She'll have us killed," the musician whispered thickly. Her profile didn't look any older than sixteen. "Or at the very least our tongues cut out."

"She?"

"First Imperial Princess—"

"Sh-h-h!" one of her companions hissed.

Silence fell, and remained so as, on the other side of the imperial garden, Second Imperial Princess Gaunon finished crossing the garden and burst into the pavilion of her mother, Third Consort Pirag. Then she caught herself up, witless with surprise, for there instead of her mother alone sat all three consorts in company with the emperor. Gaunon had forgotten the day!

She composed herself, straightening with a snap and bowed deeply; it is difficult to say who terrified her more, her father or Second Consort Su, the mother of First Imperial Princess Manon. "Daughter," Third Consort Pirag lisped, with a lizard-quick glance at the second consort, "you interrupt us."

First Imperial Consort Ran Renyi smiled at the child, saying peaceably, "Ah, it is a harmonious spring day, and court resolved early. Let us overlook such refreshing spontaneity. It will end all too soon."

Second Imperial Consort Su's exquisite mouth tightened. She remained silent as all three turned toward the emperor to see his reaction, the dangles on their elaborate golden headdresses catching the light; only the third imperial consort's betrayed a little tremble.

The emperor looked past them to his youngest daughter. "You look as if you'd encountered a ghost, Gau-Gau."

"I *wish* I might see a ghost," Second Imperial Princess Gaunon whimpered in a little-girl voice, eyes wide. "Unless it curses me! But I did not. I planned a *gift* for you, Father Emperor, but now it is *spoilt*, for I know the musicians will not *dare* to come again, and it took so *long* to get the artist."

The emperor was ready to wave off his daughter's little tempest. Suppressing a laugh, he observed, "Court Artist Yoli must be more fleet than I could imagine, coming straight from court to serve you."

"I did not ask *him*," Second Imperial Princess Gaunon declared, a new idea forming as she perceived her elder sister approaching sedately. "This silly daughter dared only ask the lowest of the low, for she knows she is young, and stupid, and should be humble."

"Oh?" the emperor prompted, brows raised.

"So this unworthy daughter asked for the newest apprentice, who made such pretty drawings for us on our sky lanterns, and the court artist sent him to draw me dancing, because that is the only talent this poor daughter has, and Mama let me have her musicians, though she likes music in the afternoons. But First Imperial Princess interrupted us, and now it's spoilt."

The emperor looked past her to First Imperial Princess Manon, who was at that moment bowing low, graceful and immaculate as always. "Is this true, Manon?" he asked.

"Forgive this ignorant daughter, Imperial Father," Manon said in her low, sweet, well-modulated voice. "Perhaps I am mistaken in my belief that our faces as imperial princesses do not retain the purity of respect if anyone outside of our own imperial circle sees us as . . . performers."

The three consorts' heads turned toward the emperor, golden chains dancing around their faces. He understood, or thought he understood, how Gaunon's natural impetuosity exacerbated Manon's craving for order, grace, and decorum.

But there had been that use of the word "imperial" three times in two sentences. "Let us look into this," he said, rising.

The three consorts rose, but he held out a careless hand. "No need to disturb the tranquility of the day a moment longer than necessary. Consort Pirag, might I trouble you to ring for fresh tea? It should be ready by the time I return."

No one mistook that "should" for a suggestion.

With his two daughters trailing him, he walked out into the soft spring air. The elder imperial princess remained silent as her younger sister chattered the entire way, explaining through at least twice, and then adding with a telling glance toward her older sister, ". . . and I don't want anything to *happen* to them, just because I wanted to give you a gift for Spring Festival."

The emperor said nothing to this, and as the pagoda appeared through the budding trees, Second Imperial Princess Gaunon's fluting voice faltered, and at last fell silent.

The emperor walked in. The four people there had remained prostrate, as ordered. He saw at a glance, which First Imperial Princess Manon belatedly saw, that this scene was not even remotely an assignation.

The emperor strolled to the table to glance down at the drawing. He saw the jolt of ink across the unfinished painting, and imagined Manon bursting in on them without her usual careful grace, assuming — what? That this situation was Afan Yskanda's idea?

He stood in silence, taking in a drawing that could not have been more innocuous. All that was visible of his daughter's actual self were fingers in a classical pose, and a sliver of a rounded cheek — but that rounded sliver suggested the shape of Gaunon's own cheek. The rest of the drawing captured the flow of long black hair, and the stylized complexity of draperies rippling with her movement.

Something in the line, and in the details of the butterflies captured on paper — which he could see in his daughter's over-robe — arrested the eye, suggesting vitality and spring grace. It was in pretty much every respect an entirely conventional drawing, almost too conventional in its exhibition of drawing skill in the details, except for that single curve of a cheek, and the dance of the butterflies.

He gestured, and a graywing appeared to take the drawing, then immediately withdrew.

"My daughter," he said, "I will take your wish for the deed. First Imperial Daughter, I acknowledge your devotion to duty." He lifted his glance then, catching a moment of confusion that was quite rare in First Imperial Princess Manon.

Perhaps she was merely beginning to test her powers. He had done the same once. It might be time for a small lesson. "Rise," he said to those still motionless on the floor, heads hidden behind the strong, clever hands of trained artisans. Losing them to what amounted to an afternoon's whim was akin to throwing away wealth, which was not infinite, though it might seem that way to the young. "We shall regard this incident as one that never happened, shall we?"

Down all four went again, in a billow of service dull blues and grays.

"Go on. You three musicians, her highness the third imperial consort is sadly missing your expertise. You, apprentice court artist, will find Court Artist Yoli restored to his chambers, where you no doubt have your own lessons waiting."

Yskanda's heart banged against his ribs as he rose, bowed with the silent musicians, and then all four took up instruments and drawing tools respectively and departed for the side paths that kept them from polluting the sight of their superiors in their scrambling retreat.

Court Artist Yoli was indeed waiting, and at first sight of Yskanda, he raised his Essence wards. "Talk," he ordered.

Yskanda did. As the court artist listened, he imagined the unfinished artwork. As ordered, Yskanda had used the most conventional of poses, but Yoli strongly suspected that what ought to have been stodgy came to life through the dynamic twist of fabrics. This in no way would draw attention to the little princess—she could scarcely be said to be present. A true artist could bring to life banners snapping in the wind over a line of riders, or curtains billowing in storm winds through an open window. The attention drawn directly to the embroidered silks.

When Yskanda faltered to a stop, Yoli grunted. "May the God of Wisdom grant she has learned something. But don't count on it. You learned to be more watchful, I trust."

Yskanda bowed assent, and was dismissed.

He returned to his dormitory mates, saying nothing to anyone as usual. As he followed them to the dining hall, he trusted that would be the end of it—but again, as always, the dread of the emperor's eye on him lingered and instinct warned him that the episode was not over.

So it proved.

The following day, Court Artist Yoli once again put on his court clothes, packed up his supplies, and trudged the relatively short distance past the Hall of Glorious Virtue to the great Hall of Glorious Harmony, with its vast hall and great throne.

Yskanda sat with other apprentices as the instructors reviewed the classics. This morning was focused entirely on recitations of Kanda's Virtues, and the chief of the Conversations, without which no one would have a hope of passing the Imperial Examination. Yskanda had long ago memorized the passages that many stumbled over now, which made the class an exercise in enduring tedium.

It was a relief when it ended. At the midday meal clumps of apprentices crowded together to test each other. To those trying to cram those passages into their heads, what was boring when one had to sit still and silent, or recite in unison, was vitally involving when shot like cannon balls at each other in a memory competition. He found this anomaly more interesting than the actual passages.

Afterward, he went to the court artist's studio, where he was able to sink into the soothing task of grinding colors. Oh, such rich colors! Everything was fresh, and plentiful, so that he could mix and emulsify every shade imaginable. The time sped by. Yskanda was not aware of the changing light, or the small sounds of his brush dipping in paint and testing it (imagine being able to test colors on Snow Wave paper, which in Master Bankan's had only been permitted to the advanced students for their calligraphy), but the sound of footsteps on the gravel outside the windows startled him, awakening the anxiety that slept like a curled creature within him.

He laid down his brush as the door opened, and the court artist beckoned to a small page. "A graywing is coming for you from the Golden Dragon Pavilion," the little girl murmured to Yskanda, then fled.

Yoli sighed heavily. "You'd better go at once."

Yskanda took a moment to make sure his clothing was straight before he walked out to discover an unknown graywing awaiting him, the fiery red ball of the sun sinking beyond the rooftops behind him, rendering his face in shadow. "His imperial majesty summons you."

"I should probably wash my hands," Yskanda said, looking down at his inky fingers, and trying to suppress the tremble that had already begun.

"The emperor is waiting."

TWENTY-TWO

IN SILENCE THEY PACED up a side path through the imperial garden, Yskanda thinking about the numerous people crowding past each other beyond the walls to the east, all with soft step. A visitor set down in the middle of the imperial palace could gain the impression it was mostly deserted, the gardens and buildings maintaining themselves somehow — those who repaired, tilled, weeded, snipped, and swept appeared at times when the owners were elsewhere, did their work, then vanished by labyrinthine byways, never presuming to step through those beautiful round moon doors in the garden walls. However, that same visitor, put down amid that tangle of byways of the periphery, would gain an impression of bustle and crowds.

When they reached the Emperor's Golden Dragon Pavilion on its hill, they climbed up the narrow stairs in the servants' entrance, and then Yskanda passed a duty graywing, and the imperial guard on duty at the door, and walked alone onto the balcony. He stopped the requisite ten paces from the emperor and faced east, a distance and direction now habitual, and prostrated himself on the rain-swept balcony.

"Get up," the emperor said. "Come here."

Yskanda rose, stilling the impulse to wipe the wet blotches from his garments.

The emperor had just come from a very long and tiring session at court, very rare two days in a row; the weight of the five-piece head-covering of the emperor, with its swinging curtains of jade beads, still throbbed across his brow.

He had left that behind, along with the heavy silk dragon robe, but all the vexations of the day had come right along with him—and duty was not over yet. Ever since the days of the first reigning Sage Empress, who established order after the devastating Years of Island Wars, directly following court the ruling empress (or emperor) would visit their consorts above a certain rank to discuss the issues of the day and share their wisdom.

This tradition had waned and waxed over the centuries, as all customs do. There was no empress now, though that might change if he chose an heir. Tradition dictated that the heir's mother would be elevated to empress. Until then, the emperor called on the consorts one a day, in order of seniority.

Late as it was, the three consorts sat awaiting him in the pavilion of First Imperial Consort, Princess Ran Renyi. This duty rotated between them, and it was her turn today. He sat alone on the balcony of his Golden Dragon Pavilion, which overlooked the court, the palace, the city, and the bay.

He was in a vile mood, and though it was not a conscious thought, he wanted someone to toy with—someone who could not possibly cause repercussions. Consciously, he had been thinking these past few hours of that drawing of Yskanda's, and how what ought to have been a student effort, utterly forgettable . . . wasn't.

He studied Yskanda. There were Alk Hanu's intelligent eyes, her exquisite brows. But this was not Hanu, who had been short and rounded, her mouth small and studious. Yskanda's sensitive mouth even in obvious dread curved with the shadow of a humor that Hanu had not even remotely possessed, and his person was tall and slender. Thin. Too thin.

"Don't you ever eat?"

Yskanda's eyes widened. "Your imperial majesty . . . ?"

The question had just slipped out. The emperor waved a hand. "You will be taking the Imperial Examination, of course."

Yskanda quickly looked down, then out over the garden, as if he longed to fly away on the rising wind. "This stupid apprentice believes that his youth and ignorance make it impossible."

The emperor issued what might, in a less exalted person-age, might have been a snort. "In my experience, people your age use the excuse 'I'm too young' only when they don't want to confess the real reason they don't want to do something. The rest of the time it's *Why won't you let me? I'm plenty old enough!* Or *You treat me like a child.*" But that thought led toward Jion, and the emperor refused to let his mind go down that painful path.

He said, "Has anyone actually forbidden you to sit for it?"

"No, your imperial majesty."

"Then you will sit for it."

Another brief glance, hastily suppressed. "I . . . this humble apprentice does not presume to be ready . . ."

The emperor cut in, "Are you intimating that I am not the best judge of who can take it and who can't?"

Down Yskanda went again, right into a puddle. "No, your imperial majesty."

"Stand up. Let's see what you know. To begin with, what is the Golden Point of Balance?"

Yskanda's gaze diffused as he enunciated in cadenced words, "In *The Five Virtues*, Kanda taught that the golden point of harmony is that place at which we maintain balance and harmony by striving to bring the mind, heart, and soul to a state of constant equilibrium."

He paused, and glanced up in mute question. When the emperor motioned to go on, he did. "Kanda taught that men must lead and women follow, but the Sage Empress Lan Renti wrote that the person, male or female, who follows the golden point of harmony is on a path of duty and must never leave it. A superior person is cautious, a gentle teacher, and shows no contempt for his or her inferiors, and does what is natural according to her or his status in the world. Even common men and women can carry the mean into their practices, while respecting natural order. The qualities of harmony include moderation, rectitude, objectivity, sincerity, honesty and propriety, with a guiding principle that one should never act in excess."

He took a deep breath and went on, "The Golden Point of Harmony is divided into three parts . . ."

Not knowing when it was proper to stop, he talked on, hearing the whisper of Ul Keg's voice overlaid by Mother's, and saw not the graceful complexity of the imperial garden, in which something was always blooming except at the very depth of winter before the plum blossoms came, but in memory the proliferation of plantain trees and bamboo, as the somnolent spring air intoxicated one with the heavy scents of

flowering fruit trees and shrubs and herbs. He saw First Brother leading the way, a guiding hand on Mouse's messy topknot, and there was Mouse, short, always lost in clothes that
Yskanda himself had been wearing until recently, her cheeky
grin as she glanced back . . .

"You do not," interrupted the emperor's dry voice, "need
to quote the entire book to me. I believe I am familiar with it. I
gather you can probably discourse on *The Roots of Virtue*."

"This ignorant apprentice would never dare to discourse
on any subject, but is aware of the text, beginning with, 'We
begin by observing that for the common people, filial piety and
respect for elders constitute the root of virtue, and for the ruler,
virtue accumulates through good character and acts of
kindness and generosity. Subjects willingly follow a ruler with
Virtue, without the need for coercion, and although Virtue was
once thought something only a true king could possess—'"

The emperor suddenly did not want to hear that soft voice
on the subject of royal virtue and the responsibility of kings.
"Yes, I believe you." And then, "Are your brothers and sisters
as well read as you?"

Yskanda's heart lurched against his ribs, but he'd had himself under control since stepping onto the balcony, except for
the shivers from the cold wind off the sea, and two layers of
thin spring garments sticking damply to his limbs. "This lowly
apprentice and his common family were taught much the
same," he said. "But I, that is, this apprentice has neither seen
nor heard from his family since apprenticed many years ago."

All that corroborated Chief Fai's report—and yet still told
the emperor nothing.

"Shall we bring them to you? Would you like to see them?"

The emperor watched the words hit Afan Yskanda like a
slap. But of course he would feel that way, having been snatched suddenly off the street of his faraway island, and brought
all this distance. Never told why.

Never had asked why. The impulse to query that rose, to
be quashed. If he asked Afan Yskanda why he'd never
questioned his abduction, of course he would get back the
usual self-deprecation about not presuming to question the
orders of those exalted above him. The ritually approved line
of defense.

"Would you like to see them?" he asked instead, sharper.

Yskanda's lips, purpling in the cold, moved, though no
sound could be heard over the rising wind.

"What is that?" the emperor said, leaning forward. "Lift your head. I can't hear you."

Yskanda raised his head, looking pale and wretched. But he answered with dignity, "This ignorant apprentice does not know which temple his sister was sent to, your imperial majesty, nor where his brother. . ."

Suddenly the emperor was tired of this game that could only have one winner. Clearly the bewildered boy had one thought: to protect his brother and sister. Just as clearly he was not aware that he was a lamb staked out on the mountain to lure the tiger: Danno.

If, of course, Danno really was Afan Olt.

It had begun to rain again. The emperor looked at that thin, shivering figure; even he felt the cold, though he wore five layers of very fine silk. And in moments graywings would be out offering him screens and extra clothing, as if a spring rain might melt the imperial flesh. Aware of the silent reproach of all those awaiting his duty rounds, he raised a hand in dismissal. "Never mind," he said, deciding not to point out that he could find out easily where both were, and have them brought, with no more than a word spoken.

And it might still happen.

"We'll leave the question for the future. I expect they are leading exemplary lives where they are," he said. "I look forward to seeing what you write on the Imperial Examination. You may retire."

Grateful to escape, Yskanda bowed and retreated.

Dark was falling. Yskanda, now thoroughly soaked, was not certain whether he ought to report to Yoli. But when he reached the crowded corridor, everyone hurrying to the evening meal, the decision was taken out of his hand at the approach of a page. "You're to go to the court artist," the child said.

When he got there, Yoli paused in his work and studied Yskanda from under those wild, snowy brows. "Drink this wine. It seems that you are to take the Imperial Examination."

Yskanda bowed from where he sat, though inwardly his bow, and his vow, reverberated through his body, mind, and soul. If a miracle happened and he gained his freedom, he would walk straight out to the first ship he could find and get as far away from the imperial capital as he could—and yet he wanted, badly, to stay to learn from this artist he so admired.

He picked up the wine he did not want. But it was heated,

mellow in flavor, and it did warm him within. He took a bigger sip, and that settled his still-churning stomach.

Yoli went on, "You need to understand first that for all its vaunted tradition of being unchanged for centuries, the Imperial Examination has been evolving all along. In the former dynasty it was held every year, until peculation and corruption got to be too blatant, and the first Jehan emperor reorganized it—after a few heads rolled to underscore his intent."

Yskanda flinched inwardly at the image, as the court artist leaned over to refill the wine cup, and went on. "In the dynasty previous, it took place every five years, and the imperial family was directly involved in the questions and the evaluation. In those days the regional examinations were more frequent, but by the time the candidates came to the capital, there were only a hundred at a time, so the competition, and the attendant corruption and bribery, eventually reached unprecedented levels. Long before that, as you know, only the children of nobles could sit the examination. Before that, scholars, and before that, only sons."

Yskanda bowed—none of this was new. Ul Keg had told him much the same.

"Its contents have also altered, though not materially. The classical books—and the key commentaries—are always the basis, though the questions might change: one year it's mostly Kanda and moral rightness in governing, the next year it's the *Ancient Annals* of Mana Ta, the following year First Empress Lan Renyi, the next time it's back to the most ancient teachings about the Path and the importance of law. And there will always be at least one question based solely on your knowledge of the great poets."

The court artist sighed, rubbing his eyes. "That pompous old fart Grand Historian Bolu Kan is meticulous, that I'll give him, but he also seems to delight in turning up obscurities to make life difficult for the other departments that have to administer the examination. For a time there were departmental examinations, not the two we now have, military and civil. Corruption again, some departments wafting their cherished apprentices through, others imposing grueling tests. Now, everyone gets the same questions, but once the judges have gone through the papers with no names attached, and weeded out the incompetents, then they are divided between departments, and evaluated again. For our section of the scribe department, for example, we might read for awareness of symbol and how it's used, and shrug away a weak answer about matters and meaning of court ritual. Over at the archival scribes' bureau, it would be the opposite."

Yskanda listened patiently, because he always listened patiently.

"I'm telling you all this in order to emphasize that you need not worry. Unless you have all the great books memorized, you won't know everything. But once you've seen the questions, and heard the instructors discussing the top-ranking examinations, you'll have a better notion of what to expect three years from now." Yoli scowled. "You're still shivering despite the two cups of wine I just got into you. Go change your clothes, and get some hot food into you. Also, you're to drink medicinal tea — I won't have you sick again. There is too much work."

TWENTY-THREE

SPRING RIPENED, IN THE lesser gardens tea olive trees and osmanthus bathing the air with their fragrances — the tea olive fragrance reminding Yskanda of home. Around Yskanda, the Spring Festival began to be talked of as often as the examination, and then, in the few days before, a fatalism appeared to set in about the examination, and it was all Spring Festival all the time.

Yskanda ignored all the talk, assuming that he would not be permitted to leave the palace for Spring Festival, though apparently the apprentices who had earned sufficient merit could all go out of the palace that day, due back through the east gate the next morning.

The days passed in a flurry of frantic studying, praying, incense-lighting, charmed objects worn or placed around beds to attract luck and ward bad luck, ghosts, and demons. Finally, Examination Day arrived. A secondary auspicious day had been chosen in case the wind gods scowled and sent rain, but they did not.

The sky was blue overhead, the air warm as Yskanda joined the other examinees in their walk toward the Hall of Glorious Virtue. Despite his inward insistence on not caring — the court artist had accepted him even if he failed, with the expectation he would try again in three years — Yskanda found his palms damp and his heartbeat fast. He attributed it to the general atmosphere of tension as all the palace apprentices testing joined the two hundred or so candidates who had passed up through the local then regional examinations, and who wanted to try for placement in the imperial government.

They walked two by two to where a pair of imperial guards administered the search.

Yskanda had to set down his case containing his brushes and ink-stick to be examined while a guard ran brisk, impersonal fingers over him, probing pockets, and he was bidden hold his arms out to either side as the guard patted his inner sleeves. Then the guard shoved his sleeves up and his arms were examined for ink. His robe was also hiked up and his underclothing glanced at for same.

He was waved to the line, where he joined with a short, round young woman who came from the shorter line administered by female imperial guards. He stood behind the girl, who never gave him a glance. Yskanda couldn't help smiling down at the top of her head. He could not but think of how very proud Mother would be to see all these women testing. A few of them even looked Mother's age, as there were some men with lined faces and graying hair among the men, back for another try. And here and there, as Yoli had said, were a couple of youths who couldn't be more than fourteen.

The candidates waited for their names to be called out, then they took their places on mats that had been laid on the stones of the Hall of Glorious Virtue's vast court. As graywings brought out jugs of water, one to a mat, the chief examiner began issuing the rules: anyone seen turning his head to either side would be instantly failed, and sent to the Hall of Correction.

Graywings then moved swiftly to the front, where two great banners had been rolled up. A graywing rang a gong, the two banners were loosened, revealing the questions in very large writing, and the chief examiner bawled, "You may begin!" Yskanda's stomach knotted when he reached the third question, which concerned commentaries on the state, works he had never heard of much less read. Clearly these were covered in the classes for the older apprentices. But the first two questions—one taken from commentaries on the last five of the Twenty-Five Virtues, and the other on poetry of the Lan Dynasty—he was confident about: the problem would be writing too much.

Gongs rang twice during the long day, indicating that examinees ought to move on to the next question. Fast as

Yskanda wrote, he left both first and second questions unfinished. He wrote what little he knew for the third, which was only basic texts about the Virtuous Ruler, then used the rest of the time to finish his thoughts on the first and second questions, as no one had told him he couldn't.

When the last gong rang, the chief examiner called out, "Pick up your ink and brushes. Leave your paper. Do not linger. Any seen still writing when I finish speaking will have their papers burned, and they will report to the Hall of Correction."

Yskanda stopped mid-word, picked up his supplies, and walked out, feeling absurdly lighter, considering that he had no expectations about his result, or what they would mean. It was just good to have it done.

He was dazed by afternoon light slanting down. The candidates from outside the palace were escorted toward the east gate by imperial guards and graywings. Yskanda looked after them, tempted to try to join that line, until he saw familiar graywings waiting for the palaces apprentices. Eyes met eyes: he sensed himself counted.

Light-headed from hunger, he followed the other apprentices to the dining hall, where everyone discovered ravenous appetites now that the tension had been released. The conversations were all about the questions, and what various people had answered.

Yut Hak sat next to Yskanda. "How did you do?" he asked.

"I spent most of my time on the first two, and probably failed the third," Yskanda said. "And you?"

"I was not expecting poetry," Yut Hak said morosely. "I mean, I guess I was, but I gambled on the asking for poetry from the earlier dynasties. I did poorly on that one. But I made up for it on the third," he added with faint triumph.

Court Artist Yoli asked about the questions the next morning, grunted a noncommittal answer, then sent Yskanda to class, as he had to attend court once more.

The emperor, of course, saw the results before anyone, as he was always the final arbiter in any question.

Those chosen to judge did not trouble him with the failures, most of which were by a considerable margin. They gave him the three that they were debating for the cherished first rank, and the pile of passes. They withheld the borderline group, in case he wished to make the decision on those.

The emperor read through the candidates for that cherished first rank, leaving the one he thought the best on top, after looking under the cover strip at the names. He only cared about impartial judging insofar as competence was concerned. The clever ones had to be considered for clan as well as for what they said.

He glanced through the passes, looking at the names of each one. He said nothing to the judges, but having not seen the name he was curious about, he held out his hand for the problematic ones, though he suspected Afan Yskanda had been among the failures. He was quite young after all. But there, nearly at the top, was one written in an exquisite scholarly hand—could only have been written by an artist. This had to be Afan Yskanda's paper.

He glanced at the preliminary judges' comments on the excellence of Afan Yskanda's answers to the first two questions. Then he looked at the third question, which had to do with writings on statecraft.

The chief judge, seeing the direction of his gaze, said, "We did not recognize the name of this candidate, but believe he's younger than most palace candidates. It's clear to us that he has not yet trained in any of the readings we give to the scribe apprentices . . ."

The emperor let him talk on, without listening. He was reading Yskanda's first two essays. There were moments where passion overcame prudence, especially in choices of quotation—always favoring the more visual metaphors. Exactly what one might expect from an artist. But Yskanda's deep appreciation for art as the method by which the invisible could be made visible, thus underscoring the innate harmony of the world under Heaven—his awareness of art's need to communicate as well as to please the eye—his passion might be considered overly fervent, but it was genuine.

This same appreciation shone through the essay on literature, which again supported Yskanda's conviction of art's place in the civilized world. The two essays adhered strongly to the form called five-talon, and clearly came from a young mind, but one far from facile, much less stupid. Every quotation was impeccably chosen, and reproduced word for word.

Finally, there was that scant attempt at the third essay, nothing more than a restatement of the history of court, which is mandated by Heaven to support the emperor. Children were taught that along with their first brush strokes. Yskanda offered no opinion, just a series of general quotations.

The emperor took time to read these through, aware that

he might not have taken so strong an interest if Jion were . . . *here*. (His mind violently rejected the word *alive*, as if there were a question. Of course he must be alive.) The emperor's mood swung between rage at Jion's unaccountable action, and worry. He missed his exasperating son terribly — but he was not here. And this boy, who might or might not be Danno's son . . . he was interesting. And his knowledge of the inner workings of court was completely innocent.

As he looked down at the deftly written paper, another whim evolved in his mind. Call it a different sort of revenge.

He read quickly through the rest of the problematic examinations, rejected three outright, and placed the remainder in order. Yskanda's, in spite of that barely attempted third question, was not at the very bottom, though near it.

The morning of Spring Festival, the results were posted outside the Hall of Virtue as well as outside the Justice Court in the city for the candidates who had come from other locations. Both lists inspired the expected results — pride from those who ranked highly, congratulations from friends and sycophants, lowered heads and even groans from the failures.

Yskanda waited until the crowd had lessened, then made his way to the board, and again wondered at his heart accelerating as he scanned the names.

Then the small burst of surprise when he saw that he had passed. Barely. Senye Tan came up and dug an elbow in his ribs. "Not bad for an infant — which you are. You've netted yourself a hat, at any rate, and the lowly apprentices have to get out of your way. In three years, take it again and you'll be a tassel man. Six years, and you'll rank with the moon and stars." He clapped Yskanda on the shoulder. "You have to celebrate with us!"

"What — I — "

Senye Tan peered at him. "Do you have family here?"

"No — "

"Didn't think so. Then you'll come with us!"

Yskanda thanked him, wondering when he would be stopped, and by whom — and what they would say to Senye Tan, who was the dormitory's biggest talker.

And so began a day that was superficially pleasant, as all the apprentices lined up on the court outside their buildings, and the examinees who had passed were awarded their hats and their new waist tallies, beginning with the top ranks who had won the cherished tassels affixed to the tops of their hats.

Yskanda looked at his name carved and painted into the new tally, which was still mere wood, but carved into a simplified tiger-eye shape, suitable for the lowest level of post-imperial examination appointment. He looped it into his sash, and let it fall. Then came the hat. Its unfamiliar weight of stiffened fabric pressed gently into his forehead. At first he tried not to move his head lest the hat fall off. But when he saw some of his fellows moving peculiarly, as if they had huge vases balanced on their heads, he knew how ridiculous he looked. Those used to wearing hats moved naturally, suggesting that the hats stayed on firmly enough.

The New Hats, as they were laughingly called, stood in a circle bowing to one another until Senye Tan's voice came from behind. "Afan! We're going!"

"Where?"

"Where, he asks," Senye Tan addressed the sky, as if only the gods could answer. "To the city!"

"I don't think . . ." *I'm allowed out*, he began to say, but bit it off, reluctant to say anything to Senye Tan. Let the imperial guards say what they liked when he reached the gate.

Senye Tan shook his head at Afan Yskanda's more than usual wooly-mindedness. "Think what? Ayah, never mind that. Hurry!" he ordered, hustling Yskanda back to their dormitory, where the others were gathered.

By now Yskanda had seen that many, if not most, apprentices had some sort of stone, whether carved or not, as a luck stone, or a gift from relations. His ward stone was so plain that it drew no attention—though he suspected an Essence master would know it for what it was. Still, if he really did get outside, how wild was the celebration? He did not want to lose his ward stone.

At least I won't be painting, he thought as he tucked the ward stone under his pillow. Then he followed the others, wondering if this might be the shortest attempt at a festival celebration in his life.

The day was another cold one, with intermittent spits of rain that belied spring. They joined the line at the East Gate, where waited two guards with a graywing from the Household Bureau.

To Yskanda's amazement, none of these stopped him as he walked with Senye Tan's friends, a group that had swelled to about twelve. He felt the searching eyes of the gate guards as the group passed, and he wondered if he were actually free.

They strolled slowly along a street full of colorful sights, laughing as the crowds compressed to let the parading musicians, dancers, tumblers, and palanquins bearing images of the gods paraded by.

Yskanda loved everything, from long streamers unfurling slowly in the breeze, to the flower-decorated palanquins. He had paused to admire the subtleties in shades of yellow blossoms decorating the image of the Phoenix Moon God when the palanquin itself shook and tipped as one of the bearers stumbled. Yskanda leaped to help hold up the corner of the palanquin lest it fall and be ruined.

The bearers got going again, and passed by in a heady swirl of flowery fragrances.

"Afan!" Senye Tan called from ahead. "Stop dawdling!"

Yskanda hurried to catch up, longing for his sketchbook. Around him the boys chattered about the examination, about liked and disliked instructors, about senior apprentices full of themselves. "We're *scholars* now," one or another would say, look at one another, and make exaggerated faces or begin to strut—as the day went on, and the hot rice wine flowed, this happened more and more often, no one ever tiring of it.

After one cup of wine for courage, Yskanda broke away, claiming a need to go to the privy. Yut Hak did not stop him—and for a few, exhilarating steps Yskanda's mind filled with wild images of ditching his clothes and running for freedom. But what would he wear instead, and how would he get it? He had no money whatsoever—

And then he spotted a familiar gaunt figure, not fifteen paces away, walking parallel. In spite of his wearing the dull blue robes of a laborer or servant, and a shapeless cap covering his hair, Yskanda immediately recognized Melonseed, second to Bitternail in the graywing hierarchy.

The two looked at one another, ignoring those passing around and between them. Despite the clothing of an ordinary person Melonseed did not look at all like someone enjoying the festival. Yskanda had given no thought to the graywings, other than avoiding them on sight, ever since that terrible first day he ventured into the corridor leading to the Hall of Glorious Virtue. *Did* they celebrate Spring Festival? Or was Melonseed there as a guard . . .

Yskanda turned his gaze away, and kept walking to the privy as if he'd intended to all along, though he doubted the graywing was fooled.

After visiting the privy, he returned to the group, who were already well on the road to giggling drunkenness.

Yskanda had been made drunk once before, his first year at Master Bankan's. He had blithered and snickered until he puked down himself—not the only one. Apparently it was time-honored custom for the older apprentices to make the first years drunk until they were sick. He'd woken the next day feeling vile, but far worse was wondering what he'd said. Luckily it became apparent that whatever he'd said, no one had paid him the least heed, but ever since he'd avoided taking more than a cup or two.

When the bottle passed from hand to hand, he poured no more than a drop into his cup. Five, six, ten toasts later at last it was decided to walk again. The older, rowdier boys flirted clumsily with some girls in ribbons and silk giggling behind fans. Yskanda found himself stared at by some of these. He looked away quickly, blushing, suspecting that they were laughing at him.

The day seemed never to end . . . until at last night fell, and the rain had stopped.

There were fireworks.

Irritations of the day forgotten, Yskanda stood with the others, staring upward until the edges of his vision glittered. He was giddy, drunk on the coruscating brilliancy of the colors, and as he stared open mouthed, the laughing, airy golden dragon appeared, dancing in rippling grace through the star bursts, which showered around him like a river through the sky.

He watched that dragon, his fingers twitching with the desire to grab for his brushes and colors, and he never noticed when certain of the older scholars vanished in the darkness, pairing off with the flirting girls, or with one another.

He stood until a blow on his arm smashed through the vision, and he staggered, bewildered, to look into Senye Tan's face. "Drunk, Afan? Come on, time to go home. Sleep it off."

Yskanda followed, dizzy, exhilarated, puzzled. Was that the same dragon from the previous image? What did it mean?

The next morning Yskanda made his way back to Yoli's chamber, the ward stone safely in his sleeve as usual. The court artist surveyed him from under questioning brows. "Feeling the wine?"

"I'm fine," he said, deciding that he'd better keep the vision to himself.

TWENTY-FOUR

By the time Ryu, Shigan, Matu, Petal, and Yaso had been a few days on the road, they had fallen into a new habit. They woke with the sun, and wherever they were, they warmed up. At first this was the Redbark warmups until Ryu caught Shigan at his dance stretches one morning early. "Teach me that," she demanded.

Shigan slanted a challenging smile at her. "You won't be able to do it—and you will be hobbling for a week afterward."

"Try me."

Matu ranged up. "I'd like to try as well."

Petal stepped beside Ryu, silent, but willing.

"Very well," Shigan said. "We'll start easy."

He sat down, spread his legs wide, so they were a single line east to west. Ryu sat down, spread hers, and winced as her inner thigh muscles twinged. She got hers to maybe a third of a circle. Matu was even less, and Petal about the same.

"Ready?" Shigan asked, then bent forward, back straight, and touched his nose to the ground. And stayed there.

Ryu bent—and let out a squawk. Matu grunted a curse.

"Grab your toes," Shigan said. "Don't bounce. Just stay there and breathe. Your muscles will loosen."

That was true—though not by very much.

It went on from there; they were thoroughly warmed up by the time they sparred, but Ryu noticed she hadn't her usual force without using much more Essence. The others (except

Shigan) seemed to feel the same, so they set out walking . . .
and by nightfall she could scarcely hobble.

The next morning, she could barely get her legs apart
before her muscles started aching.

She gritted her teeth, grabbed her toes, and hung on,
grunting with each breath.

A few days later she was still wincing when she got up in
the mornings. They came in sight of their first village, which
they hailed with relief. For days they'd seen nothing but rocks
and the variety of tea trees that flourished among rocks. As
they worked their way over the peninsula and then north
along the shoreline road, they began to encounter lines of tea
trees, meaning someone was cultivating them.

Second Uncle had given Matu a pouch of coins to start him
off, but coins were useless if there was nothing to buy. Petal
had packed up the food the family had set aside for them, but
between four healthy young appetites, it was soon gone.

At least it was four, not five — at first Petal set aside a
portion for Yaso at each meal, to be told, "Thank you, but I've
already eaten."

When? She never asked — she was still afraid to put questions to anyone but Ryu, and then only when she had to. Her
life had been shaped by the suddenness of blows coming out
of nowhere, or for the simplest of words, making her reluctant
to speak unless necessary.

Yaso ranged the slopes and fields in the mornings while
the others practiced, and brought young carrots, and a few
spring berries, though it was too early for much else in this
wild, rocky environment.

The last couple of days they had little to eat besides what
Yaso scavenged. The sight of the village in a small valley surrounded by rows of tea trees heartened them, and they ran the
last of the distance, scanning past cottages until they spotted
one with streamers hanging from the eave, indicating an inn.

It was small and dark inside, with four rough tables. Everyone in there was very still, staring with unnerving fixedness.
The group shrugged that off, assuming the interest of strangers. Their minds were entirely on the smell of pepper-fish soup
wafting from somewhere.

One table was free, so four of them sat on the floor around
it, as Yaso took their various packs to hold. The other patrons
sat very still, which Ryu, Shigan and Matu noticed peripheral-
ly as they looked around for the proprietor.

Several figures came out of the back room, none with an apron. Ryu and companions gazed past them—until on a short, "Now!" the four pulled weapons from behind their backs, and held them to the necks of the young gallants. Two swords, two knives, all steel.

"We'll take those packs now, boys," the spokesman, a big, brawny fellow with a huge jaw and an absurdly wispy mustache grated, eyes cold.

Yaso silently handed over the packs — containing not only Matu's small bag of coins, but the two wooden swords and the two sets of knives the Ki clan had loaned them — to a smirking bandit with red ribbons braided into his hair. Ryu winced. Now they would have nothing at all to buy food with.

"Get moving, rats," the spokesman said, poking Matu in the back with his sword. "If you run, you might make it to the cataract before the rain comes."

The others laughed.

"Wait," Matu exclaimed. "I know you—I saw you, at the competition—you were in the knife fights—"

Wispy Mustache glared, then snarled, "Cut their throats."

Hunger—and inexperience—had made Ryu slow, but not stupid. She exchanged a strained look with Shigan. Then called out a Heaven command: "Upward two!"

They snapped elbows up on the inside of the wrists holding knives to their necks. Ryu's enemy scraped his knife past her ear, which stung. She launched to her feet, knocking the enemy further off-balance, then kicked out his knee. He stumbled, and she brought both fists up under his chin. His head snapped back. He let out a yelp, and fell heavily, groaning.

She whirled. Matu grappled with his enemy, swaying back and forth. Shigan had dropped one, using the same method Ryu had used—by now they had drilled it at least five thousand times—but before she could leap over the table to tackle the fourth, who was bringing his sword down toward Petal, Shigan turned and his back leg came up in a kick that cracked against the bandit's jaw, sending him flying.

Petal remained where she was, shoulders hunched, her back bowed—the position she had taken for countless beatings. Furious, Ryu stomped around, kicking the weapons free of hands.

By then all the other patrons had risen to their feet, and, yelling angrily, moved to the bandits, punching and kicking until the proprietor came out bawling for them to stop destroying his furniture.

"Tie them up," he shouted. "We'll put them before the elders!" Then, as the patrons slowly began following his orders, he turned to the newcomers, his gaze sweeping them all before coming to rest on Shigan. "Thank you, young gallants." He bowed low. "A thousand lifetimes are not enough to thank you! May I be reborn as your donkey, and serve you well. They have terrorized us for two days. We tried to send someone to get help, but they have another pair watching the roads out."

"We can deal with that," Shigan said.

Another deep bow. "How can I serve you?"

"Ayah! We haven't eaten since—"

"Say no more! It would be my pleasure to lay a feast before you."

Four young appetites woke with a roar, but Matu, ever prudent said, "Perhaps not a feast. We only have a few coins."

"May ten thousand demons sour my wine and rot my flour if I touch one tinnie of your money. You will eat like kings. And drink like them, too!"

The patrons, with the bandits tied up by then, endorsed this with a hearty shout.

With that the proprietor whisked himself into the back room, as Yaso silently picked up their belongings. "That kick," Ryu said to Shigan. "That was new."

Shigan shrugged. "You could do it."

Ryu was going to deny, then paused as her inner thighs twinged. "Maybe I could. Someday. After a lot more dance torture. Stretches. Ayah!"

The first dishes—food the proprietor had been forced to provide the bandits—came out then, and conversation died as they set to enthusiastically. The soup tasted as good as it smelled, and there were five types of dumplings, each more delicious than the last.

But once the worst hunger was appeased, Ryu was the first to put down her spoon and say, low-voiced, "We walked right into that."

The others' faces made it clear they were thinking the same thing. "It was very nearly the shortest wander in history, and not the least gallant," Shigan observed. "I think we need to start scouting as a habit."

"I recognized one of them," Matu said low-voiced, though by then they were alone in the inn's front room, the locals having all helped to muscle the bandits out the door to somewhere else. "That one with the mustache, he was in the knife fighting competition. Defeated the first day. By my Second Father Cousin Li."

"They must have left before the competition ended, to be bothering these villagers for a couple days," Shigan said.

"Might have even been some of the ones trying to get recruited by those Shadow Panthers," Matu muttered. "My cousin had one trying to interest him in leaving Eagle Island for them. He said they only take those who win rank in the fights."

Ryu shrugged, having no interest in who, or what, the Shadow Panthers might or might not recruit. She leaned forward, whispering, "They said that about the paths being guarded. Does that mean they expect us to clear out the last of these bandits?"

Shigan's mouth twisted. "Ayah! As if we didn't run *that* sort of plan a hundred times at Loyalty! We sneak out, spot the scouts, waylay them. As long as they don't get warned, my guess is they'll be snoring away. We didn't exactly see a lot of traffic on that path when we were on it."

Ryu nodded. "So, who wants to sneak?"

Petal spoke for the first time. "I'll do that."

Everyone turned her way, and she reddened. And stiffened her back. Day and night she dreaded that the others—who did *everything* better than she did (except cook, and Matu was actually very good at that, having traveled a lot with his cousin Tenar)—would one day turn and send her off as a burden. "I can sneak," she said in a gritty voice, as though they'd already accused her of lying. "You never noticed when I watched you doing Redbark."

Before Shigan could retort that they'd never bothered looking—Ryu could see he was about to say something flippant—she said, "Great idea. You scout in one direction, I'll in the other. We spot them without alerting them, return, get the others, and take them one at a time."

And that's exactly what happened.

By the time they got back with the last bandit, they could see two of the erstwhile bandits fitted with heavy wooden racks around their necks, sweating up the hillside with pails of night soil to be carried to the tea trees.

Ryu was also the one who insisted they leave the next morning.

"We could have waited a day," Shigan pointed out, squinting upward at the mackerel sky, which usually promised rain.

Ryu shook her head. "I know village people. More days of feeding us for free, and they'd expect something from us, or start giving us looks."

Shigan laughed. They rounded a hillside, and he pointed out that this was a great spot for morning Redbark drill. He dropped down, and flowed into the stretches that the others still grunted and winced through.

At least, Ryu noticed grimly, she could get her face close enough to sniff in the pungency of grass. A couple of blades tickled her face as she tried to get the muscles along the backs of her legs to loosen.

When they'd stretched, three of them stood up to begin Heaven and Earth, as Petal concentrated on an imaginary circle in which she did her footwork. Ryu led while scanning the environment. No danger anywhere on a peaceful summer morning. The only living thing in sight . . . no, the only moving thing, as the ground and air was full of life: grasses, plants, herbs, flowers, and the tea trees higher up. Insects and birds darted or hovered purposefully. In the middle distance Yaso ranged up the hillside to where a meadow could be seen growing wild.

They'd completed their first sword form when Matu said, "They wanted us to stay and protect them. That wouldn't be so bad."

Ryu scowled, and started the second — they always did Heaven and Earth three times.

Shigan's grin was crooked. "I saw your face when the elder came to you asking for a judgment about the bandits. You acted like someone had cheated at the Circle table."

Ryu's scowl deepened, and, hearing Ul Keg's voice in her head, she muttered, "I was told once that as soon as you start passing judgment on others, you start setting yourself up as a king."

"Clearly a fate worse than death!" Shigan cracked, laughing.

"Do you want to be a king?" Ryu retorted, her whirl and kick snapping the long panels of her robe with a crack!

"Eh, I can take or leave kings," Shigan said, and snapped *his* clothes. "Right now, I'll leave them — far, *far* away." And on finishing his third of what he thought of as Redbark Sword form, he flipped up his legs into a handstand, did the splits, and brought his legs down to hover just above the ground.

Ryu, goaded by this wordless challenge, also flipped to a handstand, but when she tried to do the splits her legs waved, each midway between horizontal and vertical, and then she fell over. She rolled to her feet, did a couple of back hand-springs, then sent a challenging smirk at Shigan.

Matu and Petal exchanged glances — those two were at it again, doing tricks they couldn't hope to compete with.

"Let's work on your footing," Matu said to Petal.

Ryu heard that, and abandoned the tricks. "You're doing great, Petal. Your footwork is so much better. Why don't we start the first moves?"

Petal flushed with pleasure, and silently joined Ryu as the two boys squared off with the swords.

Ryu had made a silent vow to train Petal out of that bowed back waiting for a stick. Petal never asked for anything, nor did she complain even when worked until her face was crimson, her braids damp with sweat.

TWENTY-FIVE

ON THEIR DEPARTURE FROM that village, the inhabitants had loaded a basket not only with fresh produce, but also tea cakes, which brightened their evening and morning camps.

They made their way up the coast to the bay. The imperial geomancers centuries earlier had rejected it for its north by northeast opening, and the imperial navigators had rejected it on account of the large conical island named Glass Rock not far from the bay, like a medicine ball dropping toward a mouth, behind which pirates or other attackers could hide. The small island had been left to itself.

Mindful of what they'd learned at their first village, the Redbark gallant wanderers had begun scouting ahead by turns, once they'd done their daily training. It being Shigan's morning, he left his gear with Ryu and ran on ahead, as they walked more slowly. When he returned, it was to report that he'd spotted the harbor over the next ridge. All looked peaceful from the top of that vantage.

Peaceful, they discovered shortly after their arrival, meant without any need for young would-be defenders.

The traders living there now had developed their own defenses; the Redbark wanderers learned by talking to a weathered hot-buns vendor that the harbor had a council of merchants who pooled resources to hire the big, brawny individuals in bright green tabards and broad-brimmed green hats, seen strutting along the street. All carried cudgels that they swung or twirled.

As four of the five Redbarks wolfed down their buns, for their basket had gotten down to a few withered greens, the chatty vendor informed them that all the merchants contributed to the upkeep of a lookout tower on top of Glass Rock Island.

They looked up and down the busy street, seeing all kinds of wares amid the many, many tea houses and sellers. The island mostly produced dark and red teas, compressed into cakes for ordinary trade—the locals did not try to sell to the wealthy, who insisted on seeing perfect leaves unfurl in their cups, often with flowers.

The Redbarks also saw a lot of young people more or less like them, all looking for ways to earn food and board. The wealthier establishments had their own guards, standing by the doors. Then there were those bravos in green with the cudgels.

They spent the day wandering about and listening. Matu told them that inns on gallant wanderer islands were used to gallant wanderer custom, but on islands with imperials, inns friendly to wanderers hung a white strip of cloth from the eave, or a tree, or a doorway.

"If it's mostly an imperial island, the white strip will be almost disguised, usually among blessings hanging from trees, or decorations," he told them.

Finding inns in this city was not a problem. By the time the shadows blended toward evening, they'd discovered that prices were stiff. Too stiff. The only coinage they had was what Second Uncle had given Matu to get him started. While that would go a long way for one, for five it wouldn't last a week.

They finally found a room at a dockside inn, with one window that brought in the smell of brine and fish. Dinner was extra. "Less than a week," Matu said with a sigh after he'd paid.

The next day they all went out looking for work. Shigan actually found a storyteller willing to hire him to play a battered guzheng, but only for tips. However, he soon discovered that the storyteller was, like the rest of her peers, the first to discover the latest news. She spent mornings and evenings scouring the quay and the taverns for gossip, and then spun it into tales for passers-by during the day.

Ryu had no luck—everyone chased her away, some scolding her as a useless, lazy urchin before she could even speak about being a watch guard. Finally she used one of the coins that Matu had shared out and bought a steamed yam from a vendor, whom she asked, "Where are the fights?"

"Fights?" the man repeated.

"For wagers," Ryu said, figuring every town had to have something like Old Rock's ring — if not more than one.

The vendor's thin brows drew down over his long nose. "That'd be Master Fin's house, way up the other end of the quay. But you, a young boy, you stay away from that place. It's bad."

"Bad? Why?" Ryu asked.

"No one wins but the house, there. You're better throwing your earnings into the water and hoping a magic carp springs up to snatch it and wish you luck." The vendor shook his head, his long gray braid switching like a donkey's tail. "As for the fighters, some come out feet first. Don't go there."

Ryu thanked the man, annoyed that once again she was looked down on as if she were ten years old, and she dodged the crowds as she ate her yam.

She found Master Fin's. Even during daylight there were big red lanterns with sun-crystals in them so that the light shone through the painted silk panels like some kind of demon eye. Each was painted with huge characters spelling out *Master Fin*.

At first she rejoiced, hoping that "Fin," which was Shigan's personal name, might be a sign of luck. But she was not certain what kind of luck as she entered. The place was crowded, the ring built up on wooden supports so that all could see. The air was thick with the acrid stench of sweat, with an iron tang beneath that made her shoulder blades twitch.

The two men fighting in the ring were both bloody, one staggering. They both fought with a steel knife each. As she watched, they flung themselves at each other, grunting and cursing, then one danced away, his knife dripping, as the other howled, "My eye! My eye!" and clapped a hand to his bleeding face.

"You lost," a big brawler grated, coming out. "Next!"

They didn't even clean the floor, which was smeared with blood, sweat, and spit. Ryu watched another match, appalled. This was as different from Old Rock's ring as day was from night. Old Rock had never let anyone get seriously hurt — he knew that the harbor guard would land on him fast if it happened. And even so, Ryu had gotten to know him enough to suspect that Old Rock would not hurt anyone if he could help it—not this way.

Worse, these men seemed to be fighting each other just to be fighting, or maybe they were part of the wagering crowd, but there were no coins tossed to them. Everything went through the equally big bruiser taking money and handing out slips of paper at the side. *The house always wins.*

Ryu knew that if she had to, she could win, but by using all her Essence—and for what? Her gaze followed the previous winner, who had three bleeding cuts. A couple of friends tied strips of cloth around the cuts, and then they all three went over to the betting table.

Ryu backed up and ran. What could she do now?

She was in a bleak mood when they all met up at their fishy-scented inn again after sundown. Ryu was already hungry again, but she was so disgusted at her inability to earn money she refused to admit to it.

Shigan appeared last, and in an extravagant gesture, tossed down the few very small coins he'd earned. "I know. It might cover half a very small bun, but at least I do have news. Not that it's any surprise. The Shadow Panthers are recruiting." His sour smile conveyed his opinion of the Shadow Panthers.

"We already knew that," Matu said. And grinned. "I have something better. There's someone hiring tea pickers. No experience needed. Apparently the leaves ripened, or flushed, or something. I didn't really understand the words."

"Tea pickers," Shigan repeated, eyes wide. "How hard can picking leaves off trees be?"

Matu said, "It doesn't pay much, but it's something."

Shigan said with a grin, "And it won't stink like fish. Let's do it."

They all showed up at the town center, where there was the expected notice board, to be found all over the Empire, though only the government or respected town leaders were permitted to put notices there. A crowd already waited—but the two people in charge, a man and a woman, both gray-haired, took them all. "Depending on how much and how well you pick, there will be a second day," the man bawled.

The pair led them up a path behind the city. It took all morning to reach a walled manor with a sun-drenched south-facing door. Over it, a sign, Benevolent Sun. They were led all the way around to the east gate, to discover a cluster of cottages in a dip between tree-covered slopes. In a courtyard

they found baskets of tough fronds, which they were
encouraged to weave into conical hats while they listened to
instructions. No one argued. While there had been a pleasant
breeze near the water, the south-facing slopes received the full
face of the sun, and those with experience knew they'd be
grateful for the hats by noon.

Ryu listened because she had been raised to respect her
elders. She was surprised to see Shigan leaning forward as if
listening to secret orders back at Loyalty Fortress on how to
beat the year ahead. They learned that not all leaves are picked
during harvesting, but only a few top young ones, with a
portion of the stem on which they have grown, and the so-
called bud, or tip, an unexpanded leaf at the end of the shoot.

A few leaves, part of the stem, and a tip are called the
"flush." They were here to pick flushes. They learned that a
flush with two or three leaves was called a "golden flush."
Flushes were collected with three, four and even five leaves.

What was so interesting about that? Ryu bent over her half-
made hat, wishing one of these people would turn out to be an
Essence martial artist. How long was it going to take to find
one? She had thought her search would end at the Sky Island
competition.

Presently they were divided into teams, issued baskets and
flasks of water, then dispersed to different areas to begin
picking. Shigan ended up on another team, one with a lot of
giggling older teens who reminded Ryu of those flirty Ki
cousins. The owner's daughter was also on that team. The rest
of Ryu's group were with her and a couple of strangers.

Picking was simple, as she'd figured. By the time she had
been reaching and stooping over and over, she began to
understand the difference between *simple* and *easy*. This work
was not easy. Their team chief came around with a sloshing
bucket to refill their flasks, saying, "Speed it up, speed it up!"

An older boy muttered, "Why are you harassing us when
it's so hot, and my back is breaking? We get paid exactly the
same."

The team leader looked all around before saying, "True,
but the owners let the teams with the best baskets first at the
food. And the good stuff always vanishes first."

Ayah! That was incentive. Ryu set to with a will, which
drew the other younger members into putting in more effort.

Ryu had seen how strong Yaso was when building the
Eagle Island tent. She saw it again in how tirelessly the orderly

continued picking the leaves, sometimes pausing to sniff them, eyes half shut.

Their group and Shigan's came in first, which put them first with the food. Ryu settled down contentedly at a free table. Petal quietly sat with her, and a couple of teammates joined them. Ryu ate ravenously, aware of sore neck and back muscles. And she'd just begun recovering from all the stretching!

They were finishing up with dessert, which was fresh-picked plums and lychee, when Shigan and Matu showed up, standing side by side, one startlingly handsome, the other snub-nosed and square-faced, his eyes and smile reflective of a good nature.

"Redbark Brother Ryu! There's a hot bath," Matu said. "You'll feel a lot better after a soak."

Ryu stared up longingly, tempted — sorely tempted — for the first time to throw away her disguise. But then she wouldn't be sitting with the others in comfortable friendship. In fact, she wouldn't be with them at all. There might be a women's bath too (from the sound of giggles behind them, there was) but it would of course be screened from the men's side.

"Naw," Ryu said, forcing a laugh.

"Got anything else to do?" Shigan asked, brows aslant. "You've got to stink as bad as I do." He sniffed the air above her head, and promptly and noisily gagged.

The teenage girls behind him giggled ingratiatingly.

Ryu had heard a familiar clinking sound. Trying not to choke, she mumbled, "Thought I'd play some pitch-pot. Keep my hand in."

"Join us if you change your mind," Shigan said and turned away.

The giggling teens followed him, one saying, "Just as well. Leave the little boys to mother's milk."

"Redbark Brother Ryu would surprise you," Shigan's voice came floating back. "He's the toughest of us all. But he was monk-taught. One of these days he'll figure out he's not actually a monk."

Ryu groaned inwardly. Sure enough, a gangling nineteen-year-old, judging by his sparse mustache that he kept fingering, and his knobby joints that he was still growing into, turned and eyed Ryu challengingly, saying in a goading voice, "How tough?"

Ryu backed away from her empty dish as she said, "Right

now, after bending over that basket all day, a hundred-year-old tortoise could beat me blindfolded. I think I might be able to manage some pitch-pot, though you might have to help me hold the arrows."

There was laughter at that, the bathers departed, and Ryu continued on to the pitch-pot game, feeling that now she had to play. At least she hadn't forgotten the trick of it, and while she was by no means the best, she wasn't the worst.

Sooner than she expected, Shigan and Matu showed up again, their hair damp, faces glowing after their relaxing soak. They were still trailing giggling girls, who had been flirting with them over the divider between the baths. They circled determinedly around Shigan.

He picked up a stack of arrows, hit the pot ears with every single one, then said, "That's it! I'm done."

That effectively broke up the party.

There were bare cottages with nothing more than sleeping mats and straw-stuffed pillows, but everyone rejected the stifling spaces still holding the heat of the day, in favor of sleeping in the court under the stars.

The five of them laid their sleep rolls in a row as usual. It was so good to lie down. Ryu stared upward at the constellations, askew from what she had grown up with. Her heavy eyes closed as she thought her usual prayer to the south. She was already drowsing when she heard Matu say, "Redbark Brother Shigan, I didn't know how good you are at pitch-pot."

Shigan snorted. "It's amazing what you can learn when you have nothing else to do during the long winter."

Ryu was not the only one who thought of winter work being just as hard as any other season, but she was too used to Shigan, Petal never spoke unless she had to, and Matu was too good-natured — besides, he had something else on his mind. "It's just that, if there was one of those wagering games going on, wouldn't that make money faster?"

Shigan gave a single, bitter laugh. "Fast, yes, and just as fast would be the crowd who chased you shouting *cheat*, though how you can cheat at that game, I still don't know. What they don't like, I learned the hard way, is a stranger coming in and taking all their money off them. Why do you think I ended up in the army?"

"Really?" Matu asked. "I thought families sent you in. Or that you wanted, I don't know, to be a captain, but then changed your mind."

"I was about fifty steps ahead of a gang wanting to rip me apart for fun before taking their coins back," Shigan said. "And there was the test going on, so I thought, why not try something new? It was far better than night-soil hauling, which was the only other way I'd found to earn my daily rice bowl. As for earning money, you should be pestering Ryu here, who very annoyingly always wins at Circle—when anyone can get him to play."

"Really?" Matu asked, turning wide eyes toward Ryu. "I don't remember seeing you play on Ten Leopards."

"That's because he's so much better than anyone else," Shigan commented, goading.

Stung at having attention unexpectedly thrust her way, Ryu snarled, "That's because it's *boring*."

Matu sat up, his silhouette turned her way. "How could Circle ever be boring?"

"Not at first," Ryu mumbled. "It's after the first ten moves or so, when I always know what's going to happen . . ." She snorted. "It's just a stupid game. I'd rather be outside doing Heav—Redbark Sword. At least that will get you somewhere."

The others fell silent, too tired to argue.

The next day most of them woke sore in muscles unused to constantly reaching upward. The only ones not sore from the unfamiliar motions were Petal, who had been doing three people's worth of back-breaking work ever since she was small, and Yaso, who seemed to glide through everyday life.

Ryu forced herself to do stretches, though it hurt so much at first that her eyes stung. But that didn't last. Stretching actually helped.

And so began another day, full of hot work, followed by two days, three, then a week.

To Petal, leaf-picking in the fragrant summer air, with no stick beating her and no threats or exhortations to stop being lazy and work harder made the days pass by in a blur of . . . not sweetness. There were too many dreads and worries for that. She was used to dread and worry beneath every breath. But those just made awareness of the present more to be cherished.

TWENTY-SIX

FAR TO THE SOUTH, the weather was even hotter, humid with almost daily storms passing through. Ul Keg stepped off a ship heaving on slow swells, drew in a breath redolent of burgeoning greenery, and peered up at massive tumbles of shiny black rock.

Not long after he first came to Sweetwater, when Olt and Iley's children were very small, Iley had insisted on there always being a place to retreat to if danger caught up with them. She and Olt had planned the retreat: snatch whichever child was nearest, and use temple resources to make their way to remote Burning Rock Island, the southern islands' largest temple to the goddess Suanek, who left the Snow Crane as Guardian of the Islands, most well known in the aspect of God of the Abandoned. Second Imperial Prince Enjai would never think to look for them there—the Alks had venerated Kanda and the Way, and Danno had been raised to be obedient, not religious.

Ul Keg had not even tried to find his way to Imai Island. He was certain that Olt and Iley would have left Sweetwater as soon as they discovered through Granny Anise that Yskanda had been snatched by mysterious men without raising an alarm. Men who possessed their own ship. Master Bankan would have been told by the governor himself, most likely, that the kidnappers had been imperial ferrets, which would stop inquiry—even commentary—cold as death.

Ul Keg's fellow passengers were mostly clerics and

pilgrims, all bringing gifts to the temple, which supported an enormous community of orphans, refugees, and impoverished people as well as those suffering chronic diseases no one else could diagnose.

He waited while the ship's crew unloaded his trunk of carefully packed inkstones, hoisted it onto his back, and set out. He had never been to Burning Rock Island, but a temple was a temple. It ought to be easy to find Olt and Iley, even under false names, surely?

He followed a stream of folk making their way up the path between the enormous shiny-sided stones. As he walked, he looked in wonder at other weird rock formations, like fantastical playthings for the gods. Perhaps they even were, though this, the largest island in the cluster, appeared to be what was left of a very large volcano. That in itself might have been a game to some whimsical god, who knew?

As he toiled in the humid heat toward the top of the trail, his stomach growled, and he trusted he would easily find the pair—an assumption that withered as soon as the rocks parted and he looked down into a valley shaped like a bowl, with a deep-water lake in the middle. All around this lake lay the community, built in the usual winding streets, as everyone knows demons like best to travel in straight lines. And on the steep slopes above the city, it appeared that every available bit of land, between the clumps of shady willows, had been terraced for rice and other crops. What turned an otherwise austere scene to stunning beauty were the wild orchids of every imaginable hue growing everywhere, apparently living on air.

He took one last, appreciative look at all this wealth of beauty gifted by the gods, then turned his attention to the many small huts. How would he search through all that?

He wouldn't. His gaze lifted to the temple on the other side of the water, built of white stone around a huge, serene statue of vaguely female form: the Sun Goddess of Mercy, oldest of the gods. This temple was *ancient*, even more ancient than worship of Suanek—who many maintained was a form of the Sun Goddess, come in human form to teach of peace.

Followers of the Snow Crane did not build statues of their own, but honored any statues already existing—Suanek most often—working their white cranes into decorations, clothes, and furnishings. Seeing the willows, the blue, the statue, caused a great uplifting in Ul Keg's heart. While he had not

been raised to follow the Snow Crane, he appreciated this path
to wisdom and knowledge.

Presently he began seeing Snow Crane shamans and their
acolytes, distinguished from other clerics by their robes of light
eggshell blue, representing the waters over which Suanek
(who also is depicted in white and blue robes) was taken
beyond the rising sun, on the back of a golden fish. The blue
was emblematic of the Snow Crane's guardianship.

Sometimes he envied the Snow Crane shamans these
robes, just because they were so cheerful: not only the
brightness belonging to the new and eager dedicates, but the
much worn, much washed and sun-dried robes of the old,
their dyes faded to soft blues the color of summer's dawn, of
ice, of tranquil sky-reflecting pools.

The temple was crowded, but he found plenty of young
acolytes on duty sorting people, and he soon found himself in
the correct area to donate the inkstones. Which were much
welcomed by a shaman as old as he was, her hair white.

After that he was free, but at first unsuccessful. A trip to
the smithy did not furnish Olt. The same at the carpenters'. He
tried the temple's medicine dispensary, but no sign of Iley.

In desperation he made his way to the all-important archive where Suanek's teachings were gathered along with healing and divination texts. He approached a monk who seemed
to be on duty and asked, "Do you have a much-scarred
scholar?"

"Oh, you mean Brother Yan?" The young monk lowered
his voice. "Some of the children call him Brother Mask, but
we're trying to get them to understand how terrible it is to be
burned in a fire."

Ul Keg was going to turn away, when he glimpsed a
familiar outline in a far doorway. Strange, how quick the
human mind is to recognize lineaments even in someone
wearing a mask and gloves, and dressed in voluminous light
blue—none of which Ul Keg had ever seen Iley wear. And yet,
in spite of the boyish topknot, he knew her outline instantly.

"Brother Yan, yes," Ul Keg said, raising his voice slightly.
"I bear a message for him."

Olt, it turned out, worked with the construction crew,
making bricks from mixing sand with the white clay from the
other side of the island. Mostly, though, they repaired
everything, materials being scarce, Olt explained as they
walked up one of the twisting paths past people laboring in

the terraced gardens. Being strong, he tended to be the one delivering loads of bricks, and so was known as Brother Brick.

When the gong rang the hour, he sat with Olt and Iley in the shade of a broad raintree, each with a bowl of rice balls in crisped cabbage leaves, clear cold water from a deep well to drink. No one was in earshot.

Before he took his first bite, he looked into those wary, tense faces, and said, "Yskanda is alive. I saw him myself."

Iley's shoulders dropped half a handspan, and she sat back, eyes closed. Tears leaked from between her eyelids and streamed down the corrugated scars on her face. Which looked somewhat better, or had Ul Keg remembered them as worse than they were?

Olt flushed, then ran shaking fingers over the top of his head, knocking his topknot askew. "I thought you came all the way to inform us he was dead. We have been mourning him ever since Granny Anise returned and . . ." He shook his head. "What we do not understand is how they found him."

Ul Keg bowed. "I ought to have said something the moment you saw me. I was afraid to. I did my very best, but I am not at all trained at skulking, and I have been living as if the imperial ferrets shadow my heels even now. Though I tried to avoid drawing notice."

Olt gave him a pained smile. "If the ferrets had shadowed you, they would have scooped up the three of us by now." And then, though he had a thousand urgent questions crowding his mind, he forced himself to be hospitable to this man who had traveled so far to bring news. "Please. Eat, you must be hungry."

Yskanda was alive! Yes, questions could wait until the monk was ready.

Ul Keg drank some of the delicious water, then began. "It was the Spring Festival. I had been tasked to serve in the imperial city, where I was one of the legs of our Phoenix Moon palanquin in the parade along the main street. Without any warning whatsoever, I found myself staring directly into Yskanda's face. He was scarcely an arm's length from me!"

"Did he see you?" Iley asked, eyes wide. "Did you speak?"

"No, and no. There is a decorative cloth hanging down, shrouding us to the knees. *He* never knew I was there. *I* was so shocked I tripped over my own feet, and nearly dropped my end of the palanquin. Yskanda helped steady it — his hand was almost on top of mine — then a young scholar called him away."

"How did he look? Was he a prisoner?"

"He seemed well. Tall, though he's very thin."

"Thin," Iley said softly. "Was he ill?"

"That I could not discover—I did not dare to be too inquisitive, lest someone wish to find out why." Ul Keg saw a covert glance pass between the two parents that he could not understand, so he went on with the news he knew would please at least one of them. "Yskanda wore scholar's garb—and the hat of one who has passed the Imperial Examination."

Both parents stared, Iley in delighted surprise, Olt in muted shock.

"The following week I spent trying to find out more. It's fortunate that our temple has had cordial relations with the imperial city's temples. It took a few days, but I was able to learn that Yskanda is apprenticed to no less an august figure than the Court Artist."

"Is that Yoli Jiwa?" Olt asked. "Is he still alive? He was old when I was there." He reflected, then added, "Of course, to twenty, anyone over thirty is old. But he had gray hair back then. He must be very venerable by now."

"Yes, and yes."

"Hush, let him speak," Iley whispered.

"There is little more to tell. I did see him once more. Yskanda was sitting in a garden outside the Sun God shrine, sketching alongside an old man with frosty eyebrows out to here, who I assume is the court artist. From what my gabby young novice guide said, Yskanda is well regarded as an artist by the young scholars and scribes. There was a temple ship full of pilgrims, and I made my way to that. It has stopped numerous times along the way, which gave me the chance to change ships twice. Just in case I might be followed. I did watch the new passengers each time, and no one was familiar from the previous journey." Ul Keg spread his hands—that was the extent of his capabilities at sneaking.

Iley breathed in relief that Yskanda was not in pain or durance, but beneath that was the old struggle to accept that none of her children had chosen the true scholar's path. At least he was alive!

Olt's expression remained shuttered as he looked down into his bowl.

They finished their meal, and in walking back down, Ul Keg saw that everyone worked, much like at any poor temple.

He labored through the remainder of the day alongside Olt in repairing a sagging wall, until the brassy gong reverberated through the valley announcing Dragon Hour.

The sun was setting. They ate with others, and Ul Keg departed to stay in the dormitory set aside for Ul monks. Olt said he would accompany him.

They walked in silence for a time, then Olt said, "Iley persists in believing he was ill over winter. She was praying day and night to keep his soul from wandering toward Heaven." His skepticism sharpened his tone to caustic, then eased. "Perhaps her feelings were a result of guilt in our having left Sweetwater. And she did get over it." He sighed. "Is there any sign he will be permitted to leave?"

"He was followed, that day on Spring Festival. That's why I dared not speak to him. He's guarded, even I could see that much."

"Ah." Olt looked down at the ground. No, at this moment he was no longer Olt the wood-carver. He was Danno, former imperial bodyguard. "I suspected as much. Yskanda. I almost wish it would have been one of the others. Yskanda is such a dreamer, and small as she is, Mouse is far better at handling herself in a dangerous situation." His voice had flattened.

He turned to Ul Keg. "I know you finished your Ul."

"Actually I seem to still be on it," Ul Keg replied with a smile.

Danno bowed. "You made this long journey solely for us. But on your return, if you could do one more thing for us, I promise I will light incense for the next year, and beg the Jade Emperor of Heaven to permit me to serve you for my next five lives."

Ul Keg waved that off. "My divinations and dreams all reminded me of my guilt in losing sight of Mouse that day. This is a small act of expiation."

"Crossing half the empire is not small," Danno said, bowing again. "If you can, tell him we are here. That's all. I don't want him burdened with worry."

Ul Keg bowed back. "I can try."

Danno bowed a third time, very low, hands tightly clasped. Ul Keg lifted him, protesting, "I don't dare promise more."

"I know." Danno looked skyward. "And I'll start preparing Iley to face the prospect that even if Yskanda is permitted to go, he might not choose to."

Ul Keg gazed at him in surprise.

Danno's face was half in shadow as he repeated, "I know Enjai. If he didn't have my boy put to death outright, then it has to be my second fear, that he's seducing Yskanda, while laying a trap for me."

"*Seducing* him?"

"I don't know the right word," Olt said with frustrated impatience. "You know what I mean. Showering him with special attention, honors, art. The way to Yskanda's soul was always art. And Enjai could beguile anyone when he wanted to exert himself. Anyone but Hanu," he added under his breath. "I can see him enjoying the prospect of turning Yskanda away from his fugitive father."

"Yskanda has a loyal heart. They all do."

"So says Hanu. She sees Mouse in dreams. Insists Mouse talks to her every night. That gives Hanu peace — I won't argue with that, any more than I did about the prayers for Yskanda over winter. At least I can take some comfort in knowing that my daughter is with First Son. But Yskanda . . . he could see a life of art as more desirable than returning to a scrabbling life with fugitive parents." He looked down at his hands, rough from years of hard work.

Ul Keg cut across that to what mattered. "You won't go to the imperial island." It was not a question but a warning.

"No. Though when we heard, I was going to find a ship. Iley — Hanu — figured out what I was doing, and we endured the worst argument of our lives. The conflict is still there. It's one of the reasons we live apart right now, though another is that she is trading for healing by treating others. And we're both conscious of staying apart to make it more difficult to find the both of us. I want to rescue Yskanda, she wants to pray." He looked away. "It's a terrible thing, to be torn between the worries over the safety of a child and over one another. And as I could not guarantee I could rescue him successfully, I had to promise her I would not go. Now that I know where he is . . ."

Ul Keg said quickly, "The imperial island is crawling with imperial guards. The other monks at the imperial city temple told me that shortly before my arrival that autumn, the measures for security tripled for some reason. With a few questions, I put that time around Yskanda's arrival."

"It's not the imperials I'd worry about, it's the ferrets," Danno said. "Maybe it's impossible. I haven't sparred seriously, beyond teaching my children, since the day I left the imperial island. But if Yskanda is well, truly well, even happy . . ." He looked away, his face lined with conflict.

Then he passed a hand over his forehead. "My only hold on sanity is my belief that First Son is still out there, safe and flourishing as he protects Mouse. The phoenix feather is a reminder of *his* path, at least. He will look out for the others. I have to believe that," he breathed.

Ul Keg was going to remind him that it was only his assumption that the phoenix feather was predictive of military success—and for their first son. He offered what comfort he could, but when he left, he was wondering how long before Danno broke away to rescue his son the dreamer.

TWENTY-SEVEN

ONE JOB LED TO another, tea picking having become both simple and easy.

When at last the island's tea trees had been harvested, summer had settled in, dry and hot under days of brilliant sunlight. Ryu and her companions forced themselves up each morning before dawn to do their drills. In the evenings, Ryu usually made her way to whatever stream could be found, where she could bathe in peace, though these were measurably smaller each day.

Finally word spread that picking was done until the next flush. Before the five of them could discuss what to do next — three of them talking, and two listening — the latest owner pulled Shigan aside one day, having determined that they were a band. Of course Shigan had to be their chief.

The next morning, when the four met for their morning routine, he said, "I volunteered us to crew on the boat taking last year's tea cakes to one of the Fragrance Islands. They trade for cloth, but we don't have to come back."

"I'm ready to go somewhere new. But . . . crew?" Ryu repeated doubtfully.

"On a ship?" Matu swallowed.

Petal's good eye flicked between them. Yaso was already gone, climbing the path upward in search of wild herbs.

"We take charge of the cargo, and help the sailors when they need an extra hand," Shigan explained. "We unload and deliver the tea to its destination. We'd see a new island, and not have to pay for the trip. Instead, we get paid!"

Yaso made no objections, as usual—and quietly visited the herbalist to trade some rare herb finds for plenty of ginger medicine for Matu.

A couple of days later, as summer's heat pressed down on the harbor, the five toiled alongside the rest of the ship's crew trundling barrels of tightly packed tea cakes that they had helped pack themselves up the ramp to the ship.

Once they got the barrels to the deck, they tipped them one by one into nets, which were lowered to the hold, and then rolled into their assigned compartment. After that, they returned to the deck, where Yaso stood with Matu as the latter drank his first dose of ginger medicine.

"Hold!" The captain halted a string of bearers carrying bulky hemp-wrapped packages.

Ryu looked around, then upward, at where a couple of boys chattered as they hung the usual red flags inscribed with talismans to ward angry sky dragons and their typhoon winds. The bright summer sun lit the cinnabar dye to fiery crimson.

"Way! Way!"

Ryu skipped aside as burly, sweating porters muscled some very heavy barrels up the ramp. "Stow those on deck, midway along, either side," the captain bawled.

Relieved, the porters slowly bumped the barrels along the deck. "What's in those?" Ryu asked a passing porter.

"Iron hooks for cauldrons," one said, briefly pausing to wipe his forehead across his sleeve. "Sends 'em twice a year to his brother . . ." His voice was smothered by the rumble of his barrel as he and his partner pushed it to where the captain indicated. When he upended it, it fell into place with a deep *tunk* that made the entire ship shiver. A second *tunk!* From the opposite rail shivered the deck beneath their feet once more.

The burly porters thumped down the ramp, one muttering, "That's done till winter!" before they disappeared into the busy crowd on the quay.

"All right, that's the big ones," the captain said. "Now the smaller cargo comes in."

The porters with the hemp packages moved up the ramp, and other cargo carriers crowded behind. Ryu and the others offered to help, though they were only responsible for their tea, but their offer was gratefully accepted by a harried round ball of a merchant, who was also carrying tea, though in smaller packages instead of barrels. "No! No! Keep it upright—don't shake it—yes, that's . . . Careful of that corner, do you see the corner? Just so ..."

She kept up an anxious flutter of words that her harassed helpers seemed to bend against, the way people bend their backs to a bitter wind.

After her cargo was settled to her satisfaction, the last of the holds were filled, and the captain walked the length of the ship. "Top of the tide, excellent. Cast off!"

Shigan was already at one of the huge hempen ropes bent around the chain that kept the ship next to the dock. Ryu ran to join him. They were overseen by the ship's single guard, a brawny fellow with a toothy grin below a fierce mustache. His braids had been tied up with black and yellow ribbons, which swung as he gestured the others into place along the heavy rope. He alone lifted the loop from around the post, his muscular arms flexing.

He waved at the others to carry the rope to where it would be coiled down. Ryu followed his broad back—he wore only a vest, over a broad crimson sash and billowing green trousers stuffed into boots. Ryu blinked—was that a tattoo on his neck? The vest shifted, and it was gone.

All kinds of people got tattoos, she had discovered while walking about the harbor. It didn't have to be a Shadow Panther tattoo—and even if it was, she shouldn't assume he was evil. Nothing had happened during the competition, except attempts to recruit people. The Shadow Panthers weren't to blame for those bandits who'd apparently gone to the competition in order to get into the sect. The Shadow Panthers had rejected them.

"Why are you frowning? You seasick too?" That was Shigan, straightening up from placing his coil of the rope.

"Fine," Ryu said. "But hungry."

"Don't mention food around Matu," Shigan said, gazing down the length of the ship, to where Matu stood at the rail, pale and stiff, his face into the wind. "It takes guts, walking onto a ship, knowing what it's going to do to you."

"I know. He always says he's ready, but you can see how much he hates—"

"Got a sick one?"

The deep voice came from behind them. They turned to see the big guard smiling down at them. He was huge! "I'm Tiger Teg," he said, tapping his broad chest with a hand as big as a dish. "You?"

Shigan and Ryu introduced themselves, then Tiger Teg grinned. "Soon's we get out to sea, we'll have a tot to celebrate. But first, we need to get around Glass Isle. Get ready — we'll be shifting the sails soon."

"I like this part," Shigan confided as they were motioned to one of the rope-pulling parties.

"What's to like about rope-hauling?" Ryu grumbled. She was already overheated. The thought of drinking hot rice wine made her stomach close.

"What I like is watching how the sails spill wind into each other. You can feel it working," he said.

Ryu wiped her damp forehead. "That part I like, too. When we don't have to haul ropes!"

They weathered the island and began plunging into a green sea full of restless whitecaps, as the wind picked up. The wind at first felt deliciously cool after the stunning heat, then cold as rain moved in swiftly, the first in two weeks.

Ryu was actually glad of the heated rice wine that Tiger Teg brought around after the meal was served. It warmed Ryu from within, and made her eyelids heavy. She took a quick look at Matu, to discover him holding his own, though still pale. Petal and Yaso sat with him, ready to bring more ginger medicine.

That night set the tone for the next several days.

Nothing extraordinary happened during those days. Shigan had been right. Being on the crew was easy enough. The wind stayed steady, so they seldom had to help the sailors with the sails. They merely had to walk about once each watch to make certain the ropes holding the cargo in place were taut and secure.

The rest of the time they watched islands emerge from the horizon, grow, gain detail, slide by, and vanish behind them. There were two people who played bamboo flutes, who often entertained at night, and the captain had a Circle board. The augur was a veteran player, relishing all comers.

Tiger Teg wandered along the ship, chatting with all. He knew everyone by name, and insisted on sharing rice wine every evening. Even Matu got coaxed into trying a couple of sips—he loathed being the only weak one, another bit of evidence that he was far from strong enough to go rescue his father. And find out what had happened to his mother, who had been the training master before Second Uncle took over when she did not return.

As he lay back, enduring the ship-induced vertigo, he reminded himself that strength would come.

Ryu did not like wine when she was already warm. She did not understand how most of the men seemed to drink just because it was there. She discovered that if she took the cup and lifted it to her lips, Tiger Teg assumed she was downing it, and he turned to the next person, so she could pour out the liquor behind her leg and step on the wet spot to hide it. That was if Tiger Teg even found her. She had discovered a single sealed compartment that had no cargo but a couple left-over rice barrels, so she did her drills there. The routine was soothing.

They remained in sight of one or another island until the sixth morning, when they woke to clear skies and deep blue seas. The wind had died down to uncertain gusts, which left the ship wallowing, more adrift than sailing.

By the third hour of Phoenix watch, the heat beat down mercilessly. Most of the ship's people tried to hide from the sun, including the old augur, who they learned had spent his entire life on the sea. Even Shigan was longing for the journey to end — or at least that day to spend itself.

All except Tiger Teg, who ranged around as always, full of jokes and laughter.

"This is the middle of our journey," Tiger Teg said when the sun finally began its downward curve. "We must drink to the sky gods tonight to waken up the wind imps!"

Shigan muttered to Ryu, "I've got the worst headache. I'll puke if I even smell that rice wine of his."

Ryu said, "I've been hiding."

"He comes looking for me."

"Then dump it out." She mimed pouring a cup on deck.

Shigan looked askance. "How do you keep him from seeing the puddle, or smelling it?"

"Stay on deck between two lanterns."

"And if he watches? He always seems to."

Ryu's mouth opened. She hesitated. It was true, Tiger Teg paid more attention to Shigan, and to the other young men among the crew, than he did to Ryu or the other younger ones. Petal and the two gray-haired people, both merchants, he'd pretty much ignored, except for a friendly word now and then.

And the times Ryu hid, Tiger Teg hadn't come looking for *her*.

"I'll try to distract him," Ryu said.

Shigan nodded gratefully as he thumbed his temples. "Don't forget."

Ryu didn't. Tiger Teg made his rounds later than usual, right before Ghost Moon was to rise, and Phoenix Moon, in its basket-shaped phase, sank toward the opposite horizon. Ryu had to lock her knees, she was so tired of standing at the rail in her chosen spot, but at last he stamped along the deck, tiger-braids swinging, his teeth gleaming in the lantern light. "Ho, there, Little Redbark Brother Ryu! Toast to the sky gods, and may the wind imps favor us, ha ha ha!"

Ryu took her cup, tapped it to his, and raised it to her mouth. Maybe it was the hot sun, but the wine smelled even sharper than usual. "Good!" She pointed behind him. "Say, is that a kraken?"

Tiger Teg whirled around. "Where?" he barked, peering over the rail.

Ryu dumped out her wine then stepped to the rail, lunging out as if that might bring her nearer to the imaginary kraken. "Out there . . . I was sure I saw something. But it must have gone down below the surface again."

Back was the broad smile. "Right where they belong, says I. Krakens belong in the deeps! Now, where's—"

"Here I am," Shigan said, drifting up, the light sharp over the fine bones of his face, hollowing his eyes. "To the sky gods!" He raised his cup to Tiger Teg's.

And Ryu said, "I see it again!"

Once more Tiger Teg whirled around, as Ryu said, "Did you see it? Have you ever seen one? Of course you must have, being so traveled."

"Twice," Tiger Teg said, his shoulders relaxing. "I missed it, I guess. I see nothing out there at all. Not a thing. All is peaceful. Just the way we like it, ha ha!" He yawned. "It's been a long, hot day. I'll just finish my rounds . . ." He yawned again—one might even say he yawned with intent—then continued on down the deck, exhorting each person he met to toast the gods, as Ryu and Shigan leaned against the rail, staring out, each wondering what the next island might bring.

Ryu stared after Tiger Teg, aware that the only real humor she'd heard in all that laughter and brag had been after the words *just the way we like it*.

TWENTY-EIGHT

A SHORT TIME LATER, Petal emerged on deck, looking around uneasily. By now her habit was to turn to Eagle Island Brother Matu first if she had something to say, as they were so often left to one another while Brothers Shigan and Ryu argued, or challenged each other doing tricks, or practiced Redbark at a speed Petal was grimly certain she could never match.

But Eagle Island Brother Matu had fallen deeply asleep — as had every single member of the crew she passed as she made her way up to the deck.

There she paused, straining to listen. There it was again, a soft hiss and splash that countered the rhythm of the sea. She knew her hearing was better than most people's. Maybe it was caused by being one-eyed. More likely it was due to the way her stepmother had, when in bad moods, enjoyed creeping up behind Petal, and if she caught her sitting down or resting or even standing still instead of working, would swing that withy cane of hers and cackle as Petal jumped violently at the first blow.

Consequently it had been a couple of years since her stepmother had been able to catch her out, no matter how softly she stepped. As soon as Petal heard the slightest alteration in ambient sound around her, she'd leap up and vigorously busy herself. The beating usually came anyway, but it never caught her by surprise.

She bypassed slumped figures. Was *everybody* asleep?

Overhead the sails hung slack.

Petal rounded the stern — and there, to her profound relief, she found two familiar figures at the rail. She recognized their lineaments immediately, and hurried forward. "Someone's coming," she said.

The two turned to face her.

"Someone?" Ryu repeated, bewildered as she looked up and down the deck.

"Coming from where?" Shigan asked, peering around then upward at the slatted sail gently bumping the mast.

Petal pointed out at sea, sick with worry that they wouldn't believe her.

Both turned to peer into the thick darkness. Clouds had covered the sky, making it impossible to discern the horizon, much less anything else.

"Uh, did you tell the captain?" Ryu asked.

Petal clutched her hands close to her ribs, her shoulders hunched. "I didn't . . ." She was afraid to say she didn't dare disturb the captain, lest she be wrong and someone blame her. "Everyone I saw is asleep. Including the guard — I almost tripped over him when I came around the back end." She pointed.

"Tiger Teg asleep?" Ryu repeated. "He was here not half an incense stick ago. Less — "

Yaso drifted up then, and joined them. "I think he forgot to add his herb to his own flask. So I added it for him."

"I don't understand," Ryu began.

"I believe I do," Shigan muttered. "I smelled it. Thought it was just the heat and my headache, but . . . Yaso. Tiger Teg put some kind of sleep herb in the wine?"

"Yes," Yaso said equably. "The captain is awake."

"Should we get him?" Ryu asked.

"What can he do if everyone else is asleep? Except us. Because we didn't drink it." Shigan thumbed his temples.

"But why would Tiger Teg . . ." Ryu turned to Yaso. "Wait. Did he want everyone but him to be put to sleep?" Then she heard a soft sound, coming from the sea on the opposite side of the ship. And the pieces began to come together. "Duck!" She crouched down.

Shigan stared at her, then crouched down, their knees touching. Petal knelt a couple paces away, hunched over, hands clasped tightly. Only Yaso stood, but in the shadows.

Ryu said to Shigan, "I think there's a plot. And Tiger Teg is part of it." In a quick voice, Ryu explained about the tattoo.

"I'm not saying all Shadow Panthers are pirates, or robbers, but the sleep herb, the two boats coming, I think we're about to be under attack."

Shigan's mouth twisted. "Ayah, it was a good life while it lasted." He sighed under his breath, then, with a laugh, "We may as well fetch out our wooden swords, go to the prow, and go down fighting."

"Not the prow." Ryu saw it all, exactly the way she saw the paths laid out in black and white stones of the Circle game. "There's two boats. One for either side. Board at the same time." She turned to Petal. "Can you hear how many oars?"

The weak lantern light from overhead barely reached her eyes as they narrowed. "Six . . . no, eight . . . Not always together . . . eight to a side?"

"Thirty-two," Ryu whispered.

"What are you thinking?" Shigan asked, but Ryu had gone remote, the way she had that night on the wall of Loyalty Fortress when the mercenaries attacked.

She looked along the deck, up, down. Then stilled. "Ha." It was barely a soft breath. To Petal, "Which one is closer?"

Petal tipped her head, then pointed to the opposite rail. Ryu said to Shigan and Petal, "Stay down in case they shoot," bent over, and vanished in a few quick steps.

Ignoring the order, Shigan vaulted to the hatch and leaped down to Tiger Teg's cabin, where he overturned everything until he spotted a bow and arrows. He grabbed these, then ran back to the deck, and stopped when he saw Ryu, now faintly glowing, standing before one of those barrels of iron implements.

"Ryu. You can't shift those . . ."

Ryu didn't hear him. Anger and desperation ignited the ball of Essence burning in her core. It flared into a fierce sun as she eyed the barrel. Her hands slipped along the wood, then dropped — even if she used all her Essence, her bones would shatter before she could lift this dead weight as a dead weight.

But . . . she heard her father's deep, quiet voice, repeating the Four Pillars, and reminding them that *a finger can move an iron spear . . .*

It just has to be already moving.

The ship wallowed, sinking, rising on the lazy swells. When the ship rose to the top of a wave, her body twisted into the many-thousand-thousand times practiced earth stroke Bird Rises from the Grass. There was just enough lift from the deck heaving the barrel upward for her to continue its rise by bringing Essence up from her core as she smacked the barrel into a slow ascent. That rise was very slow, and minimal, but it was all she needed. As the barrel reached the top of its short arc, she risked a glance down. There were the bandits in their longboat, swords bare, eyes on her . . .

Her hips torqued and her opposing hand swept up in a circle, leaving a trail of scintillation. Then she smacked the barrel in Lightning Strikes From the Sky.

The barrel shot down to the middle of the longboat, splintering it. The bandits yelled as they were thrown into the water, their weapons vanishing in the inky waters.

A few started for the ship, in order to climb up the side, but Shigan was there at the rail. He drew aim and shot. Once, twice. Both times his arrow struck, once in a shoulder, the second in a kicking leg. Howling imprecations, the bandits began swimming away —

Shigan looked for Ryu, but she was already gone. He sent one last arrow after the bandits, heard a gratifying yelp, and bolted after Ryu to the opposite side of the deck. He had three arrows left. He nocked and aimed as he raced to the rail. The second barrel was already gone. Splinters floated on the water, would-be boarders thrashing and bobbing about. He shot one reaching for the side of the ship.

From behind, an incoherent shout, "Ayah! What? What? How?"

Shigan glanced back, to see the captain bustling up, still gobbling, "I—I—I. . . What are you—who is that? Where is Teg Nan?"

Shigan turned to shoot again, and then again with his last arrow—as all the bandits, or pirates, or whatever they were, swam away, two towing those with arrows bobbing in their flesh. He lowered the bow to look for Ryu. "We should—"

He stopped speaking when he saw Ryu sitting against a stack of cargo, hands loose, head drooping. "Ryu?"

His question collided with the captain's arrival.

The captain halted, waving his arms as he exclaimed, "That's astonishing! Pirates—where did they come from—where is my guard?"

Ryu hadn't moved, so Shigan said, "Asleep. Drugged, thanks to Yaso, who added to Tiger Teg's flask whatever it was that Tiger Teg put in the drink for everyone else. Yaso must have thought the herb was necessary, I don't know why he did it. But my guess is, Tiger Teg is part of this attack."

Ryu flung back her head. "Their ship."

"What?"

Everyone turned to Ryu.

She breathed deeply. Some of her strength returned, but her Essence was gone. Her limbs felt heavy as boulders as she forced herself to her feet. "They're swimming. Means there has to be a ship. Right? We need to ready for attack."

"We? Not if you bring on the thunder again," Shigan joked. "I never thought to see Lightning Strikes from the Sky used . . . like that. You didn't even use a sword."

Ryu just squinted at him — and he remembered how wan Ryu had been after the mercenary attack. He peered into her face. "You all right?"

She stepped back, turning away. "Fine."

"I'm very glad to hear that, Young Firebolt," the captain said, his voice high with disbelief. "Pirates — Teg Nan — I've known him four, five years. But ever since he came back with that tattoo . . . Ah, I don't want to say something about an old friend, but . . ."

"I think we should tie him up now, and ask questions later," Shigan said.

The captain nodded unhappily, passing his hand over his face as if he could clear his thoughts. "Attack," he muttered once or twice. "What if they . . . what is that?"

He looked over the rail. They all did, Shigan bracing for a pirate ship bristling with steel. Maybe even cannon.

He peered, trying to blink away the murk, and then realized he was staring into vapors rising from the water, swirling into rapidly increasing mists. The captain issued several disjointed orders, though his crew snored below. By the time Shigan, with Petal helping, got Tiger Teg's thick limbs trussed up, the ship was enveloped in thick, damp fog. From the sound of water running down the sides, the ship was still moving.

The captain bade everyone keep silent, lest the pirate hear them — and so passed the rest of a tense night.

When the eastern horizon began to blue, the air had cleared. They were alone in the ocean. The augur woke, blurry and shaking, but, harried by the captain, soon restored them to the correct bearing.

The captain prowled his ship, furious and betrayed. He had set aside the cup of wine Tiger Teg had given him, meaning to drink it when he finished writing up his log — and then had accidentally knocked it over, so he'd gone in search of the guard, in time to see the smallest person on board crash a barrel of iron into a boat full of attackers.

When Ryu woke to bone-aching tiredness, it was to discover to her intense embarrassment that everyone on the ship had begun calling her Young Firebolt. After the fourth wide-eyed, emphatic thanks—and repeated bows—she decided against breakfast and slunk back down to the hold, where she found Petal coaxing Matu to eat and drink a little.

"You look like I feel, Brother Firebolt," Matu said. "Did you get anything to eat?"

"Don't call me that," she mumbled, her ears prickling with heat.

Matu said, "You got a name. They gave you a hero's name."

"But I wasn't a hero. It was just self-defense."

Matu waved a hand, shut his eyes, and Petal said in a low voice, "You saved our lives. If you scoff it off, it might sound to the others as if our lives don't matter."

"No, no, no, I don't mean that."

"I know," Petal said. "You know. But they don't know."

Ryu bent her head, and decided to live out the rest of the trip in the hold—she needed more sleep anyway.

But she couldn't sleep forever. She'd had time to think, and late that night, thoroughly tired of naps, she ventured up on deck, hoping the rest were down for the night.

She found only Shigan and one of sailors patrolling the ship. Doing Tiger Teg's duty. No more nasty rice wine forced on them. She went up to Shigan, who said, low-voiced, "Tiger Teg told the captain everything. Said he was all but crying. He joined the Shadow Panthers two years ago. I guess if a senior brother gives you an order, you have to obey. And, well, that senior brother recently got a ship and wanted to commence piracy. This was to be their first go."

Ryu sighed. "What's going to happen to him? Tiger Teg, I mean. I don't care what happens to the pirate captain."

"He gets turned over to the harbor chiefs, our captain said. But since nothing actually happened to us, and some of those chiefs are afraid of Shadow Panther retribution, probably nothing to Tiger Teg. Short of his losing his position with the captain."

Ryu brooded. "If they got on board there would have been

plenty happening. But we wouldn't be alive to talk about it."

"Tiger Teg says that they weren't going to kill anyone, just take the best cargo. Oh, and play around with us Redbarks, as revenge for our interference."

"Do you believe that?" Ryu demanded.

"No. But it doesn't matter what *we* think," Shigan said, brows aslant.

"That's not justice," Ryu muttered.

Shigan leaned against the rail, arms crossed. "What would justice look like to you in this situation, Redbark Brother Ryu?"

Ryu opened her mouth, then closed it. The ship had lost only two barrels—both used by Ryu as a weapon. The attackers had lost their two boats, plus any who had drowned. And then there were the arrows . . ."

"Did you kill any of them?"

"I tried not to. Went for limbs, since the pirates were already in the water. But I can't say for certain." He didn't sound as if he cared one way or the other.

Ryu brooded some more, and was still brooding later on when she rounded the nearly empty deck, and discovered Yaso looking out at the sinking Ghost Moon. "Yaso," she said. "That fog. It . . . smelled of Essence, like dank water, sort of. You made it, right?"

"It's easy enough," Yaso replied. "You could do it."

Ryu was going to scoff, then remembered her mother using fog to get away from the evil prince in The Story. "I don't have any Essence paper," she said.

"You don't need Essence paper," Yaso replied. "Bring Essence through you."

"So I'm still not doing it right?"

"How do you feel?"

"Worn out," Ryu admitted. "But I thought I was doing it right. I work on my breathing every day . . ."

"Is it not written, *Water fights not to be first, it fights not to be strongest, but merely to flow unceasingly?*" Yaso said equably. "It will come, but you must learn the consequences."

"I think I'm feeling the consequences," Ryu said.

Yaso nodded. "That is true. But there are also consequences in the world."

Ryu stared upward and then around her. "There are? Where? What?"

"From last night, there is little to be seen, though the effect can be felt, and that was mostly my fog. The currents are moving slowly over the waters and dissipating. But that was not true the night on the wall at Loyalty Fortress."

Ryu's memory shot back to that horrible night. Consequences? But she hadn't seen anything strange—and then when that sudden storm hit, she couldn't see at all—

She gasped. "That storm? That was . . . me?"

"Yes. It became a typhoon, mostly at sea."

Ryu fell against the rail, horrified. "I don't understand! Then . . . then I shouldn't even use Essence at all?"

Yaso's voice was patient. "When you lifted those barrels, you did not smash your hand against them to lift, did you?"

"No."

"You sensed the rise of the ship, which did most of the work of raising the barrels, and then you merely continued the arc, yes?"

"Yes, that's right."

"So it is with Essence. You understood how to get the best effect with the least disturbance. Is that not your First Pillar?"

"Yes," Ryu whispered.

Yaso smiled. "Water is not your natural element the way fire is, but that does not mean you cannot learn to use it. Air as well. And earth, as well as metal, your second strongest element. But your instinct with water, it was well." And, again, the quotation, "Water fights not to be first, it fights not to be strongest, but merely to flow unceasingly."

Ryu shut her eyes, hearing those words whispered in her mother's voice, and again in Ul Keg's, as she sat writhing with impatience at the tedium of studying *The Five Elements*.

She blinked, the voices vanished—and Yaso was moving away down the deck.

Ryu was so very weary. She yawned and yawned again, shuffling back to her bed. She had nearly reached her blankets when it occurred to her that Yaso was not just standing around, but was on watch. For that ship to attack? For that matter, how much Essence training did Yaso have? Enough to be an Essence master? And if Yaso was an Essence master, why did Commander Weken not say so?

Ryu turned around to put all these questions to the orderly, but when she got to the deck, she couldn't find Yaso. She yawned again, gave up, and went back down to the hold.

When she did see Yaso again, it was in company, and there was no time for any more talk about Essence, but by then she had come to the realization that she needed to think out, and practice, what she had already heard.

Two days later they reached their destination, where everything pretty much happened as Shigan had predicted.

At least, Ryu thought as they set out on the road (Matu already looking less like a ghost), they had money in their pockets.

As soon as they left the harbor behind, "Let's practice and scrap," she said. Even if nothing else made sense, it was always a relief just to *move*.

TWENTY-NINE

AFTER THAT MOMENTOUS SPRING Festival, Yskanda stumbled after an unknown graywing as soon as the group got to the gate. He was hurried along to the court artist's suite, but instead of finding Court Artist Yoli in the workroom, Yskanda discovered him in the never-before-seen reception room, a fine small space decorated with screens.

Court Artist Yoli was adjusting the long sleeves on his crimson court robe, the emblem of a fifth ranker stitched across the breast and back.

"I—" Yskanda began, appalled at how grubby he was.

"Edict," the court artist said. "You'll do as is."

What did that mean? One night of freedom followed by Lotus Blossom Square? Imperial edicts could only be terrible things.

Or, it turned out, promotions. It was no less a figure than Bitternail who arrived bearing a golden scroll, which meant he was at that moment the Voice of the Emperor.

Court Artist Yoli sank to his knees with a wince and a grunt. His duty pages flopped to the floor in the background, and after a heartbeat's hesitation Yskanda also knelt behind Yoli and to the right.

Bitternail then read out the edict, which was written on silk woven of golden thread, appointing Yskanda to the ninth rank of service, and making him Assistant to Court Artist Yoli. Bitternail then gravely gave the edict into Yskanda's nerveless hands. Yoli cast a covert glance behind in obvious hint as he bowed and intoned, "This obedient servant gives thanks to his imperial majesty for his graciousness and benevolence," obediently echoed by Yskanda, whose wits had flown to the winds.

Bitternail then withdrew, and Yskanda, still on his knees, looked a little wild-eyed.

Court Artist Yoli grunted to his feet, saying. "You can rise now, my boy."

"Is this . . . is this . . ."

"You are a Talent, Afan Yskanda. Talents move up the promotions quickly, everyone expects it. The benefit is that I will be able to train you, and your days will be filled with art. Unless you wish to take classes again in order to prepare for the examination in three years. If you would like a better court appointment."

"No! I mean . . ." Yskanda didn't know what he meant.

The court artist's brows lowered over his nose. He began again. "It seems," he said slowly, "that his imperial majesty's beneficence has bestowed an assistant on me for whom I am not only teacher, but master. Do you want to become a court artist?"

Yskanda opened his mouth to say what he assumed the court artist wished to hear, for that kind of flattery was part of politeness, but more importantly it was about the only weapon of defense that he had. And yet, when he raised his eyes to meet the court artist's steady gaze, he could not lie. "This undeserving wretch is too stupid to understand the question of want, only what is expected, that is, he admires the esteemed court artist—"

Court Artist Yoli rescued him from that tangle of words. "Our students grow up learning the set phrases of formal talk," he said wryly. "What I want from you is what you think, not flattery couched in traditional polite dissembling. I'm to gather you don't want to be here, or is it you don't know what you want?"

"It's that," Yskanda said numbly, too afraid to add that his true want was to escape as soon as possible. And yet, and yet.

Court Artist Yoli, a close observer for well over half a century, saw the fear followed by the yearning, and said easily, "It's to be expected that someone your age would be unsure. I gather you do not dislike our lessons?"

Yskanda's eyes widened, so that he looked like a startled deer. "I love being in here."

"It's when you go out the door that you're unsure," the court artist said. And when Yskanda flushed to the ears, the court artist hastened to add, "Never mind that. I have no control over what happens outside my door, and don't try to. This is one of the chief reasons I've survived as long as I have. Understand?"

"Yes, Court Artist Yoli."

"Excellent. Now, to our matters. I'm certain you are aware of the difference between scholarly artists and court artists, am I correct?"

"I . . . think so?" Yskanda said. At that moment he was unsure that his feet were still attached to his legs. His entire body seemed to have turned to water.

"Let's begin at the beginning. I am a court artist, not a scholarly artist. Depending on who's talking, one is hidebound while the other achieves greatness, or else one makes contributions of importance that will resonate down the centuries while the other creates frivolities that don't last past the next festival. I don't care what the sages say, or what the nobles say. None of us can control what will be deemed valuable by our progeny. We can only do our best, always. Even if the emperor tells us to draw ducklings for his children, or grandchildren when those come into being. They will be the very best ducklings you can contrive. If you can promise me that, and believe it, then you and I can work together."

Yskanda's gaze had risen, his expression so ardent in that beautiful face that the old, skeptical court artist felt his heart bumping against his ribs.

"I can," Yskanda whispered with all the force of a vow.

"Then we might as well do it right," Court Artist Yoli said. "Page!"

The duty page appeared, was dispatched for wine and cakes, and on his return, the court artist ceremoniously poured out wine as he said, "Make your bow."

Yskanda regarded bows as another defensive weapon—except now. Alight with sincerity, he dropped to his knees, spread his arms wide so his sleeves brushed over the top of the floor, then brought them together to press to the floor, his forehead on top of his right hand.

"Rise, Assistant Court Artist Afan," Yoli said.

The page served the cakes and wine with proper ceremony. Yoli and Yskanda ate, drank, and then returned to the workroom.

There, Yoli said, "Your first duty, my new young assistant, will be accompanying me when I am summoned to attend court." The court artist gave him a wry look. Yskanda's appalled expression made clear what he thought of that idea.

The court artist did not give Yskanda time to say anything to that, which was probably just as well. He nodded at the edict. "I'll see to this—we'll store it with my own. Page! Take Assistant Court Artist Afan back to see to his arrangements."

Yskanda got back to his dormitory to discover all his things packed up, and a tall, gaunt graywing who introduced himself as Goldneedle waiting for him with another, younger graywing standing next to him. "Assistant Court Artist Afan," Goldneedle said with a short bow. "Now that you have been promoted, Juniper will see to your needs. He will show you to your new quarters."

Juniper bowed respectfully, then indicated Yskanda should follow.

A rapid journey through the labyrinth took him to a set of buildings he had only glimpsed, not far beyond Bright. These were set around a bare, raked-gravel court. Each door opened into a small sleep-chamber obviously set up for two, with just enough room for the bed, a clothes tree, and a trunk that could be used as a desk and as a table for eating.

Yskanda entered to find it already occupied by Gloom—Xek Arkanda—the tall, serious scholar who always reminded Yskanda of a bamboo shoot bent in the wind. Everyone in their dormitory had expected Gloom to win the tassel, ranking first in the examination. They were not to know that all the close-written text Gloom had poured forth had been tedious in the extreme, especially the question on poetry. He was given a pass, but he was nowhere near the top.

Subsequently he'd been assigned to the archivists, which was exactly where his heart lay; Gloom was most comfortable among lists and texts, never pretending to understand people.

Yskanda and Gloom now each had a new robe and a finer sash, Gloom's trimmed with silver edging, but Yskanda's trimmed with blue. They both had passed the imperial examination, earning them their loaves and tallies, which brought them within the "outside" court, that is, serving the "inside" court. But Yskanda, having received an imperial edict that appointed him assistant to the court artist (who was at the fifth rank), had entered the ranks himself, at the very bottom. That put him one degree above Gloom, who was now merely one of many assistants to under-secretaries of the eighth rank.

The hems of their robes were embroidered with the lines that symbolized standing water, distinct from the moving water pattern on the robes of those in power, the ministers of court. Ministers wore the green, crimson, or the especially coveted purple robes and the hats with the extensions bent up behind, meeting at a graceful point; their ranks were further distinguished by embroidered ornamental patches on the breasts and backs of their robes.

Yskanda was immediately uncomfortable at the idea of a servant, even one shared with someone else. He hated the thought of another handling his personal things, though he never dared write an inward thought, or even borrow a book that might raise a question. He knew his things could be, and probably had been, searched at any time, but Gloom had three white stones sitting in the window sill. Yskanda figured from this no one would question his ward stone also sitting in the window sill while he was in the bath. He carried it with him the rest of each day.

Much as having a personal servant made him uneasy, after a few days of arduous lessons with Court Artist Yoli, he had to admit that it was a relief not to have to find time to take dirty clothes to the laundry, then remember to go back and stand in line for the laundry servants to find his clean clothes, after which he must check them over in case they needed repair.

As before, his new clothes had his name stitched inside the left seam. Juniper laundered them, and saw to their repair with tiny stitches as deft as Yskanda's own. He also kept the little chamber spotlessly tidy, and Gloom's and Yskanda's brushes cleaned and ready for use by the time they woke in the morning, no matter how late their masters kept them. On their waking they found their clothes laid out, their hats or "loaves" brushed and ready for wear, and hot tea waiting to rinse their mouths. It was rather nice, though even thinking that made Yskanda uncomfortable. But he soon discovered that trying to do any of it for himself caused Juniper distress, lest he be punished for not performing his tasks well enough.

Court Artist Yoli shook his head over the orders thrusting a beardless boy into the dangerous precincts of power called the imperial court. The only other time he recollected the emperor doing so was when he'd brought the First Imperial Prince to court or, less often, First Imperial Princess. And those two were kept behind a screen.

There was no screen to protect the scribes or the artists.

As a result, over the next few days Yoli showered Yskanda with so many warnings that what had seemed like a possibly interesting, more likely boring duty became so fraught that the court artist realized the day before they were to attend court together that he'd managed to terrify his apprentice nearly into witlessness. "Once more. Tell me the order of ranks, and show me the bows for early morning encounter," he began.

Yskanda's eyes widened. "Bow . . . early-morning . . ." His voice suspended and he just stood there in the middle of the court artist's chamber, as though some evil Essence-master had come along and slapped an invisible talisman on him, turning him to stone.

Yoli thumped down onto his cushion and sighed. "Perhaps . . . I believe I've gone about this all wrong."

Yskanda sat down as well, looking as miserable as he felt.

"Let's start over. No, *don't* forget all I told you, just . . . you needn't recite it all for me anymore. You know enough. More will come with experience. Instead, let's consider tomorrow in the practical sense. What will actually happen is our being thoroughly ignored, once the minsters and the attendants get used to the sight of someone new. If you sit quietly and keep your eyes on your work, they will ignore you as they ignore the familiar furniture of the chamber, which includes me. And the scribes."

Yskanda let out a trickle of a breath.

"Let's begin simply. The custom is for court to be held every fifth and tenth day, unless the emperor either sends a summons, or cancels. Occasionally court will extend into a second day, and even rarer, a third. It's then that our arts tend to be truly wanted, for the long sessions often are the result of momentous occasions. Now. We will gather well before the sun rises . . ."

And so it began, pretty much as the court artist had predicted. Juniper arrived to wake him the hour before dawn. Yskanda was already awake, having slept badly. He bathed, dressed, and though Juniper had made certain his robe, sash, and hat were spotlessly clean, Yskanda inspected himself, retying his sash twice until he was satisfied that his tally hung just so, thumping reassuringly against his upper left leg.

He brushed his damp palms over his thighs — looked down in horror — there was no mark. He left without waking Gloom, and joined the court artist on the walk to the Hall of Glorious

Harmony.

Yskanda knew they must defer whenever encountering the noble ministers, but the court artist had not mentioned that while one stood with one's back to the wall, head bowed in deference, there could be very long delays. Especially when the palanquins — each of which had its owner's title inscribed on the lanterns at the front — met another palanquin, and that with the lower ranking must be halted, so that its owner could step out to bow to the superior personage. And when the superior personage saw fit to exchange remarks with the lower ranking personage, then everyone around them must wait in silence.

So that walk along the fine corridor leading to the Hall of Glorious Harmony took twice, three, even four times as long as it would have taken to walk that distance elsewhere. But the court artist had started them off in plenty of time.

At last they reached the courtyard before the steps leading up to the Hall of Glorious Harmony. They hung back as the ministers lined up in strict rank order, two by two, at the foot of the steps, looking up at the great doors carved with water dragons, coveted jade tablets held in both hands. Yskanda spotted four women among them. Court Artist Yoli had pointed out that all were silver-haired, appointments left from the empress's day.

When the sun began to rim the eastern wall, the great gong was struck, the rich sound shivering on the air.

The door guards opened the huge doors. The ministers began to mount the steps in pairs, purple robes first, exquisite jade tallies swinging at their waists, with forearm-long tassels rippling at each step as the ministers headed for those high, carved doors.

Yskanda, the court artist, and the scribes under the Grand Historian entered through a side door. The Grand Historian himself was absent, Yskanda was relieved to see — at their single meeting, when Yskanda was introduced as the court artist's assistant; the grand historian had looked down his short nose at Yskanda, his upper lip lengthening as if some-thing stank. He greeted Court Artist Yoli as if Yskanda did not exist.

Yoli later explained that Grand Historian Bolu was the third generation at his post, which required him not just to monitor court, but also to oversee the scribes working with the court's augurs and geomancers, as each day's weather and star readings must be recorded, in addition to all else. The Grand

Historian read every work his scribes wrote, and woe to he who was sloppy or inexact.

"But he has no authority over me," Yoli had finished with obvious satisfaction. "Worry not. All you need to do is bow and be polite. Any orders pertaining to art must come from me."

Yoli led Yskanda to a low table at one side, below the throne, partially obscured by the decorations around the dais. From their vantage, they could see both the throne and the hall of ministers, though they themselves were not easily seen.

The ministers filed in, their step a rhythm each incoming minister learned along with his job, so that they were all in place exactly when the sun cleared the eastern horizon and once again the great gong resounded.

"The emperor approaches," a graywing bawled.

Down ministers, scribes, and artists went to the floor in a rustling of silken robes.

The emperor entered from one of the openings at the back of the hall. As Yoli had predicted, he did not wear the imperial crown with its swinging jade beads. That and the dragon robes, the court artist had warned Yskanda, only came out when great proclamations were to be made, or when the emperor sat in judgment over mighty cases. "The black and gold dragon robe," Yoli had said, "we have many sketches of so that we can get the details precisely correct later."

Today the emperor's hair was bound up in gold surmounted by jade and pearls, and he wore a fine robe with the Jehan tiger-eye as primary motif. This was a day to listen to reports and depositions, each of which caused equally sonorously spoken commentary and debate, all couched in what was called the wind flow — cadenced speech in the classical form of the imperial language, replete with allusions and quotations.

Having been sleepless most of the night, Yskanda was stunned to find himself nearly nodding off once his dread had faded. Then he became aware of a few glances his way. He busied his hands filling in a sketch that the court artist had already prepared by laying out the appropriate proportions and making tiny dots to represent the placement, and size, of the various individuals.

That day imperial court was a mass of similar faces in similarly colored robes.

Gradually, over the following series of court sessions, Yskanda began to differentiate voices, and then faces. And then, inevitably, to discern the subtle changes in timbre, the shifts in shoulder or angle of chin that furnished a glimpse of the complexity of emotions the speaker strove to hide. "This old and worthless seeker has no talent," one declared smoothly in a tone anything but humble, "and no words of worth, but respect for this august body impels a reminder of the words of Lao Sha, who addressed this very same problem seven centuries ago in his *Militias and Rebellion* . . ."

THIRTY

TIME PASSED SWIFTLY.

Yskanda still took classes when not on duty, but these classes were all on the esoterica of art: the making of finer colors that would last, of brushes, of the reproduction of priceless art treasures as training. He now sat in the first place in all these classes, and was expected to assist the instructor from time to time. When he knew the subject, he enjoyed this, and the young apprentices discovered that the handsome young artist who had arrived so mysteriously was invariably kind and patient. Utterly unaware, Yskanda became a popular and much-discussed figure.

He was sublimely happy when he let his mind plunge into the life of color, line, and texture. His best moments were when he worked on intricate projects with the court artist, listening to him speak about artists of old.

Reality was court. As the weeks turned into months, he ceased being afraid, but Court Artist Yoli continued to lecture him earnestly lest he ever relax his vigilance. That was impossible, with the emperor seated a mere thirty paces away.

Best of all, Yoli answered his questions.

"Can the graywings do anything?" Yskanda asked one day, about the time that Ul Keg's ship was a few days out from Burning Rock Island. Yskanda and Court Artist Yoli sketched together out in the Garden of Serene Contemplation, no one in sight. "I ask because my very first day, I was beaten terribly by two of the ones tending the Hall of Glorious Virtue, not even inner palace graywings. Yet Sen—someone used to brag that the imperial guards can only arrest us, they can't take a stick to us."

"All true. The palace rules are complicated because there are those unwritten as well as the written ones you memorized your first week. For example, you'll not see it written any-where, but no graywing can give an order to an imperial guard. Only carry orders to them."

"Verbal orders? I thought everything is written down." He stopped when he realized that he himself had received verbal orders, when summoned to the emperor's inner palace.

Court Artist Yoli saw this sudden realization, and gave a nod. "To a degree," he affirmed. "And of course, where those records are stored is important. The palace archive has sections that require permission to visit. There you'll find records written about the imperial family, sometimes even by them-selves. For example, you're not likely to see in general histories the real reason behind the Era of Purification of Court."

"I thought that event was meritorious. That is, we were told that when the law was handed down that all who served at the ninth level and above must first pass the Imperial Examination, a step toward getting rid of corrupt and incompetent ministers whose sole attribute was their birth."

"Yes, but what you won't see is that the edict followed a wholesale slaughter of the denatured, after a vicious power struggle within the palace that spilled not only through the entire island, but reached as far as the Silk Islands. The graywings of that day had had a stranglehold on the imperial family by choosing very young and weak emperors, and when they reached an age no older than you, poisoning them or arranging accidents. Then another young cousin would be elevated to the throne, with graywings surrounding him and ruling as his voice. They also controlled the imperial guard, most of whom in those days were denatured."

"I did not know that."

"Also unwritten, because no one writes about the ferrets. They might have their own records that only the emperor can see—I can't imagine them being mad enough to keep records that he cannot see—but anyway, that's when they were founded. They largely investigate outside the palace now, but early on their entire purpose was internal, to seek collusion among graywings, imperial guards, scribes, even ministers."

Yskanda paused, brush in the air. "What would they get from controlling the imperial family? Power, yes, but to what end? Aren't imperials concerned with dynasty?"

Court Artist Yoli lowered his voice to a rumble that barely carried arm's length, though he had taken care to employ his silence wards. "Unwritten also is the utter bloodbath when the last empress died and the First Imperial Prince tried to take the throne by slaughtering everyone else. I still don't know how many palace servants, guards, and graywings died that night."

Yskanda looked away, deeply regretting his question.

Yoli lightened his voice. "Aside from that, every family wants continuation. As for graywings, no, they cannot establish dynasties, but they have emotions like anyone else. Including ambition and greed. Though these days they try to weed those boys out early."

"One would think the denaturing would suffice for that," Yskanda murmured, finding the subject unsettling. Though he knew knives had not been used for centuries, the effect was just as ineradicable — and one would think unfilial, when it was considered unfilial even to cut one's hair, unless one's parents specifically gave permission, as they did with cutting toe and fingernails. But then it had been parents selling children into palace service in the long-ago past. It was still considered a laudable calling.

Yoli beetled those fierce white brows at him. "You should know enough history by now to remember that people will do anything for power."

Yskanda was grateful to leave the subject.

Another reality was the changing of the season.

Letter writing happened once again. Those whose families lived far away would receive a letter sent at the expense of the state. (And most of those families would have a letter ready and waiting to go back the same way, saving them expense.)

When Juniper came to Yskanda for his letter, Yskanda was ready. He'd written another inane letter, bragging about his having passed the Imperial Examination (he wasted half a page on the first two questions), and then going on about the paintings the Easterners sent as gifts, which were being studied by the palace artists. He knew it was a stupid letter, and he also knew it would be read by at least the ferrets, and probably the emperor, before it ever got on the boat. He waited with the usual anxiety for a result. There was none, and gradually that particular worry died down, though of course there were always new ones to take its place, jostling with the deep pleasures of entire days immersed in art.

One of the lesser negatives was that cold morning walk. Yskanda knew it would get worse before it got better; at first snow, the court artist warned Yskanda that Yoli's age and rank had gained him the privilege of being conveyed in a cart, but it was so small that even so thin a form as Yskanda's would not squeeze in. "You should walk with the Grand Historian's scribes," Court Artist Yoli finished. "Being in a group is always a good idea."

Yskanda agreed. He knew the scribes by now. They were easy to converse with once they got used to the fact that Yskanda was five to seven years younger than their average. Being part of the Grand Historian's great tree of communication, they had learned much faster than the usual labyrinthine methods that though Afan Yskanda had suddenly appeared under very mysterious circumstances, and had charged up their ranks like a fireworks rocket, it had not been through any family or political benefaction. It was whispered that Afan Yskanda was a Talent. Those could be any age, male or female. A Talent earned respect — a Talent would of course receive an imperial edict appointing him to a place before anyone else could hope to get one. His handsome face and his polite, modest manner earned liking.

Court Artist Yoli signified his approval of Yskanda's progress by gradually ceasing to prepare Yskanda's papers before they entered the throne room. Yskanda had not yet been taken to the imperial study, where the emperor sometimes held meetings with the Left and Right Chancellors and the other high-ranking ministers: there was room for only a single scribe and the court artist himself. That duty lay some time off. Yskanda secretly hoped it would never come.

He could not know — none of them could — that the emperor, through the silent, gliding Melonseed and Bitternail, saw not only Court Artist Yoli's drawings of the court sessions, but Afan Yskanda's.

The emperor had expected Yskanda's drawings to be rigidly correct. He was not disappointed. But gradually, as the moons waxed and waned, their nightly journeys bringing them ever nearer the sky bridge connecting them at the next New Year's Two Moons, those drawings began to furnish glimpses of Yskanda's observations. A line here, the turn of a hand there. Once, fingers clutched on the jade tablet when the soft-spoken, sinister old Right Chancellor, Duke Su, was admonished by First Censor Huoh, the Su clan's rival for at least four generations.

Old Su prided himself on his urbanity, and yet Yskanda — as yet ignorant of the turbid waters of court affairs — had penetrated that mask. Old Su had been the emperor's enemy as far back as memory reached — he and his sons. Huoh as well, and then there was the Cor clan, ever more rampant in its climb.

All these were familiar sharks in courtly waters. What the emperor had yet to discover was the unknown force working below the surface, a malevolent eel remaining in the dark while all the rest swam in the light.

Afan Yskanda might be a toy, or a target. Until he'd seen these drawings, the emperor had not considered the possibility that he might be a weapon against more than one long-escaped traitor.

But there was work to do first.

On a blustery cold day, Yskanda switched over to his heavier winter robe, resigned to chafing from his hardier colleagues about his softness. He didn't care. Let them call him a rabbit, a turtle, and any number of other things. The fact remained he was cold, and it was going to get far colder during another long, frigid winter.

After a protracted court session, he was walking back alone, bent into a wind that seemed determined to scour beneath all his layers to his bones, when the rapid sound of footsteps caught up and he found himself surrounded by several of the Grand Historian's scribes.

They were led by Pan Nari, known as Lychee — apparently he had been particularly greedy for such treats as a boy apprentice. Lychee reminded Yskanda a little of Senye Tan, always making jokes, always the center of a group. He was far more discreet than Senye Tan, though. He talked a lot, and laughed for much of it, but he never vouchsafed an opinion about matters beyond food, drink, clothes, and the girls at his favorite dance house.

"There you are, looking like Erku the Hero," Lychee said, ranging up at Yskanda's right. "No, you're too skinny for a hero. I don't suppose you've ever even seen a sword up close. The Morningstar God, that's you." Lychee was not as tall, and much broader, with a moon face and a wide smile. "Come along. We all have a free evening tonight, tomorrow a late morning, and Orchid at Sweet Breezes wants to meet you."

"Why?" Yskanda asked skeptically. He remembered such houses on Imai. "I have no money."

"Because she likes new faces, especially pretty ones," Lychee said blithely, "and the girls' dormitories in Manifest Virtue voted you the prettiest of the New Hats. Surely you knew that."

The female apprentices and low-ranking artisans' dormitory court named Manifest Virtue was strictly off-limits to the boys.

Yskanda made a warding gesture. "No, no."

"Why not come see Orchid for yourself? It's still free food and drink, as Senior Brother Akel comes from a rich family, and his purse is bottomless. More important, if *I* bring you, and your pretty face makes Orchid happy, then Peach Blossom will be happy, and if she's happy then I'm happy, if you follow me?"

"What if I disappoint her?"

Lychee groaned, and the others laughed. "Do I really have to spell it out? Of course I do, because you're an innocent lamb ripe for the fleecing. If lambs actually do get ripe."

Another put in, "The girls won't let you disappoint them. Nor the boys, if that's your taste in wine."

The others seemed to regard this as the epitome of wit as they laughed.

"Come along, Afan," tall Gu Akel drawled. "We will take it as insult if you refuse."

The rest of them added their encouragement, amid laughing insults, and Yskanda saw that to refuse would break the easy atmosphere among them, as well as insult a senior ranking scribe. For some reason, after all these weeks together, they wanted him among them in free time. Or was this how friendship worked in the world?

His quiet evening experimenting with a new supply of colors for the court artist gave way to an unexpected evening going outside the palace walls. As always their sash tallies were examined at each gate. As Yskanda waited for the last of them to be passed, he glanced back for the expected shadow.

None in sight. But that changed when they reached the street, and wound their way among the brightly lit lanterns, vendors and night hawkers doing their best to lure custom. As he neared a stand selling painted fans, he passed a highly polished shield used as decoration for the next booth — and there, reflected in it, was a figure shrouded in a gray cloak. Yskanda's artist's eye immediately recognized that silhouette, that walk: it was Goldneedle.

He hadn't expected anything different, but disappointment still chilled him. He was glad when Lychee called out, "Here we are!" and they entered a highly decorated house full of fine silk hangings, baskets of fragrant blossoms, and colored lanterns. Pretty young people in bright, flattering clothing greeted the customers with smiles, chat, and invitations to eat, drink, sit, enjoy themselves.

They settled around a table on the balcony overlooking the stage. Gu Akel ordered a sumptuous meal and enough hot rice wine for each to have his own jug. As the musicians struck up a melody, a sudden rustle of silks and a waft of expensive perfume presaged arrivals. Three boys in bright colors joined them, followed by a bevy of girls in fluttering ribbons and layers of gauze. One boy settled on Yskanda's left as another sat with Gu Aker. The third moved about, pouring wine liberally, as the girls sorted themselves out, sitting one to a guest.

The girl with Yskanda appeared to be about his age, maybe a little older, her face paint matching the shades of aqua and peach in her gauzy, drifting robes. Tiny chimes in her hairpins dangled down, one by her cheek, another by her opposite ear, tinkling sweetly.

Yskanda sat stiffly, hands fisted on his thighs as he watched the others for clues as how to behave. On Imai he had been far too young, and too poor, for private rooms.

He left his wine untouched, until Lychee noticed, and, face flushed, roared, "Is the wine bad? Or you want another kind?"

"I'm fine," Yskanda said.

"Fine, he says! Are you a monk, Brother Afan? Who's going to squawk if you enjoy yourself? Your grandmother and aunties aren't here!"

The others at the table roared with laughter.

At that moment the music rose in pitch, and the dancers pranced onto the stage, ribbons streaming.

They began a coy fan dance as their robes swirled about their forms, concealing and revealing. The drums beat in his bloodstream, and for a time he gulped more wine than he intended, as the girl and the boy smiled and pressed him to enjoy it. "Try a sip? Don't you like it? Try the truffles — truly, the chef will hang himself if you aren't pleased . . ."

The seductive dance, the silvery laughter of the girls, the soft hands pressing him to drink, to eat food that tasted delicious, caused his senses to swim. He glanced once at the other scribes, to find them passionately entwined with their partners, ribbons and gauze shrouding them. Gu Akers had vanished altogether with his young man.

Finally Orchid leaned close, and whispered, "Is this your first time? You do know about silver milkweed?" She had opened a small ceramic jar, and with a tiny spoon measured powdered herb into the already spiced wine. "Let me give you a hint: a woman always appreciates a man who makes sure to drink his share."

Yskanda blinked blearily, recollecting Mother teaching Mouse how drinking silver milkweed kept the male and female essences from combining to make a child, and a lot more that Mouse obviously did not understand. Nor, for that matter, had Yskanda.

But he understood the invitation now.

Yskanda didn't remember the boy's name; he and Orchid smiled, and poured wine, their soft hands drifting to his shoulders to ease muscles he had not noticed were knotted. The release was delicious, the wine somehow more so, pungent with the added herb and spice. Ordinary people, he remembered Mother saying, tossed the weed fresh into boiling water if they were not ready to have a family, but the effect only lasted a day. The powdered, distilled herb would last several days . . .

"With me," the boy whispered seductively, "you need not think about how long the weed lasts."

Yskanda meant to be cautious, but he was young, at the age when the slow wink of an ardent eye can ignite desire with all the swiftness of a summer storm.

Later he was only aware of stumbling back to the palace, trying to smother laughter as his head swam. The cold air revived him a little, enough to be aware of Juniper waiting to help him to bed, speaking softly to someone at the door. Who . . . Who? Not Gloom — he was already in bed . . .

He sank into wine-sodden dreams, and woke to a throbbing head, aching eyes, and a sick taste on his tongue. Juniper was there with tea to rinse his dry, acrid mouth, looking concerned, and Gloom a little disgusted. Yskanda was sure he stank. He felt like he stank. "Bath," he said.

Once he sank into the water, with a mug of nastily bitter medicine at his side that Juniper insisted he drink, he forced himself to face the truth: he'd let himself get drunk. And, as expected, the moment he lost control of himself, another person (persons?) took control.

He did not remember anything he said, except that there had been little talk. Shards of image returned, the most persistent the quick glance of triumph Orchid had exchanged with the boy over his head. They had not concealed those smiles. And why should they? They were earning their living.

Everything had happened so fast, he whined within his own head. Yes, said cold sober Yskanda. Everything happened too fast. Lychee's sudden step toward intimacy after weeks of collegial friendship—the expensive meal—the determined seduction.

He'd been set up.

There was no true attraction between him and those two—in the cold light of day he knew they had executed a campaign from the moment Lychee mentioned his name. All as choreographed as the dance on the stage below that expensive balcony room, its steps marked by the rice wine and the spicy tidbits, the beguiling throb of music and the strong, kneading fingers.

The only thing he was sure of was that there had been little talk—the boy and the girl had been too busy glaring at one another, in competition for his attention. Which might not be the case the next time.

Because there would be a next time. Another invitation, another drunken evening. Maybe him alone in one of those private rooms, if the expense was paid for by someone with unlimited resources. Drunken talk—innocent questions: where is your home, do you have brothers and sisters, what does your father do . . . She was so pretty, and he smelled so good, her soft hands were so clever, and the boy's so strong . . .

Another campaign.

Yskanda shut his eyes, and shuddered as his senses swam. Longing warred with horror—he could not trust himself.

In the cold light of day, it was easy to think the danger was his imagination. But even if Lychee's friendship was real, Yskanda couldn't be his friend. He could not burden a true friend with the truth.

Better to end the pretense now.

He knew that consistent refusal would make him disliked, and bleakly looked down the path toward a cold, hard, lonely winter.

Thirty-One

IT WOULD NOT BE fair to say that Ryu at last had the life she had always wanted, because, unlike her brothers (and we will be revisiting Muin presently) she had seldom given a thought to the future. Other than knowing what she did *not* want to do, which was to be stuck in a temple somewhere, frowsting among old scrolls. Her imagination had come alive when reading tales of the gallant wanderers roaming freely, but she had never expected to be among them.

Yet here she was, on the road, and with companions she liked. Who would have thought Shigan Fin would be a friend? But they were, sparring together every day, along with easy-going Matu and quiet Petal, who practiced with the grim focus of one who had vowed never to bend her back to a stick again.

The only frustration was her Essence practice with Yaso, who still insisted that Ryu had to learn to breathe Essence through herself. Ryu breathed until she was giddy, always aware that she was sitting still while doing it. She needed to learn to breathe while doing martial arts! But Yaso didn't do martial arts. Ryu decided she was going to have to seek a real Essence martial artist, though she said nothing to peaceable, kindly Yaso.

The first time they stopped in the center square of a small village, thinking only of their thirst, a strong young fellow sauntered out of the one inn, swinging a spear decorated with red tassels as he eyed Shigan. "You the one calling himself

Firebolt?"

Shigan turned an ironic hand toward Ryu.

She scowled warily. "I don't call myself that."

Greatly entertained, Shigan crossed his arms over his chest as he said, "But he was named that after he beat off two boats of pirates in two moves."

"*That* sprout?" Red Tassel jerked a dismissive thumb toward Ryu, then hawked and spat in the dusty road. "*Sure* he did."

Ryu shrugged, and made to pass, but the spear dropped, barring her way. She turned her head. "We have no quarrel with you."

"I think you do. When someone six years old struts around calling himself Firebolt, it dishonors us all."

There was that word "honor" again, Ryu thought sourly.

"Speaking for the entire world, your imperial majesty?" Shigan asked, brows aslant.

He dropped his gear in the road, and Yaso silently picked it up and faded to one side. Ryu still had hers slung against her back. Petal edged behind Matu's broad shoulder as Red Tassel spun his spear in a circle, then dropped into a fighting stance. Then he brought the spear out of a spin and lunged at Ryu.

After leaving the ship it had taken her a few days to recover her Essence, but it was all there now, burning brightly within her. She let only a wisp burn through her as she feinted with her left hand and whirled the right to match speed with the spear. Then, using its own momentum, she struck the weapon right out of its wielder's hand. She caught it one-handed, whirled it up and around, point resting below its owner's throat.

His eyes widened as he dropped back a step. Then narrowed. "You . . ."

"Want to do it again?" Ryu asked as roughly as possible, trying to sound older. And like a boy only months from shaving.

She tossed the spear back to Red Tassel, whose expression faltered. She said easily, "Is the food here any good?"

As she'd hoped, acting as if nothing had happened preserved Red Tassel's face. "Try the pepper trout," he mumbled, thoroughly unsettled.

"Thanks," Ryu said, putting her hands together in the gallant wanderer greeting, and went on past Red Tassel to the door, leaving him staring after.

She hoped it all would end there, but of course it didn't.

Red Tassel had been seen by several, and the tale raced down the road ahead of them, Red Tassel adding to her formidable powers to make himself look better.

When the next several villages they came to brought similar challenges, Ryu reluctantly fought the most insistent, using either her wooden sword or just her hands. She continued addressing the challengers as if this were a practice session, no blood drawn. If she heard the word "honor" she talked about food, or pinching boots, or something thoroughly practical, leaving the ridiculous subject to wither before her friendly demeanor. Some were bewildered; others bowed to short, unthreatening Firebolt, whose speed left them blinking.

But there were always those few who seemed to have to turn a challenge scrap into a real fight, and a real fight into a feud. Shigan tried to mitigate things with his instant popularity, especially with any entertainment houses.

Within the last year he had passed beyond the age when most boys long to make the theoretical into experience. His looks assured his success. At their first inn, the three daughters of the owner competed so enthusiastically for his attention that the free rice wine one brought to the table nearly got dumped into his lap by her elder sister when she snatched jug and cup to pour it out for him.

Shigan did not have to do anything but smile; when the rest went off to peaceful slumber (Matu with some furtive looks backward, it must be said), Shigan was enticed to the private wing, plied with more expensive wine laced with silver milkweed, and introduced to a whole new world of experience.

After that, whenever they came to an inn at which handsome, eager young women formed part of the staff, Shigan discovered that offering to play pipa or guzheng, and assenting to invitations for a more private concert with young staffers, usually got them a room for free. Even if he was seldom in it for most of the night.

But they never ended up staying anywhere too long, because rumor kept racing ahead, bringing the inevitable challengers who seemed to believe they had something to prove.

Shigan and Matu offered to face these, Shigan saying to them, "You've got to go through us first before you can face Brother Firebolt."

It gratified both him and Matu a lot more than they let on

that they invariably won. They thoroughly discussed any new moves after each fight, and Ryu joined in as they incorporated their experience into their scrapping.

Nothing bad had happened, so far, but that didn't mean it wouldn't.

Ryu often thought about those boatloads of pirates, and exhorted the others to keep moving in order to outrun the gossip.

"Or maybe we should take another route?" she suggested doubtfully one morning.

Everybody turned to gaze thoughtfully at the middle of the island rising to a steep hump. This hump had been civilized over the centuries, terraced with rice planting along some slopes, mulberry trees on others. Paths there might be, but none were straight—it was more likely Ryu and the others would get lost on that massive mountain quilted by tiny rice farms. They were stuck taking the main road, which wound around the circular island, more or less paralleling the coastline.

Their walks were generally quiet—though Shigan silently longed for a horse—but each village or town inevitably brought out the challengers. After an encounter with a spoiled son whose family owned most of the mulberry trees on the nearby slope, Ryu brooded over the effects of gossip, and said suddenly one morning, "Let's take the first ship we see."

"This island is like fractured porcelain," Shigan said, surprising them. "All the landowning families are rivals."

Matu nodded soberly. "The young ones seem to have nothing to do but fight each other. And people like us."

No one disagreed.

Every so often Ryu thought of Grandfather Ki's invitation, once she was ready. What would ready look like? She strove harder at practice, convinced he'd seen something lacking in her. Shigan and Matu responded to the challenge—Petal toiled grimly behind, working hard to get the basics—and Yaso continued to exhort her to let Essence breathe through her, vanishing often in search of herbs.

They found a trade ship going west through a route called Little Dogleg. They worked as crew as the ship made its way through a thick cluster of islands, some smaller even than Imai, grouped around two so large they took up the entire horizon for a day. When Petal and Ryu commented on the strangeness of the sight, Matu laughed, saying, "Oh, there are bigger ones.

And the imperial island is the biggest of all. My aunt-by-marriage had a brother who got impressed one year into the imperial navy, when the Easterners tried to invade the Silk Islands. He told us it takes three days and nights to sail the length of the imperial island — and that in a fast wind."

They couldn't agree on where to land. Matu, of course, was all for leaving the ship as soon as possible, which he expressed with a hopeful "This one looks fine," every time the subject came up. Shigan preferred small islands, Ryu large — her hope was that an Essence martial artist would be more likely to be found where there was a larger population — the only point of agreement being to avoid islands flying the imperial tiger-eye in its harbors.

Shigan even went below if they passed imperial ships. "On principle," he said — which made Ryu laugh, as the huge warships never paid the least heed to the squat little trader with its patched-slat sails. They were looking for pirates, not runaway apprentices to traveling players.

As it happened, the decision was taken from them by the weather gods.

They woke one morning to an eerie stillness under a blue sky bright as a steel bowl. The waters were a deep blue quite unlike any shade previously seen, full of tiny white wavelets winking and vanishing.

The captain's wife was the ship's augur. "Bad storm coming," she said tersely as the ship tacked for the shelter of a harbor. "This is not a good island, according to the latest news. Pirates, some say. But we won't be anywhere near the main harbor, which is in the path of the storm. If we can get around the peninsula, we can lie up in the lee of the storm here."

So began a tense period, a silent chase of sorts. Their pursuer was the still-unseen storm and the sun traveling slowly over the sky. The wind began to pick up, the color of the sea changing to an unsettling dark green. At last she pointed to an inlet with soaring cliffs to either side. "There!"

Already the ship was bucketing badly. Matu's face blanched and he lay below limply. Ryu gazed between him and the still-clear sky, then to the restless sea. All her instincts whispered *Something's coming, take shelter.*

She said to the captain, "Why don't we try this island, then? If the pirates are not at sea, they should be tied down in the main harbor."

A shared look semaphored agreement. The tide carried

them into the inlet as the five gallant wanderers helped the ship family tie down every bit of cargo. They debarked hastily, and found a small village.

"Is there an inn?" Shigan roared over the howling gusts. "We can work for room and board."

The old woman in charge scowled warily, obviously checking them for weapons. "You'll have to go on up to the temple. There is nowhere else for you to stay." She pointed to a steep path leading up into the red-rock cliffs.

A stray buffet of wind that smelled faintly of burnt metal made everyone's hackles rise. The storm was nearly on them. The Redbark wanderers began the climb, every so often one or another looking warily at the still-cloudless slice of still visible sky overhead. Such was their worry that for once they didn't break for their usual morning martial arts practice, even though they were now on land.

The path rounded a spire, which blocked the wind, leaving the late summer sun to beat down on their shoulders and the backs of their heads. As usual, only Yaso didn't seem to mind the punishing heat as they pushed themselves up the nearly vertical climb.

Matu and Shigan fell into an increasingly hoarse-voiced, puffing conversation about the advantages of two-edged daggers over single-edged knives. Ryu and Petal pushed ahead, both eager to find shelter.

As they trod up an especially steep twist, Petal smiled thinly. "In winter I could not have walked this steep path without stopping often."

Ryu said, "You're a lot stronger now. In fact, I've noticed you're pretty good at breaking holds. You ought to ask Matu to start teaching you grappling."

Petal shot her a look that Ryu could not interpret at all, but didn't speak.

Petal and Ryu trudged on for a time. Finally Petal looked around, then said, "Matu won't teach me grappling."

"Why not?"

"Same reason he always keeps his bedroll on the other side of you or Yaso or Shigan, rather than sleep next to me. Unmarried men and women ought not to touch."

"Oh." Ryu looked away at some seabirds wheeling above the glittering sands on the shoreline.

The reminder of her disguise made her feel itchy under the skin. She knew that her pretense of being a boy wasn't going to last much longer. And there were times when she wanted to be . . . herself. Afan Arikanda. Then at other times the idea of everyone being awkward and uncomfortable, the way Petal was when she muttered that about their sleeping arrangements, made her shiver inside.

And why? That's what she didn't understand. It had to do with the boys getting older, and checking their faces for hairs. And the way they looked at girls lounging outside dance houses. Ryu had to remind herself to look in the same direction, the way a boy would, but she doubted she could mimic that fixed stare. At the same time, she had begun adding an Essence charm to the cloth she wrapped around her chest each time she dressed, to deflect attention.

These little things were annoying, but not nearly as bad as imagining the awkwardness if she confessed. She loved her present freedom, even if it was built on a lie.

Ayah, everyone had secrets. Or at least things they didn't talk about. All she was certain of, she thought firmly as she puffed and sweated in the intense heat, is that the gods would grant things never change She glanced down at her loose, bulky clothes and the reflection she'd seen in water and metal of a blob of a face dominated by a fierce pair of caterpillar brows. It was easy to see why everyone believed her to be a twelve or thirteen-year-old boy instead of a girl about to turn fifteen.

A puff of wind came from somewhere, hot and acrid. She peered ahead, scrambling for a change of subject that wouldn't sound like a change of subject, and spotted rooftops. "There's a pagoda," she exclaimed, as a fat drop of rain splatted in her face. "We have to be close to that temple. I'm so thirsty."

She bent her head and redoubled her speed up the steep, twisting path, Petal toiling behind her. More raindrops splattered on the dusty road, then a stronger gust of wind serried around the rocks at either side of the path, bringing a distinct singe of smoke.

The noonday sunlight dimmed quite suddenly, as clouds towered overhead, grayish green. Dragon light, Ryu thought, and ran faster, the boys' footsteps now thumping on her heels.

They burst past a last pile of rock — and then stumbled to a stop, staring at a broad terrace made of carved stones before a temple mostly obscured by smoke. Blood-smeared figures sprawled here and there, wearing the long braids and undyed garments of monks.

THIRTY-TWO

RYU HAD SEEN NUMEROUS temples on her travels, from ornate to bare, but they had always been places of order and quiet. She was scarcely aware of the storm breaking in a loud crash of thunder as she stared at the debris scattered around, the unmoving figures heedless of the rain that began slashing nearly sideways.

Then Yaso drifted past, into the temple, and the four followed as if drawn by an invisible string.

Here they discovered a smoky murk in which monks darted about, picking up their wounded brethren, and clearing hacked-apart cushions, scrolls, tables in order to lay out those needing care. They had clearly arrived too late to help defend the temple against whoever had attacked. They stood frozen, bewildered, not knowing what to do first.

Yaso bent over a fallen monk. "Let me help you."

Yaso's voice broke the spell. The four found themselves running to and fro under the direction of an old monk who leaned heavily on a stick, giving orders.

First they rescued all the injured monks, bringing them in from the weather. Four of them were unconscious. These their brethren cared for as tenderly as those still awake, aided by Yaso. Ryu, carrying bandages and pill bottles and pungent-smelling potions back and forth, noticed that Yaso alone didn't use needles, but touched a faintly glowing forefinger to various acupoints.

"Ryu!" Shigan called. "Over here."

Ryu ran to where a monk writhed in silent pain, and helped support the monk while he slurped the medicine held to his lips.

By the time the last of the wounded lay quietly, the storm had extinguished the fire, and a couple young monks, drenched to the skin, brought in the hopeful news that more than half their ancient, much-revered peach orchard had survived.

Shigan cut a glance toward Ryu, meeting her eyes – and they read in one another's faces what they would not say out loud: *What if the attackers come back?* But they kept that to themselves as they helped the monks tidy up.

By now they had discovered that the entire temple was carved into the side of a cliff, room after room; she glimpsed mixing cauldrons and ceramic shaping tables in some, and the earthy odor of fresh clay was stronger even than the sharp stench of dissipating smoke. Her thoughts were entirely taken up with a realization: she had recognized in wall carvings the sun-and-moon symbols of the Phoenix Moon God. These monks were from the same worship as Ul Keg!

As she worked, she looked around in wonder at the carved walls until called to help distribute a simple meal of yams stuck in a fire and congee made with of ground nuts, with fresh-picked wild berries shared out of a basket among them all.

"You know how it is with such a storm," one said soberly. He wasn't much older than Shigan. He had the wide, bright eyes of the ardent spirit, and the tattoos on his visible flesh looked new. "One cannot do else but bend to it until it moves away. So it was with the pirates."

Matu leaned forward. "I don't understand what pirates would want here."

The young monk pointed back toward their main hall. Ryu and Petal had swept the vast sacred chamber earlier, noting how sound echoed off the stone. Ryu turned to the young monk eating with them. "Is this what you make here, dishes?"

"We make the moon dishes for the altar," he said. "It is a very old process. I can praise our moon dishes as the best, since it was our ancestors who developed the method. All we do is follow directions, and the result is a purity as luminous as the moon."

Ryu nodded – she knew about the moon dishes. Ul Keg

had carried one for his offerings. His was old and chipped, but the shape was the same as those in all the Moon Gods' temples: they were made of porcelain, pure white when finished. From the side the dishes looked like half moons, and from above, like full moons. All it took was a single glance to see that the ones made by these monks gathered the light in lustrous beauty.

"We supply many temples. All those along Little Dogleg, and there are some temples from farther away that trade us for items we cannot make ourselves. Traditionally the Dal clan, whose manor lies south of Sunset Harbor, has distributed them for us, along with their regular trade."

Another young novice spoke up eagerly. "We heard that Captain Dal In ran off with a pirate when she was betrothed to a—"

"Brother Apple, that's hearsay," an older monk murmured.

Brother Apple flushed, but held his ground. "After what happened today, I think repeating what I hear when I take my basket down to Sunset Harbor is not useless. The harbor people all said that Captain Dal In came back a pirate when she got rid of old Governor Biyan. They say she leads pirates."

The elder bowed acknowledgment to his junior, then turned to Shigan and Ryu. "Captain Dal In came to us a week ago to say that the autumn tribute ought to be gold-edged, and painted with any images the god might approve, for selling to observant households. But we heard only the word 'sell' and so we said we would discuss it and do divinations to discover what the gods want. Which we did."

The first monk set aside his empty dish. "She returned with a great many armed people today, and when told that our divinations had been consistent in agreeing that we must not deviate from our traditional method—that our bowls are for temple use—they attacked us. Said it was a warning, and after they finished with us they set fire to our peach orchard."

"Peach pits being our divination method," Brother Apple put in.

"Our peach trees are over a thousand years old," an elderly monk quavered. "Some say older. But all things under Heaven die. Our lesson today was a bitter reminder."

"They didn't believe our divination as truth," Brother Apple said. "Yet the peach pits were as clear as they ever have been."

"Those who lie know not truth when they hear it," the old one intoned. "If we are all finished, let us clean the bowls."

His words were half-swallowed by a very loud crash of thunder. Outside the rain roared, sheeting down in an impenetrable wall, as purple lightning flared continuously.

Ryu glanced once toward the weird, glaring light, sensing Essence in that storm. But I didn't cause this one, she reminded herself as she helped with the cleanup, a task familiar from her orderly days. That sense of bygone days intensified later when they all gathered in the great temple carved out of living rock for the singing of the evening Sun Sutras, which in their earliest form had begged the sun to return the next day, and Phoenix Moon to protect them until morning.

Ryu was not prepared for the beauty of all those male voices rising and falling in exquisite harmony, reverberating from the stone walls. As if the centuries of music somehow echoed back, blending the voices of the monks now with those who had come before, creating a breathtaking weaving of sound.

The central melody's familiar simplicity, reaching back into her earliest years, knotted her heart. She closed her eyes, memories of Ul Keg bright in her mind. She had kept up her custom of sending a silent greeting to him along with her parents when sleeping and waking, but it had gradually become a perfunctory habit, one that only took up a very small part of her attention, especially in recent weeks.

She thought about him now, wondering where he was. Whether he still was with her parents, though there were no children to teach, for the village children her own age had fallen away by the time she was eight from lessons that their parents had never had, leaving just herself and Yskanda as his students — and Muin if he didn't go off with the fishers.

Ul Keg had always been there, living with them in trade for cooking. For the first time she wondered what had first brought him to Imai. No, why he had stayed, when he had only ended up with the three of them to teach? Two, really. Did it have to do with the phoenix feather? If so, she hoped he didn't worry about Muin. If only there was a safe way to get a message back to them all!

She looked around at the monks, wondering if any of them had made Ul journeys that might take them anywhere near Imai. She tried to image Brother Apple becoming Ul Apple, and teaching children like . . . like who? Tired, replete, she began to slide into dreams as the music wound its way around and through her, until an elbow in her side roused her abruptly.

"You're starting to snore," Shigan whispered softly, his eyes a slant of suppressed laughter.

She grimaced up at him, noting briefly that he seemed even taller these days. Then she scowled down at her hands fisted on her thighs. When were they going to notice she wasn't growing anymore? Her boy disguise constricted her yet again, like boots that were too tight. It was going to have to end . . . someday.

Not today.

"You worried about these pirates?"

"No," she muttered, surprised he would even ask.

"You look worried," he responded.

She snorted softly. "Thinking about my brother. Fifth year," she added, relieved that it was partly true—if she left out everything about the phoenix feather.

"First Ryu," Shigan said, remembering how he'd striven mightily to spy on him, Falik, and Dun when they practiced at the targets, then doing his best to emulate them. He'd never spoken to any of them; suddenly he wished he had, if only to see how much alike the two Ryu brothers were.

The Sun Sutras wound down to their end as one then another voice dropped out, leaving a single voice singing that familiar melody. Ryu closed her eyes again. Ul Keg had once told her and Second Brother that the sung Sun Sutras were the most ancient of all, from the days of worship of the Sun Mother. A very different god than the Sun God now, who was male, his realm war. The Sun Mother had ruled all living things; it was those Sun Sutras that Kanda had adapted for his Twenty-Five Virtues.

After the ritual, bedding was unrolled in lines, with a screen for modesty put up for Petal, not that anyone undressed. Though the monks talked of resignation and fate, they were human, and the attack had exhausted them in spirit as well as in body, so everyone except those tending the kiln during the night went to sleep early. Ryu, Matu, and Shigan picked spots near Brother Apple and the other younger novices and monks. Yaso vanished somewhere. The monks did not seem to mind.

As they settled down, Matu said apologetically, "Sorry if my question is an offense. I'm ignorant about so much. Like divination. I know a little about the Book of Changes. I remember stories about the Sun Mother and the peaches of immortality. And of course I know divination sticks, though only the elders use them, where I live. But I don't see how peaches and divination go together."

Brother Apple had stretched out, but he popped up again, then winced and rubbed the back of his shoulder where a pirate had clubbed him down. "Do you set out food and pour wine for your ancestors? Do you burn paper blessings to honor the dead?"

"Of course," said Matu. "I'm ignorant. Not a savage. But what has that to do with peach pits?"

"Nothing, and everything," Brother Apple said, as thunder died away in the distance. Cool, rain-washed air wafted in. The storm was passing at last. "When we put out food on the altar, we send its essence to the ancestors, the way everyday food's essence comes into you. The wine we pour out vanishes in sunlight, and its essence returns to the unseen world, bearing our message to the departed. Paper blessings burn and the smoke goes Heavenward."

"I know *that* much," Matu said. "But those are offerings and rituals. We're talking about divination with peach pits. Cultivation is important to my family, but our cultivation is mostly ourselves, to fend off the chaos of the world. We create our own path in life, or try, which is why we don't do much divination. Though some do it, elders especially," he added after a moment.

"All things are connected," Brother Apple said, and then turned to the ardent young monk. "Brother Seng, can you explain it?"

Brother Seng also sat up, wincing from the aches of the beating the pirates had given him. In the slightly singsong words of recital, he said, "The Essence of Heaven and the Essence of Earth are endlessly interacting, not just at rituals for ancestors and memorials."

No one argued with that.

"All things visible and invisible are bound together in Nature, from you and me to the birds in the air to the most distant mountain peaks and the great creatures undersea."

He paused, and when his listeners signified agreement, he went on, "And bound together, they interact with one another. The clouds shed rain, which feeds the tree, which makes fruit, which we and animals eat, and our waste becomes food for the gardens and trees. It is a circle, with no beginning and no end. The world is made up of too many circles to count, and though we are as yet too finite and uncultivated to see them all, we can see patterns that show pieces of circles, which furnish hints of the greater circles."

"The farmer knows by certain signs the exact time to plant the wheat, or south of us, the rice," Brother Apple put in. "But the shoemaker doesn't see those signs."

Ryu found herself nodding — she knew that was true from life in Sweetwater.

Brother Seng dipped his head in acknowledgment of the acolyte's words, then continued. "We here know where to find the good kaolin clay, and how to mix and pull it. A ship augur knows which star and cloud and moons' patterns will insure sailing weather. Even animals read patterns — the birds know when to fly south or north, the animals in the forest know when the Thunder Dragon below the ground is stirring before the ground begins to shake. This is one reason why we study, not just to cultivate ourselves, but to learn the old patterns and write down the new ones if they prove to be true. We also write down the false ones as ones to be wary of. The peach pits themselves tell us many things, before we ever cast them onto the board: their size, their color, their smell. Their number. All tell us things about the rain of the previous year, the insects, the sunlight. Over the centuries we accumulate wisdom, which is divination."

"Oh," Matu said, and lay back. "Thank you."

Ryu lay back, staring at the shadowy contours of the cave overhead, and as the breathing of the boys at either side slowed into sleep, she wondered how Muin was doing. Of course he would be doing great, especially as this year he and Falik and their friends would be kings of the fortress.

Kings they might be, but at that moment they were tired, filthy, and feeling like a pack of grunts as Falik and Ban Kanda of the navy training school, with his matching red armband, bent over a grubby map, dark heads almost touching as they studied the map by the light of a single candle. The red captains had all crowded into a tent, which was stuffy and smelled of dried fish as they plotted their attack.

This was not the fifth years' first time working with naval cadets, but until now the games had mostly to do with boat landings and beachhead exercises. This was their first army-navy attack on a fortress full of pirates, or thieves, or invaders — from the raucous sounds drifting down from the walls of the redoubt, the greens inside apparently couldn't decide which they wanted to be.

Cor was the green army commander, and his naval counterpart was named Ryu, which had given Muin a bad moment or two when they all first met, and this tall, gangling Ryu had pelted eager questions at him, trying to divine where they met on the family tree.

But once Dun got his attention by saying, loudly, "Ryu's family is from the south, some island even smaller than Imai, which is where I come from," this Ryu visibly lost interest — all his complication of cousins and uncles and brothers were northerners.

The navy boys were a brisk, friendly lot, pretty much like the Loyalty fifth years themselves. Everyone knew they were on the same side, and they got a lot of the same training. But as Muin watched Falik and Ban Kanda eyeing each other as well as the map, and their beginning questions with polite, face-saving expressions like, "I could be wrong, but . . ." or "If you think it might work, then . . ." Muin couldn't help but feel the underlying competition.

In spite of everything, this game was less red defenders versus green attackers, and more army versus navy. And they were all aware of it — what's more, they knew the tassels wanted it that way, as it made everyone work harder.

"You really want to divide us three ways?" Ban asked. "Two, I can see. Two-prong attacks are right up top in the list of strategies. We use it ourselves, when we can."

Falik said politely, "I don't know your Ryu, of course, but I know Cor very well. He's one of our best. He always gets his scouts to collect numbers first thing. And he delights in split forces and flanking. I think he'll be looking for a frontal attack on the gate, followed by a covert attack here on the west side."

Ban bent further over the map, as if more detail would suddenly appear in the sketchily done hills, walls, and clumps of trees. "But . . . unless we put the main force here on the west, or you people can fly, we're just going to be making noise." He tapped the map. "According to this, the walls are just as high here as in front."

"Which is why we need a third force."

Ban said doubtfully, "To do what? There's still the waterway here, which prevents us from getting scaling supplies over, much less a cannon or two."

Falik turned to Muin. "Ryu?"

Muin had gone out earlier to inspect the river himself. "If I had the boats, I could make a bridge."

Falik turned to Dun. "Can you scrounge us up some boats?"

Dun was the best forager in Loyalty. He'd perfected the art of trading and wheedling various items out of the villagers. But . . . "I could if we weren't completely alone out here."

Ban and his own captains had exchanged looks and covert hand signals. Ban said, "Say we could knock together some crude boats. That river is still right under the eyes, and the guns, of the enemy. Unless you have some sort of trick we don't know about, it won't take them half an effort to drop things on us and knock us back to our ancestors."

"They won't if the other two attacks keep their attention. They won't have time to watch the river. You give us five men, and I'll pick five of us. Muin will get those supplies over before dawn."

"With eleven men?"

Dun said, "Ryu and I come from small villages, where every man has to do the work of ten. Ryu will get it done."

It was sheer brag, and Muin suspected that everyone there knew it. But the army boys all felt that they had to live up to it anyway — and the navy boys wanted to win, brag or not.

Ban had no better idea. He was also thinking that if the whole thing failed, the honor marks wouldn't be his, for implementing such a wild plan. He said, "I'll give you my five strongest."

"I want them fast and stealthy more than strong," Muin said, glaring at that map as if he could will the river not to bend so very close to the walls.

But it did, and a short time later, he and his team stood behind cover, staring over the dark waters below, then up at the torchlit walls on the other side. It seemed Cor and his Ryu had everyone awake and alert — they were expecting a night attack, as Falik excelled in those.

Cor knows Falik as well as Falik knows him, Muin was thinking. But he raised his hand in the signal for, "Everyone ready?"

His ten stood there, each with a rope over his shoulder, tools on the other shoulder, the last four ready to bolt down to where the navy boys had been working away at a bunch of rough boats all during the last of Tiger watch. All tapped their chests: "Ready."

Bang! Away to the left, Falik's boys set off two flour cannon, then charged, roaring and waving banners.

Two, three heartbeats after, a deep *boom* echoed from the seaside cliffs, sending night-roosting birds squawking skyward in outrage. The second flanking attack was on.

Muin counted to twenty, giving Cor enough time to rally his people, send them to the two fronts, check the quiet river once more, then launch his defense . . .

"Now."

They ghosted down the hillside into the ooze. Past the cattails and into the cold, dank waters. Muin grimaced, holding his rope high. Ghost Moon was already behind them, its light weak, but Phoenix Moon gave them just enough light as long as they avoided gazing at the torchlit walls. No use looking for trouble — they couldn't do anything about it. They had to depend on the others to keep the defenders busy.

Communicating by curt gesture, the navy boys got the string of boats dragged through the murky waters to meet them, and then came the work of lashing them together, and staking the makeshift bridge on the opposite shore. Each boat had a dark cloth slung over it, to obscure the pale wood if glimpsed from above.

Then came time to get their scaling ladders over — easy — and last, their cannon — hard. The army had the fifth years practicing with real cannon, of course, but never with live people anywhere near the target. These flour cannon shot bags of coarse, gone-bad rice flour. The bags were charmed against bursting until they came into contact with the targets.

The flour bombs didn't kill, but take one close up, and they did break noses or ribs. What was worse was, the flour spread even farther than exploding bombs did, but just the same, any cadet who got doused with flour had to freeze in position and wait until a tassel came along to judge how much flour was on you, and where, and decide if you could continue the fight, though without a limb or two, or if you were dead. In which case you got to start early on collecting arrows and other cleanup, while everyone else was having fun.

Muin and his team were very aware of those cannon on the wall above them as they made their way across the makeshift bridge, utterly exposed if anyone chose to look. Keep the noise up, Muin thought to Falik as their cannon began bumping its way over the bridge, the wood groaning and clattering loud enough (or so they felt) to waken sleepers on all the surrounding islands.

The cannon wheels broke through three times, nearly capsizing the boats. The boys scrambled to repair or support, until at last, at last, they got the accursed thing over.

They only had the rise and the wall to go . . .

"They spotted us halfway up the estuary rise," Muin reported later as the tassels from both army and navy listened. "But by then we had our cannon in position, and our naval five began covering fire, supported by arrows, as the rest of us got to the walls. Two in support of the ladders, and three scaled the wall, carrying two hand-bombs each. One man was shot coming over. Three of us covered Lao until he lit and threw his bombs. Those took out twenty-six of the enemy—including Commanders Cor and Ryu. We heard the surrender drums as the rest of us were scaling the wall."

The masters turned to Cor, who nodded. "We could not see the bridge at all from above, sir. They managed to hide the boats completely. It wasn't until they reached the rise up from the estuary that we spotted them."

As a good part of the merit calculations on this exercise were for cooperation between seamen and landmen, and Cor's defensive placement was considered excellent, the green army did not come out too badly, which left everyone in a fairly good mood as they trooped back to camp, tired and dirty.

The orderlies had hot rice wine waiting—a privilege of fifth years. After the usual mutual praise toasts, tall, thin naval Ryu leaned over and addressed Muin. "Falik being called the Sun God is self-explanatory—"

"Don't let him hear you say that." Muin grinned. "He hates it."

" — and Dun over there is the Pangolin. Why pangolin?"

"It's a tough animal and it's a great scrounger. Dun is good at getting supplies the tassels won't, or can't get, for us. Falik swears he's one day going to be our company quartermaster — assuming any of us ever see one another again after we leave Loyalty."

The naval cadet leaned back; he was not particularly avaricious for a teenage boy, but he settled back, hoping for a good story. "Scrounging, eh? Is he light-fingered?"

Muin made wide eyes. "Don't let Falik hear you say that, even in jest." He tapped his glass to the navy boy's, to show he was only partly in earnest, then said, "Falik hates any kind of cheat. Especially with supplies."

Naval Ryu looked skeptical. "I don't like it either, but the things one hears about ministers in court, and certain governors. Generals. And admirals," he added in haste.

"Certain," Muin agreed. "I don't know much about that myself, but Falik hears things from his father, who insists that his men be honest *because* of those cheats, or nothing will work."

Naval Ryu turned a sober profile downward. "I know, I know. My mother came from tax people. She used to lecture us, saying every time a merchant charges three times the price for something when he knows the tax money is paying, or every tinnie some tax secretary — or flunky under a company captain — puts in his pocket when he buys horse fodder, is food taken from the mouth of some starving person after a flood, or a famine or fire. One of the reasons I went to sea was to get away from dreaming of adding columns of numbers, making sure every bit of brass came out right."

Muin stirred, aware that he was being a bad host. "Anyway, Dun — actually it's Trickle, his brother, who's his orderly — is really good at working trades. He also flirts a lot. A *lot*," Muin added somewhat bitterly, considering how often Trickle managed to get to the village on supply runs, compared to the rare liberties the rest of the older boys were given. "And the girl apprentices will give him extras, or trade for things. Everybody gets something, and not a tinnie changes hands. Trickle talks, Dun goes and makes it official, the tassels shower merits on him. Dun the Pangolin."

"But you don't have a name."

Muin realized he'd just walked into a trap. "Ayah! I don't want one," he began, sitting upright.

"Too late!" The naval Ryu chortled, unfolding his long length. "Listen, all!" He poured fresh wine from the jug into his cup as he spoke. "What I wouldn't have believed unless I'd seen it as I lay there, covered in flour, was how good you and your three are with those wooden swords." He raised his cup. "Whether you south islanders really are that good, or the training at Loyalty Fortress has gotten better than ours, I don't know. Here's to Ten-Blade Ryu. Upholding the famed Ryu excellence!"

"Ten-Blade," someone repeated, and naval Ryu's nickname passed from lips to ears — everyone from the defense on the wall agreeing with enthusiasm.

Muin groaned, hoping the ridiculous name would be forgotten with tomorrow's rice wine headache. His gaze on his cup, he didn't see Falik's sober glance: Muin's suggestions for ways to tighten up their sword drills had paid off time and again.

Falik would remember that.

THIRTY-FIVE

RYU SLEPT LIKE A rock, and woke well before dawn, shaking off dreams of the attack on the tea ship. A familiar cramp below her belly got her up.

A couple monks were moving about silently, shadowy shapes lit by a single lantern. She rolled her bedding and carried it to the shelves, then went out into a still-dripping world to find a secluded spot so that she could use Essence and charms to take care of the monthly. She had gotten used to it, but it was not easy or quick, as yet.

The storm had washed the tiled terrace clean. She passed a rain stone, a huge block into the top of which the constant drip of rain over the centuries had carved a shallow bowl. She paused to look down into the clear water, wondering how old the monastery was, then hurried up into the forested hillside beyond the terrace.

When she returned she was not surprised to recognize Shigan's silhouette coming from the pathway leading down the mountain. "You had the same thought? Those pirates, or whatever they are, will come back."

"I know," Ryu replied.

Shigan lifted a hand toward the warren of carved caves that made up the monastery. "If you were looking for the path to the harbor, it's over *this* way," he said — pointing past the terraced slope where the monks' kitchen garden and the peach trees grew. "Over there is the one we came up yesterday."

"There might be more than two paths," Ryu said evasively.

As the darkness began to lift, she could see that the temple had been built at the top of the spine of the peninsula they had sailed around the morning before. To one side, as Shigan had indicated, lay the secluded inlet where they had debarked from the trader. On the other side, below the acrid-smelling scorch of the burned trees, lay a twisting path that led down toward Sunset Harbor. Directly behind Shigan, part of the harbor town was just becoming visible, outlined by rows of tiny torches on the city walls.

Shigan glanced back. "How far down should we plant our warning trap? Fifty paces? A hundred?"

Being veterans of war games, they both had the same idea: to set up a warning system. The simplest—a buried string or a balanced piece of wood that would fall at a touch, and release a noisy rock fall—would give the defenders a few moments' notice, but it would also warn the attackers that they were expected.

Ryu said, "It seemed a good idea when I first woke. Except, then what? These monks have no weapons. Phoenix Moon monks don't take lives . . ." She stopped, biting her tongue. Was that general knowledge, or would Shigan start wondering how she knew?

He didn't. "Everyone knows that. But I heard Brother Apple last night, when he was dishing out the vegetables, reminding that acolyte with the broken arm that their Ghost Moon brothers and sisters train in martial arts. They don't start fights, but they don't seem to have a problem with finishing them."

"Ghost Moon monks and nuns are dedicated to eradicating evil," Ryu said, remembering what she'd been told as a child.

The hollow tapping sound of the instrument called a wooden fish caused both to turn—the monks were already waking and beginning their morning ritual.

Ryu said morosely, "I know they didn't ask us to, but I feel we should defend them. But there are only the four of us, as Yaso never touches the weapons." She paused, recollecting the fog on board the tea ship, then shook her head. "And this is no war game."

Shigan's chin came down in a slow nod. "Real defense. Not just a warning."

A monk's voice rose in song, beginning the morning Sun Sutras. A sharp pang of regret overwhelmed Ryu, making her throat ache and her eyes sting: she remembered, with merciless clarity, walking behind First Brother onto that ship full of cadets without the slightest thought of those at home. Oh, she'd missed them at night, but . . .

Unwilling to risk Shigan seeing her stinging eyes, she turned to face the top of the path — and there was Petal. Of course she wouldn't use the men's privy either. Ryu either had to use her bamboo method at the regular privy or, if she wanted to be alone, make her call of nature escapes at a different time from Petal so that no one would put them together. Petal, unencumbered by disguise, was in the light, Ryu in the dark. But . . .

Once again she felt as if an invisible band constricted her.

That was better than missing Ul Keg and her parents.

"Are we practicing?" Petal asked Ryu when she came near.

Ryu turned to Shigan, who cast a glance at the harbor. Ryu sensed that he was as ambivalent as she was. That had to mean they ought to go. "We're going to scout the attackers," Ryu said. "We'll be back soon."

Shigan's sudden grin flashed. Ryu's tangled emotions dissipated like fog melting before the summer sun. Yes. Planning a defense was the right decision, and the first step was always a scouting run.

Without speaking, the two jogged down the path, stopping only to drink from a stream bubbling beside them. Along the way they found wild berries and small, mouth-puckeringly sour crabapples, which filled their stomachs without slowing them down.

They halted their headlong dash when they rounded a curve and saw, directly below them, a husky guard standing with a bared blade. As one they faded back, then dropped to the ground and peered down through some weeds.

Shigan, a little farther down the path than Ryu, wriggled backward and signaled with his hand: flat palm and two fingers. Neither had forgotten the simple cadet code: two armed sentries.

Ryu scrunched back, careful not to send stones rattling down the steep slope, then crawled down to join Shigan, shoulder to shoulder. She peered down. Yes, another one. Younger than the first, though older than she was — he had a mustache sprouting. And he stood like a warrior.

They crawled backward until they were fully out of sight of the harbor below, then crouched with their heads together.

"Guarding the path or the entire harbor?" Ryu asked low-voiced. "The first is bad, the second worse." That wide a perimeter meant the pirates had an army.

Shigan turned his head, squinting against the bright morning sun as he scanned the rough, rocky terrain. Ryu was distracted by the appearance of fine dark hairs on his upper lip and chin. Just a few, which she had seen him scraping away once a week or so. But she hadn't really *noticed*. Those hairs were evidence he wasn't really a boy anymore. As if she hadn't realized that, what with all the flirting and going off with the pretty girls flocking around him in every village they came to!

She shook away the thought, and stared in the same direction. If they went back up the trail some hundred steps, there was another slope, an old landslide from the look of it. Wiry shrubs and young trees growing among the rocks made it look reasonably stable. It was not an easy trip down, and would be a worse one back up.

Bending low, they retraced their steps, found a goat path, and began the hazardous journey down. As it happened, they did not have to go all the way to Sunset Harbor that first scouting trip — they spied a force gathering on a hill above the harbor, at the base of the main path.

Moving from boulder to boulder across the landslide, they eased upward until they could hear voices. Most were men, all young, all gripping weapons. No single voice rose above the others, but they heard the word "monks" repeated, and "gold" and once an oath about books as someone brandished a torch.

They'd heard enough. With no more than a glance of silent agreement, they faded back and retreated back up the mountainside. When they reached the head of the trail, Matu was waiting for them. "Brother Song sent a pigeon to their Ghost Moon brethren last night," he said to the two red, sweaty faces. "An answer just came back." He twiddled his fingers indicating wings. "Though there's a monastery of nuns closer, it seems they are already dispersed on a justice quest, so if we can hold out for three days, some Ghost Moon monks can be here by then. Come on inside," he added. "There's a steamed bun for each of you. And Brother Seng wants to talk to you."

Matu led them into the part of the monastery where the clay began the process of becoming porcelain. A couple of monks appeared from a tunnel carved from reddish stone, their sleeves tied back and work implements in their hands.

Brother Seng led the monastery's animal handlers — including the pigeons. He was tall and thin, his expression somber. "Yesterday Captain Dal In threatened to return until we agree to make what she wants. But they won't get anything if they kill us all. We are thankful for your desire to aid us, but we cannot agree to loss of life on our behalf. We suggest you go in safety while you can. We will endure until our brethren get here. They will be able to turn the Dals away without killing."

"Do you want to get kicked around again?" Shigan asked, for he was hot, sweaty, and hungry. He hadn't expected the monks to help, but he'd thought they'd be a bit more grateful.

"No," Brother Seng said gently. "But we cannot condone anything that takes lives. There is always hope of redemption while people live, but at death their choice ends."

Ryu said, "Will you let us defend you if we just make things really uncomfortable for them so that they go away on their own?"

Brother Seng bowed, palms together. "I will consult the elders, but I suspect they will say, if you can do that, we'd welcome it."

Ryu grabbed her steamed bun and crammed it into her mouth as she dashed away. She wandered through the carved rock chambers until she found Yaso in the warm, steamy kitchen. Yaso and two monks stood around a preparation table discussing what smelled like freshly picked summer herbs.

Ryu stood nearby, finishing her bun as she waited for Yaso, who presently noted her and approached. "Redbark Brother Ryu?"

Ryu beckoned Yaso out into the corridor, then looked around before eyeing the orderly. "*Are* you an Essence master?"

"I am merely a beginner," Yaso said modestly.

"If so, I wonder what you consider a master. But all right, I don't mean to argue about what people call themselves." She looked around again. "That fog. Can you teach me to make it? We're going to try to keep those pirates from coming up the path—and they are already on their way. We don't have time to build anything."

"It is easy enough," Yaso said. "You know the Essence signs for drawing water. Write the signs in the air with your finger, if that helps your mind center. After the rain yesterday, the ground and air are full of water. It should not take long."

Yaso was right.

She was used to using Essence signs for small things, her first efforts having begun with the signs to deflect attention in the baths back at the fortress. She ran down the path alone, halting at a bend where a trickle from above ran across the path, shut her eyes, and did her breathing as she gathered Essence. She remembered the sign for collecting vapor—her mother had demonstrated it during a lesson not long after Ul Keg had first told Ryu The Story. Mother had used Essence paper, and chants, but Ryu now understood those to be merely tools to concentrate.

She focused on sensing the water all around. Yes, Yaso was right. The ground, the air, shimmered with water. She used the same mental image that once she'd employed for drawing wind imps to her, but drew moisture out of the ground.

At first she felt resistance, looked down, and to her astonishment saw jiggling droplets of water rising from the mud where the streamlet crossed the path. Her surprise broke her concentration and the water splashed down.

But that gave her a sense of what she ought to be doing, and before long she saw wisps of vapor rising from the mud. Exulting, she used both hands to help her concentrate on bringing more vapor up from pools and mud, until she had a swirling mist.

Thicker and thicker she made it, until she stood in the center of a cloud, her hair and clothes damp and cool. At first she added more Essence until she began to feel light-headed, and halted to breathe. It was then that she saw that she had set something in motion. The fog slowly thickened on its own.

Now she understood what Yaso had meant about conse-quences: once she had set the Essence flowing, it continued on, the way a rock keeps tumbling downhill once it is given a push. But this fog was not a sudden, violent expulsion of Essence. It would not accumulate forever, just as a rock tumbling downhill does not roll forever. The mist would thin and dissipate, leaving no destruction in its path.

She retreated back up the trail—stepping abruptly into bright sunlight. Two more bends in the trail, then she spotted the pagoda high atop the mountain, which meant the temple was directly below.

One more bend, and there was the terrace, with Shigan, Petal, and Matu waiting for her. "That," Shigan said, lounging against a low wall, "was interesting."

"That?" Ryu repeated.

Shigan turned to Matu, hands wide. Matu grinned. "He said you'd pretend nothing happened."

Petal added, "Look." She pointed behind Ryu.

Ryu turned. And blinked in surprise when she saw the path, the burned orchard, the rocks . . . and about thirty paces below, a soft cloud of pure white, as if the mountains had vanished, replaced by a world of snow. It was her fog.

She reddened.

"I don't know why you didn't want to tell us," Matu said, half-questioning.

"I didn't know if it would work," Ryu mumbled. "And I don't know anything. Not really. Just a few tricks. I did tell you, many times, I need to find a martial arts Essence master."

Shigan remained inscrutable, but Matu gave a good-natured shrug, and said, "I'm just glad you can do it, because I know I could not. I do have an idea, and I want to go up that side of the mountain to see if it might work. But first, shall we begin Redbark?" He began hopping from foot to foot. "It's been much too long, and if we have to face pirates . . ."

The monks had gone about their daily tasks, leaving the terrace to Ryu and her companions. They stretched, and drilled, and scrapped, Matu rejoicing in being away from a ship and on firm ground.

It was early afternoon when they halted, sweaty and warm, tired and exhilarated—they had completely forgotten to set up a watch for the pirates. They were taking turns drinking from a little waterfall above the pathway from the secluded inlet when Brother Apple scurried up to them, flushed and smiling, a basket on his arm. "The pirates came up the West Path, and got lost in a fog," he exclaimed. "Some tumbled down the slope into the mineral spring, and they went back."

"You saw them?" Shigan asked.

"Yes. There is a goat path on the far side of the hot springs that only we know about, I went to pick these mushrooms for our meal. I could see them but they could not see me! Will the fog last?"

"It will probably be gone before nightfall," Ryu said.

Brother Apple's face fell. "They'll probably be back tomorrow. Maybe even sneaking up the East Path." He pointed to the path leading to the inlet, up which Ryu and the others had first come.

"I would if I meant to attack this monastery. We'll have do something about that," Shigan muttered.

Brother Apple didn't hear him. He bowed, palms together, said, "Thank you," and trotted off with his basket of truffles.

"Let's try to figure out a way to fend off the pirates until the Ghost Moon monks can arrive," Ryu suggested.

Shigan smiled. Of course little brother Ryu would take on this task.

They split up, Ryu choosing to find a shady spot and do her Essence breathing after her exertions. Their wooden weapons lay along the wall, ready in case the pirates made a second try.

But they didn't. The sun began its downward slide toward the west beyond the fog, which swirled slowly between the soaring cliffs.

Matu had vanished up the slope opposite the temple. He reappeared before the shadows melded into dusk, running downhill toward the terrace in a skittering of small stones, his messy topknot jerking from side to side as he bounced.

When he reached the terrace, he wiped his face on his sleeve, leaving a streak of dirt, as he exclaimed in triumph, "I can do it!"

"Do what?" Shigan asked,

"Two streams up on the mountain. I can divert both with some hard digging, and wash out that path." He pointed toward the west.

"Then we just need to figure out a way to block the East Path," Ryu said.

Petal slunk up next to her. She seldom spoke unless spoken to when all were there, but now she murmured, "That East Path is so much narrower. If you can shift a boulder the way you did those iron casks. At a spot they can't get around . . ."

"Boulder and fog," Ryu said. "I'll make the fog first thing when I wake up. But the boulder, what if we block off the Ghost Moon monks?"

"Didn't Brother Apple say they have their own secret path?" Petal murmured into Ryu's shoulder, as if that innkeeper stepmother of hers lurked somewhere around with her watering can, listening.

But the boys heard anyway. "There is one," Matu said at the same time Shigan pointed, and said, "Behind the hot springs somewhere." Then he turned to Ryu. "We'd better find out exactly where it is and patrol it."

Ryu jerked her chin down the way the cadets had in agreement. "Just thinking that. Won't we look stupid if we go fumbling around to find that trail and discover the pirates waiting for us."

THIRTY-FOUR

THE NEXT DAY THE monks went about their tasks, the main of which was monitoring their kiln full of porcelain, which meant constantly tending the intense heat from a scalding-hot vent deep in the rock. Air vents were opened and closed according to the directions of the kiln masters.

Shigan and Ryu spent the entire day trading off planting booby traps on the east trail, and patrolling back and forth between all the paths. Petal alternately helped and ran messages.

But the day's true success belonged to Matu, who had learned something about mountain streams in his days on the Ten Leopards plateau. With some hard digging, he diverted a still-swollen stream resulting from the heavy storm, creating two waterfalls that tumbled right onto the West Path at tricky turns, making the ground into a slippery quagmire that sent the front runners of the advancing pirates, who were already confused by the dense fog, slipping over the cliff edge to tumble into the marsh below.

It was Shigan who discovered the abortive attack, crept down as close as he dared to observe, then ran back to report. They went to sleep that night jubilant with triumph: the pirates had been routed yet again.

Unable to sleep, the routed, angry pirates met with their leader, Captain Dal In, at what had been the City Lord's mansion on the south end of Sunset Harbor. That manor now belonged to Dal In, which she considered a right thing. Her family had been city lords in the past, only to be forced out after what they considered pure bad luck, to be replaced by the appointment of the Biyan family, whose connections among the merchant families had secured their hold on the position for four generations.

Dal In had made certain that number did not reach five: the widow of the old governor, and her daughter, were currently scrubbing the privies and floors of the Dal manor right now.

Ayah! The rest of those merchant families had been taught a sharp lesson of the sort she had learned aboard the pirate ship, and those she'd left alive bowed to the ground every time she so much as looked their way.

"But these damned monks," she said to her trusted circle of followers. "Too stupid to see how I'm *helping* them. What is the use of making the best bowls this side of the imperial city, and nobody but monks and ghosts to see them?"

She went on in this way, peppering them with rhetorical questions with the freedom of one who has never in her life had to worry about talking too much, for she had been the single grandchild, cherished by her elders until she ran away with a handsome pirate captain. And what an education that had been, ending with her first murder when he'd tried to beat her.

After cursing the monks roundly, then stoking her temper by reflecting on how many broken bones her followers had endured from tumbling down cliffs in fog and waterfalls, she said, "All we need are two or three of them — ones old enough to know the secrets of their porcelain. Kill the rest, and give those three a treasure as reward, and enough bond-servants to follow their directions. Then they get rich, and we replace the lost ships, and rebuild this town. Everyone is successful! Wouldn't that be the best gift of all?"

"Yes, Captain," the followers roared in unison, knowing their cue.

Dal In rubbed tired eyes, then put her booted feet on the table, crossing them at the ankles as she glowered at one of her lookouts. "Find another way to that temple. Then tomorrow, no more warning. We start killing."

On the mountain, even after the sun went down, the monks were absorbed with tending their kiln. The four companions were fascinated by the old monk who served as their kiln master. To them, the entire area leading down to the kiln was insanely hot, but he judged the temperature by the color of the flames, and occasionally he ventured close to the sealed wall to spit on the bricks and listen to the quality of the sizzle. Then he'd nod and either order more air or more from the fire vents to keep the kiln stable.

He talked readily about the ancient craft of porcelain-making, far more disposed to explain in exhaustive detail than his audience was to listen. Petal was the first to leave, once she'd heard enough about dyes, specifically the difficulties in making red dye that glazed to a brilliant crimson: before he became a monk, he had come from one of the elite porcelain clans, who jealously guarded the secrets that enabled them to hold onto the imperial seal for going on five generations.

Ryu left after he rambled reminiscently about his youth, and wanting to see the world, then choosing the monastic life to cultivate his spirit. Matu made it a little longer, until only Shigan was left, full of questions about the porcelain trade as seen from the inside.

"But I left home when young," the monk said modestly. "I'm certain it's all different now, and what little I know has become outdated."

"You'd still be telling me more than I know, which is nothing," Shigan said.

He joined the others at last, and Ryu, who had been drifting tiredly into slumber then jerking awake, saw him curled up in his spot and dropped into deep, dreamless sleep until Shigan poked her awake.

She snorted, sat up, and wiped her chin where she'd drooled. "What?"

"I think the fighting monks are here," he whispered, wide eyes glittering in the light of the single candle.

The Ghost Moon monks had indeed arrived, each equipped with a long staff. These monks looked little different from the Phoenix Moon monks, except that they wore simple robes over baggy trousers rather than the loose tunic-shirts and baggy trousers favored by the latter. All fabrics were similarly undyed.

The newcomers spoke very little—and not at all to the visitors—but after the eldest explained what had been happening, and that Ryu and company had been defending them, they were given a short nod of acknowledgment by the leader. Which, as Shigan murmured to Ryu later, "Made me as giddy with pride as anything in my misspent life."

The Ghost Moon monks took over patrolling — and so three of them were the first to die when a sudden rain of arrows struck from above.

All turned their heads toward where the arrows had come from before scurrying for cover: the pirates had spent an entire night toiling up the back end of the mountain, past where Matu had diverted the streams, and down to wait for enough light to see their targets.

Ryu, crouched behind the rain stone, burned with angry Essence. She made the signs and began drawing moisture to weave a fog. The air filled with drifting vapors as pirates, who had spent the entire night crawling up the West Road, burst onto the temple terrace, steel drawn.

But these were met by Ghost Moon monks, whose training, better than the pirates', leaped to the defense. One, then two arrows whizzed down until the pirates on the mountain realized they couldn't control who their arrows hit — one monk staggered with an arrow in his thigh, as a pirate let out a yell and dropped, an arrow squarely in the back of his neck.

"Something changed."

Shigan hunkered down beside Ryu. "They're fighting to kill now. At least we have these monks to plan a defense with — "

The clack of wooden staves against clubs and swords gave way to shouts, curses and howls of pain as the disciplined monks whirled their staffs with lethal expertise, knocking their way through the pirates.

Ryu blinked, her mind hovering over a map only she could see. It was nearly all there . . . She gave her head an impatient shake. "They'll stay right here to defend."

Shigan shifted to stare at her. "And we?"

The pirates, balked by the appearance of the fighting monks, would retreat now . . . "To end it, we have to take the fight to the enemy."

The clacks and shouts began to retreat down the western path. She slipped along behind them, trying to pick out the leader. Behind her, Shigan closed with Matu, who looked grim, and Petal, whose attention was on the fallen.

"Ryu wants to take the fight to the enemy," Shigan said.

Matu's face tightened even more. "What can I do?"

Shigan laughed, his mood swinging wildly between relief, disbelief, and rising tension. "Same as I'm doing. Follow him?"

He jerked a thumb Ryu's way.

Matu swallowed. Shigan saw it, and added, "Unless you want to stay. There's plenty to do here. And maybe Ryu means to scout first."

"Firebolt," Matu said, almost voicelessly — to him, Ryu was more of a mystery each day. You think you know someone, but you discover you really don't. He knew enough about Essence to recognize it, thanks to Grandfather Ki testing his progeny, but he had never seen it wielded. Making that fog was the sort of thing that Grandfather Ki was reputed to do. The only thing Matu was sure of, Ryu had the makings of a hero. "I'll come."

Petal said, "I'll stay. They'll need help wrapping wounds. That I can do."

The other two accepted that — though Petal had worked hard all summer, and was coming along well, no one expected her to be able to fight pirates after three months of drill and scrapping.

They didn't speak much as they followed the pirates down. They were too busy trying to maintain a distance close enough to hear whatever could be heard, but not be discovered. The pirates who had shot at them had also retreated, probably having to make their way by a circuitous route down the back end of the mountain. Words and phrases drifted back, and in Ryu's mind possible plans formed and collapsed. She had to see the leader, hear her. Then everything would fall into place.

Taking the path was much easier than toiling over the landslide — it wasn't all that long before the views below widened from dark slopes to the distant sea gleaming in the light of the two moons at either end of the sky, one rising, one setting. Sunset Harbor lay directly below, tiny yellow pinpoints of light glowing.

Ryu kept her gaze on the leader, trusting Shigan and Matu to watch around them. As they rounded the last bend before the road straightened, the captain beckoned someone over. She had been talking all along, her voice carrying back through the other voices, mostly cursing and anger talk of the sort Ryu remembered from her wargame days, after they finished a hard game or scrap. The way she waved off others, and walked close to the taller man as she spoke, tightened Ryu's focus: orders.

Shigan and Matu were always at the periphery of her thoughts. She turned to Matu. "That tall man," she said in an urgent undertone. "Follow him. Find out if you can what orders he was given."

As Ryu spoke, the crowd emerged onto the last leg of the path, carved through wild forest. As the pirates slouched their way toward the harbor town, Matu vanished into the leafy world beside the road.

Ryu and Shigan got into the covering forest on the other side, Ryu impatiently pushing past leafy branches and tall, later summer grasses. The pirates were too tired, angry, apprehensive, hungry and thirsty to think of looking behind them — after all, who would chase them? A bunch of monks? They had counted on being able to raid the monks' food and drink after their exertions.

Ryu had lost sight of the tall man the captain had given orders to. She'd lost sight of Matu as well. They had obviously run ahead. Ryu sketched her Essence talisman over herself and over Shigan. Who gave her a questioning look, but said nothing: the humidity, oppressively hot under a thick, low ceiling of cloud, rendered the air so still that sound carried well.

Ryu and Shigan stepped onto the path as the forest gave way to ordered plots, and then open fields. The pirates, close to comfort, food, and drink, never looked back as they approached and then passed through the harbor town's east gate. Shigan kept his hand tightly on his wooden sword, again wishing he had a real one. Ryu marched along, confident that the wall sentries, especially so very late, would pay no attention to someone her age.

And so they passed right through. Shigan waited for Ryu to peel off, but she continued on behind them, relying on the blurring effect of the Essence charm and the pirates' own exhaustion and lack of focus, as they headed straight for the largest, most elaborate building on the central square, which usually belonged to the city lord, or governor.

Ryu watched as the captain took five or six in with her and waved the others off. Before they turned away, Ryu whispered, "To the roof." She and Shigan slipped around the stone guard lions, ran full tilt toward the side. Ryu leaped to a branch of a flowering tree then to the roof. Shigan was right behind her, swinging from one branch to another, then making the leap.

Ryu had gone silent in a way that reminded Shigan of their cadet days. Back then he'd thought Ryu's aloofness mere posturing, but he'd learned that this expression was the one Ryu wore when watching the Circle board for the first ten or twelve moves, then predicting exactly how the next twenty moves would go, before wandering off, the game forgotten.

Ryu wiped her sweaty forehead on her grimy sleeve and paused at the clack and creak of windows below being pushed out to let the stuffy, candle-heated air escape. She looked around, her forehead furrowed. "I have to see what she's doing. To make sure."

"Doing? Or saying? And sure of what?"

"Both, but doing is important," Ryu murmured, staring downward.

"Why?"

"I have to see . . ." She waved a hand. "In the games. On the sand table. In Circle. It's not just the pieces that determine the end. It's how they're moved, the brain behind the fingers moving them, I mean. You see?"

"You predict," Shigan said. "How much more do you need to see? Did you notice where she's sitting?"

"That's just it." Ryu shrugged. "She sat in a chair. A carved one. It seems to be on a kang, or something, but what's important is, I can't see or hear her. I thought we'd hear up here."

Shigan held out a hand. "She's sitting in the south-facing chair, where the highest ranking person sits. Or most honored guest." And at Ryu's puzzled look, "Think of it as a throne."

"Oh." Ryu sat back. "Oh! I didn't know that. Where I lived we didn't have . . .Yes, that's *just* what I needed. I think . . . I think . . ." Ryu was looking around as she spoke—and straightened up. "There he is." She pointed down at the tall man after whom she'd sent Matu. "Let's find Matu," she said. "He has to be coming along . . ."

She ghosted along the ridgepole, and then, light as a crane feather, leaped from the roof to the ground, a faint glow around her as she leaped. Shigan sighed, not daring to leap that far. He worked his way to the tree, leaped to catch a branch, and swung himself down.

When he caught up with Ryu, Matu had just spotted them, coming from the opposite direction. At Ryu's gesture the three of them slipped between buildings behind the back door of the city lord manor.

Matu said, "He went to three houses, and told someone in each one to start bringing all the biggest and strongest of each family to the center square, with weapons. At least one fighter per household, right now. Anyone not complying, the whole family will die."

"There," Ryu said. "That's the missing piece. She's Yulin."

"Yulin?" Matu repeated.

Ryu turned to him. "Matu, you're great. I knew you could do it! Here's what I mean about Yulin, someone Shigan and I knew during our time in the army. And that is, he will never stop feuding, ever, because he thinks he deserves to be in charge because of who he is. If you win, he does something worse. If you lose, he might not do something worse, but he'll be just as mean. This captain on her throne is a Yulin. She's going to make the entire town go kill the monks. Just because they crossed her."

Matu gave a soft laugh, more grieved than humorous. "That's pretty much what I heard at all three houses."

"So, we go back to the monks?" Shigan asked.

Ryu shook her head. Everything was in place now. Except the timing. "Economy of force. Simplicity," Ryu whispered at last, the sinking moon a sliver of silver in her eyes.

Shigan grinned. "Instructor Shaz's second lecture, on the Nine Principles of War. Ayah! What is your economy of force and simplicity?"

"Everything," Ryu said, "depends on you two. Go to all the houses those three go to, and tell them that if they don't want to fight for the pirates, there is another plan. It's up to them."

"But that man was going to be sending gangs around to smash up houses where no one comes out to fight."

"Oh, they can come out to the square," Ryu said. "But if they want to be rid of the pirates, here's how it's going to go —"

She outlined her idea, finishing, "It's all up to them. If they want to keep that captain, then they obey her. If not, wait for my signal."

Matu shook his head slowly. "That threat against their families. Even if they don't want the pirates, who will be able to risk being attacked?"

"That," Ryu said, "is my part."

She said that with more confidence than she felt. How was she going to keep this pirate captain busy until everyone was gathered?

As it happened, Dal In solved that at least in part by insisting that her followers drag Widow Biyan and her daughter to the village square for, as she put it as she sauntered out the door, some entertainment. And food for Blood Drinker, her sword.

And above all, a reminder who holds the power.

Ryu watched from the roof as a couple of disheveled women, one gray-haired, were shoved into the center of the square, and made to kneel as people began gathering at a prudent distance. Both women were dressed in rags. They knelt with wan faces, their expressions dull as beached fish, as Captain Dal said loudly, "I think it's about time to behead the two of you useless offal. Your heads can join the rest of the family over the west gate, eh? You'll have a fine view of the sunset for the rest of eternity, ha ha!"

She looked around for the expected laugh, and her followers laughed.

"But first you'll be glad to know my plans for this island. Once I get control of the porcelain, Sunset Harbor will become the jewel in the crown, my capital of what will become . . ."

Ryu stopped listening, and began watching for Matu and Shigan. At one point the pirate captain stopped and gestured. Someone brought her sheathed sword.

Essence prickled along Ryu's arms and the skin at the back of her neck tightened. Essence. It was not quite a smell, or a touch, somewhere between, and yet not. It was also sharp, or flat, or sour. She didn't have the words—until the thought hit her, was this Essence bent toward evil?

The stories were full of swords, knives, caves, even castles full of evil Essence talismans. She'd asked Mother once, only to be told that such stories ought to be forbidden as they put worthless ideas into her mind, and Essence was to be respected, to be used for healing and harmony and peace.

But here was her first evidence that evil Essence—that is, Essence used for evil intent—existed. And she had no idea how to counter it. She wished Yaso had come after all. But what would Yaso do? Tell her to breathe, that Essence flows . . .

Oh. Was it possible that what flowed could recede? It sounded too simple—

The scraping of metal from a sheathe broke her reverie. Captain Dal had ripped her sword free, and was swinging it back and forth as she began describing its fame. How it could cut through anything, even rock. "One strike from my Blood Drinker," she said, standing over the two women. "And you won't even feel it. Now, who wants to go first?"

Ryu cast a glance at the periphery. Still thin of watchers. She needed more of them.

She leaped down from the roof and strode into the torchlight. "I will."

The captain whirled around. "Where did you come from, rat turd?"

Keep her talking, Ryu told herself. "Rat turd, am I?" Ryu repeated, thinking desperately for more to say. She didn't know what more to say—she didn't have conversations. Shigan was the one for that.

Insults. Back at Liberty Fortress, the boys could go on at length trading insults.

"If I'm a rat turd, you're a blowfish."

Pirates muttered, people whispered, and someone—sounded like a teenage boy—gave a caw of laughter from the back.

Ryu said, "I've never known anyone who so clearly thinks of themselves as a dragon flying and a phoenix soaring, but who sounds like a duck quacking." Color flooded the pirate captain's cheeks, and Ryu knew she must keep talking. "We have a saying back where I come from, someone who blabbers until the net is broken and the fish are dead."

"So you want action, rat turd?" the captain snarled, drawing that sword.

"What a display of bravery," Ryu shouted, thinking: that's right, look at me. Come after me. Leave those two alone . . . "Throwing stone after stone at somebody already at the bottom of the well."

Captain Dal stared incredulously as Ryu circled around. The captain turned until her back was to her victims, keeping her rage-filled gaze on Ryu.

Ryu waved one hand in a wide circle, and with the other sketched the Essence Focus. Then, on a deep breath, pulled at the Essence in that sword. She started, shocked almost witless at the thick stench of blood that flowed off it.

Essence might be neutral, as Ul Keg had taught her, but *this* Essence had been poisoned for a very long time. Yaso's lessons about consequences occurred to Ryu. She turned her gaze downward, pushing with her mind as she directed that Essence into the ground.

The captain charged at Ryu, raising the sword high, then swung in a killing stroke. The sword whooshed within a hand's breadth of Ryu, who leaped back. "You want a duel?

No, you're too weak, too cowardly." Her voice shrilled and she suppressed a grimace. She sounded like she was nine.

The captain didn't seem to care if she was girl, boy, or a pine tree. Swoosh! Swish! Two more strikes, which Ryu dodged, always moving back as the Essence poured off the blade like an invisible river of blood.

"Who are you?" the captain shouted. "Who sent you?"

Ryu was trying to frame a new insult when from the back of the crowd a voice rose, "That's Firebolt!" Matu!

The crowd began whispering, everyone asking each other, "Who?"

The captain ignored them and charged again, swinging the blade in a downward strike. "Come on, stand still," she crooned. "Let Blood Drinker kiss you . . ."

That was it. This sword had been charmed to drain Essence from people along with their life's blood. The edge gleamed greenish in the torchlight, and a fresh surge chilled Ryu's nerves. The blade was poisoned.

A quick look—there was Shigan, hand up. All right, this was as many as she'd get. Time to end this. Ryu breathed in Essence from the sky, the stars, the rising moon, and leaped, somersaulting over the captain's head. Who whirled, bringing the sword up—then staggered back as Ryu kicked her in the head.

The captain jerked around as Ryu lit behind her and sidestepped in with a swift, hard palm-heel strike to the elbow. The sword dropped. The captain dove for it, and Ryu brought her foot around in an arc, kicking the captain behind the ear. She dropped like a stone.

Ryu kicked the sword spinning. It was still leaking a river of nasty Essence. Did it really crave blood?

As the crowd shouted, uncertain whether to run or charge, Ryu looked around. Ah. She picked up a rock from the ground, set it on the blade, and then, focusing all her strength, drove her boot heel into the rock, without letting any part of herself touch that blade.

The steel chipped with a sharp crack.

The captain groaned, groping for the sword hilt. "No," she whispered, her eyes wild in the torchlight. "Not my Blood Drinker! He and I will fly, he just needs enough blood . . ."

Ryu brought the rock down again, aiming all her Essence focus at that steel. The blade shattered. Ignoring the captain's furious threats, Ryu got to her feet.

"People of Sunset Harbor," she called, reaching desperately for words. And there was Ul Keg, reading ancient poetry in memory: if she couldn't find her own words, at least there were the words of the ancients. "This is your town. As it is said by our ancestors, if you seek justice, then first you must dispense justice. If you seek vengeance, it will surely find you."

Silence met that as everyone stared. She cleared her dry throat and tried again. "If you act together, you can have the kind of town you want." She pointed at the pirates, who were still waiting for orders from their captain—now vastly outnumbered by the townspeople. "And choose your own governor."

"Correct," Shigan said, as people stirred, looking at each other to see who would act. "But first, if you want a new beginning, you have to clean up the trash." He stepped up and with three strikes, knocked a pirate down. Then turned to meet another who rushed him, a double axe raised. Shigan sidestepped, using Redbark form, flowed past the swinging axe, and brought his doubled fist down on the back of the pirate's neck. When the man dropped to his knees, a kick snapped his head back, and he lay still, the axe clattering.

Both sides had been waiting for someone to act. Someone had acted. With a roar of rage fueled by pent-up fear, the people turned on the enemy. At least a dozen charged the captain, who was moaning over the remains of her sword.

At first both Matu and Ryu ran to aid smaller groups, but arriving citizens joined them until sheer numbers prevailed. Howls and shouts rose. Ryu paused over the shattered sword—at last the Essence flow was thinning. Soon it would be just a blade, and she hoped that the Essence would disperse and not poison the ground.

She began to run, catching Shigan and Matu with her gaze. "The town is theirs. Let's get out of here."

They bolted through the gates as the crowd chased the former pirate sentries. Shrieking, angry voices faded behind them, releasing Ryu. She was giddy with relief, silent laughter running through her as she ran shoulder to shoulder with the two boys, she in the middle. Occasionally she bumped up against their arms as they pelted along in the clear moonlight. Strange, how you could know someone by the shape of a limb. So much better to think about, arms, than that crowd back there, though the pirates had probably earned whatever fate the people meted out. Probably. She couldn't know — and it was not her town.

So, arms. Shigan's slim and solid, reminding her of a hunting cat's limb. Matu's shorter, thicker, reassuringly solid. Like a . . . a boar, or another brave animal of that kind of shape and size . . .

Shigan knocked against her. "Why did you break that sword? It looked good."

"It had evil charms on it," she said, and at his skeptical glance, "*really* evil. It craved blood."

He grimaced, half-disbelieving. But only half.

They jogged up the trail at top speed, carried on the nervous exhilaration of after-action. That persisted until they spotted the temple's pagoda, gleaming softly in the moonlight. "Let's figure out what we'll say," she panted, slowing. "Maybe we should just tell the Ghost Moon monks that the problem is ended?"

They got back as the Funeral Sutras were ending for the monks slain by the pirates. Ryu threw herself on her knees at the back, praying to the Crane God wordlessly, aware that sometime, somehow, tears had begun burning on her cheeks.

THIRTY-FIVE

THE FOLLOWING DAY, WHEN Ryu and her companions said that they were going to depart, the elderly abbot blessed them with a murmured Sutra, and sketched on each forehead a sigil for a peaceful path.

When they came out, the leader of the Ghost Moon monks met them. "We can take you to our island," he offered.

They looked at each other, except for Matu, whose gaze had turned toward the ground. Ryu was going to refuse when Shigan murmured under his breath, "Free ship? Where else will we find one?"

And so they sailed with the Ghost Moon monks, who created a blanket-screen for Petal onboard the ship. When everyone but the night crew retired that evening, Ryu reflected on that screen, wondering what it was really for: to keep the monks from seeing Petal sleep, fully clothed? Or to keep Petal's female eyes from the monks? What would happen if they knew her own female self, and eyes, were right among them? As she settled down between Matu and Shigan for the night, monks to either side of them, she grinned to herself. Whatever terrible thing was supposed to happen wasn't happening, and she wondered sleepily if most of the female and male mystery was not fact but some kind of shared . . . story? Expectation? Fear? Wish?

During that relatively short journey summer abruptly ended,

plunging them into three days of gray sea, sky, and rain. During their recent adventures they had missed both moon festivals — Ghost Moon in seventh month, when people put out food for wandering ghosts, followed by Phoenix Moon or Harvest Festival. Winter was on its way, and Ryu regretted the bulky, heavy winter robe she'd abandoned along the way, finding it too much to carry during the seemingly endless heat of summer.

There was no privacy on that slim craft, between all the monks living and the dead ones being carried back to be buried among their brethren, so there was scant opportunity to speak. But Ryu and the others seemed in agreement that they would go their own way once the boat landed.

That plan changed when the Ghost Moon abbot himself met them at the inlet where the boat anchored. When they reached shore, they could see the eaves of the Ghost Moon monastery rising beyond trees.

The abbot said, "Which of you is called Firebolt by the wandering folk?"

Quick looks of surprise, then the idea occurred to all at the same time: pigeons.

Ryu said, "That's me. Though I don't call myself that."

The abbot had been looking between Yaso, Shigan, and Matu. At Ryu's words, he considered the small figure before him, the tight shoulders and lowered gaze, and said, "It was a meritorious deed, what you did in Sunset Harbor. The people there are still speaking about it."

Ryu grimaced. "It was a riot when I left."

The abbot said gravely, "Come inside. We will have sustenance waiting, once our fallen brethren are buried and the ritual completed." He indicated the monks carrying the wrapped corpses of the dead monks up the slight hill toward the monastery.

The monastery was an impressive building fitted into the rocky bluffs, on what appeared to be three levels. A look passed between Ryu and Shigan, his brows slanting in question. They were in agreement: never turn down a meal. They could depart when it was over.

The monks shrouded themselves in silence as they bore the dead up a winding trail planted with ancient dwarf trees, and through a bamboo forest. At the top of the bluff was their burial ground, everything readied.

Rain began to rustle and tap around them as the funeral

ritual was held, the monks' voices rising and falling around the silent guests, who did not know the old sutras the monks used. Ryu shut her eyes, her bones resonating to the cadences. Here was her Ghost Moon prayer after all.

Shigan closed his eyes, permitting the beauty and sincerity of the blended voices to loosen the barely-acknowledged knot in his heart.

Matu spared a glance for Petal, who looked around curiously—she had told him on the other island that she didn't mind being the only girl among monks, because they let her be. She didn't give voice to the fact that comfort for her began with no one beating her. A lifetime of being scolded for whining when in pain kept that thought between her ears.

As the silent company walked back down the trail from the burial ground, the rain became steady, cool on the back of Ryu's neck. When they reached the monastery's outer court, the abbot said, "Perhaps it was to be expected that people would react violently after enduring so much violence from Dal In and her followers. But you reminded them that the choice is theirs."

Ryu shot him a look of muted surprise. She barely remembered what she had said.

The abbot was still talking. "It appears to have roused the people to better intentions. The merchants, and the fisher folk, agreed to appoint the widow of the former governor as City Lord. Perhaps this new city lord will be an improvement. She endured much during the interim, and it is said has the wisdom to benefit from what she learned and saw."

Ryu found she was relieved, and her spirits improved as a young monk offered to give them a tour.

It turned out that the bluffs were honeycombed with caves, some of which had been dug out to connect. The refectory where they ate was in the main building, with windows overlooking the sea.

The monks waited peaceably until everyone had a plain wooden bowl of noodles and delicately cooked vegetables before them. Then they said in unison, voices rising and falling in the echoing room, "We reflect on this food we are about to eat, which we ingest not for pleasure nor gluttony but for the maintenance and nourishment of our bodies of earth, that they may serve the life of the spirit. We eat enough without denying need, which harms the body, without overeating, which harms the heart and mind, so that we may continue to live blamelessly, seeking justice, truth, and enlightenment."

As they picked up their chopsticks, Shigan turned to the abbot. "When you say they chose their new governor, does that mean there is no imperial presence here?"

He and Ryu were considerably relieved to learn that all the islands along the Dogleg — at the very end of which they were now standing — had been abandoned by the empire during the reign of the last empress, after generations of unpaid or underpaid tribute and tax. The Dogleg islands either kept their formerly appointed leaders or chose their own, and had to deal with their own problems.

"The imperial navy is on the watch for pirate fleets," the abbot finished. "Or Western invaders coming down from northern waters. The imperials sail through on their way to somewhere else. They do not interfere with us."

Ryu shot Shigan a look, to which he replied with a twisted sort of grin — it was he who had ducked every time they saw an imperial ship on their initial journey through this island cluster.

Shigan then said, "I am not in any way criticizing my esteemed hosts, or their island, but is there a reason no one has sent an envoy to the empire to remind them of their duty to defend these islands?"

"Duty?" a young monk repeated, and the abbot sent a calm look that way.

The young monk bowed, and returned to his food.

The abbot said with the same calm, "This old seeker of wisdom pretends to no knowledge of the works and ways of the empire, but to my poor understanding, the question concerns tribute."

"Tribute?" Ryu repeated. "Isn't that another name for taxes?"

"Which goes to supporting the navy, among other things," Shigan said.

"Like keeping people enslaved in mines," Matu breathed.

The abbot said, "I am no student of politics, but if you were to seek enlightenment from local councils and governing bodies, I believe that you will hear much about the difference between tribute, taxes, and trade."

Shigan saw then that twice the abbot had tried to deflect him. And indeed, Ryu was giving him a puzzled look, as if about to ask why he was bringing up the empire.

He turned his attention to his bowl. A loud clap of thunder

rattled the dishes, and hail beat against the walls and roof.

There would be no departing that day. The abbot invited them to stay, and they discovered that the monastery, like so many, had been built around a hot spring. This monastery had two living areas, one wing built in the shadow of the westering sun, where the sea breeze cooled the rooms through the open windows. There was another wing, with thick walls, behind the bluffs, where they lived during winter. Hot water had been diverted to run beneath the kangs, so that the monks slept warm. Even better, the underground spring was in an enormous cave full of astonishing rock formations, many of which had been carved into sacred representations. One could bathe in the big pool, or find one of the little nooks, as one chose; many monks came to that chamber for peaceful reflection.

Guests stayed where the monks kept their goods stored. The companions slept comfortably that night. Dawn brought the first chill of the coming winter. It was still raining, so the monks gathered in an underground hall with a vaulted ceiling made by two massive slabs falling together, bits of shiny rock glittering in the lamplight. The guests were invited to go through drills with them — and when Ryu and Shigan saw the whirling staffs, they were dazzled.

Both were experienced enough to know that though there are six basic staff moves — the jabbing point, the horizontal push, the rising strike, the lowering strike, the rotation and the cover — it was clear that these monks had developed an infinity of moves based off these.

"Can you teach us?" Ryu asked, forgetting to lower her voice.

The abbot, whose eyesight had been gradually fading, wondered if this Firebolt was even younger than he had supposed. He was already inclined to approve of these young gallant wanderers, who had spoken so earnestly of the justice the monks dedicated their lives to upholding. Perhaps he could win them to serve the Ghost Moon god . . .

Another crack of thunder rolled across the sky, and a young acolyte squeaked, "It's snowing!"

Of course the snow didn't last. But the weather had turned uncertain, the monastery was comfortable. Ryu wanted, no, *needed* to learn that staff form!

"You may stay," said the abbot. "But you must begin with the novices, to correct bad habits." And to Ryu, without any change in expression, "Master the form first before you use

Essence. Then Essence aids you instead of hiding your weaknesses."

Shigan was going to exclaim that they were far beyond that, but caught sight of Ryu bowing. She didn't like hearing about bad habits, or beginning again, any more than Shigan did, but she had been raised from her earliest memories to value the importance of foundations. If the abbot thought they had bad habits, they had bad habits.

She threw herself into the practice willingly. Matu did as well, having come from a similar background. Shigan bit down on his impatience, and was soon glad he did: at first he was astonished, and a little put out, to discover that the basics included doing the laundry for the monks, and suchlike chores. Until he discovered that the ways they carried the water buckets worked the muscles of arm and wrist to an excruciating degree, and stamped the cloth in a way that worked the legs. Even wringing was done to strengthen hands. Each chore was designed around gaining strength, balance, and above all, precision. The hardest of all was the smallest movement, extending the staff with a straight arm, and using only the wrist to turn a small knob to develop precision. Ten breaths of that one and he broke out in sweat all over.

Wielding the staff, whether in two pieces or one, required exacting focus, lest one become a danger to oneself before ever facing a foe.

And so a few days' stay turned into a winter retreat.

Petal gave up early on. Even the novices were far beyond her, and other than defending herself, she had little interest in martial arts, and none in wielding a staff. She continued to do Redbark early in the morning with the other four, while the monks prayed. The rest of the day, she worked in the kitchen, where, away from the punitive descents by her stepmother, she labored happily, impressing the monks with her thrifty habits; Yaso, as always, wandered, even when it snowed, coming back sometimes bearing rare herbs picked no one knew where.

The Year of the Pig gave way to the Year of the Rat, marked by the monks with music and chanting.

Shigan and Matu and Ryu advanced rapidly, until they were sparring regularly with the monks. Matu competed silently with Shigan—though he liked Shigan, it was still a great day the rare times he got in a touch, or an unbreakable hold. Shigan worked hard, and read everything he could find, but at night he immersed himself in the monks' music, which followed forms little changed over the centuries.

Once Ryu was strong enough to beat all the novices, the three monks who were able to use Essence worked with her after everyone else was done. She knew immediately that they commanded a fraction of what she was capable of—but closing hers to a minimum made her concentrate on developing already fast reflexes into lightning speed. She doubted she would ever have a grown man's strength, but she was faster than just about everyone, and her precision sharpened. All without any Essence used at all.

Her nights were spent lying in the cocoon of her warm bedroll between Shigan and Matu on a warm kang.

Sore, tired, warm, with the boys, familiar breathing on either side of her, she found herself wishing that these days would last forever, just like this.

THIRTY-SIX

AS WEEKS TURNED INTO months, and the moons slowly drew together again toward their meeting in the Bridge of Souls that marked the New Year, Yskanda began assimilating some understanding of courtly tensions. He knew he was as ignorant as a frog at the bottom of a well, but at least he was beginning to find the chatter between the scribes, overheard walking to and from the Hall of Glorious Harmony, somewhat more comprehensible.

He was not shunned by Lychee and the others on these walks, which he took as more proof that there had been orders about him that had little to do with their respective labors. But once he'd turned them down three times, there were no more invitations to leave the palace.

Yskanda, walking alone one blustery, cold morning, reflected how like the seepage of color into water this awareness of the court's matters had become. Many times he had passed the great map of the empire on one wall, a vast hanging painting on silk that showed the hundreds of islands in the familiar dragon-shape, the head in the north looking eastward, the tail curved westward at the southern tip. In the center, the Inner Islands, with the Silk Islands at the east, and the ancient kingdom of Ran at the west, that island nearly as large as the imperial island.

Aware of the graywing who stood motionless opposite the map, ostensibly at the command of the ministers passing into the great chamber, Yskanda forbore lingering to search for Imai in the southwestern swarm of small islands.

Over the weeks he noted the fine brush work and the brilliant hues, but the islands themselves were so many different-sized blobs, one much like another in all other respects. There was only an edge of the Westerners' islands way up in the north, and on the other side of the map, there was a slice of what he'd been taught were the Easterners' two huge islands of burning sands.

As the days passed, and he began to lose some of the paralyzing awe of court, he was able to comprehend more of what the ministers said in those sonorous, cadenced voices.

They were arguing.

They argued about taxes versus tributes, and militia, and public works, and rebels or pirates or attacks from outside the empire. As he began to understand that, various islands' import seemed to change how he saw that map he passed each court day: for instance, he could now spot at a glance the Silk Islands, considered the crown of the empire, right there in the belly of the dragon.

While he observed court, his master, Court Artist Yoli, observed him, as he listened to the prevailing gossip — reflecting wryly one morning that First Imperial Prince Jion was more present in his absence than he ever had been in person. Not that people spoke openly about him. Quite the opposite. Before, there had been spurts of gossip after this or that foolishness on the part of that prince (and, very rarely, praise for his sporadically displayed talents), but now there was that whisper-defined space.

And filling it — so the court artist feared — the emperor's growing interest in his ... hostage? Guest? Protégé?

Prisoner?

He mulled what to say to Yskanda. It wasn't until he observed a kind of coolness beneath the scrupulous politeness on the part of the scribes toward his apprentice that he decided to speak.

He got at it tangentially. One mild morning as they worked on texture by sketching a rock in the Garden of Serene Contemplation, he asked, "What happened with Lychee and those other buffoons?"

Yskanda flushed to the ears, then told him.

Court Artist Yoli reached past the superficials to the probable motivation. It took little thought to see the ferrets' interference—on behalf of the emperor. He scowled at an innocent brush, then said truculently, "I debated whether to tell you or not. I don't know which is more dangerous, your ignorance or your knowing."

Yskanda set his brush carefully down. "This foolish apprentice—"

"All right, all right." The court artist irritably waved away the formality. "The emperor seems to be making a habit of looking at your court drawings."

Yskanda looked up in surprise. "Why?"

"He seems to have forgotten to tell me in our nightly conferences," the court artist said sarcastically. "How would I know?"

Yskanda was not offended. By now he knew the more caustic his master's speech, the more something worried him.

"Then . . . what difference does it make if I know he's doing it?" Yskanda asked.

Court Artist Yoli sighed. "You're beginning to understand most of what is going on in court, am I correct? Not the deeper matters of finance and trade, and so on—none of us see everything there—but the flow of influence, let us say, between individuals? Who is allied with whom?"

"You mean seeing the ministers as individuals," Yskanda said slowly. "Their personal motivations? Reactions? Yes, even when it's so clear that one of them is lying—"

The court artist waved his brush back and forth, one tufted brow arched, and Yskanda flushed, recollecting that Court Artist Yoli Jiwa knew very much more than he did about the inner workings of the court.

"This is what's important," Yoli said soberly. "Whatever else he might be thinking, and I do not pretend to know and would not dare ask, I believe the emperor is entertained by your innocence. But innocence doesn't last, especially in a close observer such as you. Therefore. However you feel about the ministers as individuals, do not, and I'm going to repeat that, *do not* give in to the temptation to influence the emperor through your drawings. He sees the slightest hint of that, and he'll kill you for it."

Yskanda's nerves chilled. "I would never . . ."

"Good. If you find the slightest temptation to center a drawing around a liar in the midst of lying, draw someone else. Draw me. Draw the dragon screens. If the emperor wants your opinion, he will summon you and ask for it, and even in that unlikely eventuality, you had better think twice, no, five times before you actually give an opinion."

Yskanda uttered a soft, mirthless laugh. "This lowly incompetent believes he can safely promise that will never happen. Being well aware that his opinion isn't worth a worm's arm or a mouse's liver, as his old master used to say."

Court Artist Yoli eyed Yskanda. "Just remember that, because stranger things have happened when the emperor gets in one of his moods for whimsy. Though things aren't nearly as bad as they were when I was young, under the old emperor, there have been occasions when 'the dragon smiles and people die.'"

Aware that he might have said too much, the court artist sent one last reassuring glance around the garden—chosen because of the clear field of vision for at least thirty paces in all directions—then turned back to his sketch, grumbling under his breath.

Yskanda's head bent, his face red to the ears as he remembered the pair at the dance house. There was no proof whatsoever that the "emperor's whim" lay behind that incident. Just instinct, which couldn't always be trusted as it was too easily influenced by emotion. Any evidence was peripheral, such as how easy it had been for Yskanda to leave the palace moments after Lychee invited him, despite the constant checking of waist tallies, asking name and purpose for going through the gates. As if Yskanda really had freedom to move about during liberty hours. That suggested someone's orders behind it all. And who else would care?

Father had often said that though they, as children, did not yet have adult defenses, that was no excuse to throw away what they did have. Yskanda reminded himself that his present defense was to keep his mind on his work, stay away from rice wine and any other temptations, and take the court artist's warnings seriously.

He found this resolution comforting enough to enable him a good sleep that night—which was as well, because the very day after that, when he had just settled into making a new copy of a brittle scroll depicting the old royal city before the move to Mt. Lir, the open door darkened and there was one of Bitternail's staff.

Yskanda's hope that the summons was for the court artist lasted a single heartbeat. At the graywing's summons gesture his heart thumped hard against his ribs. He replaced his brushes in their stand with careful precision, as if storing his things neatly would impose order on the world, then looked down at himself to make certain he was tidy. Court Artist Yoli gave him a meaning glance as he passed.

Yskanda understood the unspoken message: *Remember what I said.*

On the long walk to the north end of the palace, Yskanda mentally reviewed the last few court drawings he'd turned in. He rehearsed what to say for each, words about ancient styles and how he and the court artist studied old scrolls for traditional symbols. Tradition dictated that writing and drawings were separate arts—if the artist wished to convey certain ideas then understood symbols would be painted in specific colors, or arrangements of objects, or relations of figures to one another, and so on. He could talk on and on about these symbols, which he'd had to memorize and recount his first year at Master Bankan's. It would be a safe subject: traditional, respectable, and utterly dull when recited in a long, long list. Dullness, he hoped, could be a defense.

He was once more taken to the balcony at the Golden Dragon Pavilion, though the air was cold, and all across the western sky a wall of cloud gradually ate the sky. At least there was no rain yet.

When Yskanda and his guide got to the balcony, they found the emperor walking back and forth, the long golden tassel hanging from his exquisitely carved jade tally swinging past his knees.

The emperor heard the soft hiss of their footsteps, his mood reflecting the weather: grim. He had woken after troubled dreams whose import needed no divination: Jion was still missing.

Ah. Here was his distraction.

The graywing bowed low and Yskanda dropped to the ground, reflecting that this abject posture was also part of his armory of defense. Despite his forehead being pressed to the floor, there was no awe in his heart. Fear, yes. No reverence, only the forced respect an enemy grants the one holding the sword. Very different from the formal bow he'd given to the court artist on his appointment; that had been the bow of promise, and of trust, apprentice to master.

"Rise, rise, Yskanda," the emperor said, waving a hand.

His sleeve flowed back in the rising wind, for a moment outlining the shape of his arm. That arm, and the emperor's trim waist emphasized by his fine jade belt, reminded Yskanda that the emperor was Father's exact age. And, it seemed, though the emperor was surrounded by highly trained guards who would give their lives to protect him, he still apparently kept himself in fighting shape. Yskanda had no idea if or when he did that—but then in all the speculation he'd listened to in his dormitory days, he'd never heard much about what the emperor actually did with his time when not seen at court or at rituals.

The important thing was that the emperor looked capable of wringing his neck with one hand. And no one would twitch an eyelid in his defense.

The emperor glanced at the silent graywing, and that personage bowed himself out—to stand at the door in earshot of a shout.

"Yskanda," the emperor said, smiling. "It is seldom I get a glimpse into the lives of the subjects I govern. Tell me about your island."

Yskanda's heartbeat quickened. "It is called Imai, your imperial majesty," he said slowly—of course they knew that much. "The harbor is also its capital, where the governor has his manor—"

"If I wanted that," the emperor interrupted, "I could have my scribes dig up the archival map and the tax lists. Tell me about your life. Your family."

By now Yskanda's heart was in his throat. All the carefully prepared, safely boring words about his court drawings vanished like smoke, useless. After an entire year, here, so unexpectedly, was the interview he'd dreaded. Interview or interrogation?

"If this stupid learner understands the question, it might be said that life centered around the growing and planting of rice." Yskanda spoke slowly, trying to find his way, using the expected formal court language. "It is my understanding that was true for most of the island where this humble student was born, though little was seen beyond the village, which also made durable mats—"

"You may forgo the extremes of court language for the moment."

"To hear is to obey; thank you, your imperial majesty for your grace. Rice and the harvest of fronds and making of mats are the center of life for the village, and so for my family, with fishing as important. My father was seldom home, as he was often out with the fishers, except during the worst of the rainy reason, when he worked wood. We youngsters were responsible for gathering the fronds that we made into mats. Then there were lessons. I escaped whenever I could, roaming the forest for herbs that I could crush to make colors for painting. I also made my own brushes—"

"Who," interrupted the emperor, "was your tutor?"

"A wandering priest offered lessons to the village children, your imperial majesty."

"You speak as if you were the only child in your family."

For half a heartbeat Yskanda was tempted to lie, but the emperor's tone, the way he surveyed the garden below, caused Yskanda's neck to tighten in warning: the emperor knew something. And of course, in a year, there'd been plenty of time for those infamous ferrets to find Sweetwater, whether or not his family was still there. Villagers would talk—though he did not think the elders would speak of everything. Such as the phoenix feather. Unless dire methods were used. Yskanda hoped it was mere gossip that the ferrets had gleaned, and not interrogation of the sort he dreaded. He couldn't bear the image of people like old Granny Anise being tortured.

He forced that thought away. He knew that his parents had never told anyone in the village anything about their background other than the story about the southern island, and as for his parents themselves, he had to believe that Mother, with her eternal vigilance, would have used her escape plan to get them safely to Burning Rock Island as soon as word came of Yskanda's disappearance.

Even if the emperor knew about the phoenix feather, what could that get him?

He said, "In a way I was an only child, your imperial majesty. My older brother was with my father most of the time, though the rest of the time he watched over us. My sister, the youngest, was taught by the monk who tutored us. She was destined for a temple, but she escaped when she could, and ran off doing whatever it was she liked to do. None of them liked to draw, so I did that alone." There. All true, so easy to remember—and nothing about Father's martial arts.

"And your mother?"

"She was often with villagers, delivering babies, listening to sick people's pulses, looking at their tongues, and curing them with herbs. There were no doctors at that end of the island. Too poor. I never even saw a needle until I was sick last winter."

"You are an artist. Give me a verbal sketch of your family. Beginning with your parents."

Yskanda said, feeling his way, "What does anyone's family look like? Their features can be so familiar one is blind to them. Father looked like the other fishers, brown from the sun. My brother as well. My mother like any mother—" A tiny movement from the emperor, no more than a flexing of two fingers, and Yskanda's breath shortened. He coughed, then said, "My mother was in a fire before any of us were born. They didn't talk about it, other than it was pirates, and destroyed their old home, so they came north and when they ran out of food landed at Imai, and the villagers welcomed them. She is very scarred."

That much came out easily, words practiced with First Brother when they'd imagined being captured, caught, and interrogated after they first heard The Story. The prospect had seemed exciting then. They were so young and stupid, lying on their pallets as rain tapped on the frond roof overhead, and Mouse slumbered in her corner.

He wrenched his mind back. "But we grew up accustomed to Mother's scars. And nobody likes to talk about things that . . . that hurt or marred people you love."

"Made them ugly?" the emperor asked. "In the eyes of others, of course."

Yskanda bowed his head, trying to divine the emperor's tone, and failing. "Yes, your imperial majesty."

His subdued voice was not intended as a rebuke—it was too patient for that, acknowledgment of a long-known truth—so it acted as one, or as near to a rebuke as the emperor had heard since his grandmother the empress died. He was surprised to feel a slight pulse of regret, which amused him. And his mood changed: this was the boy's mother whose ugliness he was talking about so carelessly, whatever her name might have been at her birth.

Here they were, and he knew exactly as much—as little—as he had at the outset. He had time, he had the boy, surrounded by vigilant guards. And he had a goal. If Afan Olt really was Danno, surely he would show up now that he knew ferrets had been through his erstwhile hiding place, and the Prince Enjai who had known him best was going to enjoy the pleasure of seeing this boy turn away from Danno before the ferrets closed the trap.

But first Yskanda's heart had to be turned. It was going to take more effort than the emperor had assumed, which made the game more interesting. Yskanda seemed to be singularly unambitious, showing no triumph whatsoever at being promoted over the heads of his seniors. He was also apparently impervious to the usual boyish revels in sex and wine.

The emperor smiled. "Court Artist Yoli has nothing to say about you but praise. Are you finding the prospect of becoming a court artist an interesting one?"

The emperor watched the tightness in Yskanda's shoulders ease a little, though there was no spontaneous expression of joy, or even relief. Yskanda, for his part, was far too wary to let any expression escape if he could help it. He certainly wasn't going to say that he loathed the court part of being a court artist. The emperor's tone made it clear he believed the promotion to be an honor, and Yskanda knew there were many who envied him.

He said what was necessary. And that afforded him the opportunity to talk about what he was learning, working in the symbols and colors and styles that he'd rehearsed on the walk to the imperial residence, all safely traditional and utterly boring.

The emperor listened as long as he had the patience, uttered a few words of praise, and Yskanda was free.

No, he thought fiercely as he walked away. He was not free. It was a stalemate in an ongoing battle mind against mind.

THIRTY-SEVEN

YSKANDA CONCENTRATED ON HIS work as the sun set earlier each day, and rose later, bringing the promise of winter. The two moons rose earlier and dominated the sky, Phoenix Moon pale as milk, Ghost Moon cold and blue as ice.

Yskanda became even quieter, finding joy only when immersed in the world of color, of graceful line and harmonious composition.

The emperor had the weight of empire occupying his mind most of the time, but on court days, when he saw Yskanda sitting there beside irascible old Yoli, he remembered his plan, and contemplated his next step. The ferrets had reported that the young scribes had failed to bring Yskanda within the circle of their private pastimes; there had to be some other way to get past that reticence to the truth, and perhaps attach his teenage heart at the same time. Attachments were always useful. But Yskanda seemed to find people easy to keep at a distance. Perhaps something related to his art.

As the year drew toward its close, another idea occurred: why not use his own children? Gou-Gou made friends with everything that breathed, if given a chance, from the butterflies in the garden to the oldsters out raking the gravel in the rock garden. Manon was quite the opposite. But he'd seen the way she stared at him that day in the garden, and he knew how much languishing from the male students had resulted when the girls separated off from the boys for morning school.

Yskanda would surely be susceptible to her beauty.

And so Yskanda was summoned again—but this time he was brought before the emperor and his daughters.

Then the emperor said, "My second daughter's project was perhaps inappropriate, but her thought was correct. I can think of no better Spring Festival gift for Her Imperial Majesty, the Dowager Empress, than a portrait of her granddaughters."

Of course Yskanda could not ask why the imperial court artist was not given this task. Granted, as an apprentice court artist, his future was supposed to lie with recording the imperial family, but he was an apprentice, not even a year in this new position. If for some reason Court Artist Yoli was not wanted, there were so many other experienced artists in the scribe wing, all of whom were qualified for this task.

Yet Yskanda could do nothing but bow, and wait while the imperial princesses discussed the best poses with their father.

The next time he came, he brought his supplies, full of Yoli's warnings cast in the form of artistic advice, beginning with the fact that he would not be permitted to take his sketches away with him when he left.

"They don't permit any drawings of their faces beyond the inner palace," Yoli said. "And when dead, those go into the ancestral shrine or the archive, unless one of the imperial family keeps one."

"I didn't know that," Yskanda said. But he had—he remembered the graywing taking his sketch of the second princess, though he'd thought it was because he was in trouble.

"It's why you've never seen pictures of them. I had to go to the archive to dig up an old sketch I'd made of the imperial family one New Year's Two Moons when the search went out for Prince Jion," the court artist added. "You'll leave your work there. The graywings will take good care of it."

So it proved.

That day, when Yskanda began to work, the emperor was not even present.

Both princesses wore their finest embroidered silks, their shining dark hair dressed elaborately in golden hairpins worked with tiny dangling chains glittering with gems.

The younger princess reveled in being drawn by Yskanda. Praised all her life, she was absolutely certain he secretly delighted in drawing her, and she cast him languishing glances that in her mind emulated the drawings of famous beauties of the past.

The elder princess watched narrowly for the slightest presumption in his gaze. Or, that was how she defined this unsettling, intense focus on his eyes the shade of teak. It was the first time she had ever felt this way. She had scorned her fellow scholars for their little gifts and hopeful looks, having been taught that only the weak-minded gave in to mere attraction.

When eyes met eyes, she wrenched her gaze away deliberately. *That* would teach him how far she was above him, and she meant to keep to it. Yet whenever he looked down at his work, she checked to see if he knew he was being ignored, and found her gaze straying to his beautiful hands, slender and yet strong. His absorbed expression, the fan of his long lashes against his cheeks.

His utter lack of expression. For he did not smile, or ask a single question. He responded to Gaunon's brainless chatter with polite formality, returning no personal comment.

"Do you think Imperial Grandmother will like this robe?"

"This unworthy apprentice will attempt to represent it as best he may." His voice was soft, and utterly without expression.

"I can send my maid for another gown if you think I'd be prettier in peach and yellow."

"This unworthy apprentice can work elsewhere on this negligible scribble if her imperial highness is not satisfied with her appearance."

Horrified at the prospect of shifting his attention to Manon, Gaunon exclaimed, "No, I recollect my mother said this robe is the prettiest on me. If you think so, too."

"This unworthy apprentice will resume with the details of the peonies on the sleeve, if the gracious second imperial princess would deign to lay her right hand on the arm of the chair once again."

"In other words," Manon whispered under her breath, "*sit still.*"

Gaunon pouted, but kept still — for about five breaths.

So it went for the next three sessions, which were pretty undistinguishable from Yskanda's perspective, as snow fell steadily outside, and the younger princess did her very best to draw his interest from the silken portrait to her.

He was aware of the older princess only by the contrast of her behavior. She sat silently, her gaze beyond Yskanda each time he glanced directly at her face, though from time to time he sensed he was being covertly stared at. But as she did not speak to him, and he knew better than to address her, he kept his mind on his brushes and inks.

Each day, Yskanda worked meticulously in relative peace, recording in exquisite detail the princesses' hair ornaments, embroidery, and jewels, always with the main door in the periphery of his vision.

The second imperial princess's chatter meant he did not have to talk, and besides, he liked the sound of her voice. It reminded him of the chuckle of a stream after a good rain. Stream . . . rain. He always made certain to eat and drink before going to the inner palace, knowing that the room would be filled with delectable foods and drink, but he would not be offered any.

From time to time the emperor spared a thought to Yskanda and the art project. He had refrained from giving his daughters any hint of his purpose. He knew Gau-Gau would not be able to resist pestering Yskanda with eager if artless questions.

As for Manon, he had to be careful. If her mother scented his interest, she was far more likely to have Yskanda abducted into one of the Su family pavilions for interrogation, then kneel and ask for forgiveness over Yskanda's bloody remains. She knew she'd get that forgiveness. Right Chancellor Duke Su would make certain of that.

If the emperor wanted Yskanda tortured to death, he would choose the time, the place, and the method, and he would be there to hear every word to the last.

The emperor was not the only one watching the progress of this project from a distance.

After the fifth session, Second Imperial Consort Su made her way toward the Hall of Drenched Blossoms at the same time as a servant in gray emerged from the just-visible side door. She paused, arrested by that handsome profile, which was vaguely familiar: ah, yes, the assistant court artist, currently executing portraits of the imperial daughters. The servant saw her in the same moment, stilled, then bowed low, effaced himself, and vanished down one of the servants' side corridors out of sight.

But not out of mind. She continued on until her daughter emerged. Manon was dressed for the throne room, another surprise. This one gratifying. How well she looked! Second

Imperial Consort Su Chafar had been raised to rule as empress, and had been thwarted twice. But she would rectify it once Manon became the imperial heir.

First Imperial Princess Manon saw her mother and bowed. At a peremptory nod from the second consort, Manon joined her.

When they reached the park, where everyone promptly withdrew to a prudent distance, thus guaranteeing them safety from listening ears, Second Imperial Consort Su reclasped her hands inside her voluminous layers of sleeves. "Was that not the assistant to the court artist?"

Manon's diction was precise, betraying how obvious she found this question. "Yes. It is he who is making the portrait for Imperial Grandmother."

"But why isn't the court artist making it? I assumed that Yoli would be summoned."

"I do not know," Manon said, even more precisely, aware of two handsome young nobles bowing, both heads turning to stare after her — then, catching her eye, hastily turning away again. They retreated down a side path and vanished behind an artful grouping of aromatic cedar.

She recognized both as sons of ministers, new appointees to various secretary positions, neither worth her time. "Imperial Father neglected to consult me," she said with measured sarcasm, then dropped into a serious tone at a warning glance from her mother. "Perhaps because Old Yoli is getting *too* old. Perhaps because Apprentice Afan is a Talent. Perhaps because that spoiled brat Gaunon thinks she fancies him. Or he her."

"She's not old enough for that," the second consort observed, then her eyes narrowed. "Is she?"

"She just wants to be admired," Manon stated with confidence.

Afan. A name distinctive only for being common and utterly undistinguished. The second imperial consort eyed her daughter narrowly. "So it is she who is protracting this project, and not you? I trust you are not stupid enough to take an interest there?"

First Imperial Princess Manon resented Yskanda for being beautiful, she resented herself for not being able to look away — and she resented her mother for not trusting her. "This unworthy daughter is unfilial," she murmured, eyes lowered, tone submissive, "in worrying her esteemed mother on her behalf."

The consort eyed her daughter sharply for irony, but saw no hint of it. Satisfied that the girl had not taken leave of her senses enough to hanker after a low-born nonentity, however pretty she found his face, she said dryly, "And does this Talent admire you?" In other words, could he be used?

Manon shrugged slightly, no more than an elegant lift to one shoulder, for she, too, had her hands hidden in her sleeves against the cold. "He studies me as a subject. There is no warmth in his gaze. He's as well-trained as an intelligent horse or hound."

The second consort accepted that with satisfaction. "As well. There's something about his face, however pretty others find it, that I do not like."

As her mother said that about most people, Manon merely shrugged again, this time inwardly. And because she resented Yskanda, her mother, and her own reaction to Afan Yskanda, she added, "He's certainly presumptuous enough, but then Talents often are."

"Presumptuous?" the second imperial consort asked, her interest sharpened. To her, encroachment was the second worst in a very long list of sins.

"You remember. New Year's Day. He sat right there in the garden, under all our noses, drawing what I thought were three dragons fighting, though when I saw it close up it was only smeared thunder clouds and a water dragon. But still, for a mere apprentice to be drawing even a water dragon on such a day, is very presumptuous, if not inauspicious."

"It's very stupid," the second imperial consort agreed. "He must be an idiot."

Manon felt that she had won this contest—for encounters with her mother were always a contest. But so it must be when one readied oneself to take an imperial throne. "Is there a point to your questions, Imperial Mother?"

Manon deliberately said "Imperial" rather than the correct "Honored" because she knew her mother liked it. But that was a title only a reigning empress could bear.

Manon went on in a firm tone, as if she could banish Afan Yskanda's image by sheer will, "The matter is tedious, but I must obey, sitting there without moving when I would prefer to be doing just about anything else, as long as it is away from that brat and her endless chatter. I do not wish to spend any more time on it than I must, which includes discussing it, unless you have orders for me, or observations to teach." She paused to bow again, always filial—especially where she could be seen.

The second consort accepted that bow, pleased at its grace, and pleased that others walking at a prudent distance saw this filial respect, because of course they would be watching. Convinced there was no incipient threat to her plans in this new whim of the emperor's, she dismissed the assistant court artist from her mind and turned it to important matters. "You have now reached the age where imperial heirs are expected to contribute to the state and earn merit."

"Imperial Father has said nothing," Manon observed.

"He still thinks of you as a child. I must remind you, the first time he receives a request for a betrothal treaty—which can happen at any time—he will regard you differently, and you had better be ready. Have you finished reading Lao Sha's thoughts on the sage king?"

Thirty-Eight

I HAVE NOT FORGOTTEN First Brother, as you shall soon see.

From time to time Yskanda thought about his siblings, usually when some spoken word, an unexpected sight (like a palm leaf fan), or the trace of a scent (fresh fruit) suddenly reminded him of home. Then he'd remember that "home" most likely no longer existed, and he'd think of his family. He saw Mouse as the small figure she'd been when trotting at his heels, and assumed she was with their parents. Yskanda liked to imagine First Brother enjoying himself on guard somewhere, perhaps a leader of a group, with tassels on his hat and his sword. He, of all of them, would surely be untroubled, his path decreed by the phoenix feather.

And to an extent he was right.

As for First Brother, whom we last left after gaining the nickname Ten-Blade from some naval cadets, he had thoroughly enjoyed his fifth year as a cadet.

Falik, he, and Dun were now known as the Three Tigers, Falik the unchallenged first in rank. He carried himself like a future general on the field and off. Those big hands of his now were in proportion to his height and the breadth of his shoulders and chest. Muin and Dun had altered between second and third rank so often that they were generally regarded by masters and boys alike as even in rank, standing at the right and left shoulders of Falik. They were Falik's tacticians, Muin the leader, fastest and best with all weapons,

Dun the master of tricky maneuvers, to which Trickle often contributed (though he never seemed to grasp the difference between innovative tactics and outright practical jokes, as the army was one big game to him).The prowess of these three, seconded at a little distance by Cor and a couple others, had surpassed most former top rankers.

It was with Falik in mind that the commander saw to it that the "spring" ceremony beginning the next year of training occurred during the first thaw, in order to make certain that Falik would reach the capital well before the imperial Military Examination. Te Gar's garrison commander had cooperated by sending a supply ship in good time.

On a cold, clear day with a sharp wind tugging at their new blue fighting robes, snow still lining the edges of cliffs where the sun did not yet reach, the Three Tigers stood before the assembled cadets, instructors, and staff, as their glories were read out. And once the ritual had been concluded, they took a last walk around the fortress that had been home for the past five years as their orderlies carried their belongings to the waiting ship. Muin and Dun traded jokes and insults with each other and with their many friends among the new fifth years, and with the younger tassels, who were sorry to see them go.

Falik was as liked as he was admired, Dun the Pangolin and Ryu Ten-Blade scarcely less so, though there were still those who added "for someone so low born" after every compliment, not always under their breath.

Falik strode along looking like a hero, all faces turning to follow him as flowers follow the sun. From time to time Muin watched him, knowing that everyone there expected Falik's fame to begin sooner than later. His merit would shed merit on them all.

Sometimes Muin wondered what the phoenix feather really meant. He knew he was excellent as a fighting captain, but Falik was the embodiment of a commander. *He* ought to have had a phoenix feather fall on him at his birth. (Though he never stopped to reflect that the phoenix feather that his family all firmly believed destined him for greatness had not fallen at his own birth, but on the day of his parents' wedding.)

"This is the last time we'll be like kings," Dun whispered when they had said their last farewell. "From now on we'll be grunts at the bottom of the ranks. Maybe for years."

Muin retorted for his ear alone, "We're used to it."

Dun dug his elbow in Muin's side as he flashed a grin.

They both knew Falik would not stay at the bottom long, and as soon as he could he would bring them along on his future path to glory.

An orderly was sent to fetch them to the ship. It was so strange to walk through the great gates one last time. Muin glanced at the spot where Mouse had landed that never-forgotten night, when they had all tasted real battle. He felt like a first-year again, his mood as unsteady as the ship that presently raised its sails and began rocking its way to sea.

There had been a lot of ship travel around the island during this past year, as the fifth years worked with the upcoming naval commanders and learned to master gunpowder and cannon. On those short journeys they had been required to study a general chart showing the principal islands of the long, dragon-shaped empire, and the most common routes between the principal islands — and the waterways that ships avoided due to krakens and reefs and other dangers. After all that experience, Muin watched the sailors knowledgeably, recognizing what they did and why.

As the light began to fade and the wind turned frigid, the five went below, where their orderlies had already set up their belongings in the spot indicated by the sailors. There, hot, fresh tea was served out, and they sat in a circle. With some, orderlies remained silent and separate, but the Three Tigers had been free and easy with their devoted orderlies, making it somewhat a fashion to diminish that line between ranks. Even tall, sharp-chinned Amna, Cor Kenek's orderly, had gradually found the change for the better, especially after they were well rid of Weed and Yulin.

"What have you heard about Te Gar?" Muin asked Cor, with whom they had made peace after the mercenary attack, when Muin's departed younger brother, the now-legendary Second Ryu, had saved Cor's life — along with the lives of many others.

"A little. But why do you ask?" Cor said. "We aren't stopping there."

Muin slewed around to stare. "I thought we were. Dun and I, I mean. Since we're not taking the Military Examination." He heard the sharpness in his voice, and saw how everyone was staring. He strove to sound casual. "I thought we were to stay with the garrison. Run exercises with them. Until the rest of you got orders."

Cor no longer used the term "barefoot," but he felt there

was a rightness in low-born Muin and Dun being left out of
the Military Examination due to their profound ignorance of
the classics. Even of reading and writing. It was the proper order of things. He said, "This incompetent ventures to suggest
that you misheard. There's a promotion and a reassignment,
someone or other at Te Gar who is transferring to the imperial
city. That's why we're stopping, but only to take on whoever
it is."

Falik spoke up. "Ryu's correct—at least, was. There *was*
talk of Dun and Ryu staying in Te Gar. But all that changed,
didn't it?" He turned to stolid Pigear, his orderly.

Pigear said, "Steward Tolu told Trickle and Fenig In and
me right before we were sent aboard ship that we weren't
landing at Te Gar. The commander didn't want to risk us
getting to the imperial island late. The ship's orders are to
stand off Te Gar for a Chief Provisioner who's being promoted,
and to carry him to the imperial city."

Falik smiled at Dun and Muin, as though giving them a
gift. "That means you two will run exercises with the imperial
city garrison. Maybe even the imperial guard! What luck! I
have to admit I envy you—riding with the emperor's chosen
while the rest of us are sweating blood over that examination."

Everyone began talking at once, until Falik noticed in that
murky light how Muin had gone silent, his face averted.
Though celebrated for his prowess, he was very much like the
famed Jong Siang, leader of the hundred and ten gallant out-
laws of the outer islands centuries ago: good to his parents, his
brothers, and his friends, and relentless against the enemy. For
Falik at this stage of his life, these distinctions were simple.

"Of course Ryu was disappointed," he said to Cor later,
when the two went to the privy. "His heart was knotted—he
surely was expecting to see Second Ryu, his younger brother,
at Te Gar."

"Ayah," Cor exclaimed. He would not go ten steps out of
his way to see *his* brothers, one greedy and lazy, the other a
lying gambler, but that he kept to himself. "Better not say
anything, then."

"Exactly as you say."

And so, a few days later, they stood at the rail looking at
the circle of Te Gar's bay, and the garrison towers at the eastern
end while a boat brought the newly promoted provisioner out.
Muin was not the only one wondering what feats of bravery
Second Ryu had been performing in that fortress.

At that very same time, far to the northeast, Ryu (who had not been "Second" since she'd left training) leaned on her staff, waiting.

Shigan stood next to her, grinning as he kicked the end of his staff, sending the fine, polished length of hardwood spinning in the air. He caught it one-handed, twirled it around himself, then grounded it with a thump. "Are you certain you want me to do your speaking for you?" he asked.

"You're better at it than I am," she muttered. "I hate speaking to a lot of people. You're good at it. You were trained at it." When he sent her a quick look, she said, "Weren't you? I thought performers were also storytellers."

"They can be," Shigan said, twirling the staff again.

"Yes, and it sounds well when you speak. I sound stupid . . ." She stopped before adding that her voice sounded in her head like a rat's squeak.

But he heard her intent anyway. "Your voice will drop," he predicted. "You're just one of those who get it late. It'll come all at once, you'll see. This spring you're here, but by next year's Sky Alliance Prize competition you might be taller than I am."

His cheery words were meant well, but only served to heighten her awareness that he was now a full head taller than she was — she didn't even come up to his chin. She faced away, twirling her own staff until it hummed, but that didn't take away the prickly, uncomfortable feeling that crowded her throat when she thought about admitting her real identity.

Later, she promised herself. Right now they had pirates threatening — she lifted her head — and there were the blotches on the horizon that meant they were coming.

They were actually coming. Pirates, the abbot had said, are seldom known for their ability to look into the future or to make wise plans. All winter, challenges had arrived from various directions, mostly from individuals who wanted to take Firebolt's fame by defeating the Hero of Sunset Harbor.

The abbot and the monks had approved of Ryu's decision to ignore those people. But the monks had not wanted to ignore more serious threats that breached the peace: once a caravan, by a new band of thieves; once a local village threatened by a larger village that wanted to expand; and once a blood feud between two merchant clans for a single seat on the town committee. They'd had to cross the island for that one, but cross they did, in spite of a miserable storm, because, as the abbot pointed out, there was no one else to see to justice.

And the people knew it. "If Firebolt only answers those challenges, then he will gain a reputation for justice and mercy," the abbot had said.

Ryu made a face, muttering that she didn't want to be known as Firebolt at all.

To which one of the elder monks had replied seriously, "Every island in the Dogleg now knows that Firebolt, who rid Sunset Harbor of a tyrant, has come to our monastery to cultivate. Can you not see that if you go with us to deal with the worst malefactors, the ones people cannot deal with themselves, your name will serve as warning in future?"

Ryu, remembering Yulin, didn't believe that anyone who wanted to cause trouble would be dissuaded by a name, even if Waoji Lion's Mane himself turned up. Make trouble, yes. And sure enough, word had recently come that the remainder of the pirates who used to rule Sunset Harbor were coming for vengeance. What's more, they seemed to have spread their intent far and wide.

"Trying to reclaim their old fearful reputation," a young monk had said earnestly.

"Not the first," murmured one of the old monks as he sat cross-legged, eyes closed, before the shrine to the Ghost Moon.

"Which is why I don't think using my name works," Ryu said, remembering all those challenges on their first island after the would-be pirate attack.

To that the abbot said, "Ayah, young one, that is because we never hear about those who do take heed, and decide to follow the orderly path. And there is a difference between a reputation as a fighter just to be fighting, and one who defends those who cannot fight."

That heartened her considerably, and she'd returned to practice with renewed determination.

What the pirates apparently didn't consider in issuing their threat far and wide was that the threat gave the monks plenty of time to prepare.

Three ships appeared on the horizon, first sails, then hulls. When the boats splashed down for the pirates to row ashore, Shigan, Ryu, and Matu walked down to the ground above the shoreline, where they had been practicing each day since the snow had melted off. Ryu's mouth dried, the way it always did before an action that wasn't practice. But she was used to that by now, because right behind that sensation was the inner warmth of Essence igniting into readiness.

Shigan twirled his staff, tossing it from hand to hand. This was the monks' preferred weapon, so the three had been training hard with these staffs.

Ryu had already decided that the staff was going to be her weapon of choice from here on. It was so much easier to disable a foe without killing, and a staff didn't raise a laugh the way a wooden practice sword did. She knew that Shigan badly wanted a sword, but he wanted to win it. That could wait for the future, for example if he won the prize at this year's Sky Alliance competition . . .

She shook her head: this was not the time for her mind to indulge distractions. Five, six, seven boats full of pirates were coming, oars splashing. Eight.

Three of the boats worked forward of the others. As they neared the shoreline, she and Matu dropped back a couple of paces — out of range of Shigan's staff — to his left and right.

The pirates from the first three boats climbed out and advanced up the sandy beach, weapons at the ready. The remaining five boats floated a little ways out, just beyond the forming breakers. Ryu turned her attention back to the immediate threat, and watched them eye Shigan, Matu, her, then Shigan again. Only one of them paid any attention to the row of monks some twenty paces back, each with a staff at his side.

After a winter of challenges, and repeated hearsay, Ryu could guess the direction of their thoughts: rumor said that Firebolt was a boy; no, that's impossible, someone just said that to explain away his defeat; Firebolt is a mighty warrior. As the pirates came closer, one by one they glanced at her and dismissed her, all attention on Shigan.

"You've got one chance to go home," Shigan called, according to plan.

One pirate with a human bone thrust through his topknot let out a roar, and the pirates charged.

Working together, Shigan, Ryu, and Matu met that massed charge and, staffs flickering in wicked arcs, scattered the pirates, who had still not learned how to work together. They got in one another's way, helped along by the end of the staff hooking behind an ankle and shoving them into one another before both went down. A smart blow behind an ear or just below the breastbone encouraged most to stay put.

The fierce warmth of flowing Essence roared through Ryu.

This was the part she liked—it was always those moments before that she hated. At the extreme edge of her vision a flurry of movement caused her to step out of the fight long enough to glance at the five boats of pirates still riding the waters beyond the breakers as they stood up, and raised bows.

She sucked in a breath to yell a warning, but the monks had been watching. The first flight of arrows hummed like angry bees overhead toward the line of monks—to meet a different hum, as the monks twirled their staffs in The Whirlwind Way. The staffs whirred so fast that they became a brownish blur, which effectively shielded the monks. Arrows bounced off harmlessly, even broke to splinters.

Then a hoarse shout from the boated pirates, and those still attacking Ryu, Matu, and Shigan dropped to the ground. The pirates shot, this time at the three.

Ryu could attain speed necessary in The Whirlwind Way using Essence, but it took time and concentration. The other two had not quite attained it.

She called up all her Essence, leaped high, and between one heartbeat and the next, the world slowed, arrows whiffling through the air, cold light gleaming on the sharpened points. Wielding her staff in a deceptively slow arc, she knocked all the arrows away, then landed lightly. The world rushed back as she turned to attack the pirates now jumping up, steel brandished.

At the same time, out in the water, some pirates put arrows to bows for a third shot, but others cursed and shouted in rising voices of panic as they became aware of their boats filling with water through holes that had somehow appeared.

They looked around—some beat the water with their swords—but the monks who cultivated breath-holding had already swum silently away, their awls in their sashes.

It didn't take long to flatten those who'd dropped to the sand.

"They didn't practice that part," Shigan said to Ryu as they passed one another.

She elbowed him in answer, hiding how heavy she felt after that expended effort. She had just enough strength left as they each knocked out a last pirate, then turned to discover that Matu stood over the groaning, writhing remainder, staff upright. He grinned.

Out on the water, pirates threw weapons away as their boats swamped. Those who could swim dove overboard, no longer armed. Others, weighed down by many weapons and knocked off balance by the others' desperate scramble, fell overboard and sank. Several tried frantically to plug the holes with tunics and shirts before disappearing into the water.

When those who survived made it to shore, the monks were waiting.

The captured pirates, gathered in a dejected group on the sand—most nursing bruised or broken joints from staff blows—watched Ryu sullenly, even fearfully. Sometimes rumors were even true. At least the ones about Firebolt were: though Firebolt did not stay to guard them, they dared not move from where they had been put. They spent a cold, miserable night outside on the sand, given only water and a handful of cold rice to eat. The next morning a train of carts appeared on the road above the temple, the pirates were fitted with bonded collars, piled into the carts, and taken away.

"And don't they deserve it," Matu said with satisfaction, his usually pleasant face uncharacteristically hard.

"Deserve what?" Ryu asked. "Execution?" Her stomach roiled.

"Works." Matu looked away, as though the word had been a curse.

Both Shigan and Ryu looked surprised. "Isn't that what happens to most able prisoners?" Shigan asked. "Repairing bridges and roads isn't so bad a thing."

Matu's lips twisted. "Depends completely on who is in charge."

Behind, Petal crossed her arms. "I know. I saw," she said. And, as the others turned to her, "Some of the Warders are worse than First Mother for cruelty. They'll add extra time on the bond sentence for anything they call an infraction, or worse, they'll sell the toughest ones to the Kings of Hell."

Ryu exclaimed, "Kings of Hell?"

"Imperial Works." Petal spat the words.

Shigan's brows slanted up. "Aren't Imperial Works for the good of all?"

Matu uttered a bitter laugh, even more unlike him, and at Ryu's and Shigan's looks of question, blushed to the ears. "I guess you never asked where my father was. I thank you for your politeness, but I'll tell you. The Imperial Works may look like they are great projects for the benefit of all—but who is really included in that all? Another temple dedicated to the emperor, where only the elderly or infirm of the nobles can go? Another artificial lake and great garden, which can only be seen by nobles?"

"I'm not defending the imperials," Shigan said mockingly. "Far from it. But I thought that Imperial Works repaired all streets, harbors, bridges, and the like, especially after typhoons and floods and other disasters."

"It's true," Matu said with rare bitterness. "But they always need bodies to do the building, especially to work in the mines. And they use prisoners, who die like flies from maltreatment, and what happens when they run out of prisoners? A call is put out for at least a hundred workers. A governor — another noble — wants the merit of sending two hundred. But there are only sixty in the prison considered able. And no one, even beggars, volunteers. *They* know few come out alive. The city guard is ordered to enforce old edicts. But of course, it's only the poor, and commoners, and especially gallant wanderers, who get arrested."

That silenced them all, as by now they all knew the story of how Matu's father had been swept up in one of those when he'd gone to visit his cousin who had become a merchant. *Lord Su, son of the duke, was made a minster shortly after that*, he'd finished bitterly.

Matu passed his hand over his face. He made an effort they could all feel to regain his normal cheerful demeanor. "We should be thinking about how to get ourselves to the Sky Alliance competition!"

"You forgot the power of rumor." Shigan clapped Matu on the shoulder. "What do you want to wager we put out the word that Firebolt and his mighty followers would like to ship out, and wait for the offers?"

"That won't happen," Ryu predicted, still believing she was largely invisible.

She was wrong. Offers did come, with the understanding that they would defend the ship in the case of trouble. As they would have done that anyway, it was easy to agree to.

They took their leave of the monks — Ryu found herself sorry to say farewell, especially after the grave old monk who was their woodworking chief presented her with a cleverly made staff that snapped into two in the middle, then locked again — and departed in so timely a manner that they were able to take the journey in slow pieces, for Matu's sake.

They were now invited to do their drills on deck, the sailors working around them. Ryu kept up the Redbark drills, of course, but she added staff work, her goal to master The Whirlwind Way without using Essence. She worked so hard she never noticed sailors stopping *their* work to watch her and Shigan in amazement. Even Petal garnered her share of admiring looks: though she still considered herself a beginner, she was advancing steadily, and both Matu (when he could speak at all past his nausea) and Ryu earnestly encouraged her to enter the competition this year.

Yaso had prepared plenty of ginger-medicine, but spring storms made for a rough journey. Petal continued to look after Matu, but Ryu found herself checking on him often, her heart wrenching when she found him lying pale and miserable, eyes closed.

They stopped at every promising-looking harbor, usually with their ship hosts spreading the word that they had been carrying the famous Firebolt . . . famous for what? And so the stories spread.

Ryu waited for Matu to say when he was ready to sail on. Somewhere between last year's journey and this — or perhaps it would be more correct to say somewhere between almost-fifteen and almost-sixteen years of age, she had not only begun to comprehend what he suffered so quietly; it had begun to matter.

THIRTY-NINE

DURING THOSE DAYS OF ship travel, far to the south and east, brother Ryu Muin was also on a ship, drawn inexorably toward the imperial island. It had stopped twice, both times without coming near a wharf. The second time, wild thoughts of diving overboard had gripped him—to be reluctantly abandoned.

While he was fairly certain he could get away—he had always been a strong swimmer, and he'd done plenty of evasion work on wargames—he knew that were he to do that, he would be considered a deserter. And it was probably his friends who would be put on the team to find him. Because they would. While anyone who left training was called a deserter, he'd learned in his five years that the few boys who ran from first or even second year training were shrugged off, considered not worth fetching back. But he was now considered a seahorse-level captain. Deserters at this rank would raise questions of conspiracy, rebellion, traitorous plans. He was in the imperial army for life, now. And he had no problem with that. Defending places like Imai was surely what the phoenix feather had promised as his future.

What he did not want was to be anywhere near the emperor.

Which is not something he could explain to his honest, loyal friends, without dragging them into The Story, and essentially asking them to pick sides. Even worse, he had heard all his life that he looked just like his father, and in his imagination the imperial island was packed with men who had once known Danno, champion swordsman and bodyguard to the former Prince Enjai.

What to do? There was no Mouse to talk it over with. This problem he had to solve himself.

And so, as they drew near the imperial island, and he couldn't figure out any other way out of his dilemma, he figured out what he had to do.

He waited until the captain ordered a pigeon loosed. That meant they were a day or two out. He chose a night when rain began to fall. He picked a time when his friends were sitting below, enjoying the precious hot wine the commander at Te Gar had sent along with his promoted Provisioner.

He excused himself for a visit to the privy, and went up on deck, pausing to enjoy the cool rain on his face. He made a business of swaying, in case the lookout happened to glance his way.

Then he moved to the piece of wood he'd already chosen. Reminding himself that pain was to be expected of a commander, he pretended to slip, and lunged forward, striking that protruding wooden piece across the bridge of his nose.

White agony clawed his breath out of his body. When he got his breath back, he found himself sitting on the deck, while Falik and three orderlies, including his own, crowded around looking down at him as he dripped blood everywhere.

"Muin!" Falik was upset enough to use his personal name. "What happened? How could you get drunk on one cup?"

"Slipped." His voice came out sounding weird—his face was already swelling.

They helped him down below, where someone offered him a cold cloth, and someone else brought bitter medicine to alleviate pain. It didn't help, but at least the blood began to dry up.

By late the next day, when the lookout announced that the outer island had been sighted, he felt his tender, swollen face with bitter satisfaction: his own mother would not recognize him now.

Muin's ship worked its way among the many others on their way to the imperial city, as far to the northwest, Yaso and Petal helped Matu from the wildly heaving boat to the wharf. Matu stepped onto the solid wood, glad of the cold rain that eased the churning of his stomach. The ground still seemed to heave under him until they reached the steep main street rising in demon-warding curves from the wharf.

They actually had money. Some of the pirates had worn golden ornaments obviously looted from past victims. These the monks had kept, to be turned into supplies. They had also carried various amounts of coinage, all of which the monks had handed over to Ryu.

"Right up there," Shigan roared against the pounding rain.

Matu was beyond question. He just wanted to lie down on a bed that didn't move. But the rest of them willingly passed by four perfectly respectable-looking inns — including the one with delicious smells wafting out, stronger than the wind bringing the rain — in favor of the one everyone on board had said was famed for its beautiful dancers, its food, and oh yes, its music.

It was the promise of famous music that got Shigan's attention, and the rest let themselves be swept in his wake.

The Heavenly Nightingale was thronged with custom. The owner, whose face was her greatest professional attribute, was in her thirties and looked twenty. She said sweetly, with the right amount of regret, "We're actually full, though there are many fine places along this street . . ."

At that moment her eyes, assessing each and passing along, halted at Shigan. It must be noted that this island, while nominally under the rule of the empire, was so far west that most of its custom was gallant wanderers. The merchants adroitly catered to both sorts, as long as the customers had money.

In the imperial world, it was understood that rules were more flexible the higher the rank of the customer, especially if wealthy. In the gallant wanderer world, wealth also paved many otherwise ill roads, but trade was understood.

Shigan had stilled like a hunting dog on the alert, listening to a trio playing pipa, harp, and guzheng, all far better than he could play. "I can dance," he offered. "And we'll pay."

The owner smiled. She liked a pretty face, and she really wanted male dancers, so much rarer than female ones. Even more rare were young and handsome ones, especially well trained. Those tended to get snapped up by well-known companies in the empire, who could command top earnings.

She therefore had low expectations. He was strikingly handsome, with those long phoenix eyes under wickedly slanting brows, and a mouth made for sin. He could strut like a barnyard rooster and her female customers, as well as a goodly portion of the male, would be pleased, especially if he flirted, and which young and handsome fellow didn't flirt?

" . . . and I think we can work something out," she finished smoothly.

They passed gratefully inside, Matu supported by Shigan and Yaso. Ryu glanced around, seeing signs of prosperity in the fine dishes, the lamps, and in the excellence of the calligraphy on the walls. She was reminded of Mother, who would approve of the pure classical form of one ancient poem as they headed for the stairs.

They were soon established in a good-sized room, Matu deposited on the curtained bed, which was big enough for two or even three, but no one wanted to disturb him until he recovered. Instead, Shigan, Ryu, and Petal trooped off to the bathhouse, which turned out to be conveniently located next door.

As usual Ryu got a tiny space curtained off, and sank back into the wooden tub gratefully.

Even though she hadn't seen where Shigan went, she sensed he was in the next cubicle. She could always sense when he was near, even before she saw him. "It's so good to have money," she sighed.

"No argument from me." Sure enough, he was there.

"But we can't waste it," she added. "I'd like it to last us until we get to the competition."

"Where we'll win the prize, and be rolling in wealth?" Shigan's voice lilted with laughter.

"We'll try," she said—always cautious, but she was thinking of the competitors she'd seen the year before. She could have beaten them with Essence. And she was so much better now. Even if she wasn't any taller. Maybe boots with heels?

"Brother Ryu," Shigan called. There was that in his voice which caused her to sit up. She couldn't name what it was she heard, except that she knew that tone. He was going to talk around whatever it was he was thinking.

"I'm here," she responded, climbing out and hastily

drying. She didn't want him suddenly pushing aside that curtain to discuss whatever it was that had suddenly become important.

"I want a sword," he said. "I realize you've chosen the staff as your weapon. At least for now. But I don't know if I want to buy one or win one."

"Win one?" she repeated, turning her back as she wrapped the binding cloth around her chest. Not that she had much to compress, but it was enough to worry about if drill included wrestling. She suppressed the urge to groan with impatience, and her voice came out sharper than she meant: "Kill someone for his sword?"

"If I meant that I'd have joined the pirates," he retorted. "No, I would never have joined them. They were too stupid. Which is very good. I don't think I want to meet smart pirates. I mean win a sword by, oh, doing some deed of high merit. Maybe even an ancient sword, with some enchantment on it."

Ryu thought of that horrible blood-drinking sword in Sunset Harbor, and shuddered. "Ugh."

Sure enough, the curtain was thrust aside by an impatient hand, and there stood Shigan, wearing only his trousers, wet hair hanging around him in shining black ribbons. "You think it's impossible, little brother?" He crossed his arms, leaning a narrow hip against the tub, which sloshed a little. "Or that you're the only one who can win high merit—the famous Firebolt."

"I don't think that," she muttered as she finished tying her sash. "When have I ever said anything of the sort?"

He snorted a laugh as she twisted up her hair. But when she went to jab her old wooden peg through the thick mat of her hair, she heard a snap and the peg came apart in her fingers.

"Ayah!" she exclaimed in dismay. "Now what do I do?"

This time Shigan laughed out loud. "Oh, no! An emergency, because there is no other hair clasp in all the empire! Here." He stepped behind Ryu and pushed her head forward. "You can have mine."

She felt his fingers work into her scalp as he gathered the mass of her hair, which had only gotten curlier over the years, twisted it expertly, and fitted it into the curve of his fine rosewood hair clasp. He slid the wooden pin through, securing it, and he stepped away. She fingered the pin, the head of which had been carved with a shape within a shape, suggestive of a tiger's eye. A typical image to appeal to boys, Ryu had thought when Shigan bought it back in Te Gar.

"This is much too nice," she protested in a gruff voice, feeling oddly off balance.

He snorted. "I have another. And they're easy to replace," he said. "But not right now. Let's get back before these clothes get soaked through."

She glanced at his river of hair flowing down his back and nodded. For some reason her mind arrowed back to when she'd first met him, and Mo Fuin teaching him how to make a topknot. How she'd despised him!

Shigan went on, "I could hear what you were thinking! That I'm a fool, that famous swords are usually unlucky."

"That, I believe," she said. "After all, nobody puts a charm on a sword to . . . to . . . make perfect dumplings, or something."

Shigan burst out laughing, and they left the bathhouse.

FORTY

THE PROPRIETOR OF THE inn, Madam Nightingale, was on the watch for them when they returned.

"We've a gap in tonight's entertainment," she said, her eyes roaming over Shigan in overt appreciation. "Let's see what you can do."

Shigan shrugged. "Let me stretch out. We just got off the ship after tossing all over the ocean."

Madam Nightingale accepted this, the mention of stretching sounding promising. She had one ear cocked toward an audience more rowdy than usual, due to the large party centered around a very wealthy scholar's son who was being feted before going to the imperial city to test in the Military Examination. Early as it was, they were already halfway to drunkenness. They had also been shadowed by all the enterprising single young women in town who hoped to marry up a rank, so every table was filled.

Shigan and Ryu mounted the stairs, Ryu saying, "I'll stretch out with you. It's been two days. Feels like two years, I'm so stiff."

Shigan grinned at the word "stiff" — unnoticed, as usual, by his predictably monkish Redbark Brother Ryu, and didn't First Ryu teach Second Ryu *anything*? They let themselves into the room, which was off the balcony directly over the stage, and shut the door on a gust of laughter from the restaurant.

Everyone glanced at the bed. Matu didn't stir, and Petal

went back to sorting laundry for washing, stuffing it into a bag.

Ryu and Shigan took off their boots, set them inside the door, and Shigan dug in his pack for one of his other hair clasps as Ryu sat down to stretch. Ryu was proud she could put her nose to her knees now. She bent again, admiring her socks, into which she'd taken to putting stuffing to lengthen the toes, so that no one could see how babyish her feet looked.

Mindful of Matu, they warmed muscles in silence, until Shigan stepped into the middle of the room and executed one of his fast twirls on the polished wood floor. He spun four, five times, then kicked his leg up over his head, stilled for a breathless second, and dropped the pose.

At that moment Yaso entered noiselessly, holding out folded cloth. Clearly a costume.

Unceremoniously Shigan began stripping right there. Petal, used to his total lack of modesty, turned her head. Ryu put her soiled clothes in the dirty laundry bag, and when she turned back, he was already wearing a robe of rich dark-red silk, woven to shimmer a golden shade. It reached to his shins, slit up the sides and back. The long sleeves were lined with yellow to match the green voluminous trousers, and there was a brilliant green sash with long fringes. "So she wants a sleeve dance?" he muttered, looked at his boots, shrugged, and walked out in his stockings.

The stairs to the right led to the front, so he turned left, and sure enough, found a cluster of female dancers waiting at the bottom. A roar of male voices rose from the room. The customers were getting restless.

"You want a sleeve dance?" he asked, holding his arms out.

Before the dancers could respond, Madam Nightingale appeared. "That's what I had on hand that might fit you. What dances do you know?"

He shrugged. "Six sleeve dances, four butterfly dances, five scarf dances, and of course the six ancient fan dances, and sword and shield —"

"Can you do the Leap?"

"I was training in it when I left," he said, impressed that she didn't use the disparaging name Barbarian Dance, as his teacher had.

She was also impressed — more cautiously, thinking to herself he might know the dances, but that didn't mean he danced well. Still, he carried himself well, and she could see in the wide, unblinking gazes of her dancers that he was going to attract female attention whatever he did.

"Give them the sword dance, and as much Leap as you can. I'll tell the musicians to follow you."

He gave a short, ironic bow and walked onto the stage as she whispered to her dancers, "If he falters or falls, go out there and make him the center of a flower dance."

They bowed their agreement, and turned to watch as Shigan took three steps, then leaped into the air in a perfect split. A collective sigh escaped the dancers, only two of whom could perform that leap, and neither at that height. The musicians had not yet received their instructions, but they were experienced, and the drummer began to pound a rhythm the moment Shigan's stockinged feet touched down again on the stage.

He never faltered. Music rose, exciting, enticing, a martial throb and thunder beneath the wild, skirling melody of the sword dance. Excellent music was like the Elixir of the Heavens to him, far better than mere wine, even the most expensive. The sight of his power and grace in turn inspired the musicians to greater efforts. They surrounded him with brilliant melody, except that when he left the ground, the musicians paused for dramatic effect, letting the drummer pound out the Leap syncopations.

The audience was enthralled, the celebrants still boisterous, but now they were entertained by what they saw, instead of entertaining themselves — which invariably leads to fights and ruined furniture and interrupted custom. The sword dance evoked appreciation, but beneath it the most basic drives. The snap of the blood-red robe accentuated the strength in Shigan's moves, making it clear even to the most indolent and pacifistic of watchers that this dancer actually knew how to use a sword.

Watching from above, Ryu couldn't look away. "I want to learn that," she said to no one in particular, her voice entirely lost in the rumble of the drums. More, she wanted to . . . to be that. No, that wasn't it, either . . . she was half-frightened, half-entranced by the intensity of the urgency she felt. So very like moving closer and closer to a very bright, snapping fire.

By the time Shigan finished that dance, Madam Nightingale was already mentally evaluating ways to entice Shigan to stay.

The dance ended, the women rushed out, their leader

whispered a few words to Shigan, and they began a sleeve dance, with him at the center dancing counterpoint to the women's circle.

It can be said that the evening was a resounding success.

Madam Nightingale had her miraculous rescue, and Shigan, after days of enforced inactivity due to the stormy crossing, gloried in movement again. By the end of that watch, among the flow of tips coming in, he had invitations from audience and dancers alike, male and female, for more private entertainment.

When Ryu retired at last, Shigan was still not back. She turned her tired face to the south to perform her nightly ritual, then finally fell asleep, knowing he must have gone off with someone, as he often did when chased; but he was back in the morning, bright and smiling.

Everyone else was awake, and Matu, after his night of slumber on a bed that didn't move, professed himself ready for drill.

Ryu commented to Shigan, "Watcher or dancer?"

His smile widened to a grin. "Musician, actually. The flute player. And there was actually dance involved—in fact," his smile diminished, "the best part of the evening, dancing alone, to music touched by the gods." The grin was back. "Then it was time to play with *my* flute, and . . ." He went on, cheerfully lewd the way boys are with one another.

Ryu had never resented it, but she had also learned that with boys that particular type of brag was *never* over. "Sure, sure, sure, you've got the tool of a donkey and your flutist swooned in gratitude. I only asked which, not what."

Shigan burst out laughing. "Very well, Monk Ryu. Just wait till you discover where your own flute is. Am I going to laugh! You're sure to be worse than Emperor Huozo of the twenty thousand concubines. Let's go—I even found us a place to practice. There's a private court behind the building, and Madam Nightingale said it's all ours."

It was a charming court, covered by a pergola supported by pillars carved with nightingales chasing upward, and trellises of aromatic jasmine just coming into bloom. It was clear that Madam Nightingale assumed that the practice was for dance, but the Redbark four were used to far worse spaces than this.

They lined up for the warmup, Matu moving slowly, then gradually gaining strength. Halfway through their sword form, they were interrupted by Madam Nightingale, who had been watching from behind a finger-sized hole in one of the windows above.

She walked up to them, and they faltered, coming to a halt. She looked around, then drew them toward the outbuilding at the back, where she knew they would not be overheard. "You're warriors," she observed warily.

"We're not here to cause trouble," Ryu said.

Madam Nightingale lifted a pretty hand in negation. "I know that. I never thought you were. But you are all so young—" She turned to Shigan. "You couldn't be . . . Firebolt?"

Shigan smiled wryly, saying nothing. It was for Redbark Brother Ryu to speak or not.

Ryu grounded her staff with a *crack!* "Some call me that."

"You?" Madam Nightingale blinked, then nodded slowly. "There was a persistent rumor that Firebolt is but a boy, miraculous in his power. That doesn't matter. What does is this: people along the street share warnings when warnings are necessary. Word has come to me from three different sources that there is a Shadow Panther scout looking for you."

"The Shadow Panthers," Ryu repeated. "What do you know about them?"

"More than many," Madam Nightingale said. "My sister unfortunately lives across a short passage from an island that for at least a century was the summer palace of a noble family. They are gone—dead, from a feud with another noble clan. The Shadow Panthers now hold that island for their cultivation. You should be on the watch. I keep hearing they recruit forcibly, though that may just be rumor."

Ryu said, "Thank you for the warning, but we'll be gone in a couple of days."

Matu said softly, "We can leave tomorrow. I'll be fine."

Madam Nightingale's sleeves fluttered as she threw her arms wide. "I don't want you to leave!" She said to Shigan, "I was going to offer you a prince's ransom of a salary if you would join my dancers."

His smile had turned sardonic, but his voice was kindly when he said, "You honor this poor beginner." He bowed. "But we are off to the Sky Alliance competition. We've been cultivating hard this past year."

She sighed. "I knew your appearance was too good to be true. Ayah, my luck! If you will dance for me until you go, I'll offer you meals in addition to the room."

"Done," Shigan said.

She left then, and they returned to practice. Matu made it all the way through, stopping before they got to staff work. "One more day on solid ground and I'll be fine," he promised, wiping his damp brow with shaking hands.

"Take two if you need it," Ryu said. "Tonight we can even enjoy the show. And free food!"

Matu smiled. "I'd like to see the players."

And so Ryu, Matu, and Petal spent an easy day wandering the streets, browsing shops and stalls and vendors, dawdling at a pleasant pace. Shigan went a little ways with them, then returned to the inn to rehearse with the dancers — but not before Ryu pushed his tiger-eye hair clasp back into his hands. She'd bought herself a plain, cheap one from a street vendor.

Matu didn't buy anything, but he waited patiently while Petal agonized over a choice between three robes. Ryu suppressed sighs of impatience. She knew that Petal was extremely careful with her money, having never had any of her own during all the years she'd worked as her step-mother's slave in all but name. Even so, who cared what clothes looked like? Sturdy, capacious, and cheap were her own criteria.

But at last Petal chose a robe of a soft peach cotton embroidered with tiny orchids, and clutched it close as they made their way back down the zigzagging streets in the gathering shadows of sunset.

Shopping aside, it had been a wonderful day in ways Ryu could not define. Colors were no brighter, the weather still uncertain, and there had occurred nothing out of the ordinary — there had even been the long wait over something as inconsequential as choosing clothing. And yet she was aware of a light sensation through her inner nerve-conduits, as if sunlight flowed there instead of blood.

They ate standing around a vendor selling braised fish on sticks between sliced peppers and browned potato. It was so delicious they all ate two, except for Matu, whose appetite had returned with the roar of a lion. He ate four, and still had room for egg cakes from another vendor.

After that they joined the crowds heading for the inn, where word was spreading fast that there would be dancing from a "famous court performer" before and after a play from some traveling players.

The famous court performer was nowhere in sight when they went to their room to put away purchases, but the place was crowded. They ran downstairs, to discover the tables had all been claimed. Most of the standing room was gone as well. Ryu pointed at the wooden divider between the kitchen and the common room, where a few teens were already perched. The three hastened over and hoisted themselves up, Matu in the middle.

The dancers pranced out to form a circle, and the drummer provided a galloping beat. Shigan whirled and leaped, a sword in either hand. Ryu could tell at once these were prop swords, but the audience roared as if they were real, as he clashed, leaped, and stamped. A flute joined the drum, sweet as bird-song, and the dancers flowed around Shigan, sleeves rippling like waterfalls. The swords vanished, and Shigan, like the women, had a fan.

Ryu watched them weaving in and out in whirling patterns, silks fluttering. Strange that there were five women dancing and only one Shigan, yet somehow when he danced alone, the stage was too small for him, too crowded; when the women fluttered and snapped the fans, their movements were rounded, making them look coy and artful, but when he fluttered and snapped his fan, the lines were straight, emphasizing his own clean, straight, powerful lines. It wasn't Essence that extended like invisible ribbons every time he leaped, or posed, or spun, but it felt somewhat like Essence, and somewhat like the sun on bright days. The crowd was enthusiastic — it was clear that a lot of them, if not most, were here to see him dance, rather than to see the promised players.

Pride suffused her on Shigan's behalf, and yet a little embarrassment, too, lest he stumble, or run into one of the screens, for the space was so very crowded . . .

She looked away — and smiled when she saw Matu's smiling profile. He was clearly proud of their Redbark brother's success.

Matu was so honest, so straightforward, like a stream running through the woods. You could see each stone beneath the water, each floating leaf. He smiled as he watched, calm and easy.

The dance ended, and the players came out. A few shouted for the "court comet" to return, but they settled down as soon as a couple of clowns began whacking each other across the stage in a parody of the dance, with plenty of boots to the butt, which sent the clowns tumbling in rapid somersaults.

The audience laughed, settled down expectantly, and the

story began. The watchers soon roared so loudly Ryu's ears rang. She laughed, too, as the greedy, obnoxious governor was enchanted, on his wedding day, his head transformed to that of a pig. When he tried to lift his bride's veil, she took one look and kicked him so that he flew across the stage, crashing into the furniture.

Everyone howled with laughter. The bride threw him out, leaving him with nothing but a farting donkey. After that, every time the donkey farted, a ripe, juicy sound, Matu laugh-ed. It wasn't a loud guffaw, or a shriek, like the customers at the table in front of them. It was a chuckle deep in his chest — Ryu wouldn't even have heard it had she not been sitting next to him, their arms pressed together. In fact, she felt it more than heard it, and before long she became aware that she had lost track of the story because she was listening for Matu's laugh.

She was now acutely aware of Matu's arm against hers, the curve of muscle, the warmth, and the inner sense of lightness pooled to a different sort of warmth in her belly. Was this . . . love?

Shigan appeared, and hoisted himself up next to her on her other side, smelling of clean sweat. They all squeezed up and she settled against his familiar arm, safe and happy and bewildered, but not in a bad way. Everything seemed new-made, the world full of promise.

As the stage hero fought the pig-man and his minions, restored justice to the downtrodden, and captivated the former bride, the sense of sunlight running through her veins mounted to her head, making her giddy. She delighted in every laugh, every clap Matu made, and when the evening ended, she went to sleep smiling at the memory of that deep, chesty chuckle.

The next day Yaso came to them, saying, "A ship is leaving for the south, and the weather is very clear."

Madam Nightingale was sharply disappointed to see them go. She had filled the house the night before, all to see the handsome dancer they were now calling the Comet. "When you come back this way, promise me you'll stay longer," she said. "I'll make your fortune."

"I promise." Shigan bowed as the others walked away down the street toward the wharf.

"And if you happen to see my sister, tell her I saw you first!"

Shigan laughed, and rejoined the others, while passers-by

stared, marveling at the notoriously choosy Madam Nightingale coming all the way to the street to see off a performer.

They continued on down to the wharf, and were soon aboard. Yaso had already prepared a wooden flask containing the ginger medicine.

Ryu was on the watch. "Let me take it to Matu," she said.

FORTY-ONE

EVERY TRIP TO THE inner palace tightened the invisible bindings of dread and tension in Yskanda.

Both imperial princesses had been difficult to capture for differing reasons — the younger because she displayed a tendency to adopt poses, screwing her face into distortions of insipid coyness. Even if the elder imperial princess had permitted Yskanda to speak, he could not tell an imperial princess not to make faces. But First Imperial Princess Manon had made it clear that servants did not speak unless spoken to, and that he was a servant. He had to wait until the younger princess distracted herself, and her expression became more natural.

Patience paid off. He finally caught her on the verge of a laugh . . . there. And there! A hint of shadow at the corners of her mouth, the beguiling quirk of eye, and he'd captured a glimpse of her true self, quick as a dragonfly in the wind.

But the older princess? Try as he might, that portrait, while meticulous in technique, was utterly empty. He had begun to discern the steel will beneath her soft-spoken words, and her conviction of the distinctions of rank as the natural order as she described the taste of first-flush tea, brewed from water collected five years ago from the branches of winter-flowering plum trees, while the younger princess carelessly splashed hers about — and he sucked his tongue in a dry mouth.

Once in a while he sensed a tangle of anger and interest, for he sensed that she stared at him while he painted. He could hear the change in her breathing. But he could not paint an angry princess. Her exquisitely rendered features remained empty of any hint of character. To his eye he had failed. Her portrait had all the life of a wooden statue.

He was damp-palmed with terror when the Dowager Empress's birthday came and he could postpone the viewing no longer. And because he had not let anyone see it until the celebration, it was not merely the princesses who came to see themselves at last, but the emperor himself appeared, escorting his mother, with the three consorts in his wake.

The youngest princess squealed with delight — until reprimanded with a cool word, and a glance, from the second imperial consort. Which annoyed the third consort, Gau-Gau's mother.

First Imperial Princess Manon looked at that empty depiction of her perfect features . . . and her chin came down in a fractional nod. Then she turned to her mother, her profile complacent.

The second imperial consort murmured, "Sufficient."

"Sufficient?" the emperor repeated. "It's excellent. Manon, my daughter, you might have smiled a bit . . . no, it really is excellent as it is. Assistant Court Artist Afan, well done. Receive my edict."

Yskanda was so relieved he didn't at first understand that he was about to be the recipient of the highest honor, an edict spoken directly by the emperor himself. A glance from Melonseed sent him dropping to his knees, his eyes so much like a startled fawn that the emperor was hard put not to laugh. "From here on, I want Assistant Court Artist Afan Yskanda to oversee portraits of the imperial family. Except Court Artist Yoli Jiwa will, of course, continue to oversee all official representations of the court."

And so, that day, as Ryu, Shigan, and company sailed at last toward the Sky Island Competition, and First Brother Muin's ship was in sight of the imperial island, Yskanda stood behind Bitternail, mirroring the graywing's bowed head and humble demeanor as he strove to hide his extreme dismay. The imperial family gathered around the Dowager Empress Kui Jin as she admired the silk screen portrait of the two princesses.

The Dowager Empress loved art. She did some drawing, though she had always confined her artistic ventures to sketching flowers for embroidery. She had even laid those aside when her nephew Pandan began to display his talent, and, honest and ruthless as the young are, had criticized her peonies for being out of true.

But she knew talent when she saw it, and she gazed down through the shimmer of tears at Gau-Gau's pretty face, caught on the verge of laughter. It was Gau-Gau to the life, sweet and innocent. Next to her, Manon sat composed and beautiful. And lifeless.

The dowager empress did not let herself dwell on that thought. She loved all her grandchildren, including the adopted one—especially the adopted one—and impulsively turned toward Imperial Sister Lily, saying, "Oh, if I could have a wish it would be that Lily were there, too. My three beautiful shining stars."

Her adopted granddaughter bowed, cheeks red above her heavy jaw; the dowager, smiling at her, missed the twin expressions of hardened disdain in the faces of the second imperial consort and her daughter, the first imperial princess.

But Yskanda saw. He noted that their expressions were as quickly hidden, and instinct warned him to drop his gaze; sure enough, he felt both of them scanning the room to see who might have noticed, like tigers surveying the forest for prey.

He kept his gaze lowered as the dowager empress turned this way and that, saying, "All my dear children. Nearly all. I will not sleep well until Jion is among us again."

"Soon, imperial mother," the emperor stated, then his voice softened and Yskanda heard a smile, though he could not see the emperor from his relative safety behind Bitternail's gray robe. "If it would please you, Imperial Mother, Lily and Vaion will have their own portraits."

Bitternail must have discerned some signal that Yskanda did not hear or see, for he raised his hand in dismissal. One of the tall, silent female guards stepped up to Yskanda's side and he followed gratefully, away to relative safety.

It was always relative, but he accepted what he could get. By the time he reached the court artist's rooms, the news of the promotion had gone on ahead.

The court artist might have been justified for private pique at being superseded, for ordinarily he would be the one to attend to the royal family. But Yskanda was a Talent. Also, not to be voiced, was the awareness that the emperor was playing some private game with Yskanda, as unspoken as it was dangerous—and he reflected on that ruined painting of the three dragons.

The wily old man regarded Yskanda from beneath wild knit brows, saying, "I don't know whether to congratulate you or commiserate. I do not wish to say too much, lest it become an evil omen, but your talent might also be your . . ." He stopped there. "No, no, even that is probably more than I ought to say."

Yskanda truly did not need any more warnings. The prospect of spending more time within the inner palace knotted his heart; tedious as court could be, he would a thousand times rather have spent his days in the Hall of Glorious Harmony. Both placed him in proximity to the emperor, but at least in court there was far less chance of imperial notice.

His mood was somber for someone promoted at so young an age to what everyone in the scribe wing agreed was a high honor. Though he remained at the very lowest rank, he was now entitled to display a modest tassel on his loaf. This promotion also came with his own bedchamber. He had not minded sharing with Gloom, who was quiet and tidy; but now he was a great deal closer to the court artist's rooms. Juniper brought him a finer robe before nightfall, the new loaf, and a new tally to hang at his waist—slightly finer wood, with a small tassel, which, as Juniper explained, "You no longer need to be accompanied to the inner palace by one of us. You will be passed by the guards, though Melonseed and Bitternail both instructed me to remind you that you must only go when you have been given a time and a place by one of the imperial family. And of course we use the outer walkways."

As if he ever would go there on his own! But Yskanda was careful never to share the slightest reaction to Juniper, who, pleasant and unassuming of demeanor, he was convinced served as the eyes and ears of the chief graywings. Who in turn were eyes and ears for the emperor.

The following day, the fifteenth and Phoenix full moon, was not a court day, so Yskanda rose, looking forward to working on his projects with the court artist. But when he emerged from the bath, there was one of the inner palace graywings. "The Second Imperial Prince requires your presence at the House of Heavenly Pleasures at the turn of Horse Hour."

The House of Heavenly Pleasures lay on the northwest side of the imperial garden, near where the imperial princes lived. Yskanda figured this summons must be for the new portrait assignment. Squashing down his disappointment, he sent the little page to fetch a roll of the specially treated pongee on which these portraits were painted, while he packed up his brushes, saucers, and inks.

He walked up the very same corridor leading in the direction of the imperial garden that had caused him to get a terrible beating his first day. When he reached the House of Heavenly Pleasures, where princes met with people outside the family, Second Imperial Prince Vaion was already there, ignoring the fine wall murals, the exquisite screens, and the carvings around the eaves representing the twelve celestial animals. He sprawled on cushions, playing with the long silken tassel attached to his belt pendant, and as soon as he saw Yskanda, he said, "Let's get this over with. Not here, though. This place is boring. Let's go into the garden."

At that moment, Muin stood with his military brethren in one of the outbuildings behind the House of Eternal Peace. They had debarked from their ship the night before, and had been led in through the west gate — used exclusively by the military — and given the chance to bathe, eat, and rest.

That morning, roughly the same time that Yskanda received his summons from the imperial prince, Muin and his companions stood before a panther-rank captain in the imperial guard, who inspected them closely. Their orderlies had done their best to make certain their masters were as spruce as possible after a longish ship journey, their new blue robes brushed clean. The imperial guard captain moved slowly along the line, his face impassive (better than a frown, the sweating young men hoped) until he came abreast of Muin.

He stopped short. "What happened to you?"

The evening before, Muin had had to endure a lot of chaffing from the younger imperial guards who had been assigned to accompany them among the bewildering tangle of buildings all looking pretty much alike. But all the humor vanished now.

"Slipped and fell during rain on board the ship, sir," Muin said stiffly.

The captain, well acquainted with the vagaries of young men, glanced narrowly at the others for telltale bruises on faces or knuckles. There were none, which meant he probably had not been fighting, but had really slipped.

Falik cleared his throat slightly, and the captain turned his way. "Speak."

"Captain, Ryu there and Dun are not actually taking the Military Examination. They're grays." Meaning: gray sea-horse—at the very bottom of command rank, with the potential to rise through the offices of the commander they served. "They were sent along as they are expected to be assigned to any company to which I have the honor to be ordered."

The captain eyed him, saying, "You're Supreme Cavalry General Falik's son?"

Falik made the military bow.

The captain's face cleared—he had everyone categorized now, and this news actually made his job easier. "That ugly face of yours can't be seen by anyone in the imperial garden," he explained to Muin. "But it seems you don't need to go to the Hall of Glorious Virtue, where these others will sit for the examination. There's another gray, from Virtue Fortress. You and . . . Dun, is it? You can join him at our drill yard. You can get a taste of real work." He smiled, if somewhat grimly, as he said this; he remembered his own training days.

Muin and Dun both bowed, Muin with suppressed relief.

And so the three candidates for the Military Examination were sent to join the other candidates who had come from other locations, and Muin and Dun were escorted by the captain himself to the drill yard.

As the captain explained to the martial instructors what was going on, the candidates were lined up by twos and marched out past the infamous Lotus Blossom Square, north of the Hall of Glorious Justice, and along the edge of the imperial garden before turning south past the Hall of Glorious Harmony which housed the great dragon throne, and over to the Hall of Glorious Virtue.

Watching from the gazebo in the garden were Second Imperial Prince Vaion, and Yskanda—Yskanda still considering the images of the imperial garden as glimpsed through the round moon door that only the imperials could use. But Second Imperial Prince Vaion had taken him through it while chattering about horses. Yskanda had marveled at the skill it took to create a perfect composition, glimpsed through that door. Then he had, for the first time, walked through it, as the full glory of the garden burst upon him.

The prince and Yskanda were now close enough to see the military candidates' faces. The candidates who dared to glance that way noted first the prince, whose splendid dress in shades of green, pink, and a soft yellow, embroidered with gold, and his braided hair ornamented in the kingfisher style, drew the eye. But there were those who glanced briefly at the exceedingly handsome young man in gray to the prince's left, his beauty emphasized by the modesty of his simple round hat and plain robe. Vaion stared back with equal interest, but Yskanda, after a brief glance, had mentally gone right back to the moon door.

Who can say what might have happened if Muin had been there? For there is no doubt the brothers would have instantly known one another, though five years had passed: each year Muin more closely resembled their father, and Yskanda's distinctive features had been planed by time and his experiences, but had not altered in essentials.

But Muin stood in the imperial guards' drill yard, where his father at his same age had beat all comers in sword competition. This palace was vast, and strange. He glanced up at the drum tower, which was apparently the only one within the imperial palace, and located here on the west or military side. Muin had heard the echo of gongs and bells from beyond the high walls that divided the guards from the emperor and his lair.

Muin thought about that as he ranged alongside Dun, who had become in one sense a closer brother than Yskanda the dreamer ever had been (though watching over his siblings had been an integral part of First Brother's sense of rightness since they were born), as they performed drills that were familiar, and some that weren't. Now that he was here, though he wasn't safe yet — anything could happen — he smiled inwardly at the idea of trespassing right under the nose of Father's enemy without being discovered.

In the imperial garden a short distance away, Yskanda, equally unaware, listened to the second imperial prince complaining as the last of the long column of examination candidates snaked between the buildings and vanished.

The second imperial prince turned away. "They all look like they're about to be beheaded. My brother always wanted to be one of them," he said. "I don't understand why. Who wants to take a long, grueling test if he doesn't have to? And we don't have to. It would never be any use."

"May this ignorant and insignificant learner seek instruction in asking why not?"

The second prince gave him an impatient glance. "You don't have to talk that way unless it's around Manon. I think she bows in her sleep if Father shows up in her dreams. And I know she's always on the watch to make sure she gets her own bows." He rubbed his backside reminiscently, then sighed. "For a scribe, you sure don't know your history, if you have to ask that question. Imperial children are forbidden to study the martial arts. It's to keep us from killing each other. One of the first edicts Father handed out, I'm told, once my First Brother was born." He shrugged. "Ayah, this pergola will serve. It'll keep the sun off me, but give me something to look at."

Yskanda winced inside when he thought of the skilled artwork in the House of Heavenly Pleasures, each piece of which represented many days of labor. But he didn't hold that careless dismissal against the prince. No matter what rank people were born to, they all, in Yskanda's experience, tended not to see everyday sights. And this prince had grown up with art all around him.

"What do I do?" the prince asked.

"Be comfortable, your imperial highness. It would be best to adopt a posture that you can easily repeat in later sessions. Also, if this is the clothing in which you wish to be depicted, I must request you wear it to all our sessions, though I'll work as quickly as I can."

The imperial prince looked down carelessly at himself. "It's fine. And I'll tell the grays to make sure I have it ready whenever we have to do this again."

With that he sat up straight, fists on his knees as he'd seen so many of his male ancestors posed in paintings at his father's residence. Silence reigned as the prince moodily watched the garden. Yskanda got a basic sketch down before Vaion got bored and started craning his neck and stretching.

The imperial prince promised to return the next week; he'd found it far less arduous than he'd expected, and while Gau-Gau's blithering praise of the handsome assistant court artist had been stomach-turning, the imperial prince was generous enough not to hold it against Yskanda. Especially as he'd been quiet, a good listener, and undemanding. Yskanda in his turn found Vaion an easy enough model, flashes of personality coming and going in his face like the sun chasing clouds. He would be easy to capture in ink.

The prince wandered off in search of entertainment. Yskanda surrendered his pongee to the waiting graywing outside the gazebo, and returned to the east side of the palace complex, where Court Artist Yoli's rooms lay.

"How was your session with the younger prince?" the

court artist asked.

"He will be much easier than his elder sister," Yskanda said as he put his brushes back on his table. "May I ask a question about the emperor?"

The court artist had made a habit of engaging the Essence charms against eavesdropping ever since Yskanda seemed permanently assigned to him. "Go on—while you get those layers done."

Yskanda had already moved to collect the work he had set aside. "The prince said that the emperor handed down an edict forbidding the imperial children from studying martial arts. According to him, it was to prevent imperial princes and princesses from killing one another off. Was there actually an attempt against the emperor?"

The court artist took the time to check his charms, though he'd already engaged them. But this was exactly the sort of discussion that could land one on the west side of the palace for a flogging at the very least. "Two that I know of," he said. "The emperor, the Second Imperial Prince then, was shot at by the First Imperial Prince, but his bodyguard managed to catch the arrow in his left arm, rather than in his heart . . ."

Yskanda got a sudden, vivid image of the puckered scar on his father's left arm.

The court artist shook his head. "If I recollect rightly, there was at least one more attempt. But those are far from being the worst. That was the Night of Blood, after the empress died. On her deathbed she proclaimed Second Imperial Prince Enjai the heir, though he'd been a prisoner in his manor for some years."

"A prisoner?" Yskanda repeated.

The court artist hesitated, wondering how much Yskanda knew of the past. And of course there remained questions about his very presence. Best to leave that subject for now. "Yes, but in a sense, they are all prisoners. They cannot leave the inner palace without an army to protect them. Even the emperor, though of course he has the power to assemble a two-hundred-person honor guard if he decides to ride out into the city. Anyway, there was a terrible bloodbath the night the empress died. We don't talk about it, though everyone over a certain age remembers it."

Yskanda paused in laying down a layer of blue-green wash over the forested mountains on the scroll.

The court artist noted his arrested profile, grunted, and said, "The emperor passed an edict forbidding his children to learn martial arts. The reasoning was that the graywings, the imperial guards, and the ferrets all dedicate their lives to protecting them, so they do not need to fight. Their time ought to be spent learning to serve the empire. So now you know, but for the sake of your own soul, never discuss that with anyone. It was a terrible time—the deaths did not stop that night, for the aftermath meant rooting out spies, or those imagined to be spies. We all walked very softly for at least a year after the emperor came to the throne."

"This ignorant apprentice is grateful for the instruction," Yskanda said formally, bowing, for the moment seemed to require no less.

They worked amicably until daylight began to fade.

On the west side, the imperial guards kept the visitors busy. Having come to the conclusion that Ryu's black eyes were really the result of being drunk and falling into the ship's privy, and that the soubriquet Ten-Blade was for prowess and not for brawling, they introduced him and Dun around and generally made pets of the pair. Dun did not need to prove his own soubriquet "Pangolin" by scrounging. They were treated to as much food and drink as they could possibly get outside of.

Falik returned that evening, tired from the long day of writing; the visitors were included in the younger guards' mess, where those who took the examination repeated as many of the questions as they could recollect, and the company discussed them in detail.

Muin thought privately that he could have dealt with these questions—they were all easy enough—if the test had been oral. He could not have written for hours without stopping, so he would have failed in any case.

Once they were dismissed to rest, he reminded himself that he had the protection of the phoenix feather, and he fell asleep wondering if that might be as influential as having a Cavalry General for a father, not that he wanted any other father than the one he had, whose future would have been very different if it had not been for that prince, no, the emperor. . .

The next day, the scores came out and Falik—as expected—was in the top five, though not first. Being as modest as he was sober, he was sincere in congratulating the first in rank, and that young man accepted, bowing and smiling, and wishing that he could trade first rank for a famous general as father.

Then the rumor spread like fire that the emperor himself

would preside over the awarding of the captains' hats – the first five with modest tassels hanging from the brass knob on the top over the edge to the top of the right ear. The kingfisher feather would come with their first actual command. Everyone else got the hat and the seahorse indicating the ninth and lowest of the command ranks.

Muin fought to hide his disgust, dread, and intense curiosity as they lined up, he and his fellow grays safely in the back row.

As Yskanda sat with Yoli Jiwa in a room redolent of paints and oils, both deeply involved in the intricate process of recopying a fragile scroll from four centuries previous, not four hundred paces away, the emperor came out, glanced skyward, and signaled with a glance that he desired the ceremony to take no longer than it needed, preferably before the black line of clouds in the west reached them. He surveyed this year's crop of promising captains, then paused to say to his current imperial guard commander (changed every few years), "That one in the back. The black eyes? How could he write his examination? He must be half blind."

"He did not sit for the examination," the commander explained. "He and the one to his right ranked second and third behind Young Falik at Weken's Loyalty Fortress. The tall one at the far end was second in rank at Virtue Fortress. They're gray seahorses."

"Illiterate," the emperor said, meaning they lacked classical education. No one would come this far who couldn't read a report. The testing in spring garnered not a few such, though rarely did any rank high enough in five years to be sent to sit the Military Examination. They still could prove to be excellent officers, especially when paired with the right comm-ander. "Did the black eyes come from us?" In other words, was this a brawler who would be better sent to the Dragon Claw Army?

"No, your imperial majesty. I am reliably informed that he was celebrating with Young Falik on the journey to the imperial island, slipped and fell into the privy."

"Fell into the privy?" The emperor suppressed the urge to laugh.

"Face first, your imperial majesty. Falik is understood to have put in a request for Ryu and Dun to be appointed his aides."

Ryu? Had he heard that name before? Of course he had – it was a common one in both army and navy. Wondering which branch of that multitudinous family young Privy Face belonged to, the emperor pursed his mouth against the amusement that wanted to escape, then his mind went to Falik, who he'd decided to send to one of his cherished commanders to gain some experience. Privy Face and the other one could earn their silver seahorses serving under Falik's command, and he issued words to that effect.

Muin stood next to Dun, his heart beating in his ears. Anger on behalf of his parents warred with a narrow-eyed interest: he was sure the emperor was staring right at him, and he wondered how many guards he could take down before they dropped him. He wouldn't go meekly, as he had done nothing wrong.

But no guards were sent to haul him off to the execution ground or the torture chambers, and the emperor looked away again.

First Orders were duly handed out along with the hats, the last few in haste as the first splatters of rain fell.

Muin let out his breath. His anger at seeing this famous figure was familiar from boyhood, more habit than hot. He didn't particularly want to kill the emperor unless the emperor actually did send someone to find and kill his family. Who he believed were all safely back in Sweetwater, except for Mouse, safely stationed at Te Gar.

That assurance enabled him to stand there next to Dun and cheer with the others when at last they were all dismissed. He cheered again the next day, boarding ship along with Dun and Falik in his new captain's hat, their orderlies carrying their new gear.

And because the gods seemed to find it amusing, or whatever it was that motivated gods to do what they do, the very same day that his ship let down its sails and plowed its way into the sea, at the other side of the wharf, Ul Keg tiredly climbed out of a boat along with a number of other monks, and trudged up the quay toward his temple.

FORTY-TWO

RYU WAS ON THE ocean at the same time, though a goodly curve of the world lay between them. We shall leave Muin on his way southward, and return to Ryu, whose reputation as Firebolt, the boy with lightning in both hands as he dispensed justice, was spreading fast through the northwest.

Formidable as she was in battle, she was singularly unprepared for the strange new world of love — or what she thought was love. The feelings she had for Matu were charming and intense, the entire world brighter as it revolved around him.

Euphoria carried her along for a number of sweet spring days, wherein she was satisfied to secretly cherish Matu's cup after he'd drunk his ginger medicine, and his plate after he'd eaten a little. She listened for the sound of his breathing at night, and after meals, when he got up, she'd slide onto the bench or mat where he'd been sitting, to cherish the warmth he left behind. One night when a cold wind came off the sea, she sprang up and offered to fetch his cloak, first hugging it against her, sniffing at the dusty cloth for his scent.

Used to keeping her own counsel, for the first time she wondered if Matu, who was so quiet and even shy, might be harboring similar feelings. But what should she say? The thought of saying anything and being wrong was too horrifying to contemplate.

She took to watching him, evaluating every slight sign that it might be so. He had only to brush against her when the ship gave a sudden lurch, causing her to spend a restless night weaving around that inadvertent encounter the magic of intent, of secret message he dared not speak.

She lay awake debating inwardly, and ruminating so much during the daylight hours that Shigan, who not for the first time found her staring at a spot on the deck at the commencement of Redbark drill, commented, "You look like a sheep about to heave up a load of grass." Then he tipped his head. "*Do* sheep puke? Dogs do. Cats do. But horses don't."

She had been staring at the spot Matu had been standing in, as he'd taken a brief walk about while the ocean was relatively still. Did he come up to see her, or was it only to get away from the stuffy air of the hold?

Reddening to the ears, she growled, "Headache is all." She spun her staff. "Come on."

The navigator put away tools of augury, consulted the chart, then announced that they'd reach Sky Island within three days if the wind held.

Ryu debated saying something to Matu before they left the ship. So far the water had been calm, the wind soft but steady, and he had been on deck more often than at any other time. She ought to speak before they reached Sky Island, and he was surrounded by his family . . .

But what if . . .

She couldn't even define the *what if*, except to look down at herself, finding the increasingly irksome disguise positively maddening.

She imagined conversations in which Matu admitted that he felt the same. Those were usually at night. In the glare of daylight all her bravery would melt away. She wanted the reassurance that he would feel the same about her before dealing with the others' reactions, the *questions* . . .

That night, both moons lay like golden crescents a hand's breadth above the horizon. The air was soft with the promise of summer, and everyone was on deck.

Passengers — mostly gallant wanderers, except for a couple of merchants — brought out musical instruments when someone began strumming a pipa.

One of the merchants had a pleasing singing voice, and sang several ballads about love and heroism amid the passing of the seasons. Shigan sat next to Ryu, and she could feel his simmering emotions, like the sun beyond the world's rim.

She had to get him out of the way. As another song started

up, she turned to him. "Dance for us."

He surveyed the deck, then shrugged. "If I break my ankle it'll be your fault."

"As if your balance weren't better than that!"

He rose, and some made a little space — then when he twirled, faltered, righted himself and leaped, the passengers gave soft exclamations and backed up, affording him a much wider space.

Everyone's attention went to Shigan, as she'd expected. He danced in the moonlight like one of the young gods in stories. Ryu turned her head, catching Matu's profile. He watched, smiling. At his feet sat Petal, also watching and smiling.

Ryu scooted a bit closer, sorting mentally for an excuse to ask Matu to walk with her, when she saw his left hand drift down. His palm curved, and rested against Petal's cheek.

Who leaned against his hand.

Shock rang through Ryu, first icy numb, then agony, followed by disbelief. That had to be a sect brother's gesture to a sect sister, for Petal had been taking care of him on shipboard since the first journey. Except so had Yaso. Who sat at nobody's feet. And did not get touched like that.

Petal! Disbelief swiftly gave way to jealousy, though the poison of that emotion lasted little longer than a pang in her heart. She did not resent Petal, who was as gallant in her own way as Matu. Petal worked hard. She never asked for anything for herself. She was a good companion, loyal to Redbark.

And Matu touched her cheek . . . like that.

Ryu forced her attention back to Shigan, dancing in the moonlight, until his outline shimmered with tears she would not permit to fall.

She was glad when at last everyone slept, and all through the next day she hid from Shigan's penetrating eye as much as possible. It wasn't until late that next night, when she tossed restlessly again, that it occurred to her that of course Matu wouldn't say anything. If he liked Petal it meant he liked girls, and he saw Ryu as his brother in Redbark.

Once he knew . . . things would be different.

She fell asleep at last, hope renewed.

When they landed, they lit incense and made their bows to the insouciant Fox God. Within the space of three breaths they were surrounded by a swarm of Matu's Ki relations. Their numbers had swelled as several of the younger cousins had finally been deemed ready for their first competition. Matu met them flushed and smiling, holding tightly to Petal's hand.

Ryu fought the hurt inside her chest at those clasped hands. She had decided after much agonizing that she would not mind sharing Matu with Petal, once he understood . . .

She didn't define even to herself what he would understand. All she had to go by were those old stories she had read as a child — and she'd skipped impatiently through the kissy parts in order to get to the duels with villains, the accolades of the saved. The establishment of justice.

As she struggled against these fresh knots in her heart, the cousins parted, and here was Second Uncle Yslu, his eyes moist with tears as he took hold of Matu by the shoulders. "If even half the stories about your Redbark ventures are true, your father will be so proud of you when he is freed."

The cousins cheered at that.

"Grandfather Ki bade me tell you how proud he is," Second Uncle finished. "Come! Our tent is in the usual place. We brought green kerchiefs for you, for all of you, in case, and we've food and fresh tea — I remember well how you felt after a ship journey. Eat, drink, and then tell us everything you have done."

He turned to the rest of them then, bowing first to Ryu, to her consternation. "We recognized you at once in Firebolt, the boy with the lightning of justice in both hands."

Ears burning, Ryu sprang to bring her hands under his clasped ones. "Please, please don't bow. That is too much courtesy."

Second Uncle straightened up, smiling. "Would you honor this humble house by staying with us once more?"

As that was what everyone had expected, they soon had their things set up in the Ki family tent, and were sporting their green kerchiefs around their heads. Last year Ryu had thrown down her gear in a pile near the others, without paying much attention to who might be at either side, but this year she agonized about how to get Matu next to her without catching Shigan's attention and getting teased.

As the day wore on, her mind and emotions whipsawed between exhilaration and anticipation and the chest-stitching agonies when Matu turned her way. And when he didn't.

As before, they gathered in the great pavilion. Usually abstemious, Ryu gulped at the rice wine until her head felt light. A faint sense of warning, and Shigan's, "How about getting drunk *after* we win?" caused her to ease up, and force food down in order to soak up what she'd already drunk.

But she was still heady when the meal was done at last, and the storyteller offered another of the famous Lion's Mane's early exploits. This year she scarcely noticed. All her attention was on Matu, who finally got up to go to the privy. She leaped up to follow.

For days she had rehearsed what to say, and how to respond. In her imagination, he'd always reacted to her confession with surprise, gratification, a smile, maybe even that hand to her own cheek.

She caught up with him halfway to the forest line, looked around, and decided that this was about as private as she could get. "Eagle Island Brother Matu," she said. Swallowed. "Matu."

He stopped and turned. "Redbark Brother Ryu? If this is about the knife contest—"

"Matu. I—" Her carefully planned words flew out of her head like startled birds. She looked up into his moonlit face, and blurted, "I'm a girl."

Matu blinked. "What?" he said.

"Girl. In disguise—me. It's—I had to, for reasons. It's a secret not my own, or I'd tell you first of anyone, because I . . ."

Love you. The words bloomed in her mind, but at the aghast expression on his face, they withered on her tongue.

He scrubbed his hand over his face. "Broth—Ryu, this has to be some kind of joke you and Shigan came up with, is it?" He was almost pleading. "You can't be." His incredulous gaze roamed down her body, then twitched away as if he'd been slapped. "I'd know it," he said—uncertainly. As if he didn't know anything anymore.

Ryu had lived around boys long enough to know what was going through his mind, and sure enough, when his gaze twitched back, and she said succinctly, "Sock. And bamboo."

He blinked, and even in the moonlight he blushed red.

"I can show you—"

"No!"

"I only meant—" She stepped forward.

And he leaped back as if she had tried to stab him.

"Matu?"

He took another step back, stiff, poised to run. "I—" In a strangled voice utterly unlike his own easy tones, he said, "I am honored with your . . . trust. I promise never to speak a word of your . . . secret." His hand passed over his face and he said hoarsely, "Forgive me. I have to . . ." He motioned toward the privy, and even in the darkness she could see that he was now even more embarrassed.

Embarrassed, and mortified. There was not a hint of the sweet fire she felt so strongly, impossible as it seemed. How could he not feel it, too?

The wine sloshed in her churning stomach, the giddy feeling souring to nausea. Afraid she was going to lose that wine, she ran off into the privacy of the woods, and though her throat ached she fiercely fought tears. Shigan was sure to notice, even if he'd drunk ten jugs, and she could not face his teasing, his questions.

When she had defeated the tears, she ran back to the Ki tent and slunk in the door. Matu was not yet back. Relief washed through her. She ran to her bedroll, and wrapped herself up so her head was covered.

"Told you to go easy on the wine," Shigan commented. "Good idea, sleep. You better be sharp tomorrow."

She was.

She rose while it was still dark, eased noiselessly, boots in hand, past the sleeping bodies, and went out to do Heaven and Earth over and over until Essence sang through her veins and she could breathe freely, though nothing reached the aching knot in her heart.

And this *is* Heaven and Earth, she thought morosely, missing her father, and the easy days of childhood lessons on the shore of Imai, as the macaws scolded overhead. She had even forgotten to make her mental bows to her parents and Ul Keg the night before, for the very first time.

Remorse knotted her heart into a ball of pain, bringing that dangerous sting in her eyes. It was not enough to bow mentally. Wishing she had incense, she located east by the fleeing stars and the faint lifting of darkness, turned southwest, and dropped to her knees, bowing forehead to ground three times.

"I was wrong not to listen," she thought miserably.

But that would not bring Mother to her, or her to Mother. The only way to go home again was to win enough money to get passage on a ship.

She leaped up for yet another round of Heaven and Earth, this time using her staff. It whistled in the air as her clothes snapped, and Essence-wind rustled the trees around her.

She stayed there until the bell rang to call them to the first competition. Where she ripped through her challengers like a hot knife through noodles.

"You'll never stop surprising me," Shigan said, appearing at her side when the midday gong rang.

She turned sick at the thought that Matu had been talking, but Shigan said, "You're the only person I've met, ever, who fights better with a hangover. Of course you would!" He clapped her on the shoulder.

She braced against it, her head throbbing. Then he said with a note of inquiry, "But we really could have used you at drill this morning. Where were you?"

"Privy," she said shortly.

He grimaced. "And now I understand the look on your face. Ayoh! If your guts decide to wring out again, don't wait on politeness."

She mumbled something about getting some water, shoulders hunched, and slunk away.

FORTY-THREE

THE REST OF THE day was an unsettling mixture of triumph and hurt. The triumph was small—she knew she could beat all the contestants in her age group. The hurt commanded far more of her attention. Matu either avoided her, or when he couldn't, was very polite, even shy—much shyer than he'd ever been, avoiding looking at her.

She strove to act normally, as she could feel silent question from Petal, and a far more focused question from Shigan. Only Yaso behaved as if nothing was amiss. But Yaso was always that way, even when pirates were attacking.

When Matu sat with them at dinner without speaking a word (having seated himself between Shigan and one of his cousins) Ryu was so disturbed she had to get out of there. She stumbled away, longing for the days when the three of them had sat shoulder to shoulder, without thinking anything of it. How could she not have remembered Matu's modesty—how he had been so careful never to throw his bedroll down next to Petal, how he'd shied away from the women's entry to bathhouses?

She walked away from the Ki tent fighting the sting in her eyes yet again—to find herself confronted by a tall, rangy boy about Shigan's age. Young man. She did not care which. He was vaguely familiar.

"You were great today, Firebolt. Waoji the Lion's Mane couldn't have been better when he was your age."

"Name's Ryu," she mumbled.

He grinned. "You don't have to pretend modesty around me. Where I come from, prowess is celebrated. Something to be proud of." He threw back his head, and she recognized him suddenly—from her very first competition the previous year. He had the Shadow Panther tattoo on his neck.

"Do I know you?" she asked bluntly.

He grinned even wider. "Enau Fan. You can call me Brother Fan. I'd like you to meet the rest of my brothers, all proven in real battles—"

"Another time," she said, as it finally hit her this was a recruiting conversation. "Headache. Drank too much last night."

"Really? No one would know it after watching you drop Kiu Kiu today. Did you know he's the son of Stinging Wasp? She used to be queen of the armored whip . . ."

Ryu cut in, "Everybody's heard stories about her. Look, I—"

"Just come meet my bond brothers," Enau Fan said. "Nothing more than that. Though if you're looking for a bigger sect than your Redbark, one dedicated to honor and brotherhood . . ."

I've destroyed Redbark. The thought hit her, an internal blow. Her face tightened with real pain, and Enau Fan said hastily, "Nah, if you're hungover still, after fighting all day, of course you should go. Drink a ginger decoction! I'll talk to you later."

By then she was so miserable she really did feel a headache panging behind her eyes, or maybe it was the effort. Of. Not. *Crying.*

She retreated to the Ki tent, glad to find it nearly empty, and once again rolled up with her head covered, though she was soon sweltering. Better than facing anyone.

The next morning she woke in darkness again, eased out of her bedroll—and Shigan sat up. She pretended this was completely normal. Maybe things might even go back to normal if she pretended hard enough, she decided as she wrestled into her socks and boots.

Things were not normal.

Shigan roused the others, and they went to their accustomed place to drill, but nothing was right. Oh, it began well enough while they took their usual spots for the warmup, but as soon as they paired off for sparring, Matu was all over the place. Ears red, eyes on the ground. And the most maddening thing was, he fought his girl cousins at Ten Leopards. And he fought girls at this competition. Not many, but it wasn't as if he had never faced one before — or as if all girls had turned into demons.

He claimed a hurt wrist, and Ryu cut in before Shigan to start in with questions, saying, "Come on! Let's get at it." And she went at him hard and fast, as though to prove . . . she did not even know what she was proving. But at least Shigan didn't have time for questions.

The remainder of the day went much like the previous. At the end, Ryu was leading her age group, and Shigan his. The evening was largely a repeat as well. Ryu hunched over her food, looking at no one. Matu sat nearer his cousins than the rest of Redbark, only Petal with him, question puckering her broad forehead.

Shigan looked back and forth, noting that Ryu had drunk nothing but water and tea. When at last she got up to go to the privy, she looked around to make certain Matu wasn't following — and there was Shigan. "Wait up, Ryu."

She grimaced, and stopped in the middle of a clear space. "What?"

Once he had her attention, he stood there, his gaze somewhere else, one hand propped on his narrow hip, the other raised to his head. His thumb ran round and round the tiger-eye in the wooden pin of his hair clasp before he said abruptly, "Is there bad blood between you and Matu?"

"No," she exclaimed, relieved that the darkness hid the color she couldn't prevent from burning up her face to her ears.

"Really?" His hand dropped, both propped on his hips as he eyed her askance. "On the ship you kept hovering around him as if he were about to drop dead, and whenever we stopped, you always harassed him for more knife practice — as if you couldn't beat him with one hand — then suddenly you're avoiding him like garlic farts."

"There's nothing wrong." Her gaze dropped as she reached mentally. "It's just that my boots pinch."

Shigan tipped his head the other way, then said, "I don't know why that would be Matu's fault. Or did he give you his last pair? Anyway we have enough left over to order you some. We both could go. Mine are pinching and I've had new ones twice this past year. I know what to ask for by now."

Ryu scowled at the ground, wishing he would go away.

She really did have to use the privy. Urgently.

But Shigan was eyeing her speculatively. She straightened up, snarling, "What?"

"You really are a short little mutt. Seems to me your brother was already two hands higher at your age. What *is* your age anyway?" And when Ryu didn't answer, "Ayah!" he remembered hearing that commoners sometimes didn't know which season or even which year they'd been born. "One of these days you'll sprout a full hand, and you'll be scraping your chin every morning with the rest of us." His encouraging tone just made her feel worse.

He saw, or sensed it. When she didn't respond, he shifted from one foot to the other and crossed his arms.

He was overheated, tired from restless sleep, but he sensed there was something deeply amiss with Redbark. Because something was amiss with Ryu. Who *was* Redbark.

But no one was talking. That was it, no one was talking, when usually they talked a lot. Oh, not about their pasts. He accepted that. But never about Redbark, the details of which seemed skimpier every time he thought about it. Ryu always seemed to be alone in that bare recitation, so how did First Ryu fit in?

This protracted silence disturbed Shigan more than he wanted to admit.

And Ryu was at the center of it. "Ryu, you've been . . . sick, or strange, ever since we left Madam Nightingale." And at her continued silence, he exclaimed, "We've shared everything since we left Loyalty. I thought if there was anyone you could trust, it was me. I feel the same about you, and I don't trust *anybody* else. What's this silence? Why won't you talk to me?"

She, too, was tired and overheated. As she stared at his angry black eyes, she wavered, seeing things from his perspective. Was this the time to admit to the truth? Except with Shigan, it wouldn't stop there. He'd want to know where Redbark really came from, he'd want to know *everything*.

She couldn't separate Heaven and Earth from Father — and The Story.

The Story.

Really, when would either she or Shigan ever be anywhere near the emperor? Never. Emperors were surrounded by imperial guards and courtly people and servants — all the stories and histories said so. You couldn't even catch a glimpse of an imperial palanquin if it paraded by because you were supposed to be forehead to the ground, on pain of death. An emperor would not be moving fast, not with all those people — and there would be plenty of warning. If word spread that the emperor was coming, she'd have the time to get herself on the first boat going in the opposite direction.

Then she remembered Ul Keg patiently going on tax days to the governor's to check the capital list, and Mother's tight lips and silence until he returned. And she remembered what Shigan had said about those ferrets. Emperors found out things, that she believed. Mother was no coward, but Ryu had seen her worry all her life.

If she told Shigan The Story, it would become his story, too. Except he didn't know Mother and Father, and so, it might be just a story to him. All Shigan would have to do is mention a part of the Story to the wrong person . . . And she could not stop him from talking to people. People talked to him. They paid attention to him. And there was nothing she could do about either of those things, except to make certain that whatever he said in the future had nothing to do with The Story.

He watched her in silence as the two of them stood there in the soft spring night. He saw the doubt puckering Ryu's familiar forehead — and he saw the chin-lift of decision.

But no words.

He drew himself up, and there was the haughty Shigan of Loyalty Fortress as he said, in the pure Imperial that she associated with scholars, "Silence is an answer, too. If you can't trust me enough to — "

"Who said anything about trust?" she cut in, too stung to realize she was responding in scholarly Imperial, which she had not used since she saw her mother last. "I've told you everything you need to know about Redbark, which is all we need." But she faltered when she realized that wasn't strictly true — because there wasn't really any Redbark.

That left them staring at one another, he slowly realizing that Redbark Brother Ryu, after all this time, really *didn't* trust him, and Ryu agonizing over what she could possibly say to get away from these paths leading straight to dragon lairs and tiger pits.

Her anger drained away, but his hurt intensified with each breath, until he said, "I see. The fault is mine, then. I won't trouble you any further."

He walked away, leaving her standing there alone, her

heart a gigantic knot of pain. She did her best to breathe it out, thinking, it's just one of his moods. He'll be over it by morning, and they could go on the way they always had.

She ran on to the privy, and when she returned, most had retreated to their beds. Shigan was there, his back turned toward her usual space.

Matu was closer to his cousins than before.

She lay down, back to Shigan, and slept badly.

When she woke at last, he was gone. She didn't call to the others for Redbark drill, but lurked in the woods until the gong summoned everyone to breakfast. She sat on the outside of a circle of cousins, well away from Matu and Petal. Shigan was nowhere in sight.

She stared out at the intense glare that meant a dragon of a storm was coming. Everyone knew it, too. The gong for competition rang early, when she'd scarcely gotten three bites. Not that she was very hungry. She drank all her tea, hot as it was, then made her way to the sword competition, where she was to face the next level of winners.

When it was her turn, she checked covertly. Shigan was not there to watch. She grimly shut him out of her mind. Shut the spectators out, everything but the duelist facing her. Resentment and regret twined together in her gut, roiling the Essence into a glowing cinder, and she launched at him so fast that he staggered off-balance. Three blows quicker than a lightning strike and his sword slipped out of his sweaty hand.

"Ryu wins!"

Ryu bowed, then walked away to get some water, aware of her clothes sticking to her skin. Behind her, the next pair squared up. Her desire to win—her interest in the competition—had faded, leaving her feeling overheated and weary. She remembered that the next level of riding competitions was also running, and was tempted to go watch, but she hesitated. Maybe it was better to wait for Shigan's mood to cool down. She didn't want to distract him. And as for Matu, how could she fix *that* mess? A mess that she made?

"Ryu."

She turned, staring as a familiar figure jogged up, panting from the heat. "Nice bout!"

It was Enau Fan again. "Do you like thunderstorms as much as I do?" he asked with a grin as he wiped a damp strand of hair off his shining forehead. His wide-spaced eyes were crescents of mirth. "I have a perfect spot to watch the gods play fireworks. And some really, really good Red Dragon."

Ryu didn't care about thunderstorms one way or another, except to avoid being caught in one. But the idea of doing something besides look for—or avoid—Shigan, Matu, and Petal-with-Matu, appealed. "Red Dragon?" she repeated.

"Only the best wine ever brewed up. You've really never heard of it? You have to have a taste. See if you agree."

"Sure," she said, looking up. She'd completely missed the disappearance of the sun, and the greenish clouds boiling up from over the palisades. "When?"

"Why not now?" he said—just as the gong beat. "There. They're calling a break. Perfect." Big splats of rain hit them in the face. "Come on. Let's run!" He waved a hand toward the forest beyond the pavilion.

She put her head down and bolted after him as the rain began falling faster, coming at a slant. She stretched her legs out to keep up. Tall Enau Fan was a very fast sprinter.

They passed trees beginning to toss their branches in the rising wind. Lightning flickered off to the right, and the first crash of thunder rolled across the sky. Enau let out a whoop, then, "This way!" he shouted.

A jig, and jag, and there was a blanket spread under an outcropping of rock beside a trickling stream. Trees sheltered the spot. You'd never know the pavilion was not a hundred paces down the trail in one direction, and the beach directly below them.

Two figures sat on the blanket, one familiar. Ryu slowed when she recognized Shigan—with another of the tattooed fighters.

"Come on, Redbark Brother Ryu," Enau Fan said. "Join us."

Ayah! Maybe it was just as well, Ryu decided. Shigan might get over his mood faster in the company of strangers.

Affecting unconcern, she asked as she sauntered up to the blanket, "I thought you were riding today."

"Already won," Shigan replied curtly.

"Which we will make our first toast," Enau Fan said, gesturing his companion, who brought out shallow dishes from a bag, and a sizable jug. "To Redbark Brother Shigan, who rides like the wind!"

Enau Fan poured out four dishes with a great flourish, and handed them around. Ryu lifted hers, sniffing cautiously. She peered at Shigan furtively over the rim of her dish, to see him dash his off carelessly; then he flushed all the way to his ears.

She tipped the liquid into her mouth and swallowed — then gasped as it stung all the way down. She coughed, as the two older boys laughed.

"Like it?" Enau Fan asked as he held out his empty cup for more. Ryu noticed he wasn't reacting at all.

Feeling like she'd was going to be perceived as a baby, she stuck her own cup out, though the taste still lingered, with an unpleasantly bitter under-taste more like medicine than anything one would seek out. She suppressed a shudder.

Enau Fan's friend poured out more. Once again Shigan drank his off as Enau Fan gave a whoop of admiration. Ryu raised hers to her lips, but peered at Enau Fan to see if he really liked that bitter taste.

He tipped the cup up, but she didn't see his throat move in a swallow. He lowered the empty cup, and she was going to ask if he kept it in his mouth, or what, but her lips tingled. She bit them twice, alarm rising when they went numb. Then the alarm faded as her tongue turned to a sodden sock inside her mouth. "Buh . . ." she said. "Buh . . ."

Her gaze met Shigan's black eyes, which were wide with shock, then they rolled back in his head as he slumped over.

"Buh," Ryu said again, vaguely aware that she was drooling. She let out a giggle and flopped back, staring up at the overhang, and beyond to the curtain of rain . . .

And then darkness closed gently around her.

FORTY-FOUR

RYU WOKE TO THROBBING inside her head, the world heaving slowly around her. Beneath her, a rotten bedroll laid out over rocks. Squishy here, sharp there. Moving.

Moving? She stirred, nausea rushing up from her roiling insides. She locked her teeth and forced her breathing to slow as one hand pressed against a fabric-bound thing contoured oddly like an . . . arm? She shifted uncomfortably, and discovered herself wrapped in rough hempen cloth that smelled like old cabbage. Beneath that the bumps of ribs, then the softness of a stomach, moving with each breath. Below that the hipbones and contour of a boy or man.

What?

She opened her eyes, to find the underside of a chin scarcely a handbreadth away. She knew that jawline. Shigan!

She was lying on top of him!

She groaned and curled up in her shroud, falling beside him onto a hard surface that smelled of damp wood and brine.

"There you are," Enau Fan said cheerfully. "First one awake? Thirsty? Drink this." A hand cupped the back of her head, and another hand pressed a clay cup to her lips.

Her mouth was desperately dry. She sucked in water that had a familiar bitter under-taste. She swallowed, shuddered, groaned as her stomach roiled again, then she slid down to the briny surface, curled into a ball around her protesting stomach as the darkness closed over her again.

She woke slowly, far more nauseated than the previous time. Voices rattled around her, but her head hurt too much to try to catch the words, much less meaning. Her stomach lurched and she moaned.

"Ho, Novice Redbark Brother Ryu is coming around."

"Quick, get the ginger into him."

Once again someone lifted her head and pressed a cup to her lips. She tried to turn away.

"It's all right," a voice soothed. "It's just morning tea. There's ginger with some peppermint and willow bark added. It'll help."

The cup pressed insistently against her lips once more. She smelled steam, and the familiar aroma of tiger tea, which she had swished her mouth out with every morning at Loyalty Island. That jerked her awake. She spat over the gunwale of a boat then sipped cautiously. Her mouth filled with tiger tea infused with ginger. A second sip began to settle her stomach.

She opened her eyes, blinking away tears in the strong sunlight made stronger by the reflections of sun splashes on water. Enau Fan's broad face loomed over her, split in a grin. Next to him his companion—and Shigan, his fine black hair spilling down over his shoulders past his elbows, a lock hanging in a blue-black ribbon over one side of his face. His narrowed eyes, set jaw, and the thin line of his mouth were expressive of anger. No, rage.

He, too, had been shrouded in a rough blanket, which was still wrapped around him from the chest down. He looked as ill as Ryu felt. Her head hurt too much to wrestle her way out of her own blanket. It was all she could do to sit against the gunwale of the boat they were in, as the companion tended the single sail.

"You'll be hungry soon," Enau Fan predicted. "I promise an excellent meal will be waiting as soon as the ship comes along. We've been watching for it since yesterday—should be any time."

Ryu cleared her throat, which still ached a little. "I don't understand," she said. "Where are we?"

Enau Fan's grin broadened even wider. "Welcome to the Shadow Panthers, Novice Redbark Brother Ryu!"

"What?"

"The Shadow Panthers only choose the best," Enau Fan went on. "That's you and Novice Redbark Brother Shigan here."

"But I don't want to be in the Shadow Panthers," Ryu said.

"That's because you don't know anything about us. Except the stupid things people say," Enau Fan stated with confidence. He waved at his tattooed friend tending the sail. "Pledge Brother Water Cat and I both heard all the bad things before we were scouted. Now all we want is to rise to the rank of a mask. Which isn't easy! For most even ten poles won't get you in reach."

The companion—Water Cat—nodded earnestly. Ryu recognized him from last year. He had been especially loud in his recruitment attempts. Her unsettled stomach boiled more, and she could think of nothing to say.

She struggled to her elbows, wincing against the demon's axe slamming in her head. Once she could see past the gunwale, she noticed other masts. Water Cat and Enau Fan's boat was second in a line of six. Theirs was the only one with four people. The rest of the boats carried two or at most, three. Judging by pale faces and tousled heads like Shigan's (and her own, Ryu suspected), each boat contained a newly woken prisoner.

It struck Ryu then that everything had been planned and prepared: the nasty herbs in the wine, the ginger tea when she woke. Even the blanket she'd been wrapped in.

She slid a glance at Shigan, to discover him glaring at the line of boats.

"There!" The boat rocked, causing both Shigan and Ryu to wince, as Water Cat leaped to his feet. "The sail! They're coming!"

"Only a day late," Enau Fan agreed. "Just as promised. In spite of that storm. Master Night's own luck is covering us."

"Master Night?" Ryu asked, as Shigan remained silent. In the few stories she recollected that had Shadow Panthers, their leader had been called King of Shadows, and the Midnight Demon. King of Demons, in one set of stories, but those had been quite old.

Both Shadow Panther recruits turned her way, their delight shining in their faces. "That's the supreme master. But First Panther Brother Banig will tell you more," Enau Fan added hastily. "Here they come!"

The ship splashed up, the sails clattering as they turned to back the wind. Enau Fan and Water Cat were already aiming their boat for the side, one straining on the rope controlling the sail and the other leaning into the tiller.

Ryu managed to get herself to hands and knees, her head crashing ferociously at the slightest movement. She began shrugging out of the noisome blanket while trying to move as little as possible, so she was unaware of Shigan until the boat rocked with a jerk and she looked up in time to see his feet vanish over the side.

Water Cat and Enau Fan both yelled, one letting go of the tiller, the other the sail. The boat began to turn mindlessly as Enau Fan launched himself over the side, Water Cat shouting a wild mix of orders and imprecations as he stared after, clearly terrified. Meanwhile the ship had halted some thirty paces off. There followed a confusion of splashes and shouts and ropes being thrown about, until Ryu saw Shigan being hoisted up to the rail of the ship, dripping wet. His head drooped — he looked unconscious.

By then she had managed to shrug her way out of her blanket. Water Cat, looking her way, leaped over and grabbed her arm. "Don't you go over the side!"

By then she had scanned in all directions, and seeing no islands, decided against trying to swim away. "Not going to," she said.

"Smart boy." Water Cat muttered in a fervent undervoice. "At least Shigan's safe out of the water. . . was he thinking? . . . so much trouble . . ."

Ryu didn't bother listening to any of this mumble. Her stomach was queasy again, the sun-splashes painful to her eyes. She leaned back, gathering strength, until the boat rocked again, and Enau Fan was back, dripping cold water everywhere as he carried the end of a rope to Ryu. "Let's get this around you. They'll heave you on board," he said.

He made to tie the rope under her armpits, but she shoved his hand away. "I'll do it," she said. And her fingers remembered the old knots from childhood as she made a loop, put one foot in it, then stood up, holding the rope.

"Never thought of that," Enau Fan said.

Ryu grimaced against the headache as the rope jerked. She swung up and out, dangling and spinning until she flung out her free hand and foot, slowing the spin. When she reached the ship rail, various hands reached for her, but she pushed them away and used all her remaining strength to clamber over herself.

"That was neatly done," a tall, husky man said, his raspy voice admiring, but a little too loud, a little too genial. With a broad grin, he added, "You must come from fisher folk. Who are you again?"

"Novice Brother Ryu," came Enau Fan's voice from behind. "We did not get any treasure, for we were at the Sky Island Competition, but we got a prize. He's actually Firebolt, with Lightning in Both Hands."

"Really? Ayoh! This *is* a prize. If he's even half as good as the rumors, Master Night will be pleased. Welcome to the Brotherhood of Shadow Panthers, Novice Brother Firebolt! I'm First Panther Brother Banig."

Ryu was going to correct him, then shrugged internally. She didn't plan to be around long enough for them to get her name right. She remained silent as she stepped out of the rope.

"Come this way. There's food waiting." The man who called himself First Panther Brother Banig extended a callused hand, and led the way. His hair was pulled up high on the top of his head, the long tail decorated with eagle feathers stuck through clasps of gold. He wore a black silk battle tunic sashed with silver silk, over more rugged clothes.

He turned aside for another group, who stood with a single drooping prisoner and three fine carved trunks. "Silk," said an eager, tattooed fellow with faint freckles and the blotchy pale skin of westerners. "Silk in this trunk, and tea in this one, all with seals, so you know it's for nobles. And books in that one," he ended with a low voice.

"Books are good, books are good," Brother Banig said. "Master Night likes books, we're told. Open the tea chest."

The entire line waited as this was done, and Brother Banig stooped to paw through the carefully wrapped and sealed packages of tea—then he stepped back and shook his head. "That goes over the side, or with us if you like tea. But not to Master Night."

"Why?" Freckle Face protested on a whining note.

"That one there, the jasmine flower, he can't drink it."

"So we toss that overboard, and—"

"All of it. He'll get sick if one tea is next to jasmine flower, don't you understand, stupid? You'll get your merit for the books."

Brother Banig stepped past, and waved the line on.

Ryu shuffled with the other newcomers down into the lower deck, where, indeed, what looked like a feast for an emperor had been laid out. She stared at flower pancakes with scallions, smoked tea eggs, steamed buns, hulled nuts, red bean cake, sweet bean curd with dried fruits, sesame pastries, and walnut cake loaded with jujubes.

Several others sat on mats, frowning and wincing as if they shared the same headache. Only Shigan sat apart, wet hair dribbling over his sodden clothes. He demonstrated no interest in the food.

At the first whiff, Ryu's stomach gave a lurch and then cleaved flat to her spine. She took one item from each plate, and after a hesitation, went over to Shigan, who had straightened his wet clothes, and clawed his hair back up into its knot. "You'd better eat," she said.

He flicked a cold look at her. "Ready to join the Shadow Panthers?"

"No." Acting on impulse, she thrust her dish at him. "Here. You look worse than I feel. I'll get some more. There's plenty. And we better get our strength back."

He took the dish, and glared at a steamed bun.

"Take it slow," a man said genially, coming up from the side as he surveyed the frowzy, blinking group. "That storm blew everyone off course. None of you have eaten for two days. Three, some. You don't want it all coming up again."

Ryu kept that in mind as she filled another dish, and then, from habit, sat down beside Shigan. He gave her another of those cold, haughty looks, and she wondered if he was going to rise and move away, but he sighed as if he hadn't the strength, and began working on a smoked egg.

Ryu bit into her own. It was delicious — the best she had ever tasted. She forced herself to eat slowly, and was glad she did when one of the others gagged, and stumbled off toward the ship's privy.

There was also more ginger tea. She washed her food down with that, and gradually the headache diminished to a slight pang. The pain tightening Shigan's forehead eased, but his mouth stayed in a thin line as First Panther Brother Banig went about making sure everyone was eating and drinking. Ryu watched narrowly, deciding that he laughed too much. No, the laughter didn't reach his eyes, that was it.

But once her headache eased, she was left feeling as if her body had turned to rock. And, despite having slept so long under the influence of that evil drink, she longed for more sleep. So did everyone else — she saw heavy eyelids and yawns at either side.

The food was cleared away, and bedrolls laid out for them.

Ryu chose the one nearest a scuttle, remembering how stuffy a ship's hold could get. Shigan slowly lowered himself down beside her. When she turned his way, he said, too low for anyone to hear, "Escape."

"Yes."

His mouth relaxed incrementally, and he stretched out, arms crossed behind his head, and shut his eyes.

Ryu turned away . . . and when she woke, it was to sunlight shafting through the scuttles, as an angry voice rose. ". . . will *not* join you. You *poisoned* us! You talk about what an honor it is, but it's no honor to be grabbed against my will. That's the act of *enemies!* Let me off anywhere, the first island we pass. I don't care."

"Novice Brother Zhiar—" began First Panther Brother Banig.

"My name is *Cor* Zhiar! You are *not* my brother! I'm fourth generation from Defender General Cor Vai, and my father is a sixth rank count! You've already got all these no-birth rats. Let me go!"

"We're all brothers here, until we make the pledge, and then we are on the way to earning the honor of the Mask—"

"Shadow Panthers are nothing but brigands! I don't want to be here!" Cor Zhiar's voice cracked. "This ship is disgusting, all of us crammed here like animals, the food is cold . . ."

A clamor of voices rose as the Shadow Panthers tried to soothe Cor Zhiar. Ryu sat up on her elbows, aware of Shigan sitting silently at her side, still except for his eyes moving between the speakers.

Ryu glanced over to see what drew his attention. It had to be the way the Shadow Panthers looked at one another, the quick hand signs as they repeated soothing words, and a lot about how pleased Master Night would be with them and their skills.

"There's some among you nearly ready to learn Master Night's own iron chain sword. He only takes a few as apprentices in that," Enau Fan said earnestly.

Cor Zhiar's diatribe halted for a breath, then he said sulkily, "Who cares?" But he'd betrayed his interest.

Ryu looked down at her hands. She'd heard of iron chain swords—who hadn't? But the context had been the infamous and dreaded Dragon Claw Army, who the emperor sent in to the fiercest battles. A chain sword, when wielded by someone with the strength, was a whip made of chain that could snap into a sword. It was a killing weapon that shredded its victims as it killed them.

Any weapon could be a killing weapon, of course. Father had said that, the instructors at Loyalty Fortress had said that. The silk strings for musical instruments could kill, if one had the intent. So could a pillow. But a chain sword was a vicious weapon. All weapons could be deadly, but some were crueler than others. This was one of the cruelest.

Cor Zhiar's smirk wavered, and Ryu wondered why someone from a famous army family was part of the gallant wanderers.

"Lay a wager," Shigan said softly in the imperial scholar tongue, "his family got themselves disgraced. Or he did."

She shot him a look and whispered, "All that about trust. I made a vow. I don't tell *anyone* about Redbark or how I got there."

Shigan's mockery was back. "Because we'll all die if you tell me if Redbark Master Duin is alive or not?"

He'd remembered the name she'd made up for the supposeed leader of Redbark.

"Not you. Just me," she said, her gaze steady. "And my brother." She used the term for elder blood brother.

Shigan stared back, incredulous someone so young, from the farthest reaches of the empire, could possibly get mixed up in such a dire situation. But then he remembered the sight of Ryu blazing with weird light before knocking those mercenaries to the ground in a single stroke, and though by now he was fairly certain of the target, he mumbled, "This isn't the place."

"Nowhere is the place," Ryu whispered, still with that unwinking gaze. "There will *never* be a place."

"If you're done," came First Panther Brother Banig's loud, determinedly jovial voice again, "let's all turn up onto the weather deck. It feels like summer out there, a perfect day. And you'll all feel better if you get moving in the fresh air."

FORTY-FIVE

THAT DAY THEY DID easy warmups on deck, scarcely more than walking around. The exercises were as familiar as the morning infusion of tiger tea — someone among these Shadow Panthers had had at least some army training.

As the next few days passed, the drills got faster, with a lot more talk of honor and the elite brotherhood. The drills all emphasized attack rather than defense. First Brother Banig offered competitions — the best got at the food first, or got to choose which weapons drill they'd do next.

From habit, Ryu quickly appraised the best and the worst and kept her own performance aimed squarely in the middle, especially when First Panther Brother Banig began adding threats to all his flattering and praise. Not overt threats. There was less about honor and more like, "Good work, but I know you can do better! Master Night doesn't like laziness."

The next day, it was, "Master Night has a sharp way with those who don't hop right up when he gives an order."

And finally, on a day when they were working on deck with staffs under a cold rain, "You really don't want to find out what kind of penalty Master Night hands out for brothers who break the rules. In the Shadow Panthers, the rewards for merit are great. No one gives better rewards! But the chastisements are, ayah! They're imaginative, wouldn't you say?"

"Yes, First Panther Brother Banig," Water Cat shouted, echoed by the others who had drugged a "recruit" and brought him aboard. Their prompt and enthusiastic responses to every utterance of First Panther Brother Banig's began to give Ryu that crawling sensation at the back of her neck — especially the day before they landed, when she ghosted up to the deck barefoot and soundless, from childhood habit, to overhear First Panther Brother Banig talking to Enau Fan on the other side of the mast: "I don't believe that runt is Firebolt. The way you were talking, it's as if he was Erku the Hero come down from Heaven."

"He is. He was, I swear on my grandfather's head."

"He barely keeps up with the rest."

"I probably gave him too much of that sleep-juice. He's a runt, like you said. It must have slowed him double. But he was unbeaten in the Sky Alliance competition for sword, knife *and* staff, before we took them."

"May the King of Hell grant the truth of that for your sake." First Panther Brother Banig spoke with no trace of his false joviality. "Or you will be singing to him before Ghost Moon rises."

Ryu grimaced, and slunk on to the privy, careful not to make a sound. When she came out, they had gone below-deck.

Land was spotted at last. Everyone crowded to the side to see where they were going, Ryu and Shigan followed, but a pace or two behind.

"Wait for dark, then run," Ryu whispered.

Shigan grunted agreement, and she breathed easier. At least for now, they were back to where they had been. Until it was taken away, she hadn't been aware of how much she had come to relish his companionship, his strength, at her side. She had lost Matu forever. That was a hard lesson, and it hurt like poking a fresh bruise every time she thought of him.

No more "love."

And *definitely* no more confessions.

Both were on the watch when they pulled into a small cove where another ship lay at anchor. Shigan was relieved to have Ryu back to normal, though not under these circumstances.

They looked around . . . to see a crowd of Shadow Panthers come to meet them. These were armed — they were guards. Everything organized, just as the ship journey had been, with the food waiting, the ginger tea, the exercises. This capture was well-drilled. Well-practiced.

And so was their welcome. Despite the friendly talk and toothy grins, their eyes were watchful. They were waiting for someone to make a break for freedom.

The line of cheerers was mostly male, but not all. There were plenty of round faces innocent of hair — boys of fifteen or sixteen and up — but most of the Shadow Panthers were men. Their hails of "Welcome, novice brothers!" rang false to Ryu's ears as the recruits were taken up a path to the huge gates of a manor. What had probably been guardian lions had been smashed, rubble still lying about. From the looks of the stones, the destruction had not happened recently.

They were herded inside, past the first courtyard. Again, what had once been fine statuary in a rock garden had been smashed, carved posts supporting a central pergola hacked. Past that into the main hall, where young people — mostly women — scurried about, bringing food to low tables. These servants all had bowed heads, and the manner of bond-servants, though no collars. But they met no one's eyes. Many were thin and unhealthy-looking, especially the males among them.

Being on dry land again woke up appetites anew, and the new recruits fell on the food with fervor.

Once the newcomers had eaten, they were led through the back to a larger court, this one swept clean, with a formidable array of weaponry in racks and stands along all four sides. Here, they were treated to a display of Shadow Panther prowess.

Perhaps a third of the recruits had already decided they would go right along with the summary recruitment, and those whirling weapons, the impressive shooting, the sparks shooting upward when metal weapon met metal weapon, warmed them to enthusiasm. Others watched with expressions ranging from narrow-eyed doubt to reluctant admiration.

Ryu, watching to gauge the Shadow Panthers' expertise, got that neck-gripping feeling she was being watched. Shigan lounged next to her, and murmured without moving his lips. "See them eyeing you?"

"I see," she breathed. "It's that cursed Fire — "

The *bolt* was lost in a last clatter, and the final demonstration ended. First Panther Brother Banig then came out to the middle and called, "Now, let's see what you can do. Novice Brother Firebolt, you are probably our most famous."

Ryu cast Shigan a meaning glance from beneath her straight black brows, then got to her feet. "It's rumor," she said.

Water Cat, desperate for the merit that bringing so famous a recruit would bring, called, "Your ranking first at the competition wasn't rumor."

Ryu hardened her voice, feet apart, shoulders braced. She'd had a pretty good idea why those bowed-down servants inside were mostly women. "I hadn't faced any of the masters yet."

A hitherto unseen man called out, "Let's see what he does against you, Water Cat."

Whoever it was got instant obedience from Water Cat, who had been kneeling. He rose, rolling over his toes to his feet. He grinned crazily as he went to the side and selected two nasty-looking axes.

Ryu spotted the staffs. No one stopped her as she headed that way. Sorely missing the perfectly balanced staff the monks had given her, she selected a likely-looking one and gave it a slow whirl. It had warped slightly. The wood was the wrong type.

She suppressed a grimace, thinking rapidly. Always in the middle. But what was the middle here? She had to beat Water Cat, or they wouldn't believe her to be trying. But not too quickly. She'd already seen the penalties when First Panther Brother Banig thought people slacked off.

Water Cat was all whooshes and strength-wasting slashes. She let him drive her back several steps, as the watchers booed and insulted her at each, then she gauged the right moment and got her end in under his left hand and tapped the top of his hand where the nerves connected to the most conduits. That axe went flying.

He began swinging wildly. She fell back two or three more steps, then tapped him at the join of the ribs. When his breath caught, she brought the staff around to the side of his knee and he went down.

Everyone cheered — including Banig, who came forward uttering fulsome praise. She looked at him, bewildered, then saw that she was supposed to be proud of that praise. Her stomach churned with disgust.

And so events unfolded in an unsettlingly predictable way. Someone had been in an army training camp. Ryu got a nasty jolt when she realized that, as they had in her cadet days, the recruits were expected to shower together – but when they began to go down stone steps, some of her worry eased. This manor, like so many fortresses and nobles' houses, had been built near a hot spring.

She had learned while staying with the Ghost Moon monks that the harmony of the elements was sought from relevant auguries before these places were even built. One of the first elements to consider was water in both hot and cold form. By now she was expert at raising steam and then sketching the warding Essence signs on her own body. Those warding signs were so habitual her hands were lightning fast whenever the group moved to baths or privy.

They fell into a routine that she could have predicted – but with some significant alterations.

She was not the only one who noticed. Shigan fell in step beside her one evening as they came back from a small wargame between the walls. (They were not yet permitted to go beyond the walls; only the Shadow Panthers who had made their oaths and been tattooed were trusted there.)

"I don't say that Cor Zhiar isn't annoying," Shigan breathed. "He is. But anyone can see he's trying. He doesn't really deserve the scorn he's getting."

Ryu's stomach churned, as happened often. She hated this place more each day, intensified by the sense of helplessness that she could not get away. Even worse, she hated the forced joviality, the frequent compliments, such as, "You looked great out there, Firebolt! Your sword form will make Master Night smile – and few things do!"

She and Shigan fell silent as they passed one of the many guards always watching, always listening.

When they were out of earshot, "They're dividing him off from the rest of us," Ryu whispered back. "Did you see – last night, those two with the eastern accents moved away from his bed?"

"I saw," Shigan said curtly. "Maybe it's their way of getting Cor Zhiar to try harder."

"Not those whispers about his ancestors being worms, and the rest."

Shigan's forehead tightened. "I didn't hear that. Maybe that's Shadow Panther humor?"

Ryu had never in her life heard insults of people's ancestors as humor, but she fervently hoped so because everything made her uneasy. It was all too . . . predictable, somehow. So deliberately cruel. The way they used honor and justice and brotherhood to band everyone together in order to despise one target. The drills aimed at attack, attack, attack. Except she wasn't sure what the goal was.

She worked hard at remaining exactly in the middle, taking a few nasty bruises to ward suspicion. Then she made herself lose both scraps the next day, but First Panther Brother Banig shouted, "That's all right, Novice Brother Firebolt. You got back up and in there—that's what we want to see. You'll be winning again next week!"

That was not at all the reaction Cor Zhiar got when he lost a single bout, after effort so strong his face was crimson, the tendons standing out on his neck.

The day after that, while thunder rumbled in the distance, they were pitched straight into culmination of the . . . game? Play? Not a ruse. No, it was a ploy, a deliberate strategy. Cor Zhiar might have been obnoxious, but he wasn't stupid enough to steal while on this island, so when he was accused of theft—and the evidence pointed to under his bedroll—his voice rose to an angry squeal as he denied everything.

But the tattooed guards closed in and dragged him out to the practice field.

"Cor Zhiar," one of the masked Shadow Panthers roared, cloak billowing in the wind. "Your loyalty has been called into question, for you in thieving have dishonored the brotherhood!"

"I'm loyal, I'm loyal," Cor Zhiar protested, his voice breaking. "It's Banig—he's always tripping me, making me look bad . . ."

"That is First Panther Brother Banig!"

Cor Zhiar threw himself to his knees, gobbling apologies. But this play had been set, and Ryu and Shigan, in looking at the ring of faces, could see who was smacking their lips in anticipation of the bloody end. With a sickening pretense of justice, Cor Zhiar was condemned—and beaten to death, to the sound of drums.

Ryu shut her eyes at the first strike. Shigan made himself watch, vowing that somehow, there was going to be justice.

Ryu had already made that vow back on the ship.

When it was over, the masked Shadow Panther intoned, "There is only one loyalty, to our brothers!"

The tattooed Shadow Panthers gave a great shout.

The mask then said, "You have seen that punishment is swift and just. But when our brothers are loyal and strive to earn merit, the rewards are great! First Panther Brother Banig, take these honorable brother recruits into the treasure room, and let them pick out their first treasure!"

Again, the tattooed members gave a roar of approval, and this time most of the recruits joined in.

They were led to the northern side of the manor, where the former owners' ancestral shrine would have been. The windowless building was guarded by armed and masked brethren. The door was opened, and then came Ryu's next surprise.

Shigan felt Ryu stiffen—but he waited, as they were led into a room filled with loot: gold in various forms, including imperial taels; precious jade ornaments; jewelry; even women's hairpins. It was heaped up in careless piles, glittering in the light of many candles.

Shigan's attention stayed on Ryu as the rest of the recruits wandered around exclaiming. She kept stealing looks at the tattooed young man who seemed to be in charge.

First Panther Brother Banig gave them a little longer to choose, then said it was time for the meal. The guards seemed to be watching to see what everyone chose. Shigan picked up a jade carving of a tiger at random, and noticed Ryu picking up a cloak pin shaped like a feather, profile utterly closed off.

On their way back to the main building, under cover of approaching thunder, he said, "Cor Zhiar is already on his way to his next life. We'll get justice for him."

"For them all," she whispered. "Do you think he's the first? The horrible part is, I think they do that with every group of recruits, make an utter mockery of honor and justice. Talk up this brotherhood that is not at all meant to help each other as brothers, but to compete and tattle in order to get rank. Then they come in here to give out this stuff so no one will care that it's all a mockery." She nudged a golden goblet with the toe of her boot. "Ayah, *how* I hate this place, and—never mind that. Listen, I recognized the one in charge of this treasure room. He was flogged out of Loyalty my first year."

Shigan glanced back. "Will he know you?"

"No. I was my brother's grunt. No one paid attention to us. That is, he was an orderly, too. We only knew him as Erk, which was his master's name—you remember how it was—but he and I never were in the same place together. I'd never seen him before they got rid of him."

"What was his crime?"

"Theft."

"At *Loyalty?* There was nowhere to spend a tinnie! What did he think he could do with his booty?"

"I don't know."

"Firebolt? Shigan? What are you talking about?"

Shigan opened his mouth, but Ryu was quicker. "I want to trade for that jade tiger. I like it better than this old pin. I don't even know why I picked it up. But he won't."

First Panther Brother Banig gave his harsh, false laugh. "This is only the beginning, boys! You'll have plenty of opportunities to choose better things as you gain more merit!"

Banig turned away, and Ryu tucked the feather away in her sleeve. It was made of silver, not gold, and it had no Essence feel to it, but she hated the thought of this lovely feather lying there in that horrible room full of loot—it reminded her of Ul Keg telling her The Story, and Mother's words about mercy, and Father's training, and her brothers' calm breathing in their room at night, and how easy life had been in Sweetwater, if only she'd known it.

She resolved to donate the silver feather to the first Snow Crane temple she saw.

If she got out of this place alive.

On their way to their barracks to put away their treasures, Shigan said, "Did you catch that loudmouth Water Cat's blabber? We have a year, then we either get the tattoo—with an Essence charm in it so they can always track us—or die."

"Charms can be broken," Ryu muttered. "But I don't want to be here that long."

"Anymore do I. All it would take is a storm like the one coming. We could get away."

Ryu gave her head a quick shake. "When I go, I'm taking those women with us."

A hesitation. "Do you . . . have a plan?"

"No." She said the word between gritted teeth. "Also I'm taking anyone else who wants out. But first it's the women."

Shigan whistled softly under his breath. Then said, "All right. You come up with a plan, and I'm in."

They stopped speaking then, as footsteps came up from behind.

At the doorway, watching them leave, the masked and cloaked man stood beside a pillar. He caught First Panther

Brother Banig, who was last of the line. "Those two — the runt and the handsome one. I want them separated."

Banig stared. "I thought they were arguing about the treasure. Did you hear them say anything, Chief?"

"No, no. Let's just be certain, shall we?"

Once everyone stashed their treasures in their trunks, they were then taken to the large hall, and treated to another feast. They sat at the far end, away from the dais, but they could see the tattooed Shadow Panthers, the so-called "pledge brothers." And a few of the masked ones. These were permitted to choose among the servants for their entertainment.

Ryu could not see much, but she heard very few female voices among the roars of laughter and increasingly drunken shouts. Most of those she did hear were shrill, false laughter, meant to please. When the women came around to offer wine, and some to offer themselves, Ryu looked into wide smiles below hungry eyes, angry eyes, desperate eyes. And lustful eyes.

The latter were easier to see in one sense, for at least it meant those women chose to be chosen. The desperate eyes haunted Ryu most, for they seemed to be carved by centuries of maltreatment inherited mother to daughter, their voices silenced by power, by indifference, by the inability even to write down grievances to be left behind. They did not get ancestral tombs, and descendants who prayed to them and for them; Ryu looked at those eyes and in dreams that night and in the nights after, she heard, shivering beyond physical hearing, the howl of desolation that turned into the long cry of the white crane.

FORTY-SIX

YSKANDA TRIED NEVER TO assume anything about people.

Ul Keg had taught him to observe. Master Bankan had taught them to depict what portrayed patrons wanted to see in themselves, which in its own way took observation skills. Yskanda knew better than to assume a surface expression was all there was, and yet he almost did that with Second Imperial Prince Vaion.

The painting was done except for the face, which was not coming quite right. Yskanda tried several times to capture the prince's quick, lazy grin, but the result looked vapid. The second prince sprawled and sighed and joked, yet that evanescent quality would not come right on the silk.

The Kraken Boat Festival was nigh, as spring ripened toward summer. The imperial family did not go anywhere yet again, Vaion admitted to Yskanda, though many of the others went on the famous water progress called Journey to the Clouds—which Yskanda wished he could see. It was famed not for any bloody battle or triumph, but for its beauty.

Vaion came drunk to their session. "I know I stink of wine," he said abruptly. "But this is so boring I have to do *something*."

"This tiresome scribbler would be happy to wait for a better day, if you wish, your imperial highness."

"It'll be boring whenever we do it," Vaion retorted, and at Yskanda's dropped gaze, he burst out, "It's my mood. I'll sit still. At least I can do that."

He sat brooding for a short time, his hands restlessly playing with the fine fan he carried.

It was an ancient fan, Yskanda saw, the sticks made of pale, rare jadewood, the silken screen painted with minimal strokes in the style of several centuries ago. But those few strokes expertly evoked mountains in the background, and in the foreground the graceful finger-leaves of the acacia, symbol of love and yearning.

Etiquette forbade him to ask any question that did not pertain to his immediate service. But he could always compliment and flatter. "That is a well-decorated fan."

The prince looked down, and smiled briefly — too brief to catch, alas, for it was the first hint of real expression Yskanda had seen. "It was my brother's favorite."

He spread it, and there on the right Yskanda saw a calligraphic squiggle, very much in the old style. The word, done with dry brush, looked windswept, the character midway between those for *Heaven* and *haven*. That the fan had a name increased the poignancy of the message.

"I saw my sister in there. Asked what she was about, going through his things. She said, if Jion is dead, they'll make all his things vanish. She wanted something to remember him by. I would not have believed that except she was crying."

The imperial prince looked away, his profile tight. "I wondered if she'd heard anything, but I knew she wouldn't tell me if she had. So I took this, but may the moon gods keep his soul right here in the world."

Yskanda remained still, watching the change of real expression in the prince's face, like clouds racing across the sun.

Vaion stared down at the fan. "We really want him to be alive, so that I can smack him for scaring us."

Yskanda began to sketch Vaion's pensive gaze as the imperial prince stared unseeing across the artificial lake.

"My cousins want to be imperial princes. Sometimes I want to tell them how many imperial brothers, sisters, cousins, and uncles all died around the throne, including those who never lived long enough to be married. Others who did marry were killed along with their children and consorts. . ." In a rapid flow, Second Imperial Prince Vaion went on to detail every sudden, violent death in the royal family, beginning with his aunts and one uncle, going back four generations — and then he dove into the history of other dynasties, and the wholesale slaughter in the eternal battle for the throne.

"Jion said he'd protect me. And he did. But he's gone. I'm *glad* he got away! I hope he's got two pretty girls with him, who don't know who he is, and a jug at his side, and the road beyond the door." Then came the crooked grin. "At least I can get the girls, and the jug."

And there was the real Vaion, that cocky, crooked grin, comprised of a kind of determined humor, a good nature with pain beneath.

Yskanda began to sketch the shadows around that smile.

He was able to finish in two more sessions, during which many of the prince's rambles began with *Jion says* or *Jion thinks*.

Vaion himself declared it ready, and took it with him when he left their meeting place. Yskanda rejoiced internally — this was turning out to be a good day. He had received his first (and only) letter, from no less a figure than Master Bankan, congratulating him on his achievements, and encouraging him to write again. Yskanda didn't know why he was so cheered to receive that letter, but he was. Secondly, though he was once again summoned to the inner palace, he would not have to be in the presence of the emperor.

He hurried back, trying to stay under the shaded walkways, as summer had come upon them suddenly. Even the insects in the garden seemed too somnolent to move about making noise in the heavy, sultry air.

He was mentally reviewing what he'd say to Court Artist Yoli when he caught sight of a page scudding along on tiny steps, running without actually running — which was forbidden. The boy's face was crimson from the heat, his eyes wide. The moment he saw Yskanda, his eyes widened further, and he changed course.

"It's the court artist," the boy said breathlessly as soon as the two were in earshot. "He fell. Chrysanthemum sent me to find you."

Chrysanthemum — that was the graywing in charge of Court Artist Yoli's things. Yskanda joined the page, and the two sped along byways. They passed two senior graywings who must have already heard the word, or they issued no remonstrance as the pair hurried by.

Bad sign. Sometimes lying awake at night and thinking wistfully about freedom, Yskanda knew he would leave that moment if given a chance, but he'd miss the irascible old artist. Now, with something terrible having happened, he found himself sick with apprehension.

They arrived at the court artist's private room, which Yskanda had never seen before. It was scarcely larger than his new room — but then the court artist, like Yskanda, was never in it except to sleep.

He was there now — alive, Yskanda saw gratefully.

"Ow, ow, curse it! No, go ahead, Imperial Physician, put in all the needles you like if it'll numb this accursed leg — oh, Jiwa, you old fool, when are you going to remember you are no longer young and nimble . . ."

Yoli went on rambling until he saw Yskanda, then he tried to rise to one elbow, and fell back, blanching to the color of paper.

"What happened?" Yskanda asked, and dropped to his knees beside the bed.

"I slipped and fell coming out of the bath," the old man husked. It clearly took an effort to speak. "Bones are like porcelain. Not what you want bones to be like. But now you're here, you can go straight to work. Don't let anyone meddle with anything until I can get in there!"

His eyes were over-bright, and a hectic flush entered his withered cheeks, but the court artist's eyes were very alert.

"I'll get back to work at once," Yskanda said, rising. "I'll return to check on you."

Yoli sank back, his eyes closing. "Yes. Good boy."

Yskanda did exactly that. He found nothing disturbed, as far as he could tell. He was only certain about his own area, which he always left in precisely the same way. For the rest, he was acutely aware that he wouldn't know the signs of a conspiracy without a label that said, DO NOT TOUCH: CONSPIRACY WITHIN!

But he became aware of the hereto invisible signs of the court artist everywhere. The cushion he sat on contained a dent the size of the man who sat there every day. The way the brush stand was aligned, everything evoked Court Artist Yoli. We all will vanish someday, Yskanda thought as he circled the room without touching anything. All we leave are our things. For a time those who know us will see us in those things, but gradually they will become just things, empty of intent, of meaning.

On that sobering thought, he set up his own work area, and

soothed his mind by letting it slide into the world of ink, color, and the controlled grace of line.

On the other side of the palace world, the imperial family stood about admiring the silkscreen portrait of Vaion.

"He really is a Talent," the first imperial consort said at last. "He caught our dear son Vaion to the life."

The third imperial consort, Vaion's birth mother, flushed with pleasure. To her eye, Vaion looked quite handsome — more than he did in real life, but you couldn't say the picture was unduly flattering.

The emperor said, "It is quite promising." And then added casually, "I'm always curious about the inner workings of the mind of a Talent. Did he converse much with you, Second Son?"

"He didn't talk much beyond light and shade. It was mostly I who was talking," Vaion admitted with a grin.

"It was the same with me," Gau-Gau put in, for she had not been center of attention all day, and she liked being there. Besides, she had a secret resentment festering, but it didn't do to raise it directly. And so, with a glance at her elder sister across the room, she added in a low voice, "Manon would not let him speak, and I hated the silence, so I talked and talked and talked. One day, when he drew the details of my hairpins, I must have drunk three pots of tea!"

The emperor laughed, and turned to First Princess Lily.

"He spoke on the subjects one would expect from a scribe-trained artist," she said. "Very polite, very restful person," she added. "He has patience."

Lily herself was a restful, patient person, mild in manner despite that heavy jaw and those low brows. She spoke rarely, and never in First Imperial Princess Manon's presence, unless directly addressed — that the emperor had noticed, and deplored. But he could not be watching over them all the time. He could leave that to their mothers, who were all in their own ways tigers in protecting their young.

This experiment using his children had failed to uncover anything new about Afan Yskanda, though it had succeeded in pleasing his mother. Afan Yskanda truly was a Talent — which might argue against Danno and Alk Hanu being his parents. Hanu had been a scholar, fussing over dusty scrolls, the more ancient the better, with scant attention paid to the fine art he had been collecting. And as for Danno, he'd scarcely been able to read.

"I must admit, I would like to see what he does with my consorts," he said, and presently left, knowing that Bitternail would see to it being arranged.

The consorts never banded together; the Second Imperial Consort Su exerted her considerable skills in making certain that something occurred to keep each from trusting enough to confide in the other. This, she taught her daughter, was the simplest method of insuring parity — and if one were clever, gaining ascendance.

She walked back to her own pavilion, saying to her daughter, "I am not displeased that your Imperial Father wishes for a portrait of me, but I could have done without it being a general order. Even the arts from Talents lose value when reproduced."

Second Imperial Princess Manon understood. By including the first and third consorts in the order, Father Emperor was not extending a sign of favor to the second imperial consort. "It will be deemed fair," she observed to her mother. "After all, these portraits are for Imperial Grandmother, and not for Father Emperor."

"True. And that might explain why he insists on having them done by this assistant who cannot be more than sixteen, seventeen at most. His chin is quite innocent of any sign of beard, yet one more promotion and he will be at a level with Masters!"

"The rules for Talents are different, Imperial Mother, everyone knows that."

"Yes, but I wonder why *him*," the second consort went on. "I don't think he's been here two years. He certainly wasn't chosen and trained here. I asked Melonseed, who said he was brought from outside. Ayah! The Afans are as common as mud."

Manon was aware of the quickening of her heartbeat at the mention of Afan Yskanda's name. And she knew she would be considerably disturbed when he came to their manor to sketch her mother.

Irritated with him — with herself — she said, "This ignorant daughter begs her wise mother to teach her why this subject ought to be considered for half a breath. Even Talents, without rank, can only be tools."

"Yes — but how to use them effectively?" The second imperial consort sent a sharp glance at her daughter, whose voice was a shade too emphatic. No, she ought not to worry. Manon had known from the cradle that she had impeccable lineage. She would never forget herself.

Mother and daughter parted in silence.

The third imperial consort did not spare Yskanda much of a thought beyond appreciation for his beautiful face. Her attention was entirely on which robe to wear that would outshine anything worn by that poisonous snake Second Imperial Consort Su Shafar. For she, too, had dreams of being raised to the phoenix throne, which would happen if either of her children was raised to the rank of imperial heir.

As for the first imperial consort, she and the dowager empress fell into conversation about Yskanda before the latter's pavilion. This was an alliance which the second imperial consort dismissed as negligible, as the dowager empress appeared to be merely a doting mother and grandmother — totally powerless.

"It seems odd," the first imperial consort observed, "that so many merits are being piled on that young artist. Admittedly he *is* a Talent, but Yoli is not dying. There is no hurry in replacing him, especially with a mere boy."

If there was any question implied in the first consort's mild observation, it caused no answer but the imperial dowager's comfortable, "Oh, the rules for Talents are not those for the rest of us, whatever their birth. I must go see to this being hung right away." She indicated the silkscreen portrait of Vaion, carried carefully by one of her silent ladies.

The two bowed to each other and then retreated to their respective pavilions, followed by their entourages.

Once inside her own, the Dowager Empress Kui Jin looked about, chose a place for the new hanging, and sent her servants to see to it. Then she glanced at old Topaz, her trusted graywing who had stood silently in the background for so many years. She knew the younger generation regarded him no more than they would the furnishings. Consequently he heard things that she was not able to hear.

She sank down onto her couch and shut her eyes, as Topaz took up an herb-scented fan and began to ply it gently.

Topaz gestured to the waiting women to bring tea and the wolfberries the dowager empress preferred to eat during hot weather. Though the dowager empress made no further sign, Topaz had learned to read her well, and nodded at the women to withdraw.

Topaz remained silent. It was he who had first recollected where he had seen Yskanda's features, but he had kept that to himself until a conversation with old Chief Fai, former ferret chief, and an ally from the terrible last days of the old emperor.

Not two days later, the dowager empress had woken from a dream. She summoned Topaz, saying, "I have it, where I've seen those eyes before. It was one of the five girls we chose for my son. She was the one I favored most, which choice turned out to be ill-omened enough."

Dowager Empress Kui Jin opened her eyes. "Renyi seems unsuspicious," she said.

Topaz merely bowed, and kept fanning as she sipped tea, then picked among the berries on the gold-edged porcelain plate.

She ate these thoughtfully, then said, "But Renyi was not even in the imperial city then. The one I worried might recognize Alk Hanu in that boy was Su Shafar."

"Her highness the second imperial consort was one of the five chosen for his imperial highness as he was then," Topaz murmured in agreement.

The dowager empress sent a sharp, wry glance up at him. "Oh, I am quite certain all she saw were four rivals, one indistinguishable from the next, during the little time the finalists spent in one another's company. But Su Shafar is much more observant now; if she does recognize him, she'll kill him if she can. Especially if my son shows him more favor."

Old Topaz prudently said nothing — which the dowager empress understood as agreement.

"I wonder if that wily old fox Yoli Jiwa suspects," she went on. "But then he has drawn so many people over the years. In any case, he never speaks to anyone about anything other than colors, ink, brushes, silk, and the like."

Topaz bowed again.

The dowager empress set down her cup, sighing. "Ill-omened, and yet I cannot find any resentment in me at this distance, though I was furious at the time." A look. "What do you say? You alone of anyone except Enjai were there at the time. In fact, you saw more than any of us."

Topaz had been placed by her in Second Imperial Prince Enjai's manor to oversee it, and train the young staff.

"She was . . . unworldly," Topaz said finally. "A rare quality."

"Yes. Exactly. I see not just those same eyes, but that very same quality, in the face of this boy. Whether or not he is her son."

Topaz bowed.

The dowager empress considered what could be said, even to this trusted advisor. But Topaz was old, and he would not last under questioning. Until she understood what Enjai was aware of, and what were his intentions, it was perhaps better to remain silent.

FORTY-SEVEN

YSKANDA HAD ALREADY FORGOTTEN about the imperial family. His mind was entirely occupied with Court Artist Yoli as he completed a layer of color over the scroll, then washed the brushes, tidied everything, and rechecked the wards.

It was dusk when he returned to Court Artist Yoli's room, and inquired if he might visit.

He was immediately bidden to enter. The Court artist issued a lengthy list of tasks. Just talking clearly pained him. Before he stopped, he said, "You will have to attend court alone. We are lucky there is no great debate in the offing. You know what to do."

Yskanda bowed. "Everything the most conventional. I promise to be careful."

The next few days passed with Yskanda trying to handle as much of the less important work as he could for the court artist, who by the end of the week insisted on being lifted into a little wheeled cart with cushions at the bottom. This way he was able to get to his workroom to see things himself—and he spoke of attending the next court session. "It's my leg that broke. Not my arm," he said irascibly, though the sweat at his hairline after only half an hour made it clear how much it pained him to move even slightly.

That night, he waved off the strong young graywings assigned to him, and murmured, "Can you lift me?"

Surprised, Yskanda slipped his hands under the old man's

arms. He could feel the loose skin sliding over stringy muscles, a surprisingly heavy body beneath. He could lift the court artist – barely. What if he slipped?

"I don't dare," he said, releasing Yoli carefully.

The court artist nodded, saying nothing. Yskanda was surprised at the sharp disappointment Yoli could not quite hide. At first he feared a lack of trust on the court artist's part. Then the reason struck him: as long as those graywings were on duty, their conversations must be circumscribed.

Later, Yskanda walked back to his own room, frowning. He didn't think of himself as weak. He walked so much, and spent so much time grinding paints. But he knew that neither his brother nor his father would agree. Even Mouse, who used to start every day by pulling her chin up to tree branches fifty times!

When he reached his room, he pushed aside the table, and then, for the first time in years, tried to do Heaven and Earth. He was breathless before the first pattern was complete.

This was no good! He threw off his robe, and did it again. And again, until he was streaming with sweat. His hands shook and his knees had gone watery, but he could feel his blood singing in his veins.

The next day, he got up, wincing at the ache in his muscles, and forced himself to do the first pattern of Heaven and Earth again. It was even worse than the evening before, though the room was cooler. This was exactly why he loathed that kind of physical effort. He gave it up – sadly he was useless in that regard.

Over the next three days, he began to regret that decision. He had thought himself careful when speaking even with the court artist. For example, the word "Imai" had never crossed his lips, even after he knew the emperor's ferrets had found Sweetwater.

But now, with at least one graywing always on duty around the court artist – sober, respectful, careful – there was no chance to speak of anything except work. His day was spent alone in the workroom except when summoned by a page, in which case he ran back and forth between the workroom and Court Artist Yoli's bedroom, bringing supplies for the court artist's lap desk, and furnishing his own work for inspection.

The third morning, when he got to the workroom, he set about readying things for the day's labor – and froze. He stepped back, realized what he was doing, and recovered, but his mood of anticipation had gone, replaced by a crawling sense of . . . being watched?

He whirled around. No one. He made himself pace the perimeter, looking behind every drying rack, into every nook. No one. That sense didn't diminish. It intensified until he understood it as a sense of violation. This stack of paper, slightly out of alignment as if a sleeve brushed against the top layer (he tried it, and it disarranged a little more), a gleam before the stack of old books that the court artist hadn't touched in years. Someone had wiped the shelf clean, and Yskanda knew he hadn't dusted for four days.

He returned to his own space. His whisker brush stand might look like it was left at a careless angle, but Yskanda actually aligned it with the grain of the wood of his table. It was now straight, parallel to his willow-brush stand. Someone had reached behind his brushes to examine the piles of sketches he had put at the back of the table.

He turned around, imagining unknown fingers riffling, touching, sifting through everything in the room. Yskanda did another, more cautious circle: all the Essence ward objects were still in place, visually indistinguishable from the various pots, inkstones, straining dishes, mortars, and water jars piled on shelves about the room.

Someone had searched the workroom, and thoroughly. They had replaced everything with what probably seemed like great care when done by lamplight, but to the artist's eye, telling details revealed methodical deliberation by a different sort of eye. Yskanda made another slow circuit of the room, trying to adjust to the idea that he might not be as hapless at investigation as he had first assumed.

The urge to rush to the court artist seized him. He fought it down. What could he say before those patient attendants?

He now understood why Court Artist Yoli had asked if he could lift him.

He moved again, going about setting up for a day's work, as if someone invisible stood at his shoulder. The day passed without him being disturbed, until he went to see the court artist when the gong rang the last of Horse.

Neither of them said anything that was not related to work, but that night, Yskanda threw off his clothes and forced himself through Heaven and Earth until he collapsed on his bed. When he caught his breath, he got up and did it again.

And the next morning, he did it twice. Then, when he

reached the workroom, he went to the back, and used one of the drying racks to pull his chin to the wooden bar five muscle-straining times.

Once Yskanda made a decision, he was as single-minded as his siblings.

He could not talk to the court artist about anything but projects. Surprising, even unsettling, how much he felt like the frog at the bottom of the well, being denied even their limited exchanges.

But by the end of a week of assiduous exercising, he was less sore, and faster at it. He still loathed it, but getting it over with first thing on waking made it easier to turn into habit. As he walked up to keep his appointment with the first imperial consort, he was convinced he was walking faster. Stronger.

Then he was summoned to commence the portraits of the consorts.

Even though the emperor was nowhere in sight, his presence was everywhere: in the triple-eaved hip-roof of the Golden Dragon Pavilion, in the ubiquitous presence of armed and armored imperial guards, even in the sweep of the garden, whose lines and even some plants evoked the dragon. He also sensed the emperor's presence in the decorated pavilions his consorts lived in, where he might be expected to walk in at any moment.

The first imperial consort, a princess in her own right, had been arrayed in five layers of green, gold, and white silk, the top robe embroidered with tiny birds hiding among bamboo shoots, her long dark hair twisted and braided up into a fabulous structure surmounted by a golden ornament decorated with emeralds and pearls, with golden chains dangling by one ear.

She received him with unexpectedly kind words, then stunned him by offering him something cool to drink. He bowed three times as he stammered out his gratitude, though of course he refused. Surely it had to be a vast breach of protocol to actually accept!

But she only smiled at him as she said, "How am I to arrange myself?"

"This humble assistant begs the exalted First Imperial Consort Princess Ran Renyi to be as comfortable as she wishes," Yskanda said awkwardly. But after a few repetitions of *Is this all right? Is this?* he could almost hear Yoli Jiwa's irascible voice in his ear, and managed — after a lot of fumbling at courtly flattery — to suggest an appropriate pose that reflected the poses of queens, empresses, and consorts through the ages. Traditional was predictable, but safe.

She was very cooperative, sitting as still as she could; her maid fanned her as sweat sheened her forehead under the heavy headdress and all those layers of silk.

Presently she said, "I was sorry to hear about Court Artist Yoli's fall. I trust he is recovering?"

Yskanda reassured her and thanked her for the blessing of her interest on Yoli's behalf.

After another pause, she said, "I don't believe I have ever seen you before the Two Moons Celebration beginning Year of the Pig."

"This lowly apprentice of no talent or interest was indeed elsewhere, your imperial highness."

"I'm curious where his imperial majesty found you, Court Assistant Afan."

Despite the heat of summer, Yskanda's blood ran cold. He managed not to pause in his sketching, or betraying his dismay by any other sign, as he said, "This ignorant assistant is grateful for the notice, your imperial highness."

The first imperial consort waited, expecting an actual answer. In spite of her exalted lineage, young people usually chattered in her presence, especially if she was encouraging. As she had tried to be. But this reticent assistant court artist remained quiet, busily working away so that all she could see was the top of the hat that marked him at the eighth level of the nine.

She tried again. "How did it come about, your arrival here? Your talent is such that I feel very certain you won some kind of competition."

Yskanda bowed from his chair, thanked her in formal terms, and then said, "It was so ordered."

That was quite a surprise. She considered further questions — there was nothing else to do while she sat there, and her curiosity was increasing by the moment — but she did not want to sound too inquisitive, without knowing the emperor's mind on the subject. For she sensed that the emperor's wishes lay somewhere in the background here. How else would an outsider be wafted within the palace, and promoted like a comet crossing the sky?

Her third question was more general. "Where were you trained before you came here? Have I ever heard of the school?"

Yskanda had been thinking fast. He would not say any more than what he knew the emperor had found out from the ferrets. Once again, he spoke a long, formal thanks for her interest, then said, "This assistant of little talent or value was born in the south, on an island called Imai, and learned from Master Scribe Bankan." And then, because she seemed to want him to talk, he went on to describe Master Bankan and his classes in excruciating detail, striving to maintain as pleasant a tone as possible.

She listened—at least this intriguing, beautiful boy was talking now. Yskanda had a soft speaking voice, and of course that face. The first imperial consort had never heard of either Master Bankan or Imai Island, but the boy's chatter was just what she would expect from someone of so obscure a background who wished to impress his auditor. He offered a wealth of details about his art, always properly self-deprecating.

And so she told the emperor when he made his next visit to her, and the subject somehow came up. "I found him very conversable," she said. "Very respectful, but full of chatter."

"Chatter?" the emperor repeated, brows rising. "Really? I have never found him so. But you have always had a gift with making people comfortable."

She flushed, pleased, for he did not hand out compliments often. "All I did was offer him some wolfberry punch from the cold room, which he turned down very humbly, though it was unspeakably hot. Then I asked him where he came from. And after he finished talking, and drawing—I don't see how he could do both at the same time, but he did it—I felt I knew as much about the differences between cinnabar, ochre, azurite, malachite, and large, medium, and small wash layers to aid Court Artist Yoli myself. This old mother believes that boy was trying to impress," she finished, smiling.

The emperor smiled back, and encouraged her to talk to Assistant Court Artist Yskanda again when next he came.

Yskanda had gone back to his own territory by then, with the usual sense of relief on leaving the inner palace. His mind was now entirely on the court artist. Bolstered by his sense of newfound strength (however minimal that might be) he did offer to try to help the court artist, and to his surprise, Yoli Jiwa exclaimed approbation with a readiness that made it clear he had been hoping for something of the sort.

It was not easy, but he managed.

Between the two of them and the cooperative graywings, Court Artist Yoli soon had a little cart made over to him, well supplied with cushions, that Yskanda could pull from the bedroom to the workroom. There, with the court artist's accustomed seat piled high with more cushions, and a little table so that his leg—bound to a stick of wood—could rest comfortably, they at last were able to face one another in their own space.

"Go along," the court artist said to his graywings. "My assistant will return me to my room at First Dragon hour." And then, with the relative freedom of his years of blameless service, "He can see to me during the day—you have no idea how behind I am, and I don't want my workroom cluttered with extra people. It's crowded enough as it is!"

Once they were all gone, the court artist silently pointed to the Essence wards, which Yskanda went to one by one. He disliked the tingling feeling of Essence on his fingers, but said nothing; when they were alone at last, they spoke at the same time:

"You've no notion how frustrating it is not to talk to you—"

"Court Artist Yoli, this room was searched."

"What?" Yoli broke off, and scowled, then sighed. "This is exactly why I am so careful. The graywings, or the ferrets, or both, regularly investigate any and every room in the palace, it being part of their duty to root out any seeds of conspiracy or rebellion."

As he spoke, he reflected that it had been years since the last thorough search behind his back. No doubt the impetus was Yskanda. He sighed, thinking of the poet Fe Da, who had written a bitterly ironic poem when he was exiled after a clash between two court factions (neither of which he had belonged to), observing that in spite of the great walls of fortresses, and armies of thousands, the most dangerous enemy was mostly at home.

Yskanda still seemed to be wary of confessing who he was. If he was who Yoli Jiwa thought he was. But perhaps it was much better so: at no time in his life had he been less able to defend someone he had come to care about.

Court Artist Yoli scowled at his broken leg, then looked up at Yskanda's expectant face. "Let's see what you've done with the Mountains scroll. Bring it over here—you'll have to be my legs and arms for a while, my boy. I don't trust the pages to handle my work."

Yskanda worked far more contentedly, reunited with the court artist. And on the way back to his room, he glanced up at the silvery light, remembered it was full moon, and veered to the Ghost Moon temple to burn some incense and pray for the safety of his family.

"I'll add in my master's name as well," Yskanda thought as he picked out sandal and lakawood incense. He lit them, knelt down and went through the bowing ritual, before closing his eyes. The ancient carved image on the altar was fine, of course—this was the imperial palace, after all, though this modest temple in the southeast corner was mainly used by servants and lower ranking staff—but the image in his mind was larger, truer, more benevolent. He'd tried to paint it in the past, but the face never came right. Maybe when he was better trained, or had more experience . . .

The crack of joints and the hiss of cloth indicated someone kneeling right next to him. He shifted a bit the other way, wondering how the temple had gotten so crowded all of a sudden. Then he breathed in a faint, familiar scent of honeybush incense rising from someone's clothes—

His eyes opened as he turned his head, and he stared straight into Ul Keg's eyes.

Yskanda's mouth opened. Ul Keg's eyelids flickered down, and Yskanda caught himself before exclaiming. His breath exited shakily as his heart labored.

"Your parents are well," Ul Keg whispered in the ancient tongue, which Yskanda had not heard since taking classes before the Imperial Examination.

Relief washed through Yskanda, leaving him heady with euphoria. "You saw them?"

"I did. At Burning Rock Island." Ul Keg looked around quickly. He had two sympathetic acolytes who were guarding the doors, but of course they could not prevent anyone from entering. At least they could make a noise if anyone approached. "We are monks. No one knows anything about how to get someone past the many guards here. But if you can manage to get yourself to the Phoenix Moon temple in the city, we could dress you as a monk and send you on an Ul-journey."

For a few exquisite moments Yskanda pictured himself shrouded in monkish clothing, stepping aboard a ship. Free. His throat ached, and the knot in his heart tightened as he struggled against hope.

Ul Keg rose, then quietly patted his shoulder. "I must go where I am called, so I might not see you again. Go in peace, child. Remember, you are loved," he said, and went out.

FORTY-EIGHT

FOUR TIMES SHIGAN SAW opportunities to escape the Shadow Panthers. But no, Ryu had said, "I'm not leaving without those women."

Shigan had to admit that as much as Ryu frustrated him, there was an equal measure of admiration. If not more than equal. Because though he had not been raised to think that way, once Ryu spoke those words, he could not unhear them. Or get away from the unsettling idea that he ought to have been the one to say that.

And so life ground on, both of them careful to remain in the middle of the pack, until the new mask who had arrived began handing out orders. This was Chief Brother Screaming Hawk, tall, brawny, with jug-handle ears and huge, strong hands. He wore his long hair braided with golden ornaments, like a prince.

First Brothers, it turned out, were captains under three Chief Brothers, who reported to Master Night. Screaming Hawk was in charge of recruitment, and as they soon found out, he had a taste for imaginative punishments, which formed his favorite evening's entertainment.

The worst of his cruelties was his cleverness in keeping his victims guessing. For Master Night had taught that if you were predictable in handing down drastic punishments, then people just gave up. But if you enjoyed watching them do anything, anything at all, including begging and pleading, and betraying those closest to them, you held out the chance of survival—even of reward, and let people see occasional mercy. Then they tried much harder. Mercy might not be as fun, but the reward was how very grateful the spared would be.

The first time Ryu had to sit through one of those evenings, it wasn't long before she claimed to have diarrhea, then went straight out and threw up behind the ornamental hedge. After that, she never watched, but kept her eyes focused on the back of the head of the recruit in front of her, and mentally reviewed the *Book of Herbs*, or Kanda's *Conversations*, always striving to pull Mother's soft voice, or Ul Keg's rusty, humorous one, from memory.

Those memories were becoming a little threadbare, but she held onto them determinedly, the fire in her heart burning brighter with each day endured.

Her isolation worsened when she and Shigan decided to avoid one another, as friendships were the first stage of Screaming Hawk's entertainments. It never seemed to fail to send him off into paroxysms of laughter when some trembling, miserable wretch chose self over a friend—and even took the first cut.

This agonizing stretch of days was the worst crisis of Shigan's life.

Each time he saw a chance to escape, he struggled. It wasn't just self-preservation, though he was very aware of that motive. There was more than that, particularly when he had to sit and play the pipa, or the guzheng. First Brother Banig came around once asking who played an instrument, and Shigan immediately spoke up, thinking that if he played for them, he'd get out of some of the worst excesses.

Wrong.

The evenings started easily enough. Screaming Hawk liked music while he ate dinner. But once he had enough to drink, he talked, and then the players, male and female both, were a captive audience. And he had to have an audience.

Shigan kept reminding himself that what he heard might be useful. To someone. Someday. And he kept listening, not to the petty cruelties and the tiresome repetitions of sexual prowess, but to the hints about the Night Master—and the Grand Plan.

The manor's part of the Grand Plan seemed to be confined to recruitment: tattoos promoted to masks were tested elsewhere; then those who survived were shipped off to the

Night Master, at which time pledges who wanted, or had just gotten, tattoos, had to prove themselves by recruiting expeditions in order to gain a mask, which meant full acceptance into the sect. The Sky Island Alliance was considered one of the prime locations for recruitment of the best in the wandering world.

Shigan brooded about that—and Ryu saw his brooding as he gazed narrow-eyed into the distance, his finger sometimes rising to run over the carving of the tiger-eye on the pin of his hair clasp.

She struggled as well. All around her was injustice, and she was not strong enough to fix it. Both endured the worst six weeks of their lives—endless while they lasted—until there was a change no one had expected: a bad summer thunderstorm swept a nearly wrecked boat up onto the beach.

"There's a girl in it," said a messenger sent by one of the lookouts. "Shall we kill her?"

"No!" First Brother Banig exclaimed, pausing his demonstration on using the big sabers he liked to call the Headsman's Honeys. "Unless she comes waving a weapon, we can always use more girls." And he uttered a coarse laugh.

Sourness rose in the back of Ryu's throat, and she braced herself to see yet another victim dragged in—but nothing prepared her for the shock of recognition.

It was Petal, wearing an eyepatch, her hair worn in many braids, and a bedraggled robe that Ryu had never seen before. Petal glanced once at Ryu and Shigan, as they paused in the middle of sword drill along with everyone else, then she looked away again.

Ryu tried not to stare in horror. She looked down, heard a hissing intake of breath from Shigan, then came First Brother Banig's bawl, "Unless you want to feel my rope on your backs, get to work!"

They practiced the sequence First Brother Banig had just demonstrated, Ryu frantic with questions. Presently Shigan came up next to her and whispered, "Petal gave us the wait signal," turned his back and walked away.

The wait signal was from their Redbark drills, a flat palm, for when they were too breathless or moving too quickly for talk. Ryu forced herself to lose two scraps in a row—both times taking bruising hits—which netted her kitchen duty for the next day. Then they ran out to play one of the chase-tackle-and-pummel war games First Brother Banig and Screaming

Hawk loved to watch.

That lasted all thousand years of the afternoon. At last the sun sank, or more to the point, one or the other of the leaders got hungry and called it quits for the day. Ryu straightened gratefully, rubbing her elbows and her right shoulder.

The others had, of course, first tried to make her a target, as she was the smallest. Now she was grateful for all that practice in contact fighting, as well as all she had learned about pain acupoints after rubbing salve into Muin's bruises from Yulin, for she had put her elbows and third knuckles to good use on would-be attackers.

Now they mostly avoided her, or pushed her to lead the attacks so she bore the brunt of the melee. It was during one of those that she'd landed on her right shoulder—but her assailant was limping badly, one knee already swelling.

On their way back from the far field, she overheard Screaming Hawk say to First Brother Banig, "If I don't see some improvement, let's invite the laggers to one or two entertainments, mmm?"

Her neck crawled; she strongly suspected she was meant to overhear, after losing those scraps that day. Her heart burned with hatred.

But it was worth it the next day, even though she got stuck with night soil duty and scrubbing pots. All new women got stuck with the worst work—and there was Petal, hauling water for the stacks of breakfast dishes. At least Enau Fan and Water Cat had not recognized her from the Sky Alliance competition, or they would have been instantly suspicious.

Ryu brought her stack of pots over to the tub of water, and they began to work side by side.

Before Ryu could say anything, Petal began whispering so fast that Ryu knew she had to have rehearsed it all. "Matu's first cousin was walking on the beach when he saw two of those neck-tattoo Shadow Panthers carrying unconscious people. Recognized you and Shigan. Returned and got the Kis and us Redbarks. We followed in a borrowed boat."

Ryu cast an astonished look at her, and bit back an exclamation.

Petal clapped another stack into the water, straightened up to wipe her hand across her brow as she looked around—and Ryu suspected she was seeing how Petal used to keep watch for her stepmother.

She went on, "We saw the ship, and one of the cousins said

he knew where it was going — he almost got recruited once, but a storm separated off their boat, and he got away. We sailed back. Raised the Ki family. We got some other volunteers, and hired a ship. How many here?"

"About sixty that I know of," Ryu said. "Not including the kitchen and laundry women who don't fight. How many do you have?"

"Thirty-two. Including me. They were arguing about who ought to scout, and I said I would, and no one listened, so when that storm was nearly done, I got two cousins to help me lower the lifeboat. We'll have to pay for it," she added. "I crashed it on the rocks."

"Petal, you are the biggest hero I have ever met," Ryu said under her breath.

Petal went right on scrubbing, her thin lips even thinner, but she blushed to the ears with pleasure.

"Two to one," Ryu said. "More, if we can recruit some of those women. Most are prisoners."

"I know," Petal began, then shut up moments before heavy footsteps trod up.

A fist swatted Ryu on the shoulder. "First Brother says that's enough, and to get out to sword practice, Firebolt."

Petal watched Ryu go, and returned to her job, having decided not to tell Ryu how many arguments had broken out among the Ki clan about what to do.

Petal had figured what sort of reception she'd get from the Shadow Panthers after crashing the boat on the shore, but she hoped that her scrawny form and her wandering eye would protect her somewhat. But she had no illusions about the darker side of human nature — she'd learned that by the time she turned fifteen, during her days at the inn.

Her eyesight was not strong, even on the good side. The world blurred, but she had learned to recognize people by the way they moved, before she could see their features. She glimpsed Shigan's extravagant grace and Ryu's tightly leashed power running past, and then again at the shooting range, when she was required to carry out fresh buckets of water for them to drink.

When Ryu came to pick up the dipper, she murmured, "Have they got arrows?"

Petal breathed, "Yes. Many."

"Then I've got a plan."

Both felt eyes on them, and Petal walked away without a

backward look.

One of the tattoos smacked Ryu on the shoulder. "Got your first hankering for a girl, Firebolt? You can do better than that scrawny thing!"

"I asked if there's hot water," Ryu said, striving not to sound truculent.

"You want tea? It's not hot enough out here?" Several turned their way, guffawing.

"For ginger tea. I've a gut ache," Ryu said. Then made a face, and clutched the front of her tunic over her stomach. "Oh, I need the privy," she moaned. "I think I got the squirts."

"Go, get out of here," the drill captain bawled.

Ryu threw down her bow and waddled away, clutching her butt as the Shadow Panthers howled with laughter.

She caught up with Petal just before the blind spot that she and Shigan had figured out before. Though there was a lookout post on a hill, the guards were mostly watching the bay, and the house. They could not see this turn in the road, which passed through a grove of great, spreading cypress whose shade was a brief but welcome relief while running back and forth.

Ryu put out a hand, and Petal stopped. "You look that way, I'll look this way," Ryu said, panting, and they stood shoulder to shoulder, facing the path in either direction as she got out the question she hated most. "Did Matu . . . say anything? About me?"

There was no mistaking Petal's surprise. "What should he say? Other than that you would probably have a plan, and that you'd need our numbers, and our weapons count. Which is six barrels of arrows, along with all the Kis having their knives, and most with swords as well. Four fighting staffs. Besides yours. We made sure to bring it."

"Thanks." Ryu wiped her damp face on her grimy arm. "Shigan and I will deal with the lookouts, and we'll signal. One half of your group comes in to attack, the other shoots overhead at the manor defense. I want to give you as much time as I can before the alarm goes up, so everyone has to be quiet. No talk, quiet oars."

"Be sneaky," Petal said. "I'll tell them. And my part?"

"How are you going to get the plan to Matu and the Ki clan?" Ryu asked. "The Shadow Panthers aren't going to let you go back."

"Yaso promised to find me," Petal said. "Actually, that's

why they let me go. They think Yaso is a secret Essence shaman. An augur at least."

"Yaso is . . . something," Ryu agreed. "All right. If you can get back safely, then find out from the women who wants to escape."

Petal jerked her head in a nod.

"You're a lifesaver," Ryu said. "I hope in your next life you get to be a . . . a princess."

Petal blushed, believing that Ryu was the real hero. But it was just like Ryu to make sure others' merit got recognized. That was the best thing about Redbark.

"We'd better part. I think I hear someone coming and I'm supposed to be in the privy."

They both hurried into the hot summer sun, moving in separate directions in case the lookouts turned their way. Ryu was thinking about Yaso, who had always said to her remarks about Essence mastery, "I am only a learner." She didn't believe Yaso to be a liar, it was just . . . Yaso seemed to belong to the world of, oh, scrolls, or something. Not quite the same world as everyone else.

She shook that off, and turned her mind to finding a spare moment to talk to Shigan.

That was made easier by Screaming Hawk, who could not resist those nights of wild drinking and his idea of entertainment. Once the carousing was well under way, Ryu slipped up beside Shigan, and told him what she'd learned.

"Plan?" he asked.

"Easy one we used back at Loyalty, the Hop of the Frogs. But first you and I have to take out the lookouts. I found rope, so we can tie them up."

"Tie them up? Alive?" Shigan regarded Ryu intently. "You know they will kill you if they get the chance. And they are going to go on to kill others when they get free."

"Maybe they won't," Ryu muttered. "Anyone can change . . ." She grimaced, looking away, until a female cry followed by raucous laughter tightened her face. "And some . . ." She breathed hard. "I really hate Screaming Hawk. I won't call him my brother. It makes the word obscene."

Shigan wordlessly clapped her on the shoulder—the surprisingly small shoulder, even after all this time. But he remembered Ryu's power when power was needed, glanced at that straight line of dark brows across Redbark Brother Ryu's frowning face, and shrugged.

FORTY-NINE

THE STRATEGY, THE READER following our tale may have noticed, was the same the pirates had used when attacking the monks' temple. The Hop of Frogs was one of the first the young cadets at Loyalty practiced. It was basic, so basic it was common throughout the world, but Ryu understood what the pirates hadn't: that surprise was the key element, especially if the forces were equal in number (as it was when pirates against monks) or there were more defenders than attackers (as now).

Ryu had no interest in war. She wanted justice, especially for the weak who could not get it for themselves. She did not consider (as Muin had been learning, for example) that the last run of boats to shore and the disembarking was the weak point of any water-to-land attack. But in this situation, she didn't need to understand. The last piece had landed on her mental Circle board, which was Screaming Hawk's weakness for presiding over those nightly entertainments, at which he was king, and everyone feared his slightest gesture.

The next night was full moon, and the hot, dry weather held, affording a cloudless sky. During the day, Ryu encountered Petal. All she had time for was, "Are the women ready?"

Petal sidled a glance both ways. "All. Almost all. Rosebloom said she would dose with sleep herb the ones who're likely to betray us."

Noise caused them to part, Ryu with no more than a curt

nod and a glance. She hadn't seen any sign of Yaso. She hoped that was a good sign.

Another grueling day of hated drills — it wasn't the heat so much as the wasted effort and the lack of understanding on the part of the drill masters how to effectively work together, rather than just making everyone obey — and the sun at last began its slide westward. Shigan and Ryu both fought the urge to look to the other for reassurance. These Shadow Panther tattoos might be haphazardly taught, but they were strong, and brutal. If they didn't strike to kill, they would maim for later play, which was even worse.

Petal had no problem getting to the herbs that the Shadow Panthers used for their recruiting expeditions, as they'd made her one of the cooks. The teenage girl named Rosebloom, who had been emphatic about escape, helped her prepare a punch for the few who had volunteered to become part of the Shadow Panther harem (as long as the treasure lasted), and who had tattled on others in order to secure their own place.

No one was particularly subtle, Petal had discovered. While the girls and women were required to wear the flimsy silks and ornaments the Shadow Panthers brought back as loot, the ones who relished their place wore a lot, jangling and tinkling whenever they moved, in order to draw attention. These were the ones Rose served the herb-laced punch to. The cleaning done, those women staggered to the far outbuildings they were housed in and fell into bed.

That was the signal for Ryu and Shigan, who left a short time apart to go to the privy.

They both had been trained to mark lookouts, and how often these were changed, so it was the matter of a moment to divide the inlet lookouts between them.

Ryu tucked the silver feather ornament into her sleeve for luck. Then she fetched a jug of the herb punch (into which Petal dumped a double dose) and several lengths of rope, which she stashed in a shrub. Going from lookout to lookout, she said, "Screaming Hawk sent out some punch as the night is so hot."

The lookouts all drank. By the time she'd been to her third lookout post, the ones at the first were asleep. She tied them up, and went to the next.

She'd gotten to her third when shouts from the other side of the inlet rang through the still, warm air. "Alarm," she thought, as one of the third set of lookouts peered muzzily in that direction.

It had to be now. She held her hands a little apart, then concentrated Essence into light, which glowed blue as Ghost Moon. She tossed it into the sky, and, just as she had when she and her brothers were small, burst the globe into a scattering of lights in the sky. As children, that was the closest they could come to fireworks between the very rare traveling fairs.

She watched in satisfaction as the sparkles died away, until Shigan panted up. "Replacements came out early," he said, and handed her a sword. "I did what I could, but two got away."

They lifted their heads: they could hear shouts fading, as the two ran for the manor.

She and Petal had briefly discussed trying to dose Screaming Hawk, First Brother Banig, and the rest, and had decided against it. Those Shadow Panthers used the herb too often for recruiting; if they tasted it, or felt the beginnings of the herb, they'd know, and raise the alarm.

As it was, they arrived sooner than Ryu would have believed possible—but by then the boats were landing. The arrows had only briefly been useful, but at least a few Shadow Panthers were dropped before the two sides met on the beach, and the second boatload stopped shooting and bent their backs to come ashore as fast as they could.

The Shadows Panthers were big, and brutal, but they were also drunk, a few so drunk they had forgotten to bring weapons, or assumed some grunt would be carrying them. The Ki clan scythed through them with their lethal knives.

Matu appeared out of nowhere. Ryu's heart lit with happiness as he thrust her staff into her hands. She threw away the huge, extra-long saber as a clumsy, useless thing, broke her staff apart in a quick twist, and then waded in, disabling Shadow Panthers right and left with smart blows to elbows, knees, wrists.

She was aware of everything around her in that inchoate sense: not individuals so much as the tide of battle. They were winning—some of the Shadow Panthers ran away, hoping the landscape hid them—when the women arrived, most carrying bundles of belongings.

First Brother Banig arrived, sword waving as he shouted, "Come back here!" The women mostly ignored him, except for one or two frightened, moonlit faces glancing back. They slowed as they waded out to the boats.

First Brother Banig reached the first of them, and in a slash, struck her down. The woman fell into the water, black blood flowing down her sodden garment, her armload of silk and the necklaces and hairpins she'd wrapped in it falling into the water.

With an inarticulate cry Ryu leaped over the water, and splashed down next to First Brother Banig. Who turned, and seeing who it was, gave her a nasty grin. "I always knew you were a traitor —"

He didn't get past that before she attacked. He tried to behead her with that sword, to find it tangled in one of her short staffs. The other came around and smashed into his throat. His head snapped back, and he slumped over the woman he'd just killed, dead.

Ryu swayed in horror. For a moment the world stilled around her as she sensed life lifting away from First Brother Banig, thin as smoke threading from a distant fire. But this was no distant thing: by her own hand she had killed someone. First Brother Banig would never waken again, at least in this body — some believed ardently in reincarnation; others insisted once your soul entered the domain of the King of the Dead, you were never again to enter the living world.

She did not know the truth of what came next, except that she had ended any chance he had of laughing again, enjoying a meal. Listening to music, walking the deck of a ship.

Killing the defenseless.

"Ryu." Shigan was at her side. "Come!" Her body jerked, and she heard noise again, felt her chest heaving as she panted, tasted brine on the heavy summer air. Then she saw the fight around them, and became aware that Shigan had been defending her as she stood motionless. She jerked again, swinging her staffs to the ready . . .

But the fight was over.

"We'd better go."

She looked around. "Not yet," she said.

"What? The boats are there. And there are so many of them still . . ."

She faced him. "Do you really want to leave that treasure for them to use to hire ships for recruitment? For rewards for killing and torture?"

His mouth thinned. "No. But I thought . . ."

"Tell them to go if they need to. But to leave a boat."

His lips curled. "I'm with you. Let's get it done."

Together they ran up the trail, past slumped, or groaning, or snoring, or deathly still figures. When they reached the manor, she discovered that Matu and Petal had come, and two or three others. They were in the process of removing, with murmured sutras, the shrine to the Kitchen God.

Shigan led the way to the treasure room in the main building. Ryu followed at first, but veered off as soon as Shigan and a few Kis began stacking and piling treasure in baskets and boxes and even in bolts of beautiful silk.

It wasn't enough.

Her gaze took in the massive room where the Shadow Panthers had caused so much misery. The strong pillars. If they took the gold and fine stuff, Screaming Hawk would merely replace it.

She had to bring it all down.

"Run!" she shouted to Shigan. "Get them to the boats!"

He gave a short nod, and led the way.

Her mood was strange, unreal and yet real—each sense preternaturally clear, yet her mind distant, as if she watched herself from far above—as she fetched wood from the stack, thrust it into the kitchen fire, then moved to points about the manor. "Burn," she said, cocking up her arm, and with all the strength of years of effort at pushing wind imps, sent fire shooting outward to scorch the fitted wooden beams holding up the ceiling. The flames caught hungrily.

When Shigan reappeared again, leading a trail of figures bowed under sheets and capes and silken screens bulging with treasure, Ryu turned in a circle, the flaming brand in her hand shooting fire in a bright, glowing stream to splash and ignite and join all the other little fires into one powerful conflagration.

Let the Essence go through you, Yaso says. She pulled it up through the ground beneath her feet and sent it out. Flash! Bright as liquid gold blazed the complicated charms etched into the wood by Essence geomancers to ward against the shaking of the ground when the dragons below stirred. Ryu tugged apart those charms and sent the Essence deep into the stone walls. *Burn*, she commanded voicelessly.

The manor burned.

As she stood alone, watching, the fires met and reached skyward. The stone walls uttered a thundering *crack!* and crashed slowly to the ground, hurling a fireball of sparks skyward, visible to all those waiting in the ship at sea.

You won't fix that tomorrow, Screaming Hawk, she thought.

Then she ran after the others. From the out-buildings behind her, she heard yells and curses as the drunks and herb-laced sleepers staggered out to see the manor burning. The Shadow Panthers howled with fury, fetched their weapons, charged . . . and ran straight into the Ki clan's defenders.

Shigan was waiting on the beach, watching for her. Behind Ryu, fire boiled up into the sky, sparks showering like fireworks. The flaming ruin was so bright that the glow beat on the underside of the clouds overhead.

Pinpoints of gold reflected in Shigan's black eyes as he said, "What did you do?"

"Make sure Screaming Hawk won't be recruiting any time soon."

Shigan gave his head a shake, and said, "Come on. Matu's got a boat waiting for us."

The rest of the escapees had already got the treasure loads on the boats, which sank nearly to the gunwales, then began paddling out to sea on the ebbing tide, to where the hired ship awaited them.

When the Ki clan saw what was on the boats, they stared in amazement from the massive firestorm down to the glittering piles in the boat. Were all these people prisoners? No one asked. They helped the new folk aboard—including a number of former recruits.

Shigan's first thought was to wonder how many were spies for the Shadow Panthers, ready to report wherever the ship went. Or maybe they were just following the treasure. He turned to Ryu, to find his Redbark little brother gazing skyward in a daze.

The sails clattered into place and the ship began to move the moment the boats were hoisted up.

Then cheers rang out over the water, ragged and hoarse. Ryu was still staring back toward the island until Petal nudged Matu, who strode out and waved at his relatives to quiet down. Then he turned to Ryu, his gaze checked, and he swung around and said to Shigan, "Do you know a Screaming Hawk?"

"That coward was the first to run," the oldest of the women snarled.

Petal nudged a teenage girl, who muttered something. Petal raised her voice. "Whether or not he's a coward,

Rosebloom says he sent pigeons."

Silence met that. Shigan asked, "To?"

"The masks, probably," Rosebloom spoke up at last, her eyes huge in her wan face. "They were doing some kind of attack drill thing on the other side of the island."

Silence met this, and uneasy looks. Shigan glanced at Ryu, who still stared as she struggled internally with the memory of crushing First Brother Banig's throat. Her mouth had dried. Was that really justice?

Shigan said, "In that case, let us off somewhere nearby. We're good at running. You take this ship and go wherever you were going to go." His eyes fell on a jeweled goblet fit for an imperial monarch — probably had belonged to one, his guess during the Yslan Dynasty, when fine etching replaced huge encrustations in royal tastes — and he added, "I also suggest hiding everything that isn't money, or getting a jeweler to take it apart. Some of those pieces are too distinctive, and Screaming Hawk loved gloating over it all so much he probably knows every crown and plate by sight."

"He does," Rosebloom said hoarsely, as her braid dripped on the deck.

"I don't think abandoning you is the right decision," one of the uncles began.

Matu was whispering with Petal.

Ryu looked up then. "We know how to run. We'll lead them off so you can get everyone back to Sky Island, or wherever you are going."

Shigan hid the urge to laugh when the adults all took his runty Redbark brother seriously — after looking at *him* with misgivings. Salutary!

Matu then spoke up in a grittily determined voice, "Petal and I are going, too. Redbark stays together." He was holding Petal's hand tightly, Ryu noticed, but — maybe it was this mood — it no longer hurt.

Shigan noticed as well, and wondered if that pairing off could possibly relate to whatever argument Matu and Ryu had had before the competition. Why would Ryu care — or were the Redbarks really monks?

There was no time to say anything, as the captain of the hired ship spoke up. "There's another island right off the east end of this one. We can be there before dawn."

FIFTY

SHIGAN TURNED TO RYU, who said, "Let's get off there. We'll take some of the treasure to buy us some new gear. If Screaming Hawk does come looking, they'll be sure to find that treasure in the shops. We can tell those shopkeepers we're heading north, which should create a trail for the Shadow Panthers. And we'll take the next ship south."

Matu's gaze lowered. "You'll need new gear. We forgot your travel packs on the ship."

Ryu could not look at him. Her heart knotted with a powerful mix of emotions: gratitude that he'd saved her face by not telling the others what she had confessed; lingering regret for that confession; a sharp awareness that the sweetness of hope was now no more than memory. Embarrassment, because that inner warmth when she looked at him had vanished like a candle blown out, but the confession was still there in his memory. Worst of all, it revealed to him she was a liar.

She longed with all her soul that she had kept her mouth shut.

"You remembered my staff," she said to the air next to Matu. "That's the most important to me. Thanks." She turned away. "Everything else can be replaced. Who was it who said we cannot carry our homes with us?"

Shigan saw that every one of those gallant wanderers looked blank, so he did not quote the poem from six centuries ago—but wondered how, and why, Ryu knew it.

The ship floated in on the last of the tide, two entertainer girls and Shigan having selected the gaudiest piece of treasure. They whispered together, arranging what they would say as they traded the items, and the girls promised to get on the next ship that took passengers.

"Better go fast. The tide is about to turn, and it's strong with Ghost Moon full," the captain warned.

Yaso was already in the lowered boat, imperturbable as always. Hastily Ryu scrambled down the side, the other Redbarks after—there was Shigan's thump, and two more.

They plied the oars. The ship turned the sails and the helmsman worked the rudder to catch the outflowing tide. The Ki clan lined along the rail to wish them farewell and good luck.

They reached the wharf and pulled their boat up onto the shore of what appeared to be a promising town bustling with people, at first glance more gallant wanderers than imperials, evident by the fact that they carried their weapons openly. Good, Ryu assured herself. Redbark would blend right in.

At the top of the wharf a double-tiered temple dominated the street, itself far from unusual. Ryu gazed in surprise at the crowd of merry-makers. She was used to seeing temples being quiet places, mainly peopled by monks or nuns, except for petitioners.

"Did we miss a festival day?" she asked.

Matu looked at her in surprise—then glanced away when he met her gaze. "I thought Redbark Sect would know . . ." He shook his head. "This is the beginning of harvest season, and for common folk, wedding season."

"I thought that was spring," Ryu said, wrinkling her nose.

"Both," Matu said as he gazed over at the temple.

Ryu slowed. She could see matchmaker booths under an enormous cypress that had to be centuries old, its branches hung with red ribbons on which prayers for matches had been written. Inside the temple, couples waited, some with families in tow, to make their bows and be married. Everywhere was red and gold decoration, banners, ribbons, and here and there, the red of wedding clothes.

As they passed, they heard the cries of people seeking a mate who did not want to pay the matchmakers. "I seek a wife to be mistress of my house," this man said loudly to a gaggle of giggling girls passing by.

"I am a man who owns five good laying chickens, and one goat," another man cried.

"Is it always men doing the shouting?" Ryu asked.

"Mostly," Matu admitted, and there was that muted surprise again. "People—common people tend to be more traditional, I've been told. Most of these are second and third sons. Girls' families tend to look for a match in groups." He tipped his chin toward the temple. "And likewise for older sons, if they are going to inherit."

Ryu missed the covert, curious looks the others sent her way, as if she ought to have known these things. She was thinking that it was good that the Sage Empress had passed laws making it impossible to sell daughters.

They left the great temple behind, and passed a smaller shrine to the Snow Crane.

"We'd better not dawdle," Shigan said.

Ryu sped up her steps—she could visit the Snow Crane shrine later. On her own. "A new pair of boots, that's what I need," she proclaimed in her deepest voice, stamping loudly.

That began a morning of shopping. None of them had slept, so they were heady with a kind of euphoric exhaustion that led to smothered giggling when shopkeepers saw the golden goblets and plates and pieces they pulled out for payment. Some wouldn't accept them, so they found a goldsmith who gave them money for the pieces.

"At a swingeing price," Petal said sourly as they walked away. "A hundredth of their worth. Robbery."

"Ha! We gave him an earful about Firebolt and the Redbark heroes sailing north to the secret Redbark Island, and if Screaming Hawk makes that goldsmith sweat, it's his own bad luck," Shigan pointed out, grinning.

Ryu grinned back. The Firebolt rumors had reached this island, that much was plain by the widened eyes and round mouths, which made her ears burn. At least no one suspected her. They seemed to think Firebolt was as tall as a roof, with fire in his eyes, and actual lightning bolts in either hand.

They bought new clothes, and Ryu even found new boots to replace her old ones, which were worn at the heels as well as gapping at the sides. No one said anything to her about feet not growing—they were too busy buying for themselves.

At noon, they wandered to the top of the street, as Ryu wanted to find out what ships were sailing next.

Then she stopped dead still. "Look!"

Coming in on the tide were four boats of Shadow Panthers, Screaming Hawk's gold-glinting hair ornaments winking in the summer sun.

"That was fast," Ryu said.

"Let's get out of here," Petal said tightly.

"We can't go to the wharf now. They'll see us," Matu said. "And we don't even know if there's a ship with spaces we can hire onto."

Shigan had been peering up the street toward the hill at the top. He said, "I believe I saw our solution. Come on."

No one argued — they all hoped he was right as he led them to the top of the hill, to where five streets came together. Here three very fine entertainment establishments vied for custom. Shigan headed straight for the one with an elegant banner saying SWANS' LAKE HOUSE.

Artfully draped young women danced about outside, luring custom by calling out to passersby.

Shigan went up to one, whose face brightened when she saw him coming, though her smile lessened when she took in his grimy clothes. "Is Madam Swan in?" he asked, and when she replied something about Madam being busy, he added, "Madam Nightingale sent me."

"Oh." Her expression cleared, and Ryu and Matu stared, having forgotten about Madam Nightingale.

A short time later they crowded around the fine desk of a handsome woman of forty or so very well-preserved years, dressed in silks embroidered with swans and butterflies with trailing wings.

"Are you the Comet, the dancer she wrote to me about?" she said abruptly to Shigan.

"Yes," he admitted. "That is, I danced for her. Not long, as it happens, but — "

"You'll dance for me. Tonight," Madam Swan said briskly. "It's Ghost Moon Full, and when people get done singing away the hungry ghosts, weddings are in the air. All the mountain people have come down to look around and spend. Competition is fierce for us on this square."

Shigan exchanged a glance with Ryu, then bent forward and said urgently, "I'll dance for you, but maybe tomorrow? You see, we are being chased by some Shadow Panthers, as it happens."

Madam Swan's face tightened. "Them and their recruiting again." She sighed. "It's getting so that all the likely youngsters hereabouts hide when they come strutting along. So? What's it to be? Do your leaps at the center of my Flower Dance, or find another hidey?"

"I'll dance," Shigan said, hoping the musicians would be worth it.

They were assigned a pair of adjoining small rooms. Matu took Petal's hand, put his head down, and marched into one, leaving the others to shrug and pass into the other, Yaso as quiet as usual.

Ryu gladly dumped her purchases, and began folding them into the new carryall she'd also bought. She usually walked with her staff in two pieces, but preferred to put it back together when stationary. She'd just twisted it and felt the pieces lock together with a satisfying *snick!* when the door banged open and Madam barged in, her face pale as paper.

"You did not tell me those demons are on a blood hunt!" Her voice dropped to a hiss.

"What?" Ryu squawked. Shigan just stared.

"By any chance, is that huge smoke plume the fishers reported from the north side of the island your work—oh, never mind. We don't have time to argue. If I'd known, I would have thrown all of you out, but the panther tattoos have not only the entire street blocked off, they have the bay blockaded as well. And there's one out in the square, ready to squawk if they see you coming—and then burn us down for retribution. Come on." She grabbed Shigan by the ear. "They are looking for *you*, Firebolt. You are still going to dance, but you will do it as a girl."

"A . . . girl?" Shigan asked, his voice rising. "But I'm not Firebolt."

"Doesn't matter. When I'm done with you, no one will recognize you, which does. You, too," Madam Swan snapped, pointing at Ryu.

"Shouldn't we avoid the stage?" Ryu said, backing away. This was disastrous!

"No! The best place for you *is* the stage," Madam snapped. "The custom is used to looking at bodies, not faces. Especially if you dance in mask. Some padding here and there, some gauzy drapes, plenty of eye paint and rouge on lips, and thank all the gods you have good hair. You'll do." She tugged at Shigan's topknot.

"Ouch," he said in a subdued voice.

"I can dance," Yaso spoke up unexpectedly.

Madam swung around, eyeing Yaso uncertainly. "You are a dancer?"

Yaso said — as usual — "I am only a learner. But I observed very carefully when we were at the Heavenly Nightingale."

Madam threw up her hands. "Just as well, I guess. I'll need to get you *all* on the stage. You! I take it you are the runt Firebolt?" She glared at Ryu.

"I don't call myself that—"

"That's the only good piece of news," Madam cut in. "If you are even half as good as rumor promises, then I count on you to defend my house if those tattoos do try tearing the place up. So let's put you at the back of the stage with the magicians. And take that," she added, pointing at the staff. "They will no doubt be searching the house. Is there anything that will identify you to them?"

Ryu thought of the treasure distributed through the town, and took out the bag of coinage from her carryall. Sliding it into her loose, rumpled clothes, she said, "Nothing now. Everything here is new, bought today."

Ryu broke her staff apart again, and took it with her down a narrow back stair, pushing through crowds of nervous, excited dancers and servants. She discovered that Petal had already been put into a musician's outfit and issued a hand drum. She was in the midst of having her face painted.

Matu was another musician — since the Shadow Panthers did not know him, he would be at the outside of the line of musicians. Madam put Shigan into the hands of a cloud of laughing, cooing dancers to be transformed to one of them, then she turned on Ryu. "Can you dance?"

"No."

"Play an instrument?"

"No."

"We can put you in a girl's outfit, and station you at the back with a fan. We just need to trim these eyebrows of yours . . ." Madam advanced on Ryu, who was backing away, shoulders hunched.

Madam stopped short, her experienced eyes narrowing as she stared down at Ryu's neck completely innocent of the protuberant larynx of a male, then the smooth chin that would never grow any beard. "I . . . see," she murmured, mostly to herself. *This* was the deadly Firebolt? Either rumor was more garbled than usual — and she was a mistress of garbling them — or the gods were mixed up somehow, because this girl could be no older than fifteen.

Either way, she would not deal with it now. "We'll fatten

you up with padding, girl's dress, and a mask," she stated firmly. "You'll ply a fan. Now, where is that other one?"

Yaso had vanished, but reappeared as the dancers were finishing up with Shigan. Who looked . . . odd, to Ryu, those long masculine bones softened by extravagant makeup, the strength of his lean form also softened by fluttering ribbons and gauzes. His outline had been judiciously padded.

Two dancers were quickly demonstrating some coy little fan moves, and how to twist at hips rather than shoulders, when Yaso appeared, equally tall, but far more convincing as a female.

There was no time to stare. The first dance was already in place when the door banged open and the Shadow Panthers streamed in, led by Screaming Hawk himself.

"Firebolt!" he roared. "If I have to rout you out you'll die in pieces!"

An insistent hand shoved Ryu into place, and she began fanning the players with an enormous decorative fan made of peacock feathers, matching the movement of a legitimate fan dancer on the other side of the stage, masked like Ryu.

The regular dancers had begun earlier. Male voices bellowed angrily, led by Screaming Hawk, "Get out of the way! Let's see your faces!" followed by the crash of dishes and tables and the thud of booted feet. Madam pushed Shigan onto the stage.

Yaso brushed by Ryu, a vision in white draperies. Ryu stared. Those curves suggested above and below looked real, not padded like Shigan's. And Yaso's round face . . . could Yaso possibly be a *she* instead of a *he*?

How could Ryu not have noticed? Except she had! She remembered Yaso quite well in summer tunics — never tight clothing, which certainly would have revealed a hint of those curves. Same with Yaso's face. Hands. Neck. All the things she was conscious of hiding herself.

Shigan was posturing away, almost but not quite comical in those exaggerated hip swings, the coy flutterings of the dance fan. It was those breathtaking leaps and turns that kept his dance from turning awkward — that, and the fact that Yaso, mirroring everything Shigan did, danced like a god of air and water spirits come among them.

Voices hissed in reproach as the Shadow Panthers pushed through the audience, and then, finding no one suspicious, thumped up both stairways. Ryu kept fanning as footsteps stamped back and forth overhead. Then the rumble of boots thundering downstairs, and someone shoved their way through behind the screens of the stage. Out front, there was Screaming Hawk himself, peering around the room — and at the dancers.

Ryu forced her gaze away. She did not want him feeling someone was watching him, and look more closely at the plumply padded fan dancer at the left. The tattoos joined him, uncertain what to do next as Shigan whirled and flirted, but then Yaso floated to the front of the dancers and drew all eyes.

Strings thrummed and drums throbbed. Shigan whirled and leaped. Then Yaso leaped, soaring overhead, poised for an impossibly still heartbeat high in the air, arms flung up and back, and for that instant, Ryu's breath caught in her throat as she gazed up at a swan in flight.

Not a swan. A crane.

An eyeblink, and that suggestion of a great snow-white crane dissolved into fluttering draperies as Yaso landed softly. Out in the audience, the tattoos stared, many of them blinking open-mouthed. A few heart-hungry for the beauty they had forgotten existed.

Screaming Hawk gazed, too, but then saw his searchers fascinated, and an angry flush rose in his face, as if he sensed a turning away from his lethal purpose. "Come on," he said roughly, smacking and kicking his followers into action. He needed to get away from this place and its uncanny feel. "We've got two more to search!"

Another rumble, and they were gone. The audience erupted into cheers, amazement mixed with exhilaration and relief.

"Free drinks for everyone!" Madam called. "As my humble apology for the interruption!"

The mood had changed to exhilaration and bright laughter. Another cheer rose, the wine flowed, the dancers danced.

Ryu fanned until her arm felt like it was going to fall off. Then at last, at last, it was over.

Customers still milled about, well-lit with the fine yellow wine. None of them, it seemed, wanted the amazing evening to end. Even the dancers crowded around one another, and ringed Shigan, exclaiming and admiring.

Yaso, Ryu saw, had slipped away.

She set down her fan, took up her staff, which she had laid against the back wall under a folded screen, and went in search. When she got to the room she was to share with Yaso and Shigan, she found all her neatly packed new things dumped all over the floor, along with Shigan's new things. She was glad she'd kept their money in her clothes, as more padding.

Yaso was there, but no longer carried a bag of herbs. He turned at Ryu's entrance. "It is time for me to say farewell."

"But—you can't—" She stopped, hearing how foolish that sounded. And added miserably, "You're leaving because I killed someone, right? Because I let passion overrule justice when I crushed First Brother Banig's throat?"

Yaso said gently, "That is a judgment you have passed upon yourself. I am leaving as I have nothing more to give you, beyond one last thing."

"But you're a . . ." Ryu stopped there. She remembered, quite clearly, that glimpse of the great white crane soaring in the air for that single moment, but she dared not sully that moment with words. So prideful, it sounded, saying that she'd had a god watching over her! As if she deserved any such thing! And what if she was horribly wrong? She amended her thought slightly. "You aren't an Essence Master, you *are* Essence."

Yaso said, "I am only a learner."

"Learning to be . . . a human?" Ryu asked, greatly daring.

"Yes." There was Yaso's bright, tender smile. "I was sent; there are those who seek protection and enlightenment for you. But very soon, perhaps, you will consider seeking on your own."

"Wait!" Ryu burst out. Questions streamed through her mind, from the frivolous (Did it really matter if Yaso was he or she—or maybe something else entirely?) to the heartfelt (Did *seek* mean people praying for her? Did the gods truly answer prayers . . . like this?) "They'll ask . . . about that dance. What ought I to tell them?"

"They will not remember it," Yaso said with a reassuring smile.

"You can wipe memories?"

Yaso laughed softly. "It is more that memory itself re-shapes on its own, cleaving to comfortable forms, those that fit everyday experience. A few might remember, perhaps."

"*I* will," Ryu stated stubbornly.

"You will," Yaso agreed, and then held out a locket on a long chain. "Here is the last thing I can give you. I made three Restoration pills. Keep them safe."

Yaso pressed the necklace into Ryu's hand, opened the door, and was gone.

FIFTY-ONE

RYU STOOD THERE ALONE, then slipped the long, sturdy chain around her neck and let the locket fall inside her clothes. It thumped below her ribs.

Then she paced around the room for a time impossible to measure, until Shigan turned up suddenly. Awareness of the here and now snapped back. Ryu noticed that the candle was guttering. Her eyes, which had not closed in sleep through two nights, stung with exhaustion as the aches in every joint and muscle finally reached her awareness.

"You look lost." Shigan's face was clean, his wet hair braided back—he'd just come from the baths.

In addition to exhaustion and a strange sort of grief, Ryu was now intensely aware of being sticky and grubby. "I'll sleep on the floor." she said as Shigan padded barefoot toward the bed. "I stink."

Shigan, also beyond exhaustion, uttered a husky laugh. "You just thought of that, after two years of kangs and inns and ships and monks and . . ." His voice cracked as a violent yawn seized him. "And Ki cousins?"

"What does that mean?" She crossed her arms over her chest, only aware of them being alone. And that was not a kang with a row of bedrolls, or the ground under the stars. It was a *bed*. With one quilt.

She'd be alone. In a bed. With Shigan.

"I always stink?" Her voice came out a squeak.

Shigan heard that high note, which registered as little-brother-too-tired-to-be-teased. He remembered then that neither of them had slept for how long? And there had been that fight, during which Ryu had killed First Brother Banig. Shigan was *glad* of that. He only wished Screaming Hawk's body lay back there on the beach, too. But Banig in his way had been just as bad — it was he who organized Cor's death, and Shigan remembered Banig's little grin, his glistening lips while it was going on.

He shook that away and glanced up, surprised to see Ryu still standing there.

He shed his outer robe, and stretched out in his loose undershirt and trousers. "Ryu. You've slept beside me for two years, and I remember times when we were all pretty ripe. You smell like you. I don't find it unpleasant. Familiar, yes. I — " *like your smell.* He stopped there lest it be misinterpreted. Except when did Ryu ever think in that way? "Come on." And he twitched the candle out.

Darkness fell. Ryu groped her way to the bed, which was plenty big enough for two. She really ought to sleep on the floor, but there was a pillow, and it felt so *good* to lie down. All her aches seemed to sink into the soft bed, as she listened to Shigan's familiar breathing at her side. Such a *comfortable* sound, that.

"Ryu." Shigan's voice was so close to her ear.

She blinked her way out of the well of slumber about to close over her. "Uh?"

"Yaso. Did you . . . see what I saw?"

"Yes. But don't ask — Yaso is gone. Said there's nothing else to be done for us." Ryu found that she could no longer attribute a gender to Yaso. She herself had found the expectations of gender to be pretty irrelevant to her life, until her disastrous confession to Matu. But Yaso seemed to . . . transcend even that.

"Nothing else to . . . I don't even know what to say to that."

"No more do I." Ryu sighed.

"But . . . thinking about it . . . and everything else. I feel dirty inside, young brother."

"From dressing up as a girl?" Ryu tightened all over.

"No, of course not! I didn't mind that. In fact, I told Madam I'll do it again. I promised to stay a month, unpaid. I'll dance as a girl, at least until the Shadow Panthers go back to their island."

"Oh." She sank back.

"It's . . . I was pretending to be someone else while I was already in disguise, and I looked up at Yaso in that perfect leap, and I swear he . . . He? I swear I saw a great snow crane soaring in the sky, so beautiful. So *true*. And then I was off to the bath with a pretty dancer. Nothing wrong with her. But I kept thinking of you."

"Me?" All Ryu's drowsiness snapped away like fog before a sudden driving wind.

"Don't misunderstand and go running off in disgust. I admire you; though you're junior to me in age, you're my elder in every other virtue Kanda wrote scrolls about. It's not just your honesty, or your finding justice where someone else might have said it doesn't exist. Or your amazing powers, which still seem half a dream."

Acutely embarrassed, Ryu mumbled, "Not really."

But words kept pouring out of him, his breath warm on the top of her head. "You never dwell in the past. Or gnaw at the future. You always see this moment, and how to better it. I cannot tell you how much I admire that." His voice was light, quick. In its own way, as attractive as a voice as Matu's. More — like a singer's, a little, the way it flowed along her nerves. Like a river of fireworks in all the hues.

"Uh?" she said cautiously, and wondered when he was going to comment on the banging of her heart. Surely he could hear it.

The bed shifted — he had rolled away to lie flat on his back. He crossed his arms behind his head. Part of his long, silky braid spilled over her arm, cool and damp still from the bath. Smelling of the summer herbs he favored. She resisted the sudden impulse to stroke it, to feel if it was really that silky.

"I think I need you to know. About myself. Who I really am. Was," he amended quickly.

"You aren't a traveling player apprentice who ran away?"

"I did run away. But from . . . the palace."

"Palace," she repeated. "Which palace?"

He breathed out a soft laugh. "You are probably the only person in the world whose reaction I fear, because it won't be approval, much less avarice or expectation: the imperial palace."

She turned on her side, closer to him, but all she could see was the silhouette of his profile as he gazed at the ceiling, dark against the pale wall behind him. "You ran away from the imperial palace players?"

"Ryu, what I'm trying to tell you is that I'm a prince. The first imperial prince, actually."

Ryu had just been considering whether she could confess, too—whether an imperial player was too close to that emperor to risk, but when she heard that, her thoughts ran into a wall, and splatted flat, stunned.

"Ryu? Say something."

He rose on one elbow, looking down at her. All he could see was a pale, round face, which turned away. Recoiled.

"You're . . . you belong to *him*?" she repeated, struggling to hide the instinctive spurt of horror. The emperor was not here. Shigan was . . . Shigan. Whom she'd been traveling with and fighting next to, yes, and sleeping next to, all this time.

"Him?" Shigan repeated, a curious note in his voice now. "You know my father?"

"No," she exclaimed, too shrill to her ears. "No," she said again, consciously lower—her best boy's growl. "How would I know an emperor? It's just, when I hear the word *emperor* I think of wars and beheadings and . . ." She realized she was babbling, and stopped.

"But you heard it when we were at Loyalty, as I recall," he retorted—quite reasonably. "Swearing allegiance every festival day. You didn't seem to worry about beheadings then."

"Ayah! We weren't gallant wanderers then," she said, knowing it sounded foolish. She shifted the subject. "Why did you run away? And to Loyalty? Couldn't you get a general as a tutor, if you wanted to be in the army? No, princes command, don't they?" Though there was scarcely a hand's breadth between them, she felt as he had become an island and each new disclosure floated her on a disintegrating raft farther out to sea. "If you're a prince, you could just make yourself a general."

"Imperial princes don't command. Or make themselves anything," Shigan retorted—he sensed withdrawing where he'd meant to get closer by sharing the truth that he had hidden all this time. "We're forbidden to so much as hold a weapon. Unless it's a play one. I learned dance, and tumbling, but I never came near a real sword . . . oh, none of that matters."

He flopped back and talked to the ceiling again, in a quick, soft voice. "You know who my father is. My mother is a princess in her own right, daughter of Prince Ran of Ran Island—"

"I know," she muttered. "The only island still ruled by one family. Kings until the treaty with the empire first year of the

Yslan Dynasty."

Shigan didn't understand why Ryu sounded so wary. He felt obliged to say, a little defensively, "My parents are both excellent in their own ways, but my mother is a worrier, and my father . . . ayah, he wanted a sage scholar for a son and I was never that. My eldest sister tried hard to help me become a scholar — I realized that only later. The only one who understood me was my next sister, Manon. She's the real scholar, always obeys the rules, so I did the things she didn't dare do. It was a triumph when I could make her laugh." He smiled reminiscently.

"Manon really understood my desire for freedom. She, and to a certain extent, her mother, who is otherwise a model for decorum. It was her mother in whose pavilion I was able to take the dancing lessons, along with Manon, who took dance to gain grace. She didn't like the tumbling — they both thought it too dangerous — but they loved watching me . . ."

He sighed, remembering those happy days. "Manon used to have to go off to study, and I would work at some new trick in order to surprise her. She said waiting to see what I learned was always the best part of her day. It was also with Manon and her mother I tasted my first wine. I could be myself with them. They understood that trying to make a scholar of me was like playing a flute to a pig. Everyone else was so strict, and horrified at the idea of a prince performing before other eyes."

He sighed again, wearily. "I got into trouble. To teach me . . . something, I was to be sent off, ostensibly as a governor, as if I was a real governor at fifteen. I knew it would all be a sham. My job would be to trot out dressed in silk and gold, and speak the words they put into my mouth. Like a performer, I tried to say — the very thing they despised, but no, *this* was to be proper ritual and protocol, a *very* different thing. And yet, someone didn't want me even as a puppet — no, I don't *know* that. I don't know *anything* . . ."

He sighed his breath out a third time, more sharply. "I'm whining. Before I left, an epidemic of some sort swept through the inner palace, making my steward and my chief personal attendant too ill to travel. For a short time it looked as if they might cancel the trip altogether but then someone pointed out it might be better to get me away, lest I catch it. The next thing I knew, I was on a ship full of strangers, tended by a steward and body servant I'd never seen before. Who didn't know me."

"How could people not know you?"

"Because our faces are not to be seen by common people, except at great events. When we did go into the city, it was always in a kind of disguise, though we had guards following behind."

"Oh."

"Ayah! I'm telling this so badly. I was kept by these attendants in my cabin, for safety. Then one day, after a lot of sailing, we stopped for supplies. Could I even go on deck? I could not. The two guards at the door were firm about the risk of illness, or pirates, or comets, or dragons, and the only place I could go was to the privy, and they always walked me there and back."

"So you were a prisoner," Ryu said.

"Essentially. Though respectfully tended, with all the comforts, and all for my own safety. The ship stayed out in the harbor, you understand. All I could see was water through my single window. I could hear stamping overhead, and distant shouts as supplies were brought in. Then my door opened, and instead of the steward bringing the tray, it was a scribe apprentice, my age. He even looked somewhat like me. He pointed that out, we laughed about it, and in talking, he wished for my life. I already wanted the freedom of his, and said, why don't we try it? Just for fun."

Ryu had found her voice. "You traded places with someone?"

"Xia — his name was Xia — said we could have this meal together and he could pretend to be a prince and I the scribe. But he kept asking questions about ritual, and what kind of commands I could make and where were the tallies of command, while distracting me over the food."

"Distracting?"

"Yes — I'd be about to take a bite, and he thought he saw a rat on the floor, and I was going to drink but he pointed out the window at a passing boat. I never did get anything to eat, but I wasn't really hungry anyway. He was sweating. Something was wrong, I could sense it."

"Didn't you say someone else was supposed to bring food?" Ryu asked. "Is that a normal thing, people changing the rules? I thought there was ritual for everything, even sneezing."

"There is, though not quite as much on board a ship. His being so nervous made me nervous. I jumped to the door, saying I had to go to the privy, and he tried to stop me, but remembered the clothes. If the guards caught him in my clothes it would be instant death. I said I'd be right back. I only wanted one walk around the ship, with no one herding me back inside as if the very air was poisonous."

Ryu said, "You escaped then?"

"The last thing I saw was his face, which was very pale by then. I ascribed that to his knowing that impersonating one of the imperial family is punishable by death, but I was not going to blab. I dropped my gaze very properly, the guards saw my lowly scribe apprentice clothes, and let me pass."

"That easy?"

"You know as well as I do that clothes place you in a category. No need to look at faces. Anyway, perhaps they were distracted by the noise on deck. I just wanted that walk on deck. But then, when I saw the supply boat about to leave, ayah, there I was in apprentice scribe clothes. I knew there would be no better chance than that, and he wanted to be a prince, so I'd let him be a prince for an afternoon. I ran down just as I was, and climbed into the boat a moment before they pushed off."

"Scribe Apprentice Xia didn't know?"

"I never saw him again. In the time it took for the boats to get away I kept expecting a cry to go up, guards to boil out and arrest everyone in sight, but nothing happened. The boat went to shore. And there I was, wearing scribe clothes, without so much as a tinnie, but for the first time in my life I was free. My first idea was to have an hour or two to myself, poking about wherever my eye took me. Of course they'd come after me and I'd be locked up again, but I wanted to enjoy perfect freedom while I could. But then the ship sailed away. I thought of Xia pretending to be me. I wished him fun as a prince, and ran well away from the harbor, laughing as I went. I still couldn't believe I'd escaped."

"What did you do?"

"Mostly starve," Shigan said, smiling up at the ceiling, his voice slow and reminiscent. "Until then I'd had food whenever I wanted it. What I wanted. It never occurred to me that I might have to go out and find it."

Ryu had risen on her elbow, and they lay there, less than an arm's distance apart, as Shigan's slow, soft voice reminisced, carried her into utterly unknown waters. The window glowed silver as Ghost Moon slid downward toward the western horizon.

"People were staring at me, which I scarcely noticed, because I *had* been thinking. There was something odd about the entire incident. I kept coming back to Xia's sweaty face as he distracted me from picking up the food, as if he had to . . ."

"Add poison to it?" Ryu asked. "That's what happens in the wanderer tales. But surely he'd add the poison before the food ever got to your room."

"I thought about that. He'd be under the cooks' eyes in the kitchen area, then under the guards' eyes, so maybe he had to do it when he was alone with me? I've gone back and forth, believing and not believing. For one thing, what would he do with my body, if he really wanted to poison me and take my place?"

"He'd have to be working with someone else," Ryu stated. "Who'd do that part."

"There was that steward, who I didn't know . . . oh, it's all guesses, and I've been around and around in my own head for the past four years, and have come no nearer to any explanation. I'll just say that my instincts had prompted me to get away. So I decided that since I hated being a prince, I might as well make the best of things, whatever the truth was. Xia wanted to be a prince—let him live my life and see how he liked it."

Ryu wondered what the horrible emperor thought, but stayed silent.

"I assume he kept on being me, for . . . but let me stay with that day. My first day of freedom, which was completely unlike anything I expected. I became aware that people were staring at my golden hair ornaments, so I pulled them out. When I got hungry I sold them. I expect every single vendor regarded them as stolen, the way they scowled at me, and offered a fraction of what they were worth. Not that I cared. I was very proud of figuring out how to get a room at an inn, for I'd read those stories, too."

"I'm surprised they let you," Ryu commented, her voice too low for Shigan to hear her sour tone. That emperor surely would hate stories about justice.

"My sister smuggled them back for me when she bought scholarly books. Which I shared with Vaion, at first reading aloud, until he could read himself. I copied the way the wanderers spoke to one another. It worked! I ate off street vendors, and looked for traveling players. A day later I found an excellent company, but they would not even let me try— they didn't want strangers, unknown name, unknown family. Because I dared not say who I really was. Same with another.

A couple days after that I found a third, much scruffier. They were willing to audition a no-family stranger — for no pay, they said, until I was trained — but when I heard them play, I knew I couldn't do it. They dared to call that noise *music*."

He drew the word out on a long sigh. "It sounded like they tortured those instruments for the King of Hell. I couldn't bear the thought of living with that each day, even though by then I was starving, because I'd run through all the coins, not having any idea of their worth. To cut it all short, before long I was filthy, as I hadn't thought to get new clothes. Until I spotted someone's washing hanging on a line. I stole the clothes you saw me in when I reached Loyalty, and left the scribe robe as trade. Then I had to learn to dress myself."

Ryu suppressed an inward laugh, remembering how terrible Shigan had looked on his arrival at Loyalty.

"I learned about soil gatherers, which I did for a long day of wretched toil, which furnished earnings that would either get one a miserable box of a room that I shared with three others, along with rats, fleas, and roaches, or I could get a little food, but not both. Then I came across a pitch-pot game, being played for money. I joined, won, kept on winning until the entire group started shouting that I was a cheat and chased me, dizzy with hunger as I was. I had decided in my utter failure to go to the garrison and surrender myself when I saw the testing for the army in the outer court. So I stopped, deciding I'd try one last time. Of course the gamblers didn't dare follow me there."

"And you got in."

"And I got in. The test wasn't that hard. I'd never held even a wooden sword in my life, but my brother and cousins and I had played duel with sticks when we weren't seen, and I had a very basic sense of block and thrust. And though I had never read *The Way of the Blade* I was able to quote enough bits of scholarly texts, and I knew how to ride. Maybe they were desperate to make up their numbers, but at any rate they took me. You know the rest. As for the scribe, he seems to have been successful at being me. For a time, anyway. The first I knew of his failure was that search at Te Gar."

"It was *you* they were searching for?" Ryu remembered the drawing the searchers held, and gasped. "It *was* you! They must have found out."

"Yes — I don't know how," Shigan went on, and then in the flat voice he only used when deeply disturbed. "I also don't know if those mercenaries were sent to Loyalty to kill me."

Ryu was going to scoff, but then hesitated. If he really was an imperial prince . . . "Did the *emperor* send them to kill us?"

The bed shook as Shigan laughed silently. "If Imperial Father sent someone, none of us would be here today. And he wouldn't send a pack of mercenaries — think about how bad their training was. He'd send the Dragon Claw Army if he wanted a wholesale slaughter, or he'd send the ferrets to just find and kill me, probably in my sleep, in the hut, with no one stirring, if he wanted a quiet assassination. But he wouldn't send those fools. Though I have to admit they nearly did get to me, until you saved me."

She stared into his moonlit face, stunned. "You think someone sent them to slaughter all of us to make sure you were in the mix? No," she breathed, remembering the group that had encircled Shigan as he fought with his back to the wall. "They *did* go after you," she exclaimed. "I thought at the time you'd gotten mouthy at them and they went at you because of that."

Shigan's long phoenix eyes widened, and his brows slanted steeply, barely visible in Ghost Moon's silvery light. "Who had any time to talk that night?" The humor faded from his face. "You saw that, too?"

"I did. But no one else did. Everything was so chaotic. And I completely forgot until now. They were after you, because you are a prince? That is so . . . cruel. But why? And how did they know you were even there? And, is Shigan one of your names? I remember Ul—being told that princes have a lot of names."

"I took Shigan from my favorite play," he said. "The only person who knew I ran was the sister I mentioned. That is, I sent Manon a letter. Before I got on the ship to Loyalty, I used my last ornament, a jade ring my grandmother had given me, to hire a street scribe to write the letter for me, because I was afraid someone might recognize my handwriting. I dictated it in the ancient tongue, making references to that play she knew I liked. And of course I didn't send it to the palace, but to her favorite bookstore. Of course I could not send it by imperial courier, so someone else might have found the letter, and it never even reached her. But who would know that letter was from me? And then send mercenaries?" He shook his head. "I've lain awake so many nights, trying to figure that out — hoping I'm wrong and that attack was something else entirely."

"The mercenaries *could* have been anything. You remember, Commander Weken said often that to be in the army was to walk with sudden death as a shadow. One of the reasons why I wanted to leave," Ryu said.

Shigan regarded her in the darkness. "Afraid? *You?* I've seen you take on mercenaries and pirates and those Shadow Panthers pretty much by yourself!"

"But I chose when to fight. Not that I wanted to, always," she muttered. "Anyway I wasn't sent into battle by someone I didn't know, for reasons I could not understand. An army fights when it's told to fight. I don't want to talk about armies. Your sister likes bookstores?"

"She's a real scholar, my sister. She ought to be writing the Imperial Examination. Maybe she will be, before too long. That's my only regret, not seeing her. I wish you could meet her," he added, and then, thinking of Vaion, still round-faced at twelve in his mind. "And my brother. You'd like him. You remind me of him sometimes."

"I wouldn't know how to talk to a prince or a princess," Ryu muttered. "Especially imperial ones."

"Oh, Manon is gracious . . ." Shigan's physical exhaustion had caught up with him at last, and he was taken by a sudden, huge yawn. "Maybe that's the wrong word. I can't think of a right one."

"It doesn't matter, because I won't be meeting her," Ryu said firmly. "I've heard enough about the imperial island to know that gallant wanderers aren't welcome there. No danger of *my* trespassing!"

Shigan yawned again, and Ryu caught it, yawning so hugely her jaw cracked and her eyes stung.

"Sleep well," Shigan murmured, suppressing a last impulse to pull Ryu's small body against him. This wasn't Vaion, who had crept into his bed in their early days when they lived with their mother, and thunder had shaken the roof. This was Brother Ryu, who might not like being hugged. Yes? No? He lifted an arm . . .

Ryu curled up, back toward him, and sank gratefully into slumber.

His arm dropped back to his side.

FIFTY-TWO

RYU WOKE CURLED UP against Shigan's long back.

It felt . . . good.

Really good. The tingle with Matu had been a distant glimmer to the sun of this new sensation.

Which brought her horrible mistake with Matu to mind — Matu who might come in at any moment, because Redbark companions had usually shared rooms, coming and going without much thought about it.

She really needed to think now!

She eased away from Shigan, and slipped out noiselessly to get that long overdue bath.

The bathhouse had private stalls, and she had Redbark's treasure money still in her grimy clothes. She paid for a luxury bath, including having her clothes washed and dried. Then she sank into the tub, wondering where to start that thinking. The entire night seemed like a dream. Yaso's dance — she recollected quite distinctly Yaso's words about memory, but even so she wondered if she had dreamed that image.

No. She remembered every word of the conversation, and she had the locket with the three pills. She glanced at the bench with her hair clasp and the locket on its chain, reassured to find it still there. Three pills. What did Restoration even mean? She knew one thing: she would give one to each of her brothers when she saw them again, and the last one could go to Mother, so she could figure out how to make more, if they really did work.

Then she let herself consider Shigan's astounding confession. Her first reaction was a huge sigh of relief that she had never told him anything about her past. She believed he'd wanted to escape – who wouldn't – but still! It was much too weird, too close to The Story in a way that she couldn't explain to herself. She knew if she were to see her father here, right now, he would tell her to ditch Shigan and run. And keep on running.

But she didn't want to ditch him! He had proved himself over and over. She didn't even want to think about life without Shigan. Redbark would be nothing but a hollow mockery without him. Especially with Matu looking at her as if she had spiders crawling out of her ears. Oh, *that* was a hard lesson – never again would she let herself feel like . . .

No, *that* rice was already cooked. For an intensely sweet moment she was right back there on that bed next to Shigan, every nerve-conduit in her body alight with a feeling more powerful than the most powerful Essence charm.

But the lie she had been living lay like an invisible sword between them. Who was it who had asked about it being all right to lie? She couldn't remember, though she did recollect Ul Keg saying once that lies are knots that all untangle eventually. Father had said it was all right to lie to protect the family, but Matu had recoiled from her when she told the truth. In some ways it seemed that in relations between people, well water truly wouldn't touch river water . . .

The noon bells rang. Already? Had the others already done drill?

She hastened out, and discovered her clothes were still damp, but that would feel good in the summer heat. She dressed and pulled on her new boots.

When she got back, she found Shigan having breakfast with Madam. "Young Firebolt," Madam Swan said. "Are you going to stay as well?"

"I . . ." She looked from her to Shigan.

Who grinned. "You don't have to say anything this moment. We can't slip away until Screaming Hawk goes back to the island."

"I've paid my young rumor-mongers well to suggest that you Redbark heroes left for Cracked Bell Bay yesterday, on the east side. Gallant wanderers seldom go there as the navy has a garrison there, controlling that passage."

Ryu ducked her head, mumbling her thanks, and Shigan went on, chortling, "Guess what Madam Swan was just teaching me — how to drink like a lady, and incidentally, how to conceal poison."

Madam Swan laughed. "Not conceal poison, precisely. Watch your words, or you'll have rumors spreading that I poison my customers. No luck more fatal for my house! Merely, if you suspect someone is trying to poison you, you come prepared, of course: extra fabric in your sleeve to soak up the wine, or tea, or medicine. Then you drink properly, the way the nobles do . . ."

She lifted the cup, shielding her mouth with the wrist of the other hand, her long sleeve effectively hiding her lower face. "Any time my girls suspect some customer is trying to slip something into their wine, they spill the wine down their sleeve. And I test it with a charmed silver needle."

Shigan mirrored her movement, drinking very properly behind his wrist, as gracefully as she had, after which he disclosed a damp spot on the wrist of his sleeve.

He flashed a wicked grin. "Forcing people to drink those kinds of herbs is a favorite tactic of Screaming Hawk," he said. "Which is how the subject came up."

Ryu suspected he'd really been thinking about that Scribe Apprentice Xia and whether or not he'd brought poison into Shigan's princely room on that ship, and then she wondered what the unflappable Madam Swan would say if she knew she was sitting over breakfast with an imperial prince.

Ayah! Was a prince really a prince if he didn't have a crown and the robes and the guards and so on? Oh, they talked about imperial blood, but Ul Keg had read her some histories in which kings and princes had been reduced to commoners and exiled. Not to mention killed.

One of Madam's workers came in, and as Madam turned to her, Ryu sat down and helped herself to congee with fresh wolfberries, since it was sitting right there.

"A lot of foot traffic," the girl said, eyes wide.

Madam touched her painted nails to her bottom lip. "I thought business would dry up what with those Shadow Panthers rampaging about. It usually does until they leave again." She frowned at the girl. "Is it them?"

"No masks, no tattoos. Shiar says she checked."

"Then a fleet of merchants. No, they'd be at the stores. It must be gallants on the way to some contest or sect conclave,"

Madam said briskly. "We'll start early. You!" She pointed at Shigan. "Go rehearse, and please, remember a *little* hip-swinging entices. Waggling your butt like you're banging side drums is not enticing."

Shigan shot a rueful grin Ryu's way, and went off with the dancers.

Ryu finished off her congee, and took the bowl along the back way to the kitchen to dump it in the barrel containing dirty dishes. Then she continued out back, hoping to find a spot to practice Heaven and Earth, but the courtyard was full of rehearsing dancers and the house carpenters repairing little tables that Screaming Hawk's searchers had smashed the night before. The urge to find Matu and Petal withered as soon as it sprouted, and she wandered disconsolately out to the street.

I've ruined Redbark, she thought as she circled the square under the blazing sun. Yaso was gone, and though there had been an explanation, she still felt a twinge of guilt, as if she were at fault. She tried to shake it off, suspecting the guilt was due to her having killed First Brother Banig, who was still very dead. He would always be dead. If he did reincarnate, he would be another person entirely. Which raised the question: would it truly be *him*? What made you *you*, having a body, or having a soul?

She turned away physically, nearly bumping into a burly traveler in a dusty robe. He carried a sword. She gave him a word of apology and made the gallant wanderer bow. He returned a curt nod, and walked away.

Ryu turned in the opposite direction, sighing up at the Inn of the Five Heroes across the way from Swans' Lake House. A cluster of young men stood in front, as if debating going inside. She stepped past them, brooding on the disintegration of Redbark, which she had thought would last forever.

Nothing did! She knew that! But it had been so wonderful . . . if only she had appreciated it at the time, instead of assuming they'd all be together for . . .

Her thoughts stumbled over the memory of her conversation with Shigan. She actually shivered. What a strange, *very* strange close call. All the more reason, she scolded herself, *never* to give him or anyone else any hint of her true origin.

But Redbark. Could she save it? Was it Matu or Petal who had really raised the Ki clan to save them? Matu had said that Redbarks stayed together, but he still avoided looking at her.

Then there was Shigan, who . . . Did he really want to be a

gallant wanderer forever? Part of Redbark, a pretend sect that was really another of Ryu's lies?

Noise some streets away caused her to go still as prey scenting a predator. Men, shouting. Angry shouts. Getting closer.

She glanced down the main street toward the wharf. The heat shimmer made it difficult to see, but it looked very much like a big group of people walking up the street. Not a mob — too orderly for that. Warriors?

An army of Shadow Panthers? But they never marched in rows.

She turned again as the shouting from the other direction approached. Roars. That was a mob! When she recognized Screaming Hawk's hoarse bawling, she skirted more gallant wanderers clustered around the steamed sweet-potato vendor, and shot inside Madam Swan's like an arrow from a bow, to slip inside the common room, and down to side windows, where Shigan had told them once that many such houses put tiny peepholes in the silk between the lattices, so they could scan outside for trouble — or for wealthy prospective customers — and not be seen.

Screaming Hawk was shouting some message over and over as his bully boys rammed their way through the throng, shoving people out of their way. Once or twice they grabbed teenage boys and very young men and held them so that Screaming Hawk could look into faces, then sent them sprawling on the ground with kicks and punches.

"Firebolt!" Screaming Hawk roared. "You and Shigan get out here, and I'll give you a chance to fight for your lives! If I have to come after you, I'm going to make it last for weeks — after I burn down this entire town! But first I'll kill this rat, who I caught spreading lies that you were gone!"

And one of the tattooed men shoved a boy of ten or twelve, who had been bound with his hands behind him, the rope tight around his throat. He stumbled and choked.

Ryu debated sharply, and decided to fetch her staff — there was no chance she'd let Screaming Hawk kill that boy — but then something very surprising happened.

All the gallant wanderers clustered in front of the five emporia on the square turned, producing weapons. The vendors left their wares, pulling swords, staffs, even a bow or two from under carts or from behind barrels and baskets. Then they formed rapidly into lines. Army lines, surrounding

Screaming Hawk and his crowd. To her astonished eyes, she recognized the formation, and the flag that appeared in one's hand: ready for the signal to surround and attack!

The flag came down, a drum rumbled, and the warriors charged the Shadow Panthers.

The little boy got shoved aside as Screaming Hawk and the rest brought out their weapons, but they had been taken utterly by surprise, and they had never worked together in defense. Crack! Smash! Thud! Shadow Panthers began dropping to the ground.

Ryu slipped out and ran to the boy, dodging slumped figures and knots of fighting. She lifted up the dazed boy, who was bleeding from his nose, his face bruised.

"Come inside." She half-lifted him, though he was almost as tall as she was, and half-carried him up the stairs to Madam Swan's doorway, where a couple of the less frightened of the staff took over, untying him and cooing over his hurts.

In the square, a pile of the warriors dressed as gallants had landed on Screaming Hawk — who was now bound tightly, his face purple as he swore revenge. Ryu looked for the leader — Sky Island Sect? Definitely someone army trained —

Then the noise from the direction of the harbor resolved into the rhythmic stamp of a march, and cold serried through Ryu when she recognized the armor and brown clothes of the Imperial Army.

Ryu ran inside and back to her window peephole, but found that the staff was already crowding around. Ryu unlatched another window, and pushed it out at the bottom no more than a finger's width, so that she could peer through the crack between its frame and the window frame.

A slim man of just above medium height, dressed in black, had emerged from the swarm. He moved like a warrior, with a sharp, commanding gaze. At a gesture from him, Screaming Hawk and the rest of the Shadow Panthers who were still on their feet were led off in one direction.

A movement at Ryu's side, and she looked up at Shigan, who was damp from dancing. His breath hissed between his teeth. "That's Fai Anbai," he whispered.

"Who?"

"Head of the imperial ferrets."

"Chasing after the Shadow Panthers?" Ryu ventured a guess. "That is certainly an excellent thing. Right?"

Shigan's profile had stilled. He glanced down at her, his

mouth twisted. "I wish it was that. But ferrets wouldn't hunt down someone like Screaming Hawk."

Ryu's face rounded in horror. "They're after *you*?"

"I believe the target is my imperial lowness. I don't see how they could have found me . . ." His hand came up to wipe a damp strand of hair from his face and tuck it into his headband. His fingers shook. "They're here. They found me," he whispered.

Cold pooled in Ryu's belly.

The last of the defeated Shadow Panthers had vanished, but the armored warriors had lined up in five precise groups, one before each emporium.

The ferrets, or army warriors, or whoever they were who had dressed as gallant wanderers had also formed up, so that the entire area was enclosed.

Fai Anbai stood alone in the center. As he raked his gaze across the front of the houses, he spoke in the ancient form of Imperial, which few beyond scholars and courtiers and nobles — and royals — understood. "Your imperial highness," he said, lifting his voice to be heard. "I have no orders concerning any others you are with. It is understood that they who do not know your true identity are not committing treason. But the moment I repeat this message in the common tongue, every person intentionally or unintentionally harboring you becomes a captor in our eyes. The sentence for seizing an imperial prince is death."

And then he held up a golden tally, which gleaming brightly in the sun.

Matu said from Shigan's other side, "I don't understand."

"Don't go," Ryu said, catching at Shigan's arm. "We can get away."

His arm was like steel, he was so rigid. He looked down into Ryu's face, his eyes desolate, his mouth curved in a bitter smile. "You didn't understand? It's everyone's life against mine. He just made the cost too high." Shigan glanced Matu's way, and said in the common tongue as he turned his palm toward Ryu, "Stay with him."

"Her," Matu said. And then corrected hastily, "Him." But the crack in his voice, his red face, caused Shigan to turn violently to Ryu, his eyes wide with question.

Outside, Fai Anbai raised his voice. As he had promised, he began in the common tongue, "By order of the Emperor of the Thousand Islands — "

"Coming!" Shigan shoved the window open to shout. And to Ryu, his gaze searching her eyes as if they stood alone, just the two of them — without an army outside poised for action.

What came out of his mouth was, "But I've seen you in the privy."

"Bamboo."

Impossibly, they both laughed, but her voice cracked, half-sob, her eyes stinging, and he saw the truth there at last. She wanted to cry *Don't go*, but she'd heard the utter conviction in that voice outside. These imperials would fight to the death.

"I can't let them do it," Shigan whispered, sick to the heart. Ryu? A girl? How *could* he have missed that?

Something pressed into his hand, and he looked down to discover it was Ryu's fingers. Such a small hand, a hand he knew so well, callused like his, yet it had never occurred to him that this could not someday be a man's hand. "Inside the necklace is a Restoration Pill Yaso gave me," she said, her voice trembling as she tucked something into her sash. "Take it when there is no other . . ."

She stepped back. He looked at Ryu once more, who he knew so well, and yet didn't know at all. She? That was still Ryu in all essentials, and yet he still felt the center of the world fracturing, whirling, fitting back together in a new pattern that he could not comprehend.

With a sudden gesture he drew out the tiger-eye pin of his hair clasp. Not violently, but gently, deliberately. He pressed the pin into Ryu's hand, leaving his topknot still in the plain wooden circle of the clasp.

Then he was gone, passing through the whispering, wondering clusters of Madam Swan's staff and customers.

He left the house, and Ryu stared at the back of Shigan's head — the prince's head, no, *Shigan's* — she would always, always remember him as Shigan. Without the pin, his silky black hair had already slid out of the clasp and fallen down the long line of his back, loose like a mourner's, as he sauntered with all the old arrogant insolence that Ryu's fellow cadets had thoroughly loathed when he first showed up in mismatched clothes at Loyalty. That, she saw for the first time, was not a strut. It was the stride of an imperial prince.

A shout, and with a thump and a rattle of armor, all those warriors dropped to one knee, right fist to the ground, heads bowed.

The man in black bowed low, and there, Ryu thought miserably, the whatever-it-was that made a prince a prince closed around Shigan as relentless as chains. I don't even know your name, she thought desolately. And you do not know mine.

He said something she could not hear, then, dressed in his gallant wanderer summer tunic, riding trousers, and boots, his shining blue-black hair flagging in the rising wind, he was surrounded by the imperial army, and escorted down to the wharf to where three huge warships rode in the bay.

ABOUT THE AUTHOR

Sherwood Smith writes fantasy, science fiction, and historical fiction. Her full bibliography can be found on her website at https://www.sherwoodsmith.net.

ABOUT BOOK VIEW CAFE

Book View Café is an author-owned cooperative of professional writers, publishing in a variety of genres including fantasy, science fiction, romance, mystery, and more.

Its authors include New York Times and USA Today bestsellers as well as winners and nominees of many prestigious awards such as the Agatha Award, Hugo Award, Lambda Literary Award, Locus Award, Nebula Award, RITA Award, Philip K. Dick Award, World Fantasy Award, and many others.

Since its debut in 2008, Book View Café has gained a reputation for producing high quality books in both print and electronic form. BVC's e-books are DRM-free and distributed around the world.

Book View Café's monthly newsletter includes new releases, specials, author news, and event announcements. To sign up, visit
https://www.bookviewcafe.com/bookstore/newsletter/